THE TREASURE OF PARAGON BOOK 1

USA TODAY BESTSELLING AUTHOR
GENEVIEVE JACK

The Dragon of New Orleans: The Treasure of Paragon, Book 1

Copyright © Genevieve Jack 2018

Published by Carpe Luna, Ltd. Bloomington, IL 61704

First Edition: March 2019

eISBN: 978-1-940675-47-3
Paperback: 978-1-940675-48-0

v 3.5

AUTHOR'S NOTE

Dear Reader,

Love is the truest magic and the most fulfilling fantasy. Thank you for coming along on this journey as I share the tale of the Treasure of Paragon, nine exiled royal dragon shifters destined to find love and their way home.

There are three things you can expect from a Genevieve Jack novel: magic will play a key role, unexpected twists are the norm, and love will conquer all.

The Treasure of Paragon Reading Order

Keep in touch to stay in the know about new releases, sales, and giveaways.

Join my VIP reader group
Sign up for my newsletter

Now, let's spread our wings (or at least our pages) and escape together!

Genevieve Jack

CHAPTER ONE

Gabriel Blakemore was running out of time, which was laughable considering time had never meant anything to him in the past. As an immortal dragon, his life thus far had flowed like an endless river, each new day guaranteed by the last. Not anymore. He thumbed the emerald ring on his finger. Already the curse at its center gave the jewel the appearance of a cat's eye in bright light, a thin black pupil visible at the center of the green. His affliction was spreading.

Hunched over the seventeenth-century Spanish baroque desk in his office at Blakemore's Antiques, he sifted through the stack of papers in front of him, praying for a savior, anyone who had the slightest potential for breaking the curse. None of the candidates seemed powerful enough. He needed more options.

Anxiously, he tugged at the bond connecting him to his manservant. Richard appeared at the door to his office almost immediately, carrying a stack of papers that he squared on the desk in front of Gabriel. "More for you."

Gabriel nodded at the man. Impeccably dressed, as

always, in a pinstripe three-piece suit, Richard had proved a crucial asset these days, researching magical options when Gabriel could not. Gabriel had bought the former slave's freedom in 1799, a wise choice. Not only had Richard become a close friend over the centuries, he'd retained a sharp wit and an eye for detail.

The man dusted off his hands before rubbing his sternum. "You don't need to scream down the bond, you know. I'm in the next room. I want to find a cure as much as you do."

Gabriel grunted.

"Are all dragons as friendly and chipper as you, or was I just lucky to be bonded to the best of them?" Richard folded into the chair across the desk, throwing a lanky arm across its back.

"How are sales today?" Gabriel asked, ignoring the man's gibe. He hadn't meant to cause Richard discomfort, but he didn't plan to apologize for it either. Not when the situation was so dire.

"Strong enough that if we all live another year, we can throw one hell of a party," Richard said. "How's that plan coming along? You find a way for us to do that? Live another year? There must be something here. For God's sake, we live in the voodoo capital of America, the home and burial place of Marie Laveau herself."

A whiff of cinnamon and molasses curled off Gabriel's coffee, and he took a long, steadying drink. "Marie would roll over in her tomb if she knew who was running this city now." New Orleans was brimming with humans claiming to have supernatural abilities. Liars, most of them. Unfortunately, the voodoo priestess who'd cast the curse on his ring was the real thing, and she did not take prisoners. Anyone left with true power in the city was either on her side or too afraid to oppose her.

Gabriel snorted. Three hundred years in this realm, only to be turned to stone by the jealous rage of a woman who couldn't take no for an answer.

The thought made his fingers drum against the desk. Tap-tap-tap. Always in threes. The compulsion to tap was so strong when it hit him, not doing so resulted in pain. Muscle tremors ran the length of his arms and hands. He flipped his thumb against the corner of the paper nearest him, hoping it would curb the impulse.

Richard frowned at his fidgeting. "You should rest, Gabriel. It's getting worse. This is the third time this morning."

"Soon."

"That's what you said an hour ago."

Gabriel pulled the pile of papers toward him. His hands cramped with the effort, and the stack spilled across the walnut desk. He cursed, but the word caught in his throat. A woman's picture had been revealed in the collapse, instantly catching his eye. He lifted the folded newspaper to get a better look.

Enchanting. That was the only way to describe her. He couldn't look away. The woman had eyes the color of deep water and curly black hair as wild as the hint of trouble she carried in her smile. He had the sudden intense desire to kiss away that lopsided grin and further tangle that hair. Where had such an urge come from? A dragon like Gabriel didn't often find himself drawn to human women. He closed his eyes and gave his head a well-deserved shake.

"Who is this?" he demanded.

Richard leaned over the desk in order to get a better

look, and Gabriel turned the article in his direction. Richard groaned. "That, my friend, is a long shot."

❧

Ravenna Tanglewood opened her eyes to darkness. She blinked and blinked again, but the eyelid flutter didn't seem to help. This was new. While she'd slept, an irregular blotch had formed in her vision, partially obstructing her view. Now it painted itself like black ink against the sterile white walls of her hospital room.

A Rorschach test, she thought. What did she see in it? An oil slick. A dark cumulus cloud. A rough joke told by her brain cancer.

Cancer. That fucking bitch.

The aroma of this morning's half-eaten eggs and the tang of antiseptic brought her fully awake. She was in the exact same place she'd been every day for the past three months: the hospice at Ochsner Medical Center in New Orleans. Only the last time she'd drifted off, there wasn't a stain obstructing half her field of vision.

She rolled her head and the dark splotch followed, blotting out the left side of the room. She closed her eyes again, counted to ten. No change. Damn, that couldn't be good.

Through her working eye, she watched her mother sleep in the chair next to the bed; she at least was the same as Raven had left her. A *Cosmo* was sprawled across her mother's lap as if she'd drifted off midsentence. Though now that Raven looked more closely, the lifestyle magazine was wrapped around a disturbingly worn copy of *Surviving Divorce* by Amy Dickerman, PhD. Raven winced. So her father's pronounced absence had come to this. Or maybe it was a preemptive read, a talisman against the inevitable. As far as she knew, her parents had only separated—the burden of her illness giving rise to separate bank accounts, separate bedrooms, separate lives—in that order. Her care had become an act of full-time charity her father could not abide.

As usual, her mom was bearing the parental weight alone this morning, although the chair beside her held her older sister Avery's rosary. When had she dug that thing up? Raven hadn't seen the likes of it since their aunt had gifted it to her for her first communion. Avery had never been the praying type. Leave it to death to bring out the inner Falwell in everyone.

Did she think she could pray the cancer away? Raven snorted at the thought. *Pull the plug.* That's what she'd say if she had a say, and if she were plugged in to anything more than Mr. Drippy, her full-time fluid and drug-delivery companion. So far, she could breathe on her own and swallow, unlike the man across the hall. *Stopped the vent*, she'd heard the nurses whisper.

Lucky bastard.

"Hey, beautiful," Dr. Freemont said.

Raven rolled her head back to center, then slightly to the left so she could see him clearly out of her good eye. Dr. Freemont was a balding, portly man whose gray temples gave away his advanced age. Still, he was more fun than his stodgy contemporaries. She liked him.

"Hey, ugly," she responded, although the words sounded choked off and raspy.

His bushy silver brows sank over his bulbous nose. "What's this about? You're holding your head at an angle. Raven, can you look at me straight on?"

"No," she drawled. "Dark." Every word was like lifting a two-ton boulder from the depths of her skull and carrying

5

it through a labyrinth of synapses to finally hoist over her lips. It was exhausting.

Dr. Freemont placed one hand gently on her head, then drew a penlight from his pocket. He swung it in front of her right eye, then her left, where the light disappeared inside the dark fog.

"Squeeze my fingers," he commanded, touching her right hand. She did as he asked, then wondered why he never placed his fingers in her left, although he'd walked to that side of the bed. Or maybe he had. She could no longer feel that hand.

As Dr. Freemont continued his assessment, she noticed a trend. Her left side wasn't working. Not just her eye, but also her shoulder, her hand, her thigh, all the way to her pinky toe. Numb. Dead. She was dying in halves.

"Why?" she demanded, but she knew.

"The tumor," he said simply. "The pressure in your brain." He kept speaking, but Raven's mind couldn't keep up with his medical explanation. She did catch the word *stroke*. It didn't matter. They wouldn't treat her for it anyway.

"Donate?" she asked.

Half cloaked in shadow, his face turned grim and he lowered his voice. "Yes. The cancer is only in your brain. You'll be able to donate your organs. It's all arranged." His voice was funny, and she wondered if he was lying. Normally Dr. Freemont didn't talk to his patients much about organ donation, but she'd pressed him about it early on. For her, it was a light at the end of the tunnel. Every time he reassured her of her donation status, her heart leaped a little. She'd do something with this life. Leave a part of herself behind that mattered.

If he was lying, she didn't want to know the truth.

"Long?" she asked. He knew what she meant. How long until she died? They'd been at this for over five years on and off. Through railroad spikes of pain that left her begging for someone to bash her head in. Months of chemo that turned her inside out. There was nothing left to try. There would be no more chemo. No more surgeries. Raven wanted to live, but if living wasn't possible, she would settle for being free.

His pale eyes met hers, and he gripped her fingers on the right where she could feel his reassurance. "Not long now."

Not long now. She tried her best to smile. "Good."

Her mother roused, her magazine-wrapped book falling from her lap and clattering to the floor. "Oh! Doctor. Excuse me. I must have drifted off. How is she?"

When he turned to look at her, his eyes glossier than usual, his face changed. A mask slipped into place, clinical and authoritative. Raven rolled her head on her pillow to see her mother, and the dark splotch swallowed most of Dr. Freemont's head. She couldn't see anything above his shoulders when he answered.

"I would never put an expiration date on your daughter, Mrs. Tanglewood... Sarah. We both know how strong she is."

"Yes, I know. This one came out fighting." Her mother still believed Raven could beat this thing.

She was wrong.

"Raven's comfort measures are working. We'll maintain the course." He straightened as if he might leave.

Raven squeezed his hand. "Do it," she said. It was the best part of her day. She wouldn't let him leave without giving it to her.

He turned an impassive expression toward her, half

light and half dark as she looked at him straight on. "I have no idea what you are talking about, Raven." The corner of his mouth twitched.

With whatever part of her face was still working, she sent him the sternest glare she could muster.

Raising one eyebrow, he backed up a few steps and glanced into the hall. "You know, I don't do this for all my patients. Only for you."

She smiled lopsidedly.

He removed his white lab coat, cleared his throat, and glanced again at the door. There was no one out there. Ceremoniously, he wrapped his coat around Mr. Drippy, holding the neck in place with one hand and gripping the sleeve with the other. He squared his shoulders.

"I get no drip from champagne...," he began to sing, deep and throaty, in the style of Frank Sinatra. He swayed with her IV pole as much as the length of the tubes leading to the port in her chest would allow. "Mere Toradol doesn't move me at all, but morphine and fentanyl too... Yes, I get a drip out of you." He cradled the screen of the IV pole and dipped it below his round belly, careful not to upset the hanging medications. His lips puckered in an air-kiss toward the screen.

Raven couldn't help it. She started to laugh. Her mother did too, which made her laugh even harder. As always, the sight of that normally stiff and paunchy man dancing with her IV pole tickled something deep inside her, something that bitch cancer hadn't ruined yet. She laughed and laughed until her throat constricted like the valve of a pinched balloon.

Her laugh turned into a cough and then a wheeze.

Dr. Freemont stopped singing.

The next moment he was leaning over her, his pale

hands gently shaking her shoulders, and she realized she'd been unconscious. Not long, judging by the look on his surprised face.

"Welcome back," he murmured. He was half dark again.

"That's never happened before," her mother said nervously.

"That's just Raven's body telling us she needs rest," he said. "I'll leave you to it." He removed his lab coat from Mr. Drippy and shrugged it on before nodding his goodbye.

"Well, that sounded promising," Mom said after he was gone. "You just need more rest." She stood up and tucked Raven in, her face positively glowing with denial.

Raven adjusted her head so her good eye was pointed at the door. *Not long now*, he'd said.

That was the day cancer stole her laugh. It was the last time the doctor sang for her. The last time she was awake long enough to ask him to. There were flashes of color and light, the feel of anointing oil crossed on her forehead and wrists as prayers were whispered over her, Avery's rosary dangling from her fingertips above her chest, Dr. Freemont's humorless face as he answered her mother's questions. But most of the following days consisted of darkness.

Until, one night, *he* came for her.

CHAPTER TWO

Death stood at the end of Raven's bed, looming and dark, and she welcomed him with open arms. Open arm. Only her right was under her control. Oh, how she longed to be free of her broken body.

If any part of her had questioned the true identity of her visitor, the skepticism was short-lived. The aura of the supernatural surrounded him. Raven's first clue was his suit, or rather that he wasn't wearing scrubs. An eternity had passed since someone who wasn't a medical professional or close family had entered her hospice room. Her own father didn't come anymore. It was too sad. A lost cause.

Death's miraculous presence aside, there were stranger things about his visit. Her IV had stopped dripping. Mr. Drippy's digital face was frozen, the impossibly full belly of her next drop of morphine hovering by a silver thread at the center of the machine's plastic chamber. She shot a glance toward her mother, hoping for an explanation, but the woman was motionless and rigid, staring, catatonic, toward the darkened hospital windows. The clock had stopped. Midnight.

Raven's time had finally come.

She took stock of the man who must be Death, the new growth of her hair rustling against the scratchy pillowcase as she turned her head. It was the only sound in an otherwise silent room. Under the fluorescent lights, she studied him. This was the one who would carry her home? He wasn't what she'd expected.

Death was a babe.

Dark. Brooding. Heavy boned and unshaven. There was something handsome about him nonetheless, alluring enough for her failing body to send her a flicker of desire, something she hadn't felt in over a year. It was the eyes, black eyes that seemed to burn into her, with flecks of red and mahogany that radiated from pitch-black pupils. His substantial eyebrows were too full to be considered conventionally attractive, but they balanced a generous nose and lower jaw that had no use for frivolity. He was olive-skinned, full-lipped, and big. Really big. Professional wrestler big. Although, based on his sunken cheeks and long, tapered fingers, she got the sense he could be bigger, like he was perpetually hungry.

"Ravenna Tanglewood?" he asked, his voice lined with charcoal and grit. A Clint Eastwood voice. A burning voice. Was he taking her to hell? A whiff of campfire drifted past her nose as he neared. That was one thing cancer hadn't taken from her, her sense of smell. And he smelled like the fall, like oak leaves and pumpkin pie, like smoke and old print.

"Yes." Her voice was nonexistent, mostly lips and breath doing the work.

"You are *this* Ravenna Tanglewood." He removed a folded newspaper from his breast pocket. The pages crinkled in his grip. He thrust it toward her.

11

A large emerald ring on his right pointer finger glinted in the light, and she had trouble looking away from it to focus on what he was asking her. Eventually though, she zeroed in on the story he was showing her. It was an article by a reporter from the *Tulane Hullabaloo*. Psychic Student Saves Family. She blinked slowly, confused. Why would Death care about a piece of gossipy journalism?

Before the doctors had discovered her brain tumor, she had experienced a premonition. She'd been doing laundry when a vision of her parents' pub completely engulfed in flames brought her to her knees. Neither her father nor mother took her vision seriously, but for some reason, her sister Avery did. Avery's resulting tantrum led to the purchase of a brand-new fire extinguisher. A few nights later, an inexperienced cook set his apron down too close to the grill and the strings caught fire. Her father reached for the old extinguisher first. It didn't work. Thankfully the new one did, and consequently her father was able to save the pub and the people in it.

It didn't mean Raven was psychic. Dr. Freemont had explained that the tumor in her brain, with its octopus-like tentacles infiltrating her gray matter, was connecting different areas of her mind, making her exceptionally intuitive. She'd subconsciously noticed the expiration date on the extinguisher, and her brain had produced the vision accordingly. It was the cancer, not anything weird or unusual. The newspaper story was a bit of flamboyant reporting by a friend who hoped to use the piece to attract readers to a fund-raiser meant to help with her medical expenses, nothing more.

Death tapped his finger against the newspaper impatiently, the massive green emerald glowing like a star. "Well, is this you?"

She licked her lower lip and nodded. He slid the paper back inside his jacket. Exhausted from the effort of responding, she closed her eyes and prayed silently, *Take me. Please take me.*

※

GABRIEL STOOD AT THE END OF THE HOSPITAL BED, using every ounce of willpower he had to restrain himself. When Richard had suggested the girl was a long shot, he wasn't kidding. She was more dead than alive, a porcelain doll he was afraid to startle for fear of breaking her. Still, there was something... alluring about her, the same as when he'd seen her picture. Deep within his chest, a primal urge to heal and protect demanded his attention.

He hadn't felt anything like it in his five hundred years. Not for a human anyway. Perhaps the feeling bore a close resemblance to when he found a rare and priceless item for his collection. Yes, that was it.

She appeared nothing like the picture he'd seen. The only way to describe her now was haunting. The bones of her cheeks protruded as if her skeleton was battling her skin for rights to the surface. Ravenna Tanglewood was death, propped in a bed like a body on display. Above thin lips and a gently curved nose, her blue eyes bulged from her skull, dull and rheumy. Those damned eyes were nothing short of pleading. His chest ached. If she refused his offer, it would haunt him the rest of his days.

He stepped closer to her. Was that night-blooming jasmine? The scent was faint, but he could smell it on her skin. "Is it true you were an anthropology major with a minor in history? Honors student?"

A grunt came from deep within her throat, a warm wet

trail of saliva coursing down her lower cheek. Her throat contracted and relaxed, but she seemed unable to form words. He hissed. Damn human hospitals. This was torture. What type of creatures left their females to die like this?

He could wait no more. Already the curse on his ring was weakening his magic. His skin felt thick, like he might turn to stone from the inside out at any moment. He tapped his fingers, exactly three times each against his thumb. Tap-tap-tap. Tap-tap-tap. It was the only thing that helped, the only thing that reminded him he could still move. His magic wasn't completely gone. Not yet.

Still, if he was to save her, he must do so soon.

"I see," he said. "I would like to offer you a job, Ms. Tanglewood. It is hard work. You'll have to learn quickly and take the initiative."

She stared at him blankly. He wondered what she must be thinking, if she could think at all. It was possible her brain was as wasted as her body. From what he'd read, she had brain cancer. Even with magical intervention, there might not be enough left in her head for her to consent. And she must consent. He would not bind her if she didn't. To do so would be to divest himself of any remaining honor he still bore in his wasting body.

He approached her bedside and gently laid his hand on her chest. Those too-big eyes locked onto him. Her heart pounded against his palm. Her expression pleaded for death, but her heart begged for life.

"Ravenna, do you consent? Do you agree to work for me?"

Her eyebrows dipped and her chin twitched as if she didn't quite understand what he was proposing. A tear escaped the corner of her eye. He wiped it away.

"Say yes, little one," he said. "I cannot bear to see you like this a moment more."

Her eyes widened. "Yes," she mouthed.

He smiled weakly. "Praise the Mountain."

As he held her stare, he removed his hand from her chest, the storm of magic brewing within him. His ring glowed brighter as he drew his power to the surface, the dragon within barely contained inside his human form. Opening his jaw wide, he reached deep into his mouth, his large hand wedging itself between his teeth. He heard her gasp as the sound of tearing flesh filled the room. Gabriel grunted. He was likely scaring her, but it could not be avoided. This was part of the transition. The faster she came to terms with what was happening here, the better.

A spurt of crimson blood beaded on his bottom lip as the tooth materialized, clutched between his fingers. He tugged a handkerchief from his pocket and dabbed at the blood, then held the tooth up to the light. It was thin. Pointed. With a long root still bloody from the extraction. Clearly not a human tooth.

"Never gets easier," he murmured.

Beside him, Ravenna trembled. Her arms were covered in gooseflesh. He had to soothe her, to do something to comfort her before she had a heart attack. He closed his hand and drew on the magic of the ring. When he opened it again in front of her mouth, there was no tooth, only a slim white pill.

"Swallow," he commanded.

She must do this now. They were running out of time, her life fading in front of him, his magic sputtering under the weight of the curse. He scooped an arm behind her shoulders and lifted. Her lips parted like a baby bird's, and he dropped the pill to the back of her throat. She gurgled, coughed. He raised her head higher. Her throat bobbed and the choking stopped.

Oh, how beautiful it was shining through her stomach. The red light spread through her torso and to the ends of her limbs, warming her flesh from within. And all the time, she lay helpless against his arm, staring at him with unrestrained wonder, that jasmine scent of hers growing stronger. It made him feel like a god to hold her like this, to know that he'd given her what she needed to heal, to survive.

He watched her chest rise and fall with the first deep breath she'd taken since he'd arrived.

"What did you give me?" she asked, and this time the words were strong and true, more than the breathy whispers he'd gotten before. Good.

His shoulders slumped. The magic had taken its toll. He must get home to rest.

He brought his face close to hers. "Rest. Recover. You're no use to me like this. We are bound now. I will know when you are ready." He pressed his lips to her forehead and lowered her to the bed.

Her mouth worked soundlessly, as if she couldn't find the words for all the questions she longed to ask.

The rhythmic beep of her heart monitor started again, and a drop of morphine fell within the chamber of her IV. As he left her side and the room, he prayed to the Mountain that he'd chosen wisely. Ravenna Tanglewood was his last chance.

CHAPTER THREE

"Raven? Raven?"

Raven opened her eyes to find her mother and Avery looming over her. Her sister's fingers trembled on the bedrail, and her expression was somewhere on the road between concerned and amazed.

"She's awake," Avery said. "Mom? What's going on?"

Light washed through the windows behind Avery, framing her long, curly black hair. Raven thought it gave her a halo. Flattering. She was glowing. Filled with light. Brimming with it. An angel at her bedside. Raven's mom didn't look quite as heavenly. Nauseous maybe, but not heavenly.

"Can you hear me?" Mom asked, stressing each syllable in a loud, clear tone.

Raven smacked her lips, her mouth as dry as a stone. "Of course I can hear you. You're screaming at me."

The women gasped, staring at each other and then at her in marked confusion.

"I'll get the doctor." Avery bustled from the room.

"I need water," Raven said. Her lips were thick and chapped, and her tongue stuck to the roof of her mouth.

17

Her eyes roved to where her bedside table used to be, but it was pushed against the wall, wiped down and out of the way. Mr. Drippy was still there, but when she glanced at the port in her chest, her tubes were no longer attached.

"We think you disconnected it," Mom said with a wince. "In your sleep. I was about to call a nurse when you rolled over and opened your eyes."

Raven tried to lick her lips again.

"I'll get you some water." Mom looked frantically for the hospice-issued cup, then reached behind her and pulled a water bottle from her purse. "Here, have mine." Hands shaking, she twisted off the cap and chucked it behind her where it bounced and rolled across the linoleum floor. She slipped her arm under Raven's shoulders to tip her head up and brought the water to her lips.

The first swallow caught in her throat, sending her into a fit of coughing. Her mother frowned but gave her another sip. This one she managed to get down. If sunlight had a flavor, this would be it. She almost moaned. Her mom pulled the bottle away to give her air.

Raven's breath stank. Her limbs felt like dead weight. But in shaky increments she raised both hands to her mother's wrist and pulled the bottle back toward her mouth. She drained it dry in a matter of seconds.

"More," Raven rasped.

"Yes. I'll get you more. Something more. Juice." Her mother pounded the call button with her finger and screamed. "We need juice in here now!" By the urgency in her voice, Raven thought the perpetuation of modern society balanced on her mother's ability to provide her with juice.

"Mom, it's okay. I'm sure they're co-ming." Her voice cracked.

Mom's face fell. She swallowed. "How are you feeling?"

Raven stared and stared at her mother, memorizing every contour of her beautiful, sleep-deprived face, a face that looked far older than it should have at her age. The dark cloud that had plagued her vision was completely gone. Nothing obstructed her view. "I can see you."

"Oh, Raven." In a rush of hands, elbows, and shoulders, her mom hugged her, and with what little strength Raven had, she hugged back.

Dr. Freemont charged into the room, Avery at his side, and came up short. His eyes were wide as saucers, his face paling. "When did this happen?"

"She disconnected her IV and rolled onto her side," her mother said, rubbing Raven's shoulder supportively.

"Raven?" He approached the bed, his eyes raking the length of her body, assessing her as only a doctor could. Did he notice her left pupil constricting in time with her right? The way she clutched the blanket with both hands?

"It must have been your singing," Raven said, a slow, lazy smile stretching across her face.

He laughed, pulling his penlight from his pocket. The further he got with his assessment, the harder he shook his head. "I'm going to order a PET scan."

Raven understood what that was for. He wanted to check how much of the tumor was left in her head. Her recovery might be temporary, the eye of a hurricane. Her concern must have shown on her face, because Dr. Freemont squeezed her hand.

"The rules of the game have changed, Raven. Don't plan your next move until we know where all the pieces are, okay?" He winked.

Raven didn't have to wait long for radiology to come and get her. According to the nurses, she was a star, a hospital celebrity with an all-access pass to have any tests her doctor ordered. Before long, she found herself propped in a wheelchair in the PET scan room, staring at cottony blue images of her internal organs.

"Totally normal," Dr. Freemont said. "Not a single tumor." His mouth gaped like a fish.

"What about my stomach?" she asked slowly. "Is there anything in my stomach?"

He dug his hands in his pockets. "No..." He narrowed his eyes. "You had brain cancer. Why would you ask about something in your stomach?"

"I saw a man," Raven said. "In my room last night. I think he healed me."

"A man... In your room?" Dr. Freemont turned from the PET scan to look at her directly.

"He was dark. With... fire in his eyes. I thought he was Death. He fed me his tooth."

Dr. Freemont blinked rapidly. "Spontaneous recovery is a reality, Raven. It's rare, extremely rare, but it happens. The body finds a way. It cures itself." He sighed. "Our brains have a funny way of making sense of the things that happen to us. I had one patient who was sure there were fairies in her room. She smelled lilies constantly." His pale eyes studied her face. "You saw a man. You saw him. He existed to you. But he also may have been created by you. Consider the possibility that your mind used a vision to process this monumental *healing* that occurred."

"That makes sense." She nodded slowly. "It just seemed so real."

Raven stared at the equipment behind Dr. Freemont and convinced herself that the stranger, the tooth, and the bargain she'd struck were hallucinations cooked up by her healing brain. It was a reasonable explanation, although a small part of her wished it wasn't true. The man had been without a doubt the most intriguing person she'd ever met. Intense and powerful. When he'd been in the room with her, she'd felt safe, even in the face of her impending death. It had been years since she'd experienced that sense of security, even longer since someone had found her interesting. He'd looked at her like she was something precious, something worth saving. It made sense that he wasn't real. He was too perfect to be real.

Dr. Freemont squatted beside her chair. "You are healthy, Raven. It's going to take time and rehabilitation to strengthen your body. You've been in bed for a long time. I can't guarantee this will last or explain exactly how we got here. But here we are."

A smile spread across her exhausted lips. "Will you do me a favor? Before you take me back to my room and tell my family all this?"

"What?"

"Take me outside. Just for a few minutes."

He grabbed the handles of her wheelchair and rolled her to the elevators. A floor up, they surged past the front desk and out the front entrance. Raven's body ached, not from illness but from her lengthy immobility, but every painful bump was worth it when they finally broke from the shadow of the hospital.

Warmth spread across her exposed skin. It was early September in New Orleans, sunny and bright. The heat wrapped around her, a heavy blanket of moist air. Raven turned her face toward the sun and stared into a clear blue sky.

Beautiful. So damn beautiful. With one puffy baby cloud floating by to say hello. She pulled a deep breath of fresh air into her lungs. Tears burst through the dam of her eyelids and she sobbed. She didn't even try to hold back. Dr. Freemont, to his credit, said nothing. He just handed her a tissue. Raven wasn't sure, but she thought maybe he was crying too.

She was free, and she swore by all that was holy that she would never allow herself to be a prisoner, to illness or anything else, ever again.

CHAPTER FOUR

"Raven, hurry, we're going to miss Joan of Arc!" Avery tugged at her hand, weaving through the crowd on the sidewalk of Chartres Street.

Twelfth Night, the kickoff of Mardi Gras season, was upon them, and Raven was more than happy to celebrate with her sister at the parade, one of the few that took place in the French Quarter. Only, speed was not her strong point. It had been a little over four months since she'd miraculously recovered from brain cancer. Four months of physical therapy, slowly building up her strength from barely making it to the bathroom when she had to go, to walking up the steps to her second-floor apartment, to five minutes on the treadmill, then ten. She'd graduated this week. That meant she was free to do any sort of activity she liked. It didn't mean it was easy.

She told her legs to walk faster. Still she fell behind.

Avery circled back. "It's okay. You're doing great."

"I'm trying," she said.

The street smelled of beer and bodies and the crisp scent of New Orleans winter underneath it all.

Approaching drums and trumpets brought a cheer from the crowd. Avery squeezed close enough to the curb so they could peek through shoulders to see. Two tall men noticed they were height challenged and allowed them to move to the front. Not that it was any inconvenience to the pair. Both men had at least six inches on her and Avery and could easily see over their heads.

Raven clapped as the band passed, their red tunics standing out against the gold and white of Joan of Arc as she followed on her horse. The sound of trumpets rose in the distance. "This is amazing, Avery. I can't believe how many of these I've missed."

"We'll make up for lost time. I promise. There's a Randazzo king cake at home with your name on it."

"I can't wait."

"Actually, if you're up for it, I thought we could stop for a drink after this." Avery glanced her way, and Raven got the distinct impression her sister had an ulterior motive. At only a year apart, the sisters had been close their entire lives. Raven could always tell when Avery had a bee in her bonnet about something.

"Sure," Raven said. If Avery was buying drinks, the least she could do was listen.

As soon as the parade had passed, they walked to the Mahogany Jazz Hall. Small place. Killer lemon-drop martinis. Raven loved the smooth croon of the saxophone and the laughter of her sister as she told stories about her regulars at their family's pub, the Three Sisters. It seemed there was a local paleontologist from the university who had his eye on her.

"He asked me if I wanted to come back to his office to look at his bones."

Raven snorted. Her sister had never hurt for male attention. She made the Kardashians seem plain with her curvy figure and dark mystique. People used to say Raven resembled her when they were younger, before she developed cancer. Now Raven thought it would be difficult to tell they were related. Unlike Avery's long, sleek curls, Raven's hair remained in that awkward growing-out stage. Her chin-length bob frizzed anytime there was an ounce of humidity, a constant in New Orleans. That wasn't the only difference. Her prolonged illness had left Raven painfully thin. Bony and flat, she'd struggled to put on weight no matter how much she ate. Dr. Freemont had explained that her body had run at a deficit for so long while she was dying that it might take a full year for her to reach and sustain a normal weight.

"Avery, will you do me a favor? It's a big one." Raven played with the stem of her martini glass.

"Of course," Avery answered. "What kind of favor? How many drinks will I need to feel good about saying yes?"

"I want to go kayaking in Manchac Swamp, and I need you to go with me. I can't drive yet."

"Manchac... the haunted swamp with the alligators?" Avery shook her head. "Hell no. Why in the world do you want to do that?"

"They give tours," Raven protested. "It's perfectly safe, especially now when the weather is cool and the gators aren't moving much."

"No," Avery said, taking another sip. "Why?"

"I'm finally strong enough. I want to do something... *free*. I want to feel alive."

"Can't you feel alive on a steamboat cruise?"

Raven frowned. "No, I can't. You don't know what it's like. I was a prisoner to that bed for months, Avery. Years, if you take out my short remissions. Sometimes I wake up in the middle of the night and I climb up on the roof just because I can, because I can't stand spending one more minute under those covers. Sometimes I can't breathe."

"You go up on the roof?" Avery seemed genuinely perplexed.

Raven nodded. "I do. I have to do things I've never done before. I have to challenge myself. Life is short, really short. What if the cancer comes back?"

Avery's smile faded. "Speaking of challenging yourself, there's something I need to talk to you about."

"Sounds serious." This was it. Raven had suspected something was coming.

"Mom and Dad think it's time you went back to school."

"Dad? When did you talk to Dad?" Raven's miraculous recovery had not been enough to save her parents' marriage. Her father had divorced her mother and taken a job running a restaurant in the central business district, abandoning the Three Sisters. Her mother had kept the business going with Avery's help, but Raven could tell it was difficult for her. Raven hadn't spoken to her father in months. She didn't care to.

"Come on, Rave, it's time. You can't stay mad at him forever. People get divorced. It's time to move on."

Raven's stomach tensed and her ears grew hot. "If you think this is about the divorce, you don't understand anything."

"I know he wasn't at the hospital a lot. Honestly, I wasn't either. I'm sorry for that..." She trailed off as if she was tempted to say more, make an excuse. She didn't.

"You were there," Raven said. "Maybe not as much as Mom, but a lot. I never blamed you when you weren't.

You're not my parent. A parent shouldn't give up on their kid, and they shouldn't abandon their spouse."

Avery sipped her drink, her eyes drifting from Raven's. "No. He was wrong. Really wrong."

"Thank you."

"But you should let him apologize."

"I've noted your opinion on the matter. Here's what I think of it." Raven flipped her the middle finger.

"Nice." Avery sighed. "So, what about the school idea?"

"No."

"Why not? Aren't you going to finish your degree?"

"And have to sit in a classroom or library all day? No. I've spent enough days doing things I don't want to do. I'm alive and I plan to live every day like it's my last. I want to be outside. I want to see the world. I want to..." She looked up at the ceiling. "I want to fly. I've never even been in an airplane."

Avery groaned. "You need money to do those things. You had a scholarship to Tulane. Dad thinks you can get it back."

There was the rub. Her parents had gone into debt from her medical bills. Her mother had supported her through her recovery, allowing her to share her small apartment with Avery. But Avery worked at the pub and paid rent. Raven had done nothing to contribute for months. This was less about it being time for her to move on and more about it being time for her to chip in.

"I'll come to work at the Three Sisters," Raven said. "No school."

Avery leaned back in her chair and crossed her arms. "I can't say we don't need the help, but at least listen to what Dad has to say about school."

Raven responded by finishing off her second drink. She

was feeling a little buzzed. It had been a long time since she'd had this much alcohol, and the Mahogany mixed them strong. Not to mention, she was the definition of a light-weight. She placed the empty at the center of the table. Her sister was acting weird, sitting stiffly across from her with her arms crossed. Avery glanced over her shoulder.

"Don't be mad," she said.

Raven followed her gaze, then did a double take. "Traitor!"

"It's time, Raven. Try to find it in your heart to forgive him." Avery stood.

"No. No! Sit back down, Avery."

Avery shook her head. Raven's mouth gaped as her father, David, paused to kiss her sister on the cheek and exchange a few words before crossing the bar to sit down in Avery's abandoned spot across the table.

"Hello, Raven," he said. His voice made her cringe.

"You're wasting your time. You and Avery shouldn't have done this," she said.

"We haven't spent any time together since you left the hospital. You won't take my calls or return my emails. I want us to get beyond this. Avery was my last hope."

"If I wasn't important enough to spend time with while I was in the hospital, why would you want to spend time with me now?" She swayed in her chair, the alcohol doing its dirty work. She didn't care. It gave her the courage to speak her mind.

"Come on now!" he said, his weathered face crinkling at the corners. Her father was thin with a thick head of gray hair, but other than that, he hadn't aged well. His leathery tan and heavily lined face made him look at least ten years older than her mother despite being the same age. "You know it wasn't like that. There was nothing I could do to help you. What good would it have done for me to sit in that chair all day and all night?"

"Good? I'll tell you what good it did me when Mom and Avery remained by my side. It took the edge off the pain. It helped me remember I was more than my cancer. It was the only thing that reminded me I was still a human being." She played with the tiny napkin under her empty glass, wishing she had another martini for no other reason than the potential to throw it in his face. Emotions swarmed like angry wasps within her.

"Do you want me to say I'm sorry? Do you want me to apologize?" His eyes connected with hers. "Well, I am sorry. I am sorry, Raven. I should have been stronger. I should have... I should have been there."

She couldn't tell if he was legitimately sorry or just saying the words. Her father didn't apologize flippantly as a rule, but the sheer aggressiveness with which the words left his mouth made them hard to swallow.

"Okay," she said in a tone clearly meant to placate him and nothing more. "Is there anything else?"

He shifted his jaw. "It's time for you to move on with your life. I've talked with Admissions. Tulane is willing to readmit you. You won't have to reapply. They'll make an exception for you, given the circumstances."

"You talked to my admissions counselor without me?" Her shoulders tensed, and a muscle in her neck started hurting enough for her to rub it.

"Someone had to do something, Raven," he said softly. "You were a straight A student. An honors award recipient. You could finish your degree in a year if you went full-time. Don't you think it's time to get back on the horse?"

Everything he said was true. She knew it in her heart. Finishing her anthropology degree would be the prudent thing to do. It would be what she would tell someone else to do. But the mere thought of sitting in a classroom made her rub the cramp in the back of her neck harder. She'd spent years of her life in and out of a hospital room. Those four white walls might as well have been bars for how much freedom she'd had over herself. And the cage extended beyond the room. Her defunct immune system and constantly fatigued body restricted everything. She hadn't actually lived most of her adult life. School was just a different type of cage. A classroom all day and studying all night? She couldn't do it. Not now, maybe not ever again.

"No," Raven said firmly.

He spread his hands. "Everything will be paid for. It's all covered."

"No," she said again, this time louder and stronger. "I will not go back to school."

His hands hung in the air between them like he was expecting to catch something she was throwing. "Be reasonable. You have to do something constructive with your time. How will you keep yourself busy now that all the PT is over?"

"I want to travel. I was thinking Paris."

His eyes narrowed. "A vacation isn't a career choice. Don't you think this... break... has gone on long enough?"

A hot wind of anger whirled like a cyclone between her ears. She squared her shoulders and stood, crossing her arms. "I am twenty-three years old. I've spent almost a quarter of my life dying. I can decide for myself when I've had enough living. If you'd spent any time at all in that hospital with me, you would know why I am not ready to waste a single moment sitting in a classroom." Her voice was quiet and steady. Everyone in the bar was staring now.

She didn't care. "You don't get to tell me what to do. No one gets to tell me what to do ever again."

Deliberately, he closed his mouth and then leveled his gaze on her. "You think this is me telling you what to do?" He snorted. "I have a job. Your mother has a job. Avery has a job. You were sick; I get that. But you are not sick anymore. Life goes on. You're better than this, Raven. The world needs you. It needs your mind. It needs your skills. It needs your heart. You've been given a gift. A second chance. A damned miracle! Why are you wasting it?"

"I—" Raven revved up to hand him his ass on a platter. Didn't he understand she had a right to some freedom after what she'd been through? All she was asking for was a little understanding. But he cut her off.

He held up his hands. "You know what? Never mind. I promised your mother I'd talk to you. I talked to you. You're an adult. Do what you want."

"Wait. Mom asked you to talk to me?" A heavy weight settled over her heart.

"Yeah, she did. I'm not the bad guy you think I am." He blew out a long breath of air through his nose. "I'm just trying to help you remember what it is to live as if tomorrow isn't your last day on Earth. What will happen if the cancer doesn't come back? You could have a long life ahead of you. It's time to get busy making a future for yourself."

Her head was swimming. She couldn't listen to this right now. Whirling, she headed for the door.

"Where are you going?" her father called, rising from his seat to come after her. "Let me drive you home."

"I'll take an Uber," Raven said.

"Raven... I'm sorry. Don't leave like this."

This time she could tell without a doubt he was sincere. But she wasn't ready to forgive him. Part of her was gripping her resentment of him like a well-worn baby blanket he'd have to pry from her tantrum-tightened grip. She closed her eyes against a wave of drunkenness and shifted on her feet. "I need time."

This he seemed to understand because he sat back down. Raven left alone.

❦

THE COOL NIGHT AIR FILLED RAVEN'S LUNGS AS SHE strode aimlessly along Chartres. Between the argument and the martinis, she felt nauseous. And she'd lied. She didn't have money for an Uber. Maybe the streetcar though. She'd head in that direction once she sobered up. For now, she chose to walk along Bourbon Street, keen to take in the energy of the people and the lights.

She milled among the bars and drunken revelers, becoming invisible in the crowd. The night chilled her, even through her light fleece, and she hugged herself against it, but she kept on walking, needing the freedom, the night air. She drifted from Bourbon, from the crowds, from the bars, lost in her own thoughts. How far she'd wandered she wasn't sure, but she found herself on a dark street in a residential area. Where was she? Likely on the edge of the Quarter by the looks of it. Her head throbbed.

"Hey. Hey, little lady."

She ignored the man yelling from behind her and walked faster, trying to remember where the closest streetcar stop was.

"You there, little dark-haired chick, where you going?" His tone was crass and didn't hold the accent of a local.

She glanced over her shoulder. He looked about thirty and very drunk.

"Hey, I'm talking to you." There was a shuffle of footsteps and then a hand clamped around her bicep and turned her roughly. A fog of rum-soaked breath hit her squarely in the face.

She tried to free herself and failed.

"You wanna dance?" He forced her against him and swayed to some unheard music.

"No," she said, pushing as hard as she could against his chest. "I have to go now." A more polite response than he deserved. Why was the street so dark? A streetlight was out, she realized. Quickly she tried to turn, to walk away.

He was on her in an instant. "I asked you to dance. Don't be a bitch."

She struggled, but this time he held her tighter, pinching and hurting. She twisted in his arms. He slid his hands lower to circle her wrists.

"What do you have there, Mikey?" Another man emerged from between two houses, zipping his fly. He swaggered toward her.

This was trouble. Warning flags flew in Raven's head, and she searched for someone, anyone, to call to for help. There was no one. She tried to remember exactly where she was, but she'd been tipsy and angry and hadn't been paying attention.

"A new friend," Mikey blabbered, sending a spray of spit against her cheek.

"Stop," she begged. "Leave me alone." She twisted more forcefully. Already exhausted and still recovering physically, she was easily overcome. The harder she struggled, the more it seemed to incite them.

The first man grabbed her by the shoulders; the other man moved in fast from behind her.

"Let me go!" she shouted, but his hand slapped over her mouth.

"Do it fast, man. I'll hold her," the second man said.

Do what fast? Full panic embraced her. She bit, scratched, and kicked like a wildcat. In her weakened state, she might not be strong enough to overpower them, but she wouldn't make it easy. By force of pure adrenaline, she managed to twist out of the man's grip. Unfortunately, the other man's legs were between hers and she tripped in her effort to escape. Raven fell hard, the side of her head slapping the sidewalk with a sickening hollow thunk.

The world spun. Warm wet blood trickled near the corner of her eye. She tried to blink it away. Her head throbbed and a wave of nausea rolled through her.

"I got her," the one called Mikey said. He rolled her onto her back, his weighty body knocking the breath from her lungs. His hand worked between their bodies.

She had to get up. She needed to run. Her head swam. Spots circled in her vision.

And then Mikey was gone.

Cold air washed over her in a rush. The man ascended into the air, straight up. She watched him rise and rise into the star-filled sky until she thought he might hit the moon. His pants were open and his junk dangled from his fly. His arms and legs flailed like a newborn's.

She couldn't process what was happening. Was she hallucinating? Was it the alcohol?

Whatever power it was that had levitated him abruptly gave out. He dropped like a rock, his body slapping the street next to her with a crunch. He did not get up. Blood trickled from the corner of his mouth.

Confused, Raven tried to rise, but nothing worked right. It hurt to move, and the black dots circling in her vision were expanding. She heard feet strike gravel and pavement nearby. Someone running. She couldn't see him, but she recognized the second man's voice crying, "No, no, please no!"

There was a thud. She didn't hear that man again.

More footsteps. These were slow, deliberate; dress shoes on pavement. She blinked helplessly toward the street, her cheek pressed against the curb. Her attacker's blood spilled onto the asphalt... or was that her blood? There was so much of it she couldn't tell anymore.

A pair of polished black alligator loafers stepped into her field of vision. Expensive gray slacks draped over the tops. Whoever he was, he had good fashion sense. She had the fleeting thought that she should warn him about the blood. *Don't ruin your shoes.*

"Fuck!" a deep voice said from above.

She was too weak to turn her head to see his face. Two hands slid beneath her body and lifted her. A sharp pain; something in her neck cracked; and then everything went black.

CHAPTER FIVE

Why the fuck had his magic failed him? Gabriel held Raven tightly against his chest, anger throbbing in his temples. Her bloody body felt tiny in his arms, frail, like he could crush her if he wasn't careful. How the hell could this have happened?

He'd felt her readiness today like a tug on his bones. She was healthy and strong, ready to serve him. But no matter how hard he'd focused on that deep sense of urgency that tied him to her, he could not zero in on her location. That had never happened before. In the past, he'd followed the bond like Ariadne's thread straight to his ward. Even now, he sensed Richard in his home in the Garden District and Agnes in her apartment across the Quarter. By the energy coursing down the bond, both were happy and safe. But the woman in his arms—she'd been impossible to detect.

Until her fear beckoned him. Then it had been as if she were screaming down the bond. Thank the Mountain he'd reached her before those men had raped her or worse. Unfortunately, the delay had cost her a nasty bump on the head. Unacceptable.

It was the curse. The damn thing had scrambled his circuitry. Dragon magic was a tricky thing to wield in this realm under normal circumstances. Disrupt it with voodoo and he couldn't trust it anymore. Not consistently.

He landed on the balcony of his apartment, thankful that his invisibility still seemed to be effective. It was late, and he'd taken care to fly over areas of the French Quarter less populated than others at that hour. He tucked his wings away and used his foot to slide open the door.

Safely inside, he laid her on his bed to inspect the damage. His breath seized in his lungs. She was tiny, waifish, her body still holding an echo of the illness he'd saved her from. Regardless, she was as lovely and pale as priceless porcelain, the fragile bones of her face supporting luminescent skin. Her hair was longer now, down to her chin, and wavy. He thought she looked like a goddess lying there, bleeding in his bed.

Bleeding. By the Mountain, what was he doing? He ran to his dresser and retrieved his healing amulet, its lustrous white giving off rainbow hues like mother-of-pearl as he looped it around her neck. When he'd first come to this realm, a renowned indigenous healer had helped him and three of his siblings settle in the New World. She was a wise woman named Maiara, and Gabriel had grown to trust her implicitly. That was long ago, in another time and place. He thought of her now as the amulet that once was hers glowed in the dim light, and the edges of Ravenna's wounds began to stitch together. Three hundred years and the amulet still worked. He frowned at the black heart of his traitorous ring.

Retreating to the kitchen, he threw open the cupboards, one after another. Maiara always used a silver bowl for healing. It had to be silver. She said it staved off infection.

Nothing silver resided in his cabinets, but he owned an antique store for Mountain's sake. *Think, Gabriel. Silver.*

An idea came to him, and he rushed into his living room, snatching a fresh flower arrangement off the coffee table and dumping its contents in the kitchen sink. He'd remembered the container the blooms were arranged in was an antique Spanish silver ember bowl. He washed it out quickly and filled it with warm water. The next instant he was by her side, using a fluffy white washcloth to clean her wound. He took care to remove as much of the blood as possible. It was best if she never knew how hurt she'd been.

He suspected that her injuries might have killed her if it weren't for his tooth. Curing her cancer was only the start. She'd heal faster with it inside her, and any skills she'd had before his gift would be enhanced by its presence. He was counting on that.

Hand resting on her stomach, he turned her head to get at the blood that had dripped through her hair toward her ear. She moaned.

"Hot," she mumbled. Her eyes were still closed and her voice was groggy.

Of course she was hot. She was wearing a fleece, and Gabriel's natural body temperature kept things toasty in his immediate vicinity. Tucking the amulet inside her shirt, he cradled her head and carefully removed her outer layer.

"Is that better?" he asked.

Her eyelashes fluttered. He wrung out the rag again, mopping her forehead with cold water. Everything stopped when she opened her eyes. Sapphire blue. Intense. They cut right to his soul. All he could do was stare dumbly. Her picture had intrigued him, but a two-dimensional likeness couldn't do her justice. And although he'd seen her in the hospital, her eyes had been rheumy then, clouded with pain, their natural luster dimmed. This was so much more. She was as enchanting as a jewel in the light whose facets begged to be examined, a sleeping beauty woken with a kiss.

"It's you," she said, her lips parting in amazement. She raised her hand, letting it hover near his face like she meant to touch him but couldn't bring herself to do so. "You saved me... again."

What was wrong with him? He could feel his inner dragon coil within his torso, wanting desperately to be stroked by those fingers. Her voice spoke directly to the deepest part of him. Unsettling to say the least. As a dragon, he wasn't normally attracted to humans. He tended to find them too vulnerable. Which made him suspect his reaction to her was more about the curse than reality.

"Of course I saved you," he said, reining in the odd sensation. "Only an idiot wouldn't protect his investment."

"Your investment?" Raven wasn't sure how long she'd been asleep, but she'd woken to heat burning in her torso, starting at the base of her ribs and blossoming north until it made her flushed and sweaty. Had she lost too much blood? Hit her head too hard? When she'd opened her eyes, he'd been there. Him. Death, dark eyes smoldering with that weird internal fire.

The look in his eyes had been tender. Almost adoring. At first she thought he might kiss her, his face was so close to hers. She'd raised her hand to cradle his cheek but paused when she sensed something like a ripple travel first through him and then through her. She had the fleeting thought that she'd been electrocuted, only she had no personal experience with that. She'd read that when someone was struck by lightning, the energy entered at one point and traveled all the way through their body to exit out another. That's how this felt, like heat had rolled through him and passed to her at the place he touched her stomach. It connected them still.

But then he'd pulled away so abruptly, she might as well have been doused in ice water. He'd called her his "investment." What the hell was that supposed to mean?

"Breathe, Raven. I haven't saved you twice now to have you suffocate yourself."

Yes, she was holding her breath, her body trying to reconnect with that energy it had experienced only a moment ago. But it was gone. She filled her lungs and let the air out slowly.

He smelled of fire and spice, orange peels and burning leaves. The man was massive, his size intimidating enough for her to reflexively fist the sheets. She was lying on a nest of red silk on the right side of a mahogany four-poster that belonged in a European castle. Its size dwarfed her, making her feel tiny and insignificant. If she sank any deeper into the mattress, it might swallow her up. *He* might swallow her up.

"You're okay. Those men didn't succeed in violating you." His voice was a low rumble reminiscent of thunder.

She ran a hand down the front of her body, thankful to find her T-shirt, bra, and jeans were all in place. So he'd stopped them in time.

He turned to wring out a cloth he held and then mopped her head with it before returning it to a silver bowl on the bedside table. She touched the cool spot he left behind on her forehead. The idea of him caring for her made her heart flutter. His eyes raked over her possessively, rendering her as good as naked despite all her clothing.

"Did you kill them?" She trembled at the memory of the man bleeding in the street.

"No," he said. "Although I should have. It brings me no joy that they will wake up tomorrow, even if they do so in a hospital."

A dark cloud passed behind his eyes, and for the first time she felt afraid. He was real. A man who could bring death as easily as he could bring life. She shuddered.

He leaned back to put additional room between them. "There's nothing to be afraid of," he said. "I wouldn't have healed you if I planned to hurt you. Those men deserved what they got. It is in my nature to be protective of what is mine."

Mine. What? She swallowed twice. "Are you Death?"

He snorted, then laughed, the sound reverberating from deep within his chest and filling the room. He ran a hand through his longish dark waves and then shook his head as if he found the idea entirely preposterous.

"Of course not," he said. "My name is Gabriel Blakemore, proprietor of Blakemore's Antiques, the shop below us."

She wrinkled her forehead, an expression that hurt more than it should have.

"Careful. You're still healing. I hastened the process, but your body has to do the work. Give it a few minutes." His voice was thick and deep, with the hint of an accent she couldn't quite place. Not Louisianan or even Southern. She hadn't noticed before. Now she wondered if he was originally from somewhere else.

She rubbed her head. It was throbbing. She could barely think.

"Hmm. Sorry about that. You will heal faster with my tooth inside you, but I was worried about your head, so I used this." He lifted a disk from her chest that shone with the luster of mother-of-pearl. He set it on the table beside the bowl. Instantly her head stopped aching. "I've left it on too long."

"Better," she said.

"Good. Rest for a moment. Then I will take you home. You're safe now." He placed a hand on her upper arm.

Raven's stomach did an odd little flip at his touch and then, just as strangely, everything inside her calmed. She met his gaze again and was not afraid. A sense of peace and safety wrapped around her like a cloak.

He cleared his throat and removed his hand, retreating to a chair beside the bed and leaving her arm cold from the lack of his touch. The Louis XIV piece looked like children's furniture beneath his oversized body, but he folded into it with the grace of a dancer, smoothing his shirt. He was impeccably dressed. Raven wasn't into fashion, but anyone would appreciate the man's threads.

"How did you cure my cancer? What did you give me?" she asked. "Was it an experimental drug? Something illegal?"

"Ms. Tanglewood, I fed you my tooth. I'll thank you not to make light of it. I only have so many, and it takes years for them to grow back." He rubbed his jaw as he spoke, as if the extraction still stung.

She blinked at him, trying to make sense of what he was saying. "If teeth cured cancer, we'd all be saving our baby teeth instead of buying health insurance." Was she really arguing the impossibility of magic healing teeth?

"*Human* teeth cannot cure cancer." His long, tapered fingers tapped compulsively against his thigh. *Odd.* She was still staring at those dancing fingers when the gist of what he said sank in.

"Did you just say you weren't... human?"

He leaned back and looked at her through long, dark lashes. "I would have thought that would be obvious by now."

She rubbed her head again, feeling a little sick. She'd lived in New Orleans for years, since the day her parents had taken over the Three Sisters from her grandparents when she was nine. Rumors of the supernatural abounded in the city's history, in the air she breathed, in the voodoo shops that lined the Quarter.

She *should* be afraid. Any normal woman would be. She should leap out of this bed and huddle against the wall or race for the exit. Whether from exhaustion or because after everything, she couldn't bring herself to muster a fear of him, she stayed where she was and simply asked, "Are you a... vampire?"

His eyes widened, and he broke into deep, rumbling laughter. "No. I'm not."

"Then what are you?"

"I, Ms. Tanglewood, am a dragon." He inclined his head formally.

"A dragon." She stared at him, waiting for an explanation.

"A dragon. You and I made a deal. I cured you with my tooth and you agreed to work for me in exchange. I presume I gave you enough time to recover. It appears you are entirely whole again. Are you prepared to fulfill your debt to me?"

"You want me to... work for you?"

He raised an eyebrow in her direction. "Of course. You agreed—"

"I remember," she said. "I just... I didn't think you were real. I haven't heard from you in months."

He scoffed. "I assume my existence is no longer suspect. I gave you space to heal. That is all. Now I need you to uphold your end of the bargain."

"What do you want me to do?" She braced herself. She still wasn't sure what he meant by being a dragon. Would he want to drink her blood? Make her his sex slave? Or something worse?

"Do you see this ring?" He thrust the massive emerald he wore closer to her face. It was a large rectangle set in a thick band of gold, crafted with scrollwork along the sides of the center stone. The size of the stone filled the space between the base of his finger and his second knuckle.

"You could see that thing from space," she murmured.

The corner of his mouth twitched and then he seemed to remember himself, becoming serious once again. "At the center of this stone, you will notice a flaw." He moved the ring closer, almost to her nose. There *was* a flaw, a narrow black cat's-eye at the center of the gem. The facets hid it at a distance, but close up, it was unmistakable.

"I see it," she said.

"I need your help fixing it."

She slowly sat up, inhaling deeply. "I don't know anything about jewelry."

"You don't need to."

"Then how do you expect me to fix it?"

He rose and paced away from her, toward the end of the bed where a fireplace lay cold and unused. His fingers tapped vigorously against his thigh, and the former grace and gentleness she'd seen in him melted away. In its place was an agitation that was almost palpable.

"This is a very special gem, an important gem. The magic imbued in this ring allows someone like me, a dragon like me, to remain in this realm. Without it, I will be forced to return to my homeland or I will perish. I don't wish for either of those things to happen."

Raven tried to digest what he was telling her. "What's wrong with your ring?"

He gave a frustrated sigh. "It's been cursed. The magic is failing. I need you to use your abilities to help me find the cure, the countercurse."

"You want me to cure your ring?" She formed each word slowly, deliberately, but the elocution didn't help it make sense.

"Exactly." His tapping fingers curled into a fist. He looked somehow relieved, as if now she understood what she needed to do. As if curing rings was something former cancer patients did all the time.

She shook her head and tried to still the tremble in her hand. "There's been a terrible mistake. I don't know how to fix your ring. I wouldn't even know where to start."

With a deep sigh he approached her again. "Of course not. I haven't given you the resources to do so yet. But I will, once you begin. I'll give you everything you need." He shifted restlessly, like his entire body itched.

"Okay," she said softly. She didn't understand. Not by a long shot. But she'd try. She owed him that.

"Now, if you are well, my driver is waiting to take you home. I expect you back here by seven thirty tomorrow morning. Do not be late. Do you understand?" His voice had changed, and she winced at the harshness.

"Tomorrow is Sunday. You mean Monday morning."

"Tomorrow, Ms. Tanglewood. I expect you to start tomorrow. Is that understood?" His eyes had gone hard and as cold as ice, and his jaw tightened. He was twice her size. A human man that large could snap her like a twig. Gabriel had made it clear he wasn't human. He'd said he was a dragon. Would he burn her with fiery breath if she didn't obey? Stop her heart with the same magic with which he had resurrected her body? She didn't want to find out.

"All right." She didn't know what else to say. It was all too much, too crazy. All she wanted to do was wake up from this surreal dream she was in. She needed room to think.

He helped her up and handed her fleece to her. For a moment she was pinned by his undivided attention. The intensity slammed into her like she was a flower newly sprouted from the earth and looking directly into the sun.

Enthralled, she allowed him to guide her from the apartment into a short hallway and down a flight of stairs with a glossy, dark wood railing that belonged in another time. She oriented herself as they descended. His home was on the third floor. The second level was dark, closed up for the night, she presumed. When they reached the first floor, there was no doubt they were inside an antique shop. Every manner of Old World décor was displayed in the space, which was large by French Quarter standards. As they navigated the uneven aisle toward the front door, she tried not to gape at an ornate armoire's $40,000 price tag. She took a step away from it.

It surprised her how gracefully Gabriel steered his oversized frame through the valuable and delicate pieces in the room. Only when he opened the door for her did she realize where they were: Royal Street. She glanced up at the sign, BLAKEMORE'S ANTIQUE SHOP.

A town car pulled up beside her, and Gabriel opened the door. "Will you need a ride in the morning?"

"No," she said quickly.

"Are you sure, Ms. Tanglewood? After what happened tonight, I want to ensure you make it here safely."

"Raven," she said.

"Hmm?"

"You called me Ms. Tanglewood. You can call me Raven. It's short for Ravenna."

He nodded. "Gabriel."

Their eyes caught again, and the energy returned with a vengeance, like something in her torso had reached out and hooked something deep within his. He shuffled his feet and glanced away.

"Duncan will take you home. Good night, *Raven*. I look forward to working with you."

She climbed into the dark leather seat, and he shut the door behind her.

"Where to, miss?" Duncan asked.

"The Three Sisters. Magazine Street, in the Garden District."

The elderly man twisted around to look at her. "The bar? No. Mr. Blakemore won't like that. I'm supposed to take you home."

"That is my home. It's my mom's place. We live in the apartment above the pub."

With a single nod, the man turned back around and pulled away from the curb.

"Does Mr. Blakemore know where you live?" Duncan asked.

She shrugged. "I don't know. He didn't ask for my address."

The man made a throaty sound. "He'll know soon enough. You're working for him now."

Raven leaned back against the seat and stared out the window. "Yes, I guess I am."

CHAPTER SIX

The next morning, Raven was too nervous for breakfast. She couldn't explain exactly what Gabriel was or how he'd saved her, but today she would be working with him full-time. She hadn't even had enough presence of mind to ask him how much she'd be paid.

He'd said he was a dragon, but what exactly did that mean? The question intrigued her enough that she wanted a chance to learn more about him. She'd be lying to say that was her only desire. There were plenty of things intriguing about Gabriel, not the least of which was that he made her feel alive again, as alive as before she'd become ill.

A part of her though had an awful feeling that her debt to him would mean much more than he'd told her last night. He'd looked at her like he owned her. Maybe he thought he did. She hadn't signed a contract before she swallowed that tooth. Hadn't reviewed the terms and conditions. She took a deep breath and let it out slowly. Worrying wouldn't get her anywhere. She was alive thanks to him. Plus she had a job, a fine point she hoped would get her mom, Avery, and most importantly her father off her back.

"Why are you all gussied up?" Avery asked when Raven emerged from the bathroom dressed for the day in her favorite sleeveless floral dress. It had a scoop neck and a cut that skimmed along her body down to the knee, with a thick rose-colored belt that matched the scarf tied around her neck. It did a good job of giving her rather flat figure a little shape. She figured she should dress nicely for a job in a place where they sold $40,000 armoires, and this was the most professional thing she could find that fit her bony post-cancer frame. Normally she would wear heels with this outfit, but she found a pair of flats that matched well enough and were more practical for a day of... she wasn't sure what. She'd also tamed her wild mass of curls.

"I found a job," she told Avery. She did not offer a smile or a good morning. "I'm going to work today."

Avery scowled. "I thought you said you were going to help Mom and me at the Three Sisters."

"You didn't tell her that, did you, Avery?" Raven cut her a sharp glare. "I never committed to that. After what you pulled last night with Dad, even if I didn't have a job, I'm not sure I'd want to work with you."

"I'm sorry," Avery said defensively. "I thought I was doing the right thing."

"Well, it wasn't. He hurt me and now he wants to control me."

"Truly, Raven, I am sorry. He abandoned you. I see that now." This time she meant it. Avery was a year older than Raven, and the two had a long history of psychological co-torture and hair pulling. But this apology was full of compassion and genuine contriteness, not unlike the day Avery had made Raven walk home from the pool alone so she could make out with Jeffrey "String Bean" Pulitzer. Raven had passed out from heat exhaustion and had to be taken to the ER. Avery had apologized through the same tight lips that day.

"Apology accepted," Raven said. "Just don't try it again."

"I didn't tell Mom, but I was looking forward to you working with us. We need the help."

"This job... it sort of fell out of the sky," Raven said, leaning against the breakfast bar where Avery sat. Her mind rushed to Gabriel lifting her attacker off her and flying him toward the stars. *Not a lie.* "I couldn't turn it down."

"It's Sunday. What sort of job has you start work on a Sunday?"

"*You* work on Sunday."

"I'm a server in a pub. You're dressed for the office. Where are you working?"

"Blakemore's Antiques."

"Blakemore's? No shit? You've got to be kidding."

"What's wrong with Blakemore's? It appeals to the history buff in me."

"Have you seen Gabriel Blakemore?" Avery's eyes widened.

"Of course I have. I'm working for him."

"He has quite a reputation."

"What sort of reputation?"

Avery shook her head. "Oh my poor, sweet, sheltered sister. Blakemore is rich, sickeningly so, and mean as a badger. A friend of mine waited on him at Antoine's, and he practically chewed her head off when the food was late."

"Oh," Raven said, shocked. She remembered the way he'd comforted her and carefully cared for the wound in her head, the one that was gone now because of him. "He was kind to me."

"Probably wants to get you into bed." Avery snorted. "I've heard he's also a playboy."

If Raven told her she'd already been in his bed, Avery would have a coronary. She rested a hand on her hip and tilted her chin up, her stomach tightening with the memory of Gabriel's scent and the red sheets. He'd only touched her arm. She had no reason to believe he was anything but a gentleman.

"Who do you know who has actually slept with him, Avery?" Not that Gabriel couldn't have whomever he wanted, but she was a decent judge of character, and he didn't strike her as the type that slept around. Plus, Avery was prone to exaggeration.

"No one, personally." Her eyes shifted. "But look at him. You know that guy is getting some tail."

Raven scoffed. "I'm going to enjoy looking at him. Every. Day. Because, unlike you, I'm working for him." She snapped her fingers and grabbed her purse off the counter. "Gotta go. I'm going to be late."

"He's out of your league, Raven. Way out." There was not a hint of humor in her voice.

"Don't worry. I don't plan to do anything but work for him." She motioned at her dress. "Would you buy antiques from me?"

"Sure." Avery smiled. "How are you getting there?" It was a sore subject. Raven had never gotten around to renewing her driver's license. She'd lost it when her brain cancer made it unsafe for her to drive. With a note from Dr. Freemont and some practice, she could get it back, but for some reason she hadn't made it a priority.

"I'm taking the streetcar." She turned back. "Tell Mom about the job. I didn't get a chance to."

"Oh believe me, as soon as I get to the restaurant it will

51

be a major topic of conversation." She winked over her coffee.

"If you're going to gossip about me, make me taller and far more attractive."

"Done."

She'd reached the door when Avery called her name. "Hey, be careful tonight on your way home. Two guys were killed in the French Quarter last night."

Raven swallowed hard and turned back toward her. "Killed?"

"They found them alive. Victims of a brutal attack. Their blood alcohol level was in the danger zone, so who knows what actually happened. Anyway, they both died this morning in the hospital from complications."

Raven nodded, feeling a little sick.

"Are you okay? You look pale. You should eat something."

"I'm fine. I'll be careful. See you tonight." Raven forced herself out the door and hurried for the streetcar, grasping all at once that she was going to work for a killer.

❧

WHERE WAS SHE? GABRIEL PACED OUTSIDE HIS OFFICE at the back of the store, his fingers tapping so hard they hurt. Raven was his last hope, the last person with any potential he'd been strong enough to bind to him. She was his. His! He needed to know where she was at all times. He should have known, should have been able to track her movements, but he could not. The damned curse must be messing with his abilities.

His tapping hand bumped a Sèvres urn, and it teetered on its base. Thankfully, Agnes, his salesperson, caught it between her spotted hands and righted it before it crashed to the floor.

"Try to relax, Gabriel. She's only ten minutes late," the elderly woman said. "She's bound to you. She'll be here."

"She could be injured," he said. "What if something has happened to her?" A horrible thought passed through his mind. "What if she refuses to come at all?"

Agnes's white hair swung at a sophisticated angle. She glared at him through a pair of oversized eyeglasses and wrinkled her nose. "You will force her!" she said matter-of-factly. "Are you a dragon or one of these spineless boys that pass for men around this city?" She waved at the street.

Of course Agnes, whose bond was working correctly, would not suspect that his power over Raven had been compromised by the curse. Nor would he tell her as much. "I don't wish to force her," he said. "People achieve better results when they are invested in delivering them. I want her to want to help us, not be coerced."

"How noble of you," she said, steepling her fingers, "Or might this be about Kristina?" Agnes frowned and lowered her voice. "What happened to her, Gabriel?"

"I don't want to talk about Kristina."

"So you've said." Her frown became more pronounced, and Gabriel turned away. The less he said about Kristina, the better.

"Gabriel," Agnes repeated. She gestured toward the door with her chin.

Raven stood in the entrance, framed by the morning light pouring through the window behind her. He was momentarily speechless. She might have been an angel with her flawless skin and welcoming smile. Darkness coiled around his heart. Surely this was a side effect of the curse.

He was acting like a teenaged boy. He grimaced until his face hurt from the expression of distaste.

"I'm sorry I'm a little late," she said. "The streetcar was delayed."

He didn't say a word.

"It was an oyster truck. There was an accident. Oysters all over the track." Her voice was sweet and her smile warm and genuine.

"Streetcar?" He winced. He could feel the dragon roil within him, and he tapped his fingers to keep it at bay. "I asked you last night if you had reliable transportation—"

"I do!" she said. "The streetcar picks up near my home."

He scowled. "You have no vehicle of your own?"

She closed her eyes against the humiliation. "No. I haven't renewed my driver's license since I was ill."

"From now on, Duncan will pick you up and make sure you are here on time."

"No, really, that isn't necessary. It was a freak accident. I'll leave earlier next time."

"You will not be late again, Ms. Tanglewood." He purposely used her last name, addressing her like an unrepentant child. She had to learn her place. She was his. He'd saved her from death for his purposes, and she must obey.

"It won't happen again." Her smile faded and her cheeks flushed. Was she angry? She had no right to be angry.

"You agreed to be mine. You agreed to do my bidding. You must do it. I do not want to have to punish you, but I will if I must." His voice cracked like a whip.

"Do your bidding?" There was no smile now, just pure, unadulterated anger. "I agreed to no such thing! I agreed to work for you. That is all. And as for punishing me?" Raven marched forward, her tiny body seeming to fill a space eight times her actual size, and leaned toward Gabriel. "I'll have you know I am an adult, *Mr. Blakemore*. I am a free woman. You may be my boss, but you are not my father. You can fire me, but you sure as hell won't punish me. I suppose you have the right to chastise me for being late, but I hardly think five"—she checked her watch—"ten minutes is a punishable offense, considering the circumstances."

Her chest rose and fell rapidly, and Gabriel thought for a second she might punch him. For some reason, he had to repress a smile. She was a brave little thing.

"A dragon must manage his investments, you understand. We made a bargain, you and I. I can't have something happening to you. I need to know where you are and that you are safe. You have cost me dearly." He tapped the side of his cheek over where his tooth once was. "Has my gift benefited you?"

Her hands landed on her hips, and she raised her shoulders toward her ears. "Yes," she said, the word high-pitched and short. "Of course it has. You know it has."

"Hmm. Any woman worth her salt would show her gratitude for such a gift by upholding her side of the bargain." He raised an eyebrow and stepped in closer. "You are bound to me."

She gaped at him. "If that's your attitude, you can shove your bargain right up your—"

"Is this our new associate?" Agnes positioned herself between them and cleared her throat. Not that the sound was necessary. Her black leather skirt and silver silk blouse were hard to ignore. The woman might be seventy, but she still knew how to command a room. She nudged Gabriel. "Introduce me."

"Yes, of course," Gabriel said darkly. He'd give her hell for this later. "Raven Tanglewood, this is Agnes Rollins, my sales associate. You'll have to wait to meet our interior designer, Richard Parker. He comes in later today."

"He takes his husband out to breakfast every Sunday morning. Isn't that sweet?" Agnes offered.

Raven raised her eyebrow and straightened slightly. "Yes," she said. "Sweet. Amazing he doesn't get *punished* for it."

Gabriel felt the dragon rise inside him again. Infuriating woman.

"Would you like me to show Raven around?" Agnes asked, her hand lingering in the vicinity of her throat.

"Not today, Agnes. Since Raven was late, she needs to start upstairs right away."

Agnes folded her hands. "Would you like me to show her where Kristina left off?"

Gabriel scowled. There was no reason to bring up Kristina. "No. I will do it," he said harshly.

Agnes exchanged a glance with Raven and shrugged. "Perhaps we could have lunch together, dear, when you're ready for a break?"

She nodded. "I'd like that."

"If she has time," Gabriel snapped. "Come with me. I'll show you to your work." He reached for her wrist.

She pulled her arm away from him. "I can follow you. I don't need you to lead me by the hand."

He growled. Behind Raven, Agnes tossed up her hands, frantically motioning for him to make nice with the girl. He turned and headed for the stairs.

He'd taken her down this way last night. He wondered how much she remembered. He made a point of stopping on the second floor and pointing out where they sold antique lighting fixtures. On the third floor, he passed his apartment and led her to the adjacent room where she'd be working. Turning his key in the lock, he opened the door for her.

She stepped inside, her eyelashes fluttering as if she couldn't believe her eyes. She glanced at him once and again before saying, "Oh, wow."

❧

GOD IN HEAVEN ABOVE, RAVEN HAD NEVER SEEN A more spectacular library. The sweet, musky smell of old books and leather filled her nose, and the shiny dark wood gave off a deep luster in the dim light. There had to be thousands of books in here, some that looked hundreds of years old. Housed on shelves that ran floor to ceiling every three or four feet, the books filled the entire length of the building as far as Raven could tell.

Instantly she became excited about the job again. For a moment downstairs, when she'd come face-to-face with Gabriel's inflexible and possessive attitude, she'd thought about quitting. Now she was glad she hadn't. Her fingers itched to investigate these historical texts. She walked deeper into the room, lips parting with the absolute wonder of it.

"You like books?" Gabriel asked.

"Yes," she said. "I love books. I enjoyed reading as a child, but I grew to love it more after I got sick." Reading had been her savior, a vacation from reality with every page. Sometimes it was her only way out of her hospital room.

He stepped closer to her, until she could feel his warmth radiating against her back, and his scent wrapped around her like a balm. She blinked, suddenly aware of his looming presence. Downstairs when she was angry, hubris came easily. Now, the memory of what he'd done to her attackers made her skin prickle.

"You suffered greatly when you were ill. I am sorry for this," he said.

The compassion in his tone moved her and she glanced at him over her shoulder. Her breath hitched. Avery had been right to warn her. He was absolutely arresting. Despite her apprehension, his smoldering eyes alone made her burn from within. "Why am I here? What are these books?"

"Rare editions. Books about magic and the paranormal. Most are one of a kind."

An expert she was not, but she knew enough to question the specifics. "One of a kind? Shouldn't these be behind glass or in a climate-controlled room?"

"They are," he said. "These books are preserved... with magic. My magic."

She dropped her chin. "Dragon magic?"

"Yes."

"Ahhh." She tipped her head back. "I didn't know dragons existed before yesterday. I had no idea they used magic."

"Dragons are magical beings," he explained. "There are a few abilities inherent in our nature. We can fly... become invisible. We are faster and stronger than humans. We come from the Mountain, and the Mountain fills us with magical energy. We can perform certain spells when we need to, leveraging that magic."

"Like a witch?" Part of her wanted to deny his otherworldly nature, but a stronger part, the same part of her that had looked death in the face and known somehow it wasn't the end, believed he was what he said he was.

He nodded. "I cannot control the elements as a witch

can, but I can execute some spells and rituals similarly, and my magic will make them effective."

She moved to the first shelf, examining the spines. "You don't look like a dragon."

He leaned against the shelf. "I can change my appearance, but it would be too destructive to show you my natural form now, not to mention dangerous. I don't have the control I do in this form. I could hurt you without really knowing what I was doing."

"You seemed to do a pretty good job hurting those men last night. They're dead, you know." And there it was. Perhaps she was braver than she thought.

He shifted uneasily. "They were alive when I left them. I gave the paramedics their location."

She frowned. "They didn't make it." Needing to move, she walked down the row to the next shelf.

"Does it bother you that they're dead?" he asked darkly.

She thought about it. "I'm having trouble mustering sympathy for men who definitely would have raped me and probably would have killed me if they'd had the chance."

"Then we don't have a problem."

She stopped and looked at him. "Only that now I know I'm working for a murderer who wants to punish me. Will you kill me if I don't do what you say?"

His face darkened, and he gave her a wry grin. "Let's not find out."

A chill ran through her. Gabriel had been kind to her. Unmistakably kind and gentle. He'd looked at her as sweetly as any man had. But she could see it now. He was also dangerous. And what he'd said downstairs had been downright possessive.

"So, what do you want me to do in here?" she asked.

"I need you to examine each page of each of these grimoires."

She glanced at him curiously. "Grimoires?"

"Books of magic. Each of these books was written by someone who had and exercised the magic contained within. A grimoire is a personal book of magic and the contents of these rare editions are in most cases original and entirely unique."

Raven stared at the books. There were thousands. She was a fast reader, but it would take her years to get through every book in this room. "What are we looking for?"

"A countercurse to break the hex on my ring." He held up his right hand. The emerald seemed to give off its own light in the dim and dusty room. "I have spent the past year procuring these texts from every corner of the world at great personal cost. This room contains a comprehensive encyclopedia of magical knowledge. Something here has to be strong enough to do the trick."

She ran her finger along one leather spine. "How long do we have?"

"Mardi Gras. The curse will completely destroy the magic of my ring at midnight on Fat Tuesday."

"Mardi Gras is February thirteenth this year. It's January seventh. That's just over a month away. It would take me a year to get through all these."

"You don't have to read all of them," Gabriel said. He gestured for her to follow him toward the back of the room.

There was a ledger open on a massive library desk. He tugged the chain on a green banker's lamp in the corner, and it glowed to life, spilling a circle of light over the pages.

"My previous employee, Kristina, kept excellent records. Start where she left off. She has already analyzed the first half of the shelves. Everything is cataloged here."

Raven examined the tight handwriting and neat notes. "What happened to Kristina?"

"She has moved on," he said, his eyes slipping away from hers.

"Some of these aren't in English." She could see one spine on the shelf in front of her that appeared to be in Korean.

"Few of them are in English," he confirmed.

"I can only read English."

He huffed. "Don't limit yourself to examining them with your eyes, Raven. Use your abilities. The same psychic abilities you used to warn your parents about the fire. It is why I chose you."

"But—" How did she explain that her former vision was just a fluke? A product of the cancer he had cured? "I'm not actually psychic. I don't know how I did it before. It's not like I can hold these books against my forehead and tell you what's inside."

A slow grin spread across his face. "Is that a Johnny Carson reference?"

"Carnac the Magnificent."

"Wasn't he before your time?"

"I watched reruns in the hospital."

"Carnac you may not be, but I believe you are enough." The way he said it made her chest warm. He believed she could do this. He really did. Gabriel retrieved a volume from the shelf and opened it to a random page, then grabbed her wrist and positioned her palm flat over the words. "Anything?"

Raven tried not to laugh. She felt something all right: his strange heat running the course of her body, straight to her core. Her tongue felt thick as she answered, "Uh, no."

He released her. "Hmm. Well. There will be when you

come upon something useful." His fingers tapped against the desk. Tap-tap-tap. Tap-tap-tap. The rhythm she'd noticed before had started again, more violently this time.

"Can I ask you a personal question?" Raven toyed with the corner of the catalog.

He gave her a small nod.

"Do you have OCD? Because I know a doctor who can help you with that." She gestured toward his fingers.

He pulled his hand away, tucking it into his pocket. "OCD?"

"Obsessive-compulsive disorder. Like there are certain things you have to do to feel normal. Reoccurring thoughts or behaviors."

"It's not OCD. It's a side effect of the curse," Gabriel said.

"Hmm. It's similar to OCD." Raven fell silent when it became clear by the hardening of his jaw that she was making him self-conscious.

He pointed toward a room to her right. "Bathroom and break room are through there. I will leave you now. Get started."

"Wait, what if I have questions?"

"Write them down. I'll check in this afternoon."

"But—"

She was too late. Gabriel had turned on his heel and left the room, leaving Raven alone in the strange library.

"Okay then, have a nice day to you too, mysterious, sexy dragon man," she muttered under her breath. Her eyes fell on the books. She lowered herself slowly into the chair behind the desk.

Avery was never going to believe this.

CHAPTER SEVEN

Raven flipped pages all morning. The book she'd chosen from the list, the next on the shelf that Kristina had abandoned, was written in fine German calligraphy. She had no idea what it said. Dutifully, her eyes traced over the words and symbols ordered down the page like a recipe. It was boring as hell. With her head resting against her fist, she had to work to stay awake.

At nine a.m. she stood and did jumping jacks to keep her blood flowing. She finished the first book, logged it in the catalog, and slid it back onto the shelf. The next book, she was relieved to learn, was in English. Blakemore wasn't lying about these books being grimoires.

"Spell to remove a demon from an infant," she read. "Locator charm. Summoning of the spirit. Incantation to release inner power." She mumbled the words to herself and scratched a growing itch on the inside of her arm. She turned the page, gaining interest when one of the spells called for the "urine of a newborn boy" and the "placenta of a goat."

"Ew," she whispered to herself. As she read, she had the

passing thought that she'd caught some type of skin infection. The patch of itchy skin on the inside of her arm seemed to be getting bigger. The back of her neck had begun to itch as well, and she scratched the base of her hairline. Come to think of it, she felt itchy in a few places: the side of her calf, under her ribs. She wondered if she might be allergic to something in the room.

It was almost eleven when she heard the tinkle of a bell from the small sitting room attached to the library. "Perfect time for a break." She rose from the desk and stretching her arms above her head. Her stomach growled. She crossed into what turned out to be a well-appointed parlor. Someone had left her a tray on the coffee table with tea, toast, and hard-boiled eggs.

"Hello?" she called. No answer came. "Is anyone here?" The tea was steaming hot. Whoever had left it had done so recently.

She used the adjacent bathroom. As she washed her hands, she took in the art on the walls. If she wasn't mistaken, the piece hanging above the toilet was an Emelia Beldroit. She'd just read an article on the young local artist. Her paintings were selling for $50,000 and up. She pulled out her phone and snapped a picture.

"Avery is never going to believe I peed under this thing." She giggled, then eyed the paintings on the other three walls. Three. There was no other door to this room besides the one through which she'd entered.

Eyes narrowing, she reentered the sitting room. There was no other way in here either. Whoever had delivered the tea would have had to walk past where she'd been working. How had she missed them?

Her temples throbbed. Men with healing teeth who say they are dragons. Tea that appears out of nowhere. A room full of magical texts. Was this her new normal? It was too much. She needed air.

Walking back through the stacks, she speculated that she'd missed the tea being brought in because she'd fallen asleep reading. It was possible. The books were about as exciting as insurance contracts. A short walk outside was what she needed. Some fresh air would invigorate her.

She tugged on the door to the library. It wouldn't budge. Examining the lock, she saw a keyhole. She tugged the knob again. It didn't give. She was locked in. She rattled the knob, banging on the door with her open palm.

"Hey!" she yelled. "Someone let me out!"

No one answered.

"Hey!" she yelled again, this time as loud as she could. A terrifying thought gripped her like a vise. Had she been locked inside on purpose? When Gabriel said she was *his*, was it in a *Silence of the Lambs* sort of way? Was she locked in here for good? Forced to work for him while food dropped out of the sky?

Her heart sprinted in her chest and her breath came in pants. "No. No. No. I can't do this. *I can't do this!*" she screamed at the door. She shook her hands, but the panic attack revved up another notch. She could handle that Gabriel was some sort of supernatural monster. She could deal with a library full of magical texts. But this... this *terrified* her. In the blink of an eye, she was back in that bed in the hospital, a prisoner to the tubes and the illness. She couldn't go back there. She couldn't live in a cage. Not again. Not ever again.

She grabbed her head. The room was spinning, books blurring as the walls wavered, dipping toward her and back out again. Bending at the waist, she tried to breathe deeply with her head between her knees. It didn't help. If she didn't get out of this room, she would lose her mind.

Her gaze caught on the window at the back of the library. She rushed to it and rolled up the shades. The sun poured in across the ancient texts. It would be folly to expose them to the elements. If she opened the window, the humid air and sunlight could damage the fragile pages. Another wave of anxiety punched her, and she decided she didn't care. All she cared about was getting out, getting free.

She turned the lock on the window and lifted. Clearly it hadn't been opened in years, and it took muscle and a curse to jimmy it up one inch, then two, then as wide as it would go. She hung her head out and gasped for air. There was no balcony below her, just a straight drop to Royal Street. Only three stories. The fall wouldn't kill her, although if she landed wrong she might break her legs. She placed a hand on each side of the window and stepped up onto the sill.

Her heart raced like a jackrabbit's and sweat dripped down her temples. Her anxiety yelled *jump* while her self-preservation begged her to wait. Body and mind in this state of war, she dug her nails into the window trim.

She was still fighting herself when Gabriel's voice, soft, kind and desperate, spoke to her from the doorway.

"Raven, what are you doing?"

IF GABRIEL'S POWER HADN'T BEEN COMPROMISED, HE might have drawn her from the window using the bond and forced her to run to him, whether she wanted to or not. Or he might have moved fast as a dark wind to catch an arm around her waist and save her from herself. As it was, he stood helpless in the aisle of the library with the door propped open behind him, tugging helplessly on the bond that connected them but was as good as useless. He cursed. There was no other choice. He couldn't force her off the sill. If he was going to fix this, he'd need to find the right words to convince her to come to him.

But what could he say to make her stop when her emotional spectrum was riddled with anxiety like he'd never felt before? Her panic was what had drawn him out. He'd been sleeping in his dragon form, as he'd made a habit of doing to counteract the side effects of the curse, when a lightning bolt of fear had shot down his spine and rattled the bond he shared with Raven. The sheer terror, razor sharp and agonizingly real, had forced him to shift back into his human form. He'd finished dressing before his eyes were fully open.

It pained him to know he had caused that crippling terror. He'd locked her in this room without thinking, and right after she'd told him about her fear of captivity. He should have known better. He deeply regretted it now. An image of her fragile bones cracking like eggshells on the pavement below terrorized his thoughts. He couldn't let that happen.

She turned her head.

"Please, don't jump," he said. There was no disguising the genuine pleading in his tone. He made no attempt to hide that he was positively wrecked. He'd shifted into his human form so quickly he felt newly born into the world, and he stumbled forward, his hands outstretched toward her.

"I can't do this," she cried. "I can't stand it." Her pupils were oversized, and her nails dug into the trim around the window.

What had he done? She was half crazed.

"You can leave," he said, pointing one hand toward the propped-open door. "Please... through the front door. I don't want you to hurt yourself. I won't try to stop you. You can leave right now if you wish." He took another step toward her but stopped when she leaned out the window.

"You locked me in." Her voice cracked and tears began to flow. Gabriel sensed self-loathing in the tightness around her jaw. Did she hate herself for showing her panic? This tiny fireball of a human didn't want him to see what he'd done to her. He respected that, even as he loathed himself for causing it.

"It was a mistake."

"Bullshit. You sick, twisted bastard!"

"The books are priceless. For security reasons, the door locks when you close it. I didn't think about it. I should have warned you. I should have given you the key." Gabriel reached into his pocket. He held the key aloft like a talisman and stepped closer to her. This time she was more receptive to his nearness. Slowly, carefully, he set the key down on the desk. "You are not a prisoner here. You can leave at any time."

She let out a shaky breath and glanced toward the door. "I can leave?"

"Yes. I can see you are afraid. The door is open now. You don't have to jump out the window. I won't hurt you. I would never hurt you." He offered her his hand. Raven slipped her fingers into his, and the relief he experienced almost sent him to his knees.

Although his instinct was to sweep her into his arms, he hesitated, not wanting to scare her away. Instead, he helped her down onto her own two shaky legs. He was surprised when she collapsed against his chest, her tears soaking his shirt. Her hair smelled of vanilla and night-blooming jasmine, and he bent to place a kiss along her part. Strange, he felt as if he'd done it a dozen times, as natural as breathing. He heard her draw a long, deep inhale.

"Shhh. It's okay. You're safe now." He stroked her back with long, comforting caresses.

"Gabriel?" Agnes called from the doorway.

Without thinking, Gabriel shifted to block Raven from view. It was a protective movement. Instinctual. That was odd. Agnes wasn't a threat. Raven stepped back and met his gaze, wiping below her eyes.

"What do you want, Agnes?" he asked.

"Richard and I wanted to ask Raven to lunch. Our treat."

"Would you like that?" he whispered to her. "Get some fresh air?"

She tucked her hair behind her ears and licked her lips. "Yes."

"Go."

He respected the hell out of how quickly she pulled herself together, straightening her dress and smoothing her hair. If he hadn't known better, he'd never believe she'd been perched on the edge of insanity only moments before. She left his side and joined Agnes.

The older woman placed a hand on Raven's shoulder and guided her from the room. Gabriel sensed the girl's relief as the two made their way to the exit.

He frowned. What a sorry excuse for a dragon he'd turned out to be. He'd just let his last chance at survival walk out the door, and by the look on her face, she wasn't coming back.

"He locked me in there," Raven said over the table at the Green Goddess. She'd had half a mind to leave immediately and never look back, but Richard and Agnes had insisted she join them, and she was too flustered to say no. "I don't believe his story for a second. It was no accident. Thank you for lunch, but I'm not going back."

"Easy, Raven. I know you're upset, but there are things about Gabriel you don't understand." Richard Parker held up one manicured hand. He was a lanky and sophisticated man who had introduced himself as Blakemore's design consultant. Sitting between him and the sharply dressed Agnes, Raven felt positively frumpy. The two were striking, and even more so side-by-side.

Agnes removed her glasses and looked at Raven through small, sunken eyes. "Gabriel isn't like you or me, as I'm sure you are aware." She glanced toward Richard, who made an *mm-hmm* sound deep in his throat. "Gabriel gave you a gift, a gift that changed your life. Richard and I understand what you're going through. We, too, were recipients of Gabriel's generosity."

"What are you saying?"

Richard tapped his eyetooth. Raven had never considered that Agnes and Richard had also received a tooth from Gabriel. Was that how he obtained all his employees? That was one hell of a recruitment strategy.

"He bought my freedom," Richard said. "I was owned by the master of a tobacco plantation. The man was cruel. He planned to whip me to death as a lesson to his other slaves. Gabriel caught wind of his intentions and gave me the money to buy my freedom. *Gave* it to me. He did not buy *me*, mind you, although he could have back then. No, he gave me the money and disappeared. No strings attached."

Raven shook her head. Was he speaking metaphorically? Slavery hadn't been legal for over a hundred years.

"Living free was hungry work. I contracted yellow fever that year. Gabriel was there for me again. He offered to cure me if I would work for him, not as a slave but as a wage-earning employee. I agreed. He fed me his tooth, and here we are. I've never regretted it."

Raven rubbed her eyes. "Excuse me, but did you mean you were an actual slave? You personally?"

"We struck our bargain in 1799," Richard said.

Raven couldn't breathe. She searched Richard's face and found nothing there to suggest he was joking. This couldn't be real.

He placed his hand on top of hers. "Raven, honey, I know this is a lot to take in, but that tooth he gave you is the gift that keeps on giving. Gabriel is not a bad man. He's simply not like us. Who is? Heaven knows, everyone in New Orleans is flying their freak flag high." His fingers slid slowly off hers as he leaned back in his chair and looked at her over his sunglasses.

Raven couldn't get her mouth to stay shut.

Agnes tore a corner off a piece of pita bread and popped it into her mouth. "My husband died in 1965. The two of us were quite good at spending money at that time. Once Harry was gone, I found out we'd been living well beyond our means. We were in deep financial trouble and I thought I'd solve that problem with a bottle of sleeping pills. I used to go into Blakemore's frequently and had ordered something for the house. When I called Gabriel to cancel it, he must have heard something in my voice. He showed up at my home and picked me up off the bathroom floor. I struck the bargain with him just before my heart slowed to a stop." She sighed. "Turns out I had more to live for than I thought

I did." She lifted her wine and swirled the cabernet in the bottom of the glass.

Raven pinched her thigh. She didn't wake up. "You too?"

"Yes. And Duncan, the driver."

"And the tooth has made you live longer than normal?"

"Our lives and yours are now tied to his. We will live as long as he does," Richard said.

Chewing her lip, Raven wanted to scream. How could this be real? "But you work *for* him." Raven scowled. "Aren't you both just a different kind of slave?"

Richard scoffed. "Do I look like a slave to you?"

Agnes placed a steadying hand on Richard's arm but looked straight at Raven. "We've both come to love Gabriel. That's why we're here, talking to you on his behalf. Yes, we are bound to him, but he has never abused that power, Raven."

"We know you're scared," Richard said. "Everyone is at the start. But if you give this a chance, you won't regret it."

Raven shook her head. "Being trapped in that room..." She grabbed the base of her neck.

"It must have been terrifying for you, but believe me when I promise it will never happen again." Agnes replaced her glasses. "You are too important to Gabriel for him to do anything to scare you away. I suspect he's kicking himself right now at the prospect."

Richard straightened. "Agnes..."

"No, Richard, she needs to know. She is too important to all of us." She squeezed Raven's hand. "We can't let you quit, not just for Gabriel's sake but for ours and for your own."

"I don't understand." Raven rubbed her temples.

"The curse on Gabriel's ring is eating his magic from

the inside out. That ring allows Gabriel to stay in our realm. When his magic dies, he will either have to return home to the place he came from or he will perish here," Agnes added. "Either way, we lose."

"What do you think will happen to each of us if Gabriel's magic fails?" Richard asked.

Raven's breath caught as realization dawned. "You mean the tooth. The magic of the tooth will also fail."

They nodded in unison. "If Gabriel's magic is gone, the magic keeping all of us alive will also be gone. Richard will age rapidly and most certainly die, as will I. You—"

"I'll have cancer again."

"We're not sure how it will happen," Richard said. "If the effects will fade gradually or all at once. But, girl, the results will not be good." Richard rubbed a hand over his short curls, looking exhausted.

"You are our last and final hope to break the curse. Gabriel is no longer strong enough to bind another helper," Agnes said.

"But that's the problem," Raven said. "Gabriel chose me because he thought I was psychic. I'm not. I don't understand how I can help any more than the two of you. Flipping through books all day—books I can't even read—it isn't going to work. You must know that."

They fell silent, both staring at her, competing in an impromptu contest of who could look the most forlorn.

"What about the person who did this before me?" Raven asked. "Was she a real psychic? Maybe we can convince her to return."

Agnes nodded. "As real as they come. A medium too. She spoke to spirits."

"Why did she leave? Can we talk her into coming back?"

"She's not coming back."

"Why not? Did Gabriel heal her as well? Doesn't she know what will happen?"

Agnes and Richard looked at each other for a moment before Agnes spoke again. "Kristina was a troubled soul. Sometimes she didn't seem completely... sane. Gabriel tried to help her, but one morning she didn't come in to work. A few days later, we were visited by a police officer. She's gone missing, Raven. No one, not even her family, knows where she is."

Raven held her head. It was so much to take in, so much pressure. She wasn't a medium and she couldn't talk to spirits. There was nothing remotely magical about her. But if what Agnes and Richard told her was true, her life as well as theirs depended on her finding a way to shatter this curse.

"I hate to break it to you guys, but we are doomed. There's been a huge mistake. I don't have any supernatural abilities." A thought came to her. "How did the ring get cursed in the first place? Wouldn't undoing the source of the curse be the better option?"

Richard lowered his chin to look at her over his sunglasses. "The source of the curse is one dangerous, badass witch, and she would be the last person to lift it."

Raven leaned forward, resting her chin on her fist.

"Don't tell Gabriel I told you about this," Richard said. "Nothing pokes the dragon in the scales like talking about *her*."

"I'll keep it to myself," Raven said. "Her who?"

"Have you heard of Crimson Vanderholt?"

The name sounded familiar, but Raven couldn't place it.

"The voodoo queen of New Orleans?" Agnes clarified with a raised eyebrow.

"Uh... you don't mean the one that does bachelor parties and backyard ceremonies?" Crimson Vanderholt was nothing like your stereotypical voodoo queen. She was blond and blue-eyed and covered in tattoos. She was the type of person Avery would have commented had "led a rough life." As far as Raven was aware, she was commonly believed to be an entertainer rather than a true voodoo priestess. Her entire shtick was scammy. For fifty dollars, she'd come to your house on your birthday in a red bustier and flowing black skirt, wave a snake in the air, and call it a spell to prolong your life.

"That's the one," Richard said. "She's the real thing, darling. Into some dark shit too."

"What's her beef with Gabriel?"

"Crimson took a shine to Gabriel a few decades ago. She's much older than she looks. She's been around almost as long as Gabriel. He claims she was once an acolyte of Dr. Jean."

"Whoa, *the* Dr. Jean?" Dr. Jean Montanee was as famous as Marie Laveau when it came to the history of voodoo in New Orleans. He was considered the original and most powerful voodoo priest to have ever graced the city. If you followed the religion, he was a big deal. "So she's immortal too?"

He nodded. "A dark witch. She is extremely powerful and absolutely obsessed with Gabriel."

Agnes leaned forward and lowered her voice. "She asked him to marry her in the early 1900s. He refused. She asked again several years later. Apparently, that time he embarrassed her enough that he pissed her off royally. Over the years Gabriel had to defend himself from all manner of love charms from the woman. I caught her putting a potion in his coffee once. Completely out of her mind."

Richard leaned forward and spread his hands. "You would think the witch would give up after a hundred years of hearing no, but she won't. And every year she grows stronger. Enter women's liberation, and Crimson became even more obsessed. Now she says she just wants sex. On Mardi Gras last year, she disguised herself as another woman and tried to lure Gabriel into her bed. He refused, but because he didn't know who she was, he let her get too close. She cursed his ring."

Agnes shook her silver hair. "Now she says if he won't have sex with her, he dies. She's given him a year. That year is almost up."

"Talk about desperate," Raven said. "All this for one night with him? It doesn't make sense."

"We think it's about voodoo," Richard said.

"Oh, she claims she loves him," Agnes added. "Claims she wants to marry him. But she is incapable of love. Her true goal is power. We're not sure how the sex will make her stronger, but judging by her past behaviors and comments, we're sure magic is her motivation."

The distaste that filled Raven steeled her resolve. Even the thought of Crimson forcing herself on Gabriel turned her stomach. A primal urge to rip the woman to shreds made her fingers twitch. Raven had no right or reason to feel possessive of Gabriel, and she suspected it was their bond that was the source of the feeling, but at that moment, she pictured him hovering over her that first night in his bed, the heat of his hand radiating against her ribs, and she had the illogical thought that no one else belonged in her place.

"We have until Mardi Gras to break that curse, Raven. Will you help us? All of us?"

Raven was unable to stop the tears from rolling over her cheeks. As much as she wanted to help, she could not go back there. Not today.

"I'm sorry," she said. "I need to go home and think. Tell Gabriel I need time."

CHAPTER EIGHT

"You told her everything?" Gabriel stared over his desk at Richard, his heart dropping like a stone. The man must have drawn the short straw because Agnes had volunteered to help the customers in the store while he delivered the bad news.

"She said she needs time." Richard rubbed his palms together slowly.

"It's been almost twenty-four hours." Gabriel's fingers drummed beside his desk blotter.

"I think she'll be back," Richard said confidently.

"You think... You *think* she'll be back." Gabriel grabbed a pen off his desk and hurled it across the room where it lodged in the wall an inch deep. His fists came down hard on the desk, the handsome piece of furniture groaning under the pressure. Richard bounded from his chair in the blink of an eye.

"Gabriel, my friend, I love you, man, but your eyes are telling me you need some alone time." Richard backed toward the door. "Don't give up on her. She seems like a decent person."

Gabriel's insides coiled and writhed, his dragon's scaly flesh brushing the underside of his skin. He was the dragon and the dragon was him. Fully and completely. Only sometimes the beast demanded his own way, a crabby alternate personality that Gabriel struggled to keep under control. His inner dragon was all about primal urges and living in the now, punching first and asking questions later.

It scared him a little how close that part of him was to the surface these days. He didn't blame Richard for making himself scarce. When Gabriel got angry, the dragon knocked on his internal door. Like the night he found Raven in that alley. No wonder she'd run. He'd brutally beaten those men and left them to die, without remorse. Raven probably thought he was a killer, and she wasn't wrong. He'd killed before when he had to. And the truth was, the closer they came to Mardi Gras and the culmination of the curse, the less human he'd feel. No wonder she feared him.

He closed his eyes and rested his face in his hands.

Footsteps entered the room and the door closed. Probably Agnes checking on him.

"Leave it open. I'll be fine in a minute."

A cruel laugh cut through the room. "Oh, I doubt it."

His gaze snapped up, the cloying scent of saccharine-sweet perfume filling his nostrils. Crimson. She was leaning across his desk, her overfull bust spilling out of the front of her dress within the frame of her ratty blond hair. Another man might have found her voluptuous or simply taken her to bed for the distraction. Gabriel found her repellant.

"What are you doing here?"

"A month, Gabriel. That's all you have left. Isn't it time you were reasonable?" She drew a nail down the side of her neck and over her right breast. "One night, that's all I'm asking. I have a spell that will ensure once is enough."

"Enough for what?"

"Enough for me to harness your power. Simple as that."

Looking at her now, it was hard to believe they used to be friends. For close to three hundred years they'd lived in the same city, and as immortals, there were times they'd had to rely on each other for protection and support. At one time, he'd considered her his closest friend. It might have been more if he hadn't seen her for what she was, hadn't caught her removing the still-beating hearts of dying soldiers on the Civil War battlefield, hearts that she used to bolster her own power. These days she was a warped version of herself, whose magic was dark enough that the stink of it turned his stomach.

He looked her straight in the eye. "No. My answer hasn't changed. I will never sleep with you, Crimson. Never. Even if I didn't find you repulsive, the thought of giving you my power would be."

Her smug grin morphed into a sneer. "Repulsive?" She stood and tugged at her dress so that her breasts bounced. "I've never had a man say *that* before. As I recall, you used to find me quite comely."

"You've changed. You are nothing to me but a walking corpse."

"Could it be that your interest in the male employee out front goes further than friendship?"

Clearly she meant it as an insult, but Gabriel didn't flinch. He was completely okay with her assuming he was Richard's partner. She could spread it all over town if she wanted. "Yes," he lied. "I am gay. As gay as they come. I cannot stomach being with a woman. Now remove your curse from my ring."

"Liar." She snorted. "Besides, if that's your game, I have ways to get around it." She cupped her hands over her face and smoothed them up and over her hair, giving her body a little shake. When she was done, a male version of herself stood before him. Even her clothes had changed. She now wore a three-piece suit. "I assure you, my illusions are strong enough to fool even you." Even her voice was an octave lower.

He scowled. "What have you done to yourself? This is dark, even for you."

She swaggered toward him around the desk. "As dark as it comes, darling. Don't knock it until you've tried it."

"The answer is no. Never. Don't come back here again."

She shook herself and the illusion broke apart and dissolved around her. "Never say never, Blakemore. The worst is yet to come." She eyed his ring, stepping closer.

Gabriel rose from his chair and backed toward the wall to put space between them.

"You'll be begging me for mercy in a few short weeks."

The door opened. "Gabriel, I..." Raven stood on the threshold, her eyes darting between him and Crimson. "I'm sorry. Richard and Agnes are with customers, and I didn't know you had... company."

His chest swelled with hope. She'd returned! All was not lost. He smiled at her, pouring all the warmth he felt for her at that moment into his expression. "Crimson was just leaving."

"Who is this lovely little bird?" Crimson's artificial nails clicked as she reached for Raven.

A growl rumbled in Gabriel's chest. When had his fangs dropped and his fingers extended into talons? "Leave, now."

Crimson's eyes widened for a fraction of a second. Her gaze roved over Raven, her lip twitching. "Interesting." She snorted. "She's more pitiful than the last one, and I suspect will last half as long."

Gabriel leaped over the desk, sweeping Raven into the office and behind him. With a deadly growl, his talons slashed out and tore through Crimson's chest. Right through it. Her form rippled like water, and then she was whole again. No blood. No injury.

"Oh please," Crimson said. "I know all your tricks, Gabriel. You can't hurt me." She swaggered out of his office and disappeared.

Gabriel whirled to face Raven. "Are you all right?"

"Is she gone?"

"Yes." Gabriel could no longer detect the voodoo queen's acrid stench.

Raven let out a deep breath. "So, that's the infamous Crimson. She's a theme park princess gone wrong."

"That's one way of putting it." He scanned her from head to toe. "Thank you for coming back. You are back, aren't you?"

Her spine was straight, confident; she was not a bit afraid even though she'd watched him try to tear Crimson apart. "I have decided that I will help you, Gabriel Blakemore," she said. "On my terms."

❦

A COLD PRICKLE LINGERED AT THE BASE OF RAVEN'S neck. Never in her life had she been in the room with energy as dark and evil as Crimson Vanderholt's. The woman oozed menace. Raven got the sense that the voodoo queen had once been pretty, maybe even beautiful, but now she appeared to be someone trying too hard to cover an unsustainable lifestyle. Her makeup was thick, her hair overprocessed, and her perfume... Raven had never smelled a more sickly-sweet concoction.

The four-inch talons that had extended from Gabriel's first knuckles retracted with a shake of his hands, his partial transformation reverting before her eyes. All at once, she remembered what he was. She was in a room with a dragon. He was big and strong and had killed people without breaking a sweat. She'd watched him thrust claws through Crimson's gut. She swallowed hard. A cold ribbon of fear twisted through her, and she wondered if she'd done the right thing coming back here.

But then he started tapping again. The same pattern as before, tap-tap-tap, tap-tap-tap. His face took on a tortured expression, and he tucked the offending hand behind his back. Raven connected with that expression. She was no stranger to being a slave to compulsion. Her brain cancer had once made her arm go rigid, snapping to her side and straightening until her muscles threatened to break her bones. She'd had no control over the movement back then.

Dragon or not, Gabriel was suffering.

"Give me your hands," Raven said softly.

His gaze snapped to hers.

"It's okay. I... I understand. I used to have something similar when I was sick. Please."

Slowly, Gabriel withdrew his hand from its hiding place and held it out to her. She sandwiched his tapping fingers between her palms and rubbed vigorously. "Dr. Freemont used to say that distraction was better than any drug when it came to obsessive-compulsive behavior."

An overwhelming sense of calm rolled through her, and she smiled as his fingers eased under her touch. After witnessing those fingers turn into claws, she should have been afraid, but she wasn't. Gabriel *was* dangerous. He *was* a killer. He was massive enough to tear her to shreds. But when he'd leaped across the desk and lashed out at Crimson, he'd been protecting her. Every time he'd become violent, it had been to shield her, because if Agnes and Richard were to be believed, he needed her. She trusted in that as she remained close to him.

"How did you do that?" Gabriel gawked at their coupled hands.

"I'm not a doctor, but it has something to do with neural pathways. If you disrupt the electrical impulses from your brain to your extremity, you can ease the discomfort."

He nodded. "Thank you."

She raised her face and looked directly into those smoldering eyes. Big mistake. Avery had been right. Gabriel Blakemore was undeniably sexy. For a moment she forgot who she was or why she was standing there holding his hand. Her tongue turned to leather and her mind went straight back to his bedroom, to the feel of being under him, dwarfed by him. She dismissed the rogue thought and lowered her gaze, dragging her fingers off his. "You're welcome."

"You said something about terms."

"Yes." She collected herself, smoothing her hair and gathering her thoughts. "I need to be paid. Well paid, Gabriel. My dad has been riding my ass to go back to school, and I owe my mom a ton of money. If I'm going to put him off, I have to have a good reason."

"Done. What else?"

"I need weekends off."

He inhaled sharply.

"I know you only have a brief time left, and I will be here working when I don't have other things to do. But life is short. I promised myself the day I walked out of the hospital that I would never live like that again. I plan to live every day like it's my last. I want to help you, but my time is my own. I come and go as I please."

He stepped in closer, close enough that she could feel his breath. He didn't look happy. "I won't stop you from doing what you want to do, but I need to know where you will be. To keep you safe. With my magic in the state it is, I can't track you like I once could."

She bristled. Raven had no intention of reporting her whereabouts to him on a regular basis. She was a grown woman. "If I miss work hours, I will let you know why."

"Anything else?"

"No locks. I won't be locked in. I don't care how valuable the books are."

"I gave you the key."

"Not good enough. I want to keep the door open." Raven closed her eyes. "It feels like a coffin when it's closed. It's hard enough for me to be stuck inside all day. I won't be locked in."

He grunted. "Okay. Is that all? I want to know all the terms I'm agreeing to." His eyes tightened at the corners, and he pressed his mouth into a straight line.

"That's it."

"I accept your terms." He licked his lips, and Raven saw hunger brew like a storm around his coal-black pupils. The red flecks burned, flickering in a way that wasn't human. His smoky scent filled her lungs, and his undivided attention weighed on her like a spotlight. "On one condition."

Raven swallowed. It wasn't fear that made her heart flutter. "What condition is that?"

"As you say, life is short. I have until Mardi Gras to find a cure or I will end. My end will come before yours, in fact.

All of this means that I must live until I die as well. What purpose is there to life if we don't enjoy the time we have?"

She shook her head. "What does that have to do with me?"

Towering over her, he bent his neck until his nose almost grazed hers. "Your presence helps ease the symptoms of my curse, Raven." He stretched the fingers of the hand that was no longer tapping.

"Oh?" Her voice came out in a squeak. Why did the sound of her name on his lips make her insides quiver?

"Yes. At times I will need to be near you, no questions asked. That is my condition."

His skin was hot. Hot where his breath skimmed her cheek. Hot where his chest neared her own. That heat seeped into her, sliding down her skin like warm honey.

What was happening? She had no business reacting this way to someone like him. He was a dragon. Not even human. Not to mention he was her boss.

"Okay." The word came out husky, and she cleared her throat, her cheeks warming. "I accept your condition."

"Good. Then you will have dinner with me tonight." Not a question. A statement.

"Er, no," she said. "I'm sorry. I can't. It's my mother's birthday. I have to have dinner with her and my sister."

He stepped back, his jaw tightening as if he were supremely disappointed.

"Breakfast?" she blurted.

He paused. "Oh, I would love to make you breakfast, Ms. Tanglewood," he drawled, his eyes raking over her.

She ignored the innuendo. Chewing her lip, she said, "I'll come early tomorrow, before the shop opens."

He nodded, his nostrils flaring. "Very well. We have a deal." He extended his hand and she shook it. As he backed away, still firmly gripping her palm, his eyes dropped to her arm and he frowned. "Raven, what is this?"

She looked down and then looked again. Her arm was glowing. Not her entire arm but portions of it. It was covered in marks like she'd caught a case of phosphorescent, interconnected measles. Her other arm was normal, pale-skinned, and smooth. The glow was only on the side that held his hand.

"I don't know. What is happening to me?"

He released her and the markings slowly faded. "I'm not sure. I've never seen this before. Has anything unusual happened to you recently?"

She rolled her eyes. "What hasn't been unusual? Literally everything about yesterday was a once in a lifetime."

"Did Crimson touch you?"

"No. But wait... This arm itched when I was reviewing the grimoires. I couldn't stop scratching. I thought I was having an allergic reaction."

He cradled her arm again, rubbing his thumbs over the long blue vein on the inside of her wrist. His fingers were warm, soothing. She almost moaned. Light followed his thumbs, glowing to life where he touched. "I don't think this is an allergic reaction, Raven. Your skin is reacting to me."

"What do you think it means?" she asked. "Does it have to do with the bond?"

He looked her in the eye again. "I am not sure. But I promise you I will find out."

CHAPTER NINE

Raven had underestimated how hard it would be to reenter the library. All she had to do was look into the space and her heart raced. But she was not the sort of woman to be conquered by fear. Cancer was a shrinking room with no doors and no windows. She'd survived it because of Gabriel. She would survive this for him.

Skin slick with sweat, she propped the door wide open and crossed to the desk near the window. The drapes were open today, and the shelves of books seemed different in the full light—less daunting. Her original curiosity crept back like a skittish pet. These books were worlds waiting to be explored. And she planned to survey every one of them.

No matter what Gabriel thought, she wasn't psychic. Raven didn't have any power capable of detecting the spell that could break the curse on his ring, but that didn't mean she couldn't help. What she needed was a method to find any magical instructions that had to do with curses, then Gabriel could review her findings and they could try anything that looked promising.

She flipped to the back of the catalog and tore out a

blank page, then folded it into thin strips and ripped along the seams. The text of the grimoire still on her desk was clearly in German. She pulled out her phone and navigated to her translation app, plugging "curse" into the English to German box.

"*Fluch* or *die Verwünschung*," she whispered. Should be simple enough. She would find and mark every instance of either word. She lifted her chin. She could do this.

After quickly examining all eight hundred pages of the German text, Raven had found only eight instances of the words. She followed that up with a grimoire in a Middle Eastern language. Then one in Old English that she wasn't sure was a grimoire at all, but more likely a reference guide to the application of herbal medicine. She skimmed each page for the words for curse, noting any spells that mentioned them. She had no idea if the entries she found were for breaking curses or casting them, but she marked any promising spells for Gabriel, using the bookmarks she'd created.

Whatever Raven was allergic to came back again. She'd started to believe it was some sort of mite that lived in the pages of these books. Her current tome, with its crisp modern print, made her skin feel cold and the half-moons at the base of her fingernails darkened to a blue tint. She tried to ignore it.

"Knock, knock," Agnes said from the door.

Raven looked up. "Oh, Agnes, come in."

The old woman smiled. "Sorry to interrupt, but I was wondering if you needed a break. Gabriel wanted me to watch the room for you while you're away." She looked around at the priceless volumes on the shelves and then back at Raven, her lips pursed.

"Uh, yes, I do, but... Agnes, can I ask you something?"

"You may ask. I can't guarantee an answer." The woman grinned beneath her gigantic glasses and sidled up to Raven at the desk.

"Do you know how Kristina organized these grimoires? The categorization doesn't make sense to me. I mean, clearly she has them broken into distinct sections, but I can't tell what distinction she used to group them. I've ruled out alphabetical or by language. They aren't categorized by age."

Agnes ran a perfectly manicured nail down the list, then inspected the corresponding shelf. After a few moments, she released a deep sigh. "I'm sorry, Raven. I have no idea. It doesn't make any sense to me."

"But did Kristina mention anything to you about what she was doing? Anything that might give me a clue? It's like she up and left in the middle of her work."

Agnes gripped her chin and shook her head. "Kristina kept to herself. Unlike you, she enjoyed being locked in here. She wasn't a people person, you understand. Never joined us for lunch."

Raven frowned. "Why do you think she left?"

"Richard and I have gone rounds about it. We have no idea. The girl seemed happy here. Although she was troubled. Her gift of talking to spirits made her often... distracted. From what we'd heard, she'd had a history of being misdiagnosed with mental illness. Clearly the adults in her life never understood her gift. No one did until Gabriel."

"So, despite being happy here and Gabriel being the only one who ever understood her, she simply took off one day?"

Agnes lowered her voice. "You didn't hear it from me,

but to be honest, Richard and I think something happened to her. Gabriel can use the bond to call both Richard and me to his side, but for some reason he is unable to use that ability to track down Kristina. But then, now that I think about it, he wasn't able to call you either, was he?"

Raven shrugged. "What does the call feel like?"

"Like a sharp tug behind your breastbone. It's not something you'd be able to ignore, or to forget."

"Then no. I didn't feel anything. But maybe he didn't try. Maybe he wasn't that concerned with me leaving."

Agnes's platinum bob swung against her cheek as her head turned abruptly. "Oh, dear. Believe me, if he could have forced you back, he would have. We had one grouchy dragon on our hands."

"Oh." Raven sighed. "Hmm. I wonder what happened to her... Kristina. I wonder if Crimson had anything to do with it."

Agnes shrugged. "If she did, it seems odd to me that she wouldn't use her to get at Gabriel. Crimson isn't subtle. She would be the type to leave a ransom note. Even if she killed the girl, she'd want credit."

Raven contemplated the list one last time, then shook her head. "Thanks for having a look. I'll take that break now." She rose and headed into the attached room, pausing when she saw a fresh tray of tea on the table in the kitchenette. "Agnes?"

Raven's shaky voice must have struck a chord because the older woman came running.

"What is it, honey?"

"The tea... I didn't see anyone come in with this. How is it here?"

Agnes cackled. "Oh, that's just Juniper and Hazel, dear,

Gabriel's housekeeping staff. They're practically invisible and as silent as church mice. Enjoy it. It looks delicious."

Silent and invisible were understatements. Juniper and Hazel were miracle workers. Raven cracked her neck and tried to take Agnes's word for it. After a short bathroom break, Raven poured herself a cup of the tea and filled a plate with finger sandwiches before returning to the book she'd been working on. She thanked Agnes.

"Anytime, my dear. As sad as I am about Kristina leaving us, I'm happy you're here." She smiled brightly and left the room.

Left alone again in the library, Raven retrieved the next grimoire from the shelf. This one was in English. *The Book of Melding* contained potion recipes and associated incantations to do anything from keeping deer out of a garden to rendering an enemy lifeless. Not dead. Temporarily lifeless. Raven shuddered as she read it. Nothing about breaking curses on jewels, although there were potions used to repel or prevent them on a person. She marked those, just in case.

Out of bookmarks, she again flipped to the back of Kristina's ledger to tear another page from the binding to make into strips. Once that was removed, a drawing was revealed on the second to last page of the catalog. She paused to admire it. It was a sketch of a tree with a twisted trunk and branches that arced almost to the braided roots. A tree of life in the Celtic tradition.

Raven stared at the sketch as she sipped her tea. Damn, Kristina was talented. According to Agnes, she'd liked being in this room. What else was she good at? Why had she left so abruptly? What had happened to her?

Raven selected the next grimoire, this one in French, but she couldn't concentrate on the words. All she could think about was the tree and Kristina's meticulously cataloged library. Agnes and Richard had said Kristina was a medium, someone who spoke to spirits. Someone with a powerful gift. If something had happened to her, why hadn't the spirits warned her?

When Raven looked at her phone again, she swore. If she didn't hurry, she was going to be late for her mom's party. She scribbled a note to Gabriel to check the pages she'd marked, locked the library, and jogged down to his office.

"Gabriel?" His door was open, but Raven knocked on the outer wall before entering. He wasn't there. She placed the note on the center of his desk. A chill spider-walked up her spine at the memory of when she was last in this room, of Crimson surveying her like she was a new pet. Magic or not, that woman did an excellent Ted Bundy impression. Her cold eyes had cut straight through Raven, and her expression had been—murderous.

Frowning, Raven pulled her phone from her pocket and typed *Kristina missing person New Orleans* in the search bar. An article popped up: FATHER PLEADS FOR HELP IN MISSING PERSON CASE. Raven bookmarked it to read later. Gabriel might not want to talk about Kristina, but Raven couldn't let this go. If Crimson had anything to do with her disappearance, Raven needed to know. Besides, finding Kristina and reenlisting her help could be their only hope of breaking the curse.

☙

CRIMSON VANDERHOLT WATCHED THE THREE SISTERS from across the street, thinking she was very clever. People were always underestimating her. It was her favorite thing about life, actually. An underestimated person had far more power than one whose talents were fully appreciated.

It had taken her less than twenty minutes to figure out who Raven Tanglewood was. A short conversation with that idiot Richard had proven fruitful. She'd had to compel it out of him with a carefully spritzed herbal concoction, but the man could not resist her influence. Once she had the name, tracing Raven to the Three Sisters was easy enough. No magic needed. There were articles galore on the internet about her cancer and the various fundraisers her parents had thrown on her behalf.

The cancer was interesting. It should have killed her. All the articles said it was terminal. But clearly the girl had a new lease on life. Gabriel's handiwork, Crimson assumed. He'd used dragon magic; there was no other explanation.

A town car pulled in front of the restaurant and the girl climbed out. She had to hand it to Gabriel; Raven was beautiful. A pang of jealousy ricocheted through her. Was this the reason she couldn't win Gabriel's affections? This little slip of a woman with her woe-is-me cancerous past? He must feel sorry for her, she thought. If Gabriel did have feelings for her, there were things that could be done, actions that would neutralize the girl before she became a problem.

Crimson *needed* Gabriel. The demons she spoke to at night told her his magic was the only way she could extend her longevity. A human witch was not meant to live forever, and Crimson was over three hundred years old. The first time she'd been meant to die was at age sixty-five from a case of consumption. With the help of a close friend, she'd tapped into demonic energy and developed a ritual to give herself temporary immortality. At that stage, the spell required only blood sacrifices of animals. As time went on though, she'd started to age. And although she repeated her ritual, the spell offered diminishing returns.

Just short of her two hundredth birthday, she'd sacrificed her first human. She'd been living in Storyville, making her living as a fortuneteller, when an inebriated man hadn't been happy with her vision of his future. His anger had turned to violence and then to lust. He'd tried to rape her before she'd reached the athame she always kept in her boot and thrust it into his gut. The injury hadn't been enough to kill him, but it had weakened him sufficiently for her to force him back to her chamber. She'd performed the ritual, this time drawing on his human life.

That had renewed and revived her body far more effectively than any animal. She'd killed five men since then and absorbed the life force out of many a dying man's heart. Each had provided several more years, but the wrinkles at the corners of her eyes and mouth told her she was running out of time. The ritual needed more. Something greater.

Gabriel was a dragon. Over the years, she'd heard it was forbidden for a witch to mate with a dragon, but it was ages before she questioned why. If her sources were correct, sex with him would infuse her with power, at least enough for another lifetime. The demons had promised her as much.

Of course, Gabriel didn't need to know her reasons. No one did. As far as those around her were concerned, she spoke to spirits, the generations of voodoo ancestors who came before her. To them she was the descendant of Dr. Jean. She wasn't, of course, although she had known him once. Truthfully, she was an orphaned child of two executed criminals, raised in a convent that might as well have been a prison. Voodoo had saved her life, as had the broader practice of magic that her voodoo roots had grown into. For all her early childhood hardships, Crimson was blessed with one curious talent: she could speak to demons, and with small sacrifices she could get them to do her bidding. They'd made her powerful, and in return she'd fed them generously.

As the town car pulled away, Crimson watched Raven slip inside the colorful cottage-like pub on Magazine Street. "Malphesidak, I need an illusion," she whispered.

The demon seeped from the sewer like an oily snake, slithered around her ankle and ascended her body. It leached into her skin, filling her with its power. She smoothed her hands over her face and hair and shivered with the transformation. When she looked down at herself, she was a mousy and plump woman in her forties.

"Perfect," she cooed. "Thank you, my darling."

Crossing the street, she slipped into the front door of the bar. The Three Sisters was the type of place she would call eccentric. The walls were painted purple and cherry red with lime-green accents. There were wooden parrots hanging from the ceiling, tiki torches around the bar, and an overall ambience that would fit in at a Jimmy Buffett concert or a Tommy Bahama store. It was kitschy but homey, filled with people drinking and hugging. The smell of spilled beer, fryer grease, and candle wax hit her squarely in the face.

She navigated the crowd to the bar and ordered a beer. "What a lovely pub you have here," she said to the young man popping the cap. "Is it always this crowded?"

"It's the owner's birthday. This is a family party." The boy couldn't be more than twenty with sandy-brown hair and freckles. She sensed he wasn't related to the dark-haired group gathered in the opposite corner of the place.

"Oh, how nice," she said, sipping her beer. "Are all three sisters here?"

"What? Uh... Oh... No." The bartender laughed. "You mean the name of the place. No, it's not named after living people. I haven't worked here long, but it has something to do with the family's heritage."

"You don't say." Crimson eyed the crowd, finding Raven smiling at an older woman who must be her mother.

The bartender shrugged. "I guess they've been here since the late 1600s. There was a plantation in the family at one point, the Tanglewood plantation. That's where the name comes from. It's kind of a big deal in their family. If you're born a Tanglewood, you stay a Tanglewood. Even the girls keep the name."

She smiled as he moved on to fill another patron's drink order. "How very interesting," Crimson whispered. The demon had slithered and hissed inside her head when the bartender had mentioned the family name.

"Tanglewood," she said to herself, testing the word on her tongue. Why did that name sound familiar? The demon squirmed in response. It knew the name, but how? "Shh, my darling."

"Excuse me?" The bartender was back. "Do you need another?"

Crimson placed the empty on the bar. "Oh no. Only one for me. Thank you." She tossed a ten beside the empty. "Keep the change."

She left the Three Sisters more curious than when she'd arrived. "Who are you, Ravenna Tanglewood?" she whispered under her breath. "More importantly, what are you?"

🐉

ALL THE TINY HAIRS ON RAVEN'S ARMS STOOD AT
attention. It was like she'd been hit with an icy breeze, and
she rubbed her shoulders against the chill.

"Are you okay?" Avery asked. "It's like eighty degrees in
here and you're shivering."

"Got a chill," she said.

Raven glanced over her shoulder, her gaze snagging on a
woman leaving the bar. There was nothing unusual about
her. If anything, her appearance was understated. Short.
Maybe five foot. Mousy brown hair. Weight on the heavy
side of average. Someone's mom. Maybe someone's
grandma. There was no reason for Raven's skin to go all
creepy crawly on her. Only it did. Raven was goose-bumped
and tingly. And the source was definitely that woman. Her
intuition was doing a two-step with a sandwich sign that
said *run, run, run*. Raven had never had such anxiety, and
over a patron! She breathed a sigh of relief when the door
closed behind the woman.

"Raven, seriously, what's wrong with you?" Avery
asked. Her sister looked worried.

Raven took a sip of her martini. "Nothing. Hungry.
Tired. I'll be okay."

Avery glanced between her and the door. "It's Blakemore, isn't it? You succumbed to his siren-like charms, and
now your heart and soul are being crushed by his rakish
nature."

Raven gave her a withering look. "He is not crushing me
with his rakish nature. He's not even rakish."

"That's what they all say. Admit it, you have a crush on
him!"

With a laugh, Raven decided to throw her sister a bone.
"Maybe." It wasn't a lie. Her thoughts dwelled on Gabriel
in the most salacious ways. It was odd. She'd started

yesterday locked inside a room and thinking he was a serial killer. She'd never been so happy to be wrong. Gabriel was mysterious and otherworldly, and she found him incredibly sexy. He spoke to something that lived deep inside her. Not the bond itself; she understood he'd connected them by healing her, but that was an entirely different feeling. This was her need for adventure. Gabriel was a living, walking adventure. He was the breath of life wrapped up in broad shoulders and a tight ass.

"Why do you keep looking at the door? Did you invite him?" Avery asked.

Raven shrugged. "I had a feeling he might stop by tonight. It's stupid."

"Oh, well, he's an idiot if he passes on you." Avery wrapped an arm around her shoulders and kissed the side of her head.

The rapid ching-ching-ching of a spoon against the side of a glass called their attention to the front of the bar. Their mom was standing on a chair, looking over the heads of all her guests.

"I want to thank everyone for coming to this, my fiftieth birthday!" The crowd erupted in applause. "I never would have thought that my life would be filled with so much joy this year. My daughter is alive and well." She raised her glass and everyone turned to look at Raven who smiled widely and raised her glass right back. "The Three Sisters is doing better than ever." She nodded toward the bartender.

"Despite my husband divorcing me," Avery added in a murmur beside her.

"And I am a lucky woman to be surrounded by friends who like me enough to drink my beer and eat my cake!"

The crowd cheered.

Avery and Raven laughed.

"Now, consider this a thank-you to each of you for coming tonight. Have another round. I'm going to open my gifts." She jumped off the chair and headed for the stack on the table at the back of the room.

"She's in rare form tonight," Avery said. "Come on, she's opening ours."

Since Raven didn't have two quarters to rub together yet, Avery had taken care of the gift buying for both of them. She tugged Raven through the crowd to their mother's side to watch her rip into the present. Raven had been so distracted with Blakemore's, she'd forgotten to ask what her sister had picked out. She grinned as the gift came into view. An embossed photo album. Avery had outdone herself once again.

Her mother squealed. "Oh girls, it's perfect! And filled with pictures of Avery and Raven!" She held it up for the partygoers to see. "How thoughtful."

Raven leaned in to get a better look. The deep cinnamon-colored leather was embossed with their last name, Tanglewood, and a circular symbol. Raven squinted but couldn't quite make it out.

"What's that symbol, Avery?" Raven asked.

"It's the Tanglewood family crest, the Tanglewood tree. You've never seen it before?"

Raven shook her head.

"I guess Dad didn't want it in the house. He was always so butthurt about us taking Mom's last name. Whatever. He knew what he was getting into when he married her."

Raven had always taken for granted their family's tradition to keep the name Tanglewood generation after generation. Everyone knew the stories of the original three sisters, the Tanglewood plantation, and how their pub had come to be. But she didn't remember a crest.

"Here, Mom. I'll put it aside while you open up your other gifts." Raven reached for the album.

"Good idea." Her mother handed her the leather-bound book.

Now that it was in her hands, Raven had an unobstructed view of the Tanglewood tree. She gasped, her fingers trailing lightly over the crest. This was *Kristina's* tree. Same twisty trunk and drooping branches. It was the sketch Kristina had drawn at the back of the catalog.

"Avery?" Raven's voice was high and tight.

"Yeah?"

"This tree symbol, it's common, right? You probably just picked it from Celtic stock art."

Avery looked at her like she was losing it. "It's our family crest. As in, drawn by our ancestors... Not Celtic by the way. It was from here, a special angel oak tree that grew on the plantation before, you know..."

She shook her head.

"The place burned down or something, including the tree. After that, the Tanglewoods were out of the plantation business and into innkeeping." She gestured toward the bar.

"Why did I never know this?"

Avery shrugged. "I don't know. You were sick for a long time. It's a morbid story. Anyway, I had to upload a scanned version of it. There is nothing like this anywhere."

"Of course not," Raven murmured. Her head was spinning. The room felt hot, and she tugged at the collar of her shirt.

"Are you okay?" Avery asked.

She handed the album to her sister. "Um, I'm feeling weird again. I'm going to go to bed. Can you tell Mom?"

"Sure. Do you want me to come with you? Are you sick? I could call Dr. Freemont."

"No, no. Seriously, I think I just ate something bad. I'll be fine. Just need to lie down."

Avery nodded, her expression heavy with concern. Raven gave her a reassuring hug before heading toward the stairs to their apartment. As if Kristina's disappearance wasn't worrisome enough, now Raven had to wonder why the woman had been sketching her family's crest.

CHAPTER TEN

Paragon, 1698

Gabriel strolled down the hallowed aisle of Paragon's Great Mountain Hall, elated to be witnessing history. Tonight his uncle, King Brynhoff, having ruled for two thousand years, would step down from the throne, ceremoniously passing the crown to Gabriel's older brother, Marius.

Of course, as dragons, older was a matter of minutes, not years. The nine siblings had hatched within the same hour. Still, Gabriel was happy Marius was considered firstborn. He wouldn't want to have the responsibility for Paragon that his brother was taking on. It was too much. Even with their mother Eleanor, her consort Killian, and Brynhoff helping him rule, Marius's entire existence would revolve around protecting, defending, and becoming the final rule of law in Paragon. Talk about pressure.

Then again, Gabriel had trained as a warrior, both in the form of his dragon and his more common two-legged form. He and his brothers would be the ones leading Paragon's troops in defense of the realm, if it ever came to that. Not that *anyone would challenge them. No one had in thousands of years. Their realm was a paradise, loved by its citizens and neighbors alike.*

Taking his place to the right of Marius, Gabriel watched his younger brother Tobias stride down the red carpet after him. By the firm set of his jaw, Gabriel could tell he was still worried about Rowan, who was less than enthused about the day's events. Marius might be the oldest, but Tobias was the one they all trusted. Alexander was next. Through his spectacles, he seemed to be memorizing the historical banners lining the shiny black obsidian walls of the palace. No doubt he'd sketch the occasion in his artist's journal the first chance he got. Nathaniel, Xavier, Sylas, and Colin followed in turn, the first with the grace of a dancer, the second with his hand on his sword, and the last two looking distracted, like they had better places to be.

And then there was Rowan, their only sister and the future of the race. The crowd collectively gasped at her beauty as she descended the aisle in a blood-red gown that made her look like a mountain goddess. Dragon women were rare. Rowan would have her choice of suitors and be their race's best hope of producing heirs to the throne. Although Marius could take a consort, any children a future mate would bear would only become royalty if Rowan, as blooded queen, failed to produce young. That hadn't happened in five thousand years. Rowan's coronation was scheduled for after Marius's. She was already suffering ridicule for not choosing a mate. It was a pressure Gabriel wouldn't wish on anyone.

Once everyone was in place, the priestess began the ceremony, calling on the Goddess of the Mountain to bless Marius with the wisdom he'd need to rule Paragon. His uncle, Brynhoff, stood behind Marius, his hand on his sword.

Eleanor, his queen mother, stood off to his side, hand in hand with her consort and their father, Killian.

Gabriel frowned. His uncle did not look happy this day. The older dragon's mouth sagged, and he seemed to grow angrier with every word the priestess uttered. Gabriel's instincts urged him to draw his sword. He didn't like the way his uncle was looking at his brother, the corners of his narrowed eyes wrinkled with tension. The expression on his face was something Gabriel had never seen there before, but he had on others. If he was reading it correctly, Brynhoff was... jealous.

But that couldn't be. His mind wasn't working right. His uncle had always wanted the best for all of them. Gabriel must have drunk too much tribiscal wine. He was seeing things. He relaxed his shoulder and dropped his hand from his sword hilt.

Brynhoff's gaze darted to Gabriel. In that fraction of a second, a moment as fleeting and wispy as a spider's web, Gabriel's life changed forever. His uncle drew his sword like only an ancient dragon could. As fast as a flash of light, the weapon sang through the air and Marius's head tumbled from his shoulders. His body turned to dust just as quickly, his diamond heart hitting the floor with a bone-chilling clank.

Gabriel's sword was in his hand as Brynhoff turned a murderous gaze his way. His mother's screams echoed through the hall, her ring, a bright yellow citrine, glowing like a small sun behind his uncle. She knew Gabriel didn't stand a chance against Brynhoff. Gabriel was young, inexperienced. As Killian defended her, his mother raised her ring and uttered an incantation. Her magic plowed into him and his brethren. Gabriel's body broke apart, and he was cast into shadow, cast from Paragon, cast into the human world.

"Nooo!" Gabriel howled, springing out of bed like an overcranked jack-in-the-box. His talons and wings extended before he was fully awake, and he shredded the corner of his red sheets. How was it that even after three hundred years in New Orleans, the nightmare and the memory could come back to him as fresh as if it had happened yesterday?

To this day, he did not know why his uncle had done what he'd done or what had ultimately happened to his mother and Killian, but he suspected his mother would have come for him and his siblings by now if she were still alive and free. They had arrived in the Old World with nothing but their rings and a quartz orb the size of a grapefruit. The orb carried a message; his mother had suspected the coup and prepared the spell to hide them in this new realm. She'd warned them not to return to Paragon and to spread out across the new land in case Brynhoff ever discovered where she'd hidden them. In his effort to maintain control, his mother's message had said, Brynhoff would send hunters to slaughter them, the true heirs of Paragon. Staying together would make them an easy target.

Gabriel's fingers started to tap vigorously, and he closed his eyes against the rapid heartbeat and crawling skin that drove the compulsion. His mind immediately drifted to Raven. She could soothe this with a touch. When he'd fed her his tooth, he'd thought he was saving her, binding her. Now everything had gone topsy-turvy. Her presence was a balm to his worsening symptoms and a source of hope for him. Up until now, his only release from the ceaseless urge to tap was shifting into his dragon, a form that was mercifully immune to the side effects of the curse. If Raven could keep him from having to spend his remaining days hiding from the world within a shell of scales and fangs, he had to find a way to endear himself to her.

Raven was an anomaly. He'd had lovers over the years, but never had he been drawn to a woman as he was to her—especially a human woman. It was her fire. He'd seen it the day he'd stood in her hospital room. Her words said she wanted to die, but what she really wanted was freedom: freedom from the confines of that wasted body, freedom from that room. The same as when she'd crouched in the window of the library. She wasn't trying to kill herself. She'd believed she would survive that fall. It was all about being free, even if she broke her legs. Damn, he respected the shit out of that.

Which was why he couldn't be with her. Raven was human, and it had been a long time since he'd been with a woman. With his magic faltering the way it was, he couldn't trust himself not to injure her. His dragon had taken an unnatural interest in Raven. That was dangerous. One uncontrolled shift and he could tear her apart.

And that was simply the act itself. The real problem ran much deeper. If he loved her, and he could love her, she would never be safe. Loving Raven was an imagined future he could easily picture in his mind, as easily as he could conjure her jasmine-and-vanilla scent. But he was the eldest heir to Paragon, and this curse on his ring was only one of a million dangers that came with that honor. No, he couldn't do that to her. She deserved a human husband, a home, safety and security.

If his uncle ever found him, his head would be the first on the chopping block. The life of an innocent human like Raven would be the perfect bait and the ultimate punishment. He couldn't stand it if something happened to her because of him. If she could accept what he was at all. Big if. To humans, he was a monster. If he ever revealed his true form, she'd probably run for the hills, and well she should.

No, he'd been stupid to think of her now. He was an idiot for allowing himself to have feelings for the human. He must work harder to resist her charms.

"Gabriel!"

He turned his head. Now he could swear he was hearing her voice.

"Gabriel!"

RAVEN SLEPT FITFULLY THAT NIGHT. SHE DREAMED SHE was running through a forest of tangled branches. There was something in the darkness hunting her. A monster. Its heavy breath came ragged in her ears. Closer and closer, until a rush of scalding air roared in the gathering darkness and fire engulfed her, burning the tangled wood around her, burning it all down. The dream changed, circling and swaying, and she saw herself burning.

She wasn't the victim. She was the monster.

When she woke, she was sweating. Her heart pounded, and she stared at the silvery light of coming daybreak that shone through her window. It didn't take a professional to analyze what her dream meant. Her job was to find a spell to break a curse on a dragon's ring, a job that had resulted in her predecessor going missing under mysterious circumstances. Raven had the strangest feeling she was standing on the edge of a cliff. She understood her new reality, but until she jumped, none of it would feel entirely real. She ran her fingers along her arm where the markings had glowed the day before.

Truth was, she didn't fear the dragon half as much as she feared herself.

At once, she threw back the covers. No way could she

sleep with her thoughts racing the way they were. She needed answers, and there was only one place she could get them. She showered quickly and dressed in a pair of black slacks and a blouse she'd had from before she was sick. They were both too big on her, but they'd have to do. She couldn't afford new clothes. Not yet.

Raven had arranged for Duncan to pick her up at seven. The clock read five thirty. She couldn't wait. She wanted to search Kristina's notes again and confront Gabriel about the symbol Kristina had sketched and why it matched her family crest.

She boarded the streetcar and traveled to Blakemore's uneventfully. The front door was locked, but she knocked on the glass. It was dark inside. Raven hadn't thought of this. Gabriel was probably still sleeping like the rest of New Orleans.

Backing to the curb, she called toward the third-floor balcony in a loud whisper. "Gabriel. Gabriel!"

A man with a cart laden with goods gave her an annoyed look before rolling his bounty into a restaurant up the street. Raven placed her thumb and pointer finger in her mouth and whistled.

The curtains on the third floor moved aside, and then Gabriel was there, stepping out into the morning light. Oh hell was he there. Shirtless and in a pair of cotton pajama bottoms like something out of a dark dream. She lost her voice. Raven's breath hitched in her throat, and her brain hiccupped. Why was she here again? What did she want to ask him?

"Raven, what are you doing outside my window at this hour? Where's Duncan?"

"I—" *Stop staring,* she thought. She had to glance away to find her voice.

"Wait. Come inside." He gestured for her to go to the front door and disappeared again. By the time she reached it, he was already there, opening it for her. The smoky scent that surrounded her as she passed into the building was stronger than usual. He hadn't showered yet, she realized. He'd just rolled out of bed. God, he was hot, his torso a series of hard planes and deep shadows. What would it feel like to touch that taut flesh? He ran warmer than her. She knew that much. Making love to him would probably feel like dancing with a flame. She forced a swallow. A man had no business looking like that first thing in the morning.

"Raven?"

"Hmm?"

"What happened? Why are you here?"

Her mouth worked, but nothing came out.

He rushed to her, stroking down her arms, her back, and along her neck. Heat feathered over her skin with his touch in a way that made her scalp tingle. His movements were frantic, searching. "Are you well? Are you injured?"

"I'm... I'm fine." Honestly, she was tempted to say she was hurt so he'd keep touching her. It was intoxicating, his bare chest close, his smoky smell overwhelming her. She inhaled deeply, her head tipping back so she could look him in the face. What would it feel like to kiss him?

"Why did you come without Duncan?" he snapped.

Okay. Major mood breaker. "I had a nightmare," she said. "I woke up early and couldn't get back to sleep. I have questions. I thought we could... have breakfast and talk." She chewed her lip. Where could she get herself a World's Greatest Idiot mug? This was her *boss*, and she'd just woken him up because she had a bad dream. "Or I could work in the library until you're ready, if you prefer?"

He stopped with his hands on her shoulders, his dark

eyes narrowing. "You couldn't wait to talk to me?" The corner of his mouth lifted into a wry grin.

Raven's cheeks heated. "I have so many questions, Gabriel. My arms. The books. Kristina." She shook her head. "Crimson."

He guided her deeper into the building, his hand landing naturally in the curve of her spine. "Give me a minute to get dressed. We will eat in the courtyard."

"And you'll answer my questions?"

He looked at her, eyes smoldering. "As honestly as I can, as long as you are willing to listen."

She swallowed hard. "Why wouldn't I be willing to listen?"

"People say they want the truth, but often lies are far easier to sleep with at night."

Okay. Raven didn't like the sound of that, but she nodded anyway. He led her into a brick courtyard at the back of the building where a table was already laden with a silver tray of food and a carafe of coffee.

She stopped short. "How is this already here?" She'd woken him. He wouldn't have had time to make this or even call someone to make it.

"Please, sit. Allow me to..." He looked down at himself. As much as Raven appreciated his bare chest and thin cotton pajamas, she understood his need to perform his morning routine. She nodded, feeling flushed, and sat down at the table.

He disappeared in the blink of an eye.

The courtyard was a haven with four ivy-covered brick walls forming the boundary. Flowers bloomed in pots along the border and around a bubbling fountain that made a relaxing gurgle in the open space. It was a crisp morning, but she was comfortable in her long sleeves. She leaned back in the chair and closed her eyes, letting the sun bake her face.

The scent of smoky spices wisped past her nose, and she opened her eyes again. Gabriel, dressed in jeans and a sport jacket, watched her hungrily from the doorway. That *was* hunger she saw in his eyes, and not for the food on the table in front of her. It had been a long time and she was out of practice, but she knew when a man wanted her. He held her gaze too long and his body had stilled like a predator's.

She gave him a small flirtatious smile. With a shake of his shoulders, he frowned and strolled toward the chair opposite her, his body language going from hot to cold in a matter of seconds. She looked down at her hands, thinking she must be rusty when it came to the opposite sex. She had totally misread him after all.

"Coffee?" he asked.

She nodded. "You were going to explain how the food is ready. Agnes told me you have housekeepers, but they'd have to be clairvoyant to have prepared this in advance."

"Eat first, then I will answer." He lifted a silver dome and slid a plate of eggs benedict in front of her. "You are still far too thin. Doesn't your family feed you?"

How rude. "My mother is a phenomenal cook, thank you very much. Dr. Freemont says my metabolism is like a bank that has been overdrawn for too long. It's going to be hard for me to put on weight for a while," Raven said with no attempt to soften the edge in her tone. "I'm sorry you find my appearance off-putting."

He drew back. "On the contrary, nothing about your appearance is unpleasant. You are... enchanting. I only worry about your health and that you are happy."

"Oh," she said, sensing his words were genuine.

Maybe... maybe she'd mistaken a brotherly regard for attraction. She stared down at her plate and took a bite. Delicious.

"Agnes told you I have housekeepers. Did she also tell you they weren't human?"

Raven stopped chewing. "No. She left that part out."

"They followed me here from the Old World. They are oreads, or mountain nymphs. As long as there are natural substances from which to draw their power—wood, stone, water—they cannot be seen unless they wish to be seen."

"Oreads." Raven dissected the strange word in her mind. "And they are the ones who brought me tea in the library?"

He nodded.

"How many work for you?"

"Two. Juniper and Hazel."

"But I can't see them."

"Not unless they wish to be seen. They only reveal themselves to those they trust completely."

"Oh."

"You said they come from the Old World. Where is that?"

He eyed her plate. Raven took another bite.

With a self-satisfied smile, he answered. "When I first arrived in this realm, it was on the island of Crete. The oreads are from Mount Ida. As magical beings, they were attracted to what I am. You could say our relationship is symbiotic."

"When you first arrived in this... *realm*? What realm are you originally from?" Raven hadn't considered that he wasn't from here. After all, everything she'd ever learned about vampires and witches suggested they were once human. Why not dragons?

"All dragons are originally from Paragon."

"Paragon? Is that like another... planet?"

He shook his head. "A realm. Another realm."

"What does that mean?"

He sipped his coffee, studying his plate as if trying to find the right words. "If Paragon were another country or even another planet, you could potentially go there in a car or on a boat, right? Or maybe a rocket ship, yes?"

Raven nodded.

"No spaceship could ever reach Paragon." He pointed toward the sky. "This planet, this universe, is one realm." He held up one of the red cocktail napkins stacked on the tray. "Paragon is another." He held up another napkin parallel to the first. "Two separate realities, advancing through space and time, never to intersect under normal circumstances."

"But you're here."

"There was a political uprising in Paragon. My mother used very powerful magic to help my siblings and me escape. She saved our lives by sending us here." He held up his right hand and thumbed the emerald ring. "She was the one who enchanted my ring. This allows me to withstand the environment here."

"And without that magic, you'll die?" Her voice was hushed, although there was no one to hear her.

He shook his head. "Death is not necessarily an accurate word for what will happen to me."

Raven could feel her eyes widening. She drew her mouth into a grimace. "What will happen?" The question was more breath than audible syllables.

He licked his lips, his fingers playing across the handle of his mug. "I'll turn to stone."

Sometimes life kicks you in the teeth. Raven wasn't sure what she was expecting him to say, but "I'll turn to stone" was not it. It bothered her. Not just because the entire situation was bizarre, but because it wasn't lost on her that stone did not mean dead. She couldn't imagine being conscious inside a body of stone. Or maybe she could. Was it unlike being very ill? The horror made her shift in her chair.

"We are not going to let that happen. We'll find a way to break the curse. I have an entire room of spells upstairs."

"About that..." He reached across the table and touched her wrist, his thumb running gently along the back of her hand. Raven had a moment to enjoy the touch and the delicious feeling of warmth it elicited. Then the marks returned. Her arm lit up and glowed right through her blouse.

"It doesn't hurt," she said.

His eyebrows sank. He retracted his hand.

"Did this happen to Kristina?" she asked.

"No."

"What did happen to her?"

"She left one day and never came back." Gabriel looked down at his plate, feeding himself a large bite of eggs.

"But, I mean, do you think that woman, Crimson, had something to do with her disappearance?"

Gabriel stopped eating. "I shouldn't need to say this, but stay away from Crimson, Raven. She's dangerous."

Raven crossed her arms over her chest. "Duh. After yesterday, I wasn't planning on making her my BFF."

He snorted. "I have rescued you from a dark alley and a tall ledge. Believe me, Raven, if I thought I could apply logic to your actions, I wouldn't bring it up." He gave her a piercing stare.

"Advice heeded," she said flatly. "But there's something else I need to ask you about Kristina."

He sighed heavily. "I don't want to talk about Kristina."

"She sketched my family crest in the back of the catalog she kept of the grimoires. Do you have any idea why?"

Gabriel's expression seemed nothing short of shocked. "It must be a coincidence. Kristina was gone long before I considered binding you."

"It's a distinct design based on a tree that used to grow on my ancestors' property."

He shook his head. "I have no idea. I'm sorry, Raven."

She played with her food, her shoulders hunching.

Gabriel placed a hand on hers, warming her with his touch. The pattern on her skin glowed to life again. "I'd like you to come with me to visit an acquaintance of mine. I believe she may know what this condition is on your arms."

"Okay."

"You're not going to fight me on this?" The corner of his mouth lifted.

"What would be the point? I want answers as much as you."

The laugh that came from deep within his chest wasn't human, and it took her a second to realize what it was. It made her laugh too, and she leaned toward him without even thinking about it.

"I am not used to this level of compliance from you. So far you've resisted me at every turn. You don't want to use my car, you won't lock the door to the library, you come and go on your own terms..."

"Do you want me to resist?" She gave a teasing smile. "Do you enjoy it?"

His eyes narrowed—a predator toying with his prey. "Only in the sense that I enjoy a challenge."

Oh hell, she was playing with fire. It was as if the dragon was right in front of her, showing her his teeth, and she was standing there like an idiot admiring them.

"When would you like to go see your friend?" she said, changing the subject.

"After dark."

"Okay." She folded her napkin and tucked it next to her plate. "I should get started in the library."

"Nonsense." He stood and rounded the table. Wrapping his arms around her, he cut off another bite of her eggs and lifted it to her mouth.

His warmth surrounded her like a soft blanket, and she caught herself sagging against him.

"There's time, Raven," he whispered in her ear. "Remember, you promised me your presence. It is soothing to me."

She was feeling soothed herself at the moment. Raven opened her mouth and ate every last bite.

CHAPTER ELEVEN

D ragons, Raven thought, were mythical beasts with
scales and bony ridges, huge clamping teeth. They
breathed fire. Their reptilian brains focused on few things
other than hunger and violence, and if books were to be
believed, they had hearts of stone.

Gabriel challenged everything she thought she knew
about dragons. While she reviewed grimoire after grimoire
over the days that followed, flipping through books like her
life depended on it, which, of course, it did, her mind
lingered on him. He walked like a man and spoke like a
man, but now that she'd spent time with him, that was
where the similarities ended. Gabriel wore his magic like a
cloak. His physical body was larger than most, a size that
would fit in among professional wrestlers or NFL players,
but when he entered a room, he was far bigger than the
boundaries of his skin. Raven could feel him like an invisible force when she was near. She could smell him like a
raging bonfire. She could sense him, a connection that
lingered deep within her even now. Shouldn't she be afraid?

A deep itch ran the back of Raven's neck, and she

scratched it lightly. She was perusing a Russian grimoire, its pages stained with something suspiciously blood-like. When she flipped the page, it felt like a swarm of tiny spiders were raiding her skin. Raven brushed the back of her arms and the top of her thighs, but there was nothing there. It was all in her head. She flipped through the rest of the book quickly and was never happier than the moment she returned it to the shelf.

Kristina had left her no further clues regarding why she'd sketched the family crest. The Tanglewood tree, if that was indeed what she'd been drawing and not some random and coincidentally similar version of the tree of life, was an enigma. Raven checked every page of Kristina's notes and did not a find a single reference to it anywhere.

Engrossed in her work, she lost track of time and didn't notice at first when Gabriel appeared in the doorway later that week. She was surprised it was as late as it was. Where had the time gone?

"I brought you something," he said. He strode into the room, drawing a blooming plant from behind his back. An African violet. A mound of deep amethyst flowers smiled up at her from a glazed blue clay pot. "You said you missed the outdoors. I thought it might help to have something living in here."

Raven gazed up at his face. "They're gorgeous, thank you." She positioned the pot on the corner of the desk. "Careful, Gabriel. How can I take you seriously as a deadly dragon when you woo me with such gentle charms?" She laughed.

Abruptly, he was beside her, his face close, his arms caging her in as his hands gripped the arms of her chair. There was nothing but fire in his eyes. She stopped breathing.

"Don't be fooled, little one. A few flowers are a simple thing. When I woo you, if I woo you, you'll know. Dragons do not mate lightly." His lips brushed her cheek as he whispered in her ear, and Raven trembled. She actually trembled with desire that made her knees turn to water. Eyes wide, she realized how long it had been since she'd felt like a sexual creature. If he touched her right now in the right place, the simple trail of his fingers would make her shatter.

She forced herself to take a breath. Forced her brain to think the words *your boss. Playing with fire.* His lips were close, so close.

He drew back, a breath of air working its way between them. "That friend I wanted you to visit about the symbols on your arms, she can see you tonight. Be ready in an hour."

He was out the door before she could agree.

❧

PRECISELY AN HOUR LATER, a horn honked from below the window. Duncan. Raven marked her place in her work, locked the door to the library, and joined Gabriel in the waiting car. To Raven's surprise, Duncan whisked them away to the Old Ursuline Convent. The building was the oldest in New Orleans and, according to one of her past professors, one of the best examples of French Colonial architecture in the country. She'd toured the place before. It was a quintessential part of New Orleans history and the last place she expected Gabriel to take her.

"Are your friends meeting us here?" she asked as they made their way toward the front of the building.

"They live here."

"No one lives here, Gabriel." Raven pointed at the

copper plaque on the door. "This place hasn't been a residence since 1899."

He gave her a dark look and led her around the side of the building. The door he knocked on looked ancient, like it might disintegrate under the pressure of his knuckles. Raven stared at it, her brain trying to figure out how the door could be there. She didn't remember it from before, and it looked completely out of place.

Before long, it opened to reveal a small, wrinkled woman who wiped her hands on a filthy apron she wore over her floor-length skirt. She stared at the two of them with an unappreciative scowl.

"Gabriel Blakemore," the crone said through tight, wrinkled lips. She had an unmistakably French accent and had to crane her neck to see his face, thanks to her hunched back. "What brings you to our door?"

It was no wonder her apron was filthy. The room behind her was something lost to time. Dust covered and decorated with cobwebs, every corner of the room displayed the bodies of dead insects, curled on their backs in the thick layer of grime. Raven stepped closer to Gabriel, her arms crossed in front of her lest she accidentally touch something. There was a fire burning and dried herbs and vegetables hanging from the rafters. It smelled of lavender, wood smoke, and possibly rat droppings.

"I need your help diagnosing a malady, Delphine," Gabriel said.

She frowned. "I have told you before we cannot help you break your curse. Only the venom from the snake who bit you can counteract the poison." The crone started to close the door. Raven's eyes darted to Gabriel. Had she just confirmed the only one who could break the curse was Crimson herself?

Gabriel's hand shot out, catching the door, forcing his way inside with his large body in a way that clearly threatened the old woman. The door closed behind them, making Raven jump.

"It is not my curse I have come for but this." He grabbed Raven's wrist and pulled her toward the old woman.

"Hey!" Raven protested, but her arm had already lit up with the strange markings. More than before, she realized. They were spreading. "Oh dear Lord. Gabriel, they're everywhere." Both arms were covered as well as her chest. The light glowed through her blouse.

"You have been a busy boy," Delphine said.

Gabriel released Raven's arm.

"The price is the same. Are you willing to pay it, darling?" the crone asked.

"Yes."

"This one must be special for you to weaken yourself further." Her rheumy eyes narrowed on Raven.

"She is."

"I am?" Raven whispered under her breath. When she searched his profile, there was nothing flippant about his expression, but he did not turn his face toward her.

"Come upstairs. Antoinette has been bed bound since September. She'll be excited for your visit."

Antoinette? Who was Antoinette?

Delphine led them up two flights of stairs to a dim room that smelled even worse than the first floor. Raven breathed through her mouth and moved closer to Gabriel, hoping his smoky scent would mask the foul odor.

The old woman limped to the center of the room and appeared to pick up a tall tin from the floor. Raven couldn't be sure because only an outline was visible in the moonlight that trickled in through slats in the two windows. The tin rattled, and then a match struck its side. A flame glowed to life, bathing the space in flickering light. With a whoosh, the flame multiplied and rose to the ceiling before leveling out. Fire danced within a great crystal cylinder, the likes of which Raven had never seen before. It reminded her of a chiminea like the one on the Three Sisters' patio, but bigger and entirely made of glass. The flames burned without the benefit of wood, but she noticed a pipe leading to the base. *A massive gas lamp*, she thought.

Raven moved out from behind Gabriel as the light spread across the room. What she saw in the previously darkened corners made her blood run cold. Delphine's sisters were there all right, but they were dead. Really dead. She was in a room of corpses.

She opened her mouth to scream, but Gabriel's hand clamped over it. His eyes came into view, and he placed a finger over his lips. "Shhh." His touch calmed her, and she closed her mouth. There was no stopping the goose bumps though as they marched up her arms, or the chill that made her hug herself.

One of the sisters lay in a silk-lined coffin, nothing left but a shriveled corpse in an antique lace dress. The other looked fresher but still dead. Her body was propped in a rocking chair, her needlework still in her desiccated hands.

Delphine returned from the dark recesses of the room with a chalice that looked like it had come straight from the Vatican and a dagger that might have come straight from hell.

"Your flesh, dragon," she said in her raspy French lilt.

Gabriel rolled up his sleeve and extended his arm. *No*, Raven thought, her every instinct rejecting the course of events. But she watched helplessly as the dagger sliced into Gabriel's flesh, fast and deep. She gasped at the brutality and winced as his blood spurted into the chalice, dark red splattering against the gold sides of the cup. She needn't have worried. Almost immediately, the flow slowed, and without any pressure or tending, the bleeding stopped completely, the two sides of the cut knitting together until the wound was nothing more than a memory.

Delphine dropped the dagger and it clattered across the floor, splattering blood. She cradled the chalice in both hands. "*Mes sœurs, nous avons du sang,*" she whispered.

"What did she say?" Raven recognized the language as French and cursed herself for taking Spanish in high school.

"Shhh." Gabriel placed a finger over his lips.

"Right. Wouldn't want to tell the human what kind of supernatural hoodoo was going down." Raven sneered at him.

Delphine raised the chalice to the lips of the dead woman in the rocker and poured blood into her mouth. A bit trickled out the corner of her lips, and Raven stifled a gag. Gabriel had to steady her when that shriveled corpse swallowed. Before their eyes, the dead woman transformed, growing taller and stretching out the wrinkles in her skin. Her breasts and hips plumped and her hair changed from its gray and brittle straggles to a full mane of mahogany waves. She lifted from the chair in a way that didn't seem to use the strength of her legs, a thick cloud of dust billowing from her limbs. The ancient chair creaked, empty behind her. Arms extended like a ballerina, she twirled, sending the rest of the dust flying. When the filth settled, her rags had transformed into a flowing, knee-length blue gown that looked brand new.

Raven gulped, her gaze darting between Gabriel and the woman.

The sister curtsied. "Gabriel, always a pleasure."

He gave a small bow. "Lucienne."

"Help me with Antoinette, sister. She has let herself go." Delphine walked to the coffin, and Lucienne joined her. Carefully they cupped the back of the skull within.

"No," Raven mumbled under her breath. The thing was a skeleton. How could it swallow? It didn't even have any lips.

"Slowly, sister," Lucienne said.

Delphine dribbled the blood into the open jaw. It dripped onto the bones of the spine. Raven almost climbed into Gabriel's arms when it swallowed. The damned bones undulated without aid of muscle or flesh. Raven pressed her back against Gabriel's chest and was grateful when he wrapped his arms around her shoulders.

"It's all right," he whispered in her ear. "Perhaps you shouldn't watch."

Raven should have listened. What happened next was straight out of a horror movie. Cartilage and veins, tissue and skin formed over those bones in a reverse melting process that made her nauseous. Blood seeped from the wood beneath the corpse, hair grew, and gelatinous flesh became solid. When the process was done, a girl who couldn't have been more than seventeen, with hair the color of ripe wheat, sat up and swung her legs over the side of the casket. She brushed the dust off her tea-length cotton dress and smoothed her long, straight hair.

"Oh Gabriel." She clasped her hands in front of her heart. "You must visit us more often." She started moving around the lamp, her arms swinging, her hips swaying. Lucienne fell into step behind her.

Delphine lifted the chalice and mumbled a few words, then drank deeply. Her throat bobbed, and before long her hunch was gone and she was tearing the handkerchief from her curly black hair. With a pirouette, she transformed, her dress altering into a long column of silver. Her youthful arms began to sway with her sisters'.

By the light of the fire, the three women, now young and full of life, began to dance in earnest, not for Gabriel and Raven but for the fire. They turned toward it, shimmying their shoulders and bending backward, kicking and spinning in the light. As weird as the whole thing was, Raven was fascinated by it. A strange perfume scented the air. Their black silhouettes writhed against the fiery glow. The air grew thick, and Raven closed her eyes against a sudden and unwelcome arousal that bloomed low in her body.

"What is it you want of us, dragon?" the three sisters asked at the same time in one melodious voice.

"What do the markings on this woman's skin mean?" He ushered Raven forward gently. "Why do they glow when I touch her?"

Lucienne twirled from the light and grabbed Raven's wrists. Raven balked. The woman's eyes had gone totally white, the pupil and iris gone. The whites glowed like incandescent bulbs.

Raven swallowed her fear.

"Let us see, girl," Lucienne said, her sisters circling. They unbuttoned Raven's blouse, pulling the tails from her waistband. She glanced back at Gabriel in a panic.

"It's the only way. They have to see them. All of them. I'll keep you safe," he said.

She told herself that exposing a little skin was easier than bleeding into a chalice. She removed her blouse, then thanked the Lord above they did not attempt to remove her bra.

"Come, dragon," Delphine said. "Touch her so that we may see."

Raven looked down at herself. Nothing but smooth pale skin gleamed in the fire. She was still pallid and too thin. Her flesh gave off a faint sheen of sweat in the light. She blushed as Gabriel approached, her breath coming quicker and her sex throbbing with the anticipation of his touch. She couldn't help it. The heat, the smell, the dancing. Her body was a raw nerve.

Gabriel positioned himself at her side and made eye contact. The fire leaped and crackled in his eyes. He'd touched her before, but this time was different. Although her bra was modest and she was still wearing her slacks, she felt naked beneath his gaze. He looked at her reverently, as if touching her was an exquisite privilege.

"May I?" he asked.

"Yes," she said.

Delphine cried out, "Turn her this way so we can see."

Gabriel slipped behind her again and shuffled her closer to the flames. His heat against her back warred with the heat of the fire. All the tiny hairs along her skin reached for him, anticipating his touch. It seemed to take a million years for him to do it, but when his hand landed on her shoulder at the base of her neck, her breathing quickened. Her nipples strained against her bra as tingles of pleasure traveled from his touch straight to their tips. Her lips parted.

His breath hitched in her ear, and she felt the hard length of him extend along her backside. So, he was not immune to this. She tipped her head back against his chest, and his hand slid over the length of her arm, trailed soft and slow across her belly before sweeping under her bra. His thumb grazed the underside of her breasts, coaxing a deep ache within her. When she thought she couldn't stand it a moment longer, his coarse palm brushed over her belly again, his pinky slipping inside her waistband only to slowly circle back again.

Raven's flesh ignited. The symbols glowed neon blue in the firelight, but she was having trouble remembering why that was important. Gabriel's touch was exquisite torture. She ground her ass against him and writhed in his arms. Her hand slithered up, her nails scraping along the back of his scalp. She grabbed a thick handful of his hair and tugged, eliciting a sound from deep within his throat.

Delphine, Lucienne, and Antoinette chanted toward the fire, twirling and leaping with the melody. Raven could hardly hear it anymore. Gabriel's hand kept circling, his pinky finger brushing even lower beneath her waistband. She moaned. *Please.* Every cell in her body wanted those fingers inside her. She slid her hand behind her back and stroked his erection through his jeans.

"Raven," he hissed in her ear.

She breathed out a heavy sigh. Her hips undulated with the rhythm of the dancing. "Please," she gasped.

A rumble started in his chest, a noise she'd never heard a man make before. She knew what it meant. She knew by the way he pressed himself against her, the way he trailed his lips from behind her ear to her shoulder. Up, over, down. He swept lower this time, brushing the top of her sex as his lips brushed her ear.

"Do you like that, Raven?"

"Yes," she whispered. She ached for him, ached with a need she thought might kill her if it wasn't quenched. Instead, the lamp went out. They were plunged into darkness, wisps of white smoke curling in the moonlight that broke through the one and only window.

"*Sang interdit,*" the women shouted in their singular

voice, gasping as if they could hardly breathe. "*Femme proscrite!*"

"What are you saying?" Gabriel snapped, tightening his hold on Raven's stomach.

"She is forbidden, dragon. An abomination!" Delphine hissed like a snake and the air rattled with her menace.

"Why?" he demanded.

But Delphine had picked up the dagger she'd used to cut Gabriel's arm. Her eyes glowed brighter in the darkness as she focused on Raven.

"*Sorcière!*" Delphine charged, raising the dagger.

The silver blade flashed. Gabriel's grip tightened around her middle, and then they were moving, fast. Raven was hoisted upward and sideways. There was a crash. Glass shattered and she held her breath as she was thrown through the open window. In the next blink, the gardens swept by beneath her dangling feet. She was in Gabriel's arms, and he was flying!

She tried to look over her shoulder, but he banked left and all she saw was starry sky. He landed gently on the walkway outside the grounds.

No sooner were her feet on the pavement than she spun around, speechless but needing to see, needing to know how he'd flown her from that room. She caught a glimpse of two dark, fleshy wings tucking into his back.

"Wait!" Raven protested, raising her hands to his chest. "Let me see. I want to see them."

With a wicked smile and widening eyes, he grabbed her wrists, glancing both ways up and down the street. They were alone. "Not here."

Raven's cheeks warmed.

He quickly removed the black button-down he was wearing and gave it to her, reminding her she was standing on the sidewalk in her bra. She donned the shirt quickly. What had gotten into her? She'd practically thrown herself at him. In a public place, no less.

"Will they follow us?" she asked, looking back toward the convent.

"They can't leave the grounds. If they do, they'll turn to dust." He slid his phone from his pocket and called Duncan, saying only "come now" when the driver answered.

Raven's face tightened in disgust. "What are those women?"

"You've never heard of the Casket Girls?"

She'd heard of them. Everyone who grew up around New Orleans had. In the early 1700s, the king of France sent women to serve as wives to the men living in the colonies of what would become New Orleans. The women's long, arduous journey across the Atlantic left them pale and painfully thin. Some of them had contracted consumption, what was now called tuberculosis. It caused them to cough up blood. Those ghostly, starving women arrived in the colonies carrying casket-shaped boxes that contained all their belongings. The women were called the Casket Girls because their real names were lost to history. They became the source of vampire legend. Some said they'd inspired Bram Stoker's *Dracula*.

"Are they truly vampires?" she asked.

Gabriel snorted. "One could call them vampires, but they do not completely fit the label. They caught something on their way here from the Old World, something that lives in them still. They drink blood and are experts in fortune telling and divination, but they do not have fangs or power over the elements. They are prisoners there. The former nuns ritualistically bound them to the grounds to keep them from feeding on the townsfolk."

"What did they mean about me being an abomination? Some of what they said was in French. Did you understand it?"

His smile faded and his gaze shifted over her shoulder. Duncan was there. He pulled up beside them, and Gabriel opened the door for her.

"Come home with me. We need to talk."

CHAPTER TWELVE

Gabriel tried not to stare at Raven across the seat of the town car, although his eyes were drawn to her again and again. By the Mountain, he wanted her. The memory of her white skin in the firelight, the way she'd writhed against him, the brush of his fingers against her sex... He closed his eyes and forced himself to think of something else. His accounting procedures. Blakemore's inventory policy. The general idea of being plunged into an ice bath. As soon as the car stopped, he opened the door for her and helped her out.

"You look pale. Are you all right?" Gabriel asked.

"I'm fine, all things considered," she said. "A little hungry."

"When was the last time you ate?"

She shrugged. "Breakfast with you."

He frowned. "Raven, you must eat. Please. Didn't Juniper and Hazel bring you meals today?"

"Yes, of course they did. I ate an enormous breakfast. I wasn't hungry."

"Come. We'll eat and we'll talk." He found the curve of

her back with his hand and guided her up the stairs. She was still wearing his shirt, big enough on her to be a dress, and Gabriel liked the look of it. He wished it was all she was wearing. He'd like to see her bare legs, to unbutton the shirt slowly.

Fuck. He'd told himself he wouldn't do this. It would only complicate things, for both of them. She turned her head, her eyes twinkling, her mouth holding the promise of ecstasy. Her gaze traced the lines of the simple black T-shirt he wore. There was nothing short of abject desire in that perusal. Everything narrowed on her, all his thoughts bowing to the overwhelming need to mark her as his own. There were a dozen other things he should be thinking about now. Life-or-death things. But it had been decades since his body had responded like this to anyone.

He stopped in the hall outside the door, and she collided with his chest. It was his speed. He'd stopped much faster than she could, faster than any human could. It wasn't on purpose, but she ended up flat against him. She inhaled deeply and went limp in his arms. And wasn't that like a bowl of milk to his inner kitten?

"Are you all right?" he asked her.

"Yes." Her voice sounded husky.

He massaged the base of her neck as he searched her face. He was not alone in his attraction. She wanted him too. He could see it in her eyes, smell it like a perfume around her. If he could have her, even once, maybe he could manage this runaway desire. If he could just taste her.

Fumbling for his key, he unlocked the door without letting her go and flipped on the light. She turned in his arms and entered his home. She'd been here before, of course, when he'd saved her from her attackers, but he wondered what she thought of it. He'd taken the place down to the studs a few years ago. It was light and airy, completely modern with stainless steel appliances and clean, almost sterile lines. The floors were hardwood and the art on the walls was contemporary. Lots of gray and white with punches of red. Gabriel might be almost five hundred years old, but he liked to change with the times.

Raven stopped a few steps inside the door.

"Are you afraid of me?" he asked from behind her. He wondered if the events of the night had finally caught up to her. He closed the door. "I should have warned you about the Casket Girls. What they do is hard to explain, and I've never had a reading go like this."

"I'm not scared," Raven said, whirling around. It wasn't fear he saw in her giant blue eyes but tenacity. "Will you show me, now that we're alone?"

"Show you what?"

"Your wings."

His eyes widened and he tried to force himself to breathe evenly. "It's a very personal thing you are asking."

"Personal? It can't be *that* personal. You had them out in public."

"Out of necessity."

She sighed thoughtfully. "You don't have to, but for the record, I thought they were beautiful, what I saw of them. Are they magic? How do they come out through your shirt?"

He stepped closer and put his arms around her, sliding his hands inside hidden openings in the sides of the one she was wearing. He brushed the bare skin of her back. "Specially designed panels. Juniper and Hazel are excellent tailors."

"Oh..."

Their eyes locked again and Gabriel pulled her closer.

"Are wings the only, um, physical difference between you and a, um, human?" Raven placed both hands firmly on his chest.

He slid his hands out of the shirt she was wearing and chuckled when a blush stained her cheeks. "Are you interested in investigating our physical differences, Raven? I thought you might have felt them tonight when I was pressed against you." His dragon had locked onto her like prey. He had to be careful. He wasn't sure how long he could hold himself back.

"I love that sound," she said.

He knit his brows. "What sound?"

"You're making a sound now, a rumble." She placed a hand over his chest. "It's beautiful. Like a purr."

Shit, his mating song. It had been a long time since that particular trait had reared its head. He might as well strip down naked in front of her. "What do you expect when you look at me like that?" He tried to keep his voice even. He cupped her jaw. "You are the most singularly desirable woman I have met in my five hundred years."

She snorted. "I'm a skinny survivor with puffy, half-grown hair and a short fuse."

"You are a tower of feminine strength who might as well be a dragon the way you breathe fire. You're brave and kind."

The scent of her arousal met his nostrils and he moved in closer. He wanted to kiss her, to taste her. He lowered his lips toward hers.

"So, about those wings...," she said, backing away a half step.

"This is important to you?" He gritted his teeth.

"Very."

He took a step back. If this was the thing keeping him from being inside her, he'd give her what she wanted.

Slowly he crossed his arms over his stomach, grabbed the hem of his T-shirt, and slipped it off over his head. He didn't have to remove the shirt. There were panels built into it the same as in the one she was wearing. But he wanted her, and having one less piece of clothing between them seemed like a good choice. He was rewarded with another wave of her arousal, her natural jasmine-and-vanilla scent growing musky. His nostrils flared.

"You like what you see?" He swaggered toward her.

She placed her hands on her hips. "Not as much as I would like to see some wings."

Damn, she wasn't going to let it go. "So demanding."

She tapped her toe expectantly.

He swallowed hard. Maybe this was for the best. If she could accept this part of him, maybe she could accept the rest of the monster within. He took a deep breath, rolled his shoulders, and spread his wings.

❦

RAVEN WANTED DESPERATELY TO TAKE A PICTURE OR video of what was happening in front of her; not to share it with anyone else, but to watch it over and over. Gabriel was beautiful. The man already looked like a chiseled work of art, standing in front of her in nothing but a pair of low-slung jeans. What happened next was frosting on the cake.

Two dark wings extended from his back. Not black exactly but darkly iridescent. Smoothly scaled like the belly of a snake, they were covered in a light dusting of dark feathers. They were darkest closest to his body, jet-black with a hint of green when he shifted in the light, but the color lightened gradually toward an almost light gray tip. Raven stepped forward to get a better look, her hand extended, and he flinched away from her touch like a startled bird. She placed one hand gently over his heart.

She knew two things—Gabriel had a heart, and it was in the same place as a man's. It pounded against her palm, that rumble she'd heard before becoming more pronounced with her touch. "Trust me," she said. "I won't hurt you." She almost laughed when she heard herself. He was a foot taller than her and more than twice her weight. Surely he could wipe the floor with her in a single beat of those wings. She couldn't imagine being strong enough to hurt him.

She skimmed her hand up his chest and over his shoulder to where his left wing originated from his back. The purring grew stronger. He didn't ask her to stop, so she kept going. Gently, she stroked the outer edge, feeling the hard, bony structure that defined the wing. The glistening originated from a fine layer of scales that ran the length, smooth and soft as the layered petals of a flower. It wasn't all scales though. There were feathers... tiny feathers from shoulder to tip, dappled like the fine hairs on a human arm. The wing itself was bare flesh, framed by a support network of five long bones that she thought looked like a massive webbed hand. She gently scratched along the inner curve with the tip of her nail.

"Raven, please." Gabriel's voice broke. His eyes were closed as if what she was doing was almost painful, and the scent he was putting off—his regular smoky citrus radiance—had added another dimension. Cloves and spice. The world's best cologne. Now she understood why seeing his wings had been such a big deal. This was bare skin. This was intimate.

She removed her hand from his wing and instead

smoothed it along his ribs and down the front of his abs. "Please," she echoed.

Her feet left the ground and she was swept up in his arms, those powerful wings thumping the air on either side of her. When the rush was over, her back was pressed against the wall and he was stretched out against her. His chest was heaving and his breath brushed her lips.

"Do you know what you do to me?" he asked.

She wrapped her arms around his neck and dug her nails into his hair, her eyes on his mouth. "I think I do."

His lips connected with hers, deliciously hot. Everything inside her liquefied. She wrapped one leg around his hip and groaned into his mouth. He purred in answer, his chest vibrating against her torso, sending an electric tickle of pleasure through her. She moved her hand from his hair to his wing and felt his erection kick.

Holding her up with one hand, he reached between them for the buttons of the shirt she was wearing. Raven was temporarily blinded by the glow of her own skin. The symbols were brighter than ever and seemed to be spreading. A flood of fear rolled through her and she stilled in his embrace.

"Gabriel, what's happening to me? What did the Casket Girls say?"

He released her leg and settled her feet back on the floor, the intensity in his dark eyes cutting straight to her soul. The clink of silver on silver came from the next room, but Gabriel didn't take his eyes off her. "That would be Juniper and Hazel setting up the dining room. I had them make you something." His eyes drifted to her mouth. "I'll tell you over dinner."

He started to back away from her, but Raven grabbed him by the hips. "Wait. Tell me here. I'm not that hungry and..." She parted her lips and allowed her eyes to sweep down to his erection. "I'd like to pick up where we left off." Shameless, but she couldn't help herself.

He feathered his fingers across her cheek and brushed them through the hair over her ear, his wings flexing with his movements. "There is nothing I'd enjoy more than touching you, kissing you, finishing what we've started, but I can hear your stomach growling, and it's been a long night. You're tired and you're hungry. And clearly you're afraid." He glanced at her glowing skin.

Raven opened her mouth to insist she was fine, but he quieted her with a kiss, the tip of his hot tongue flicking across her bottom lip.

"When I make love to you, Raven, I won't rush it. I don't want to be distracted by hunger or fatigue or the effects of this curse." He held up the ring, his fingers noticeably free from tapping. "I want hours to worship you in the way you deserve to be worshipped, and I want it to mean something."

"What do you want it to mean?"

"Dragons don't mate lightly, Raven."

He'd said that before, although she wasn't sure exactly what he meant by it. She felt her knees wobble and was thankful for his steadying hand leading her toward the dining room. The spread there was something out of a dream, laden with food and candles that burned above silver holders. The gilded china sparkled.

"Do you like seafood?"

"It's my favorite."

"Good. I requested lobster risotto for you. It's the oreads' specialty. I don't tell many people this, but the chef at Commander's Palace has my oreads to thank for his prize-winning recipe." He raised the dome off her plate, and her mouth started to water.

"Mmm." Raven's stomach growled. Once she started eating, her body finally admitted it needed food. By the time Gabriel sat down on the other side of the table, she had made a sizable dent in her risotto.

"We need to talk about what happened tonight with the Casket Girls."

"Why did they freak out like that?" Raven forked a chunk of lobster and moaned at the delectable flavor. "She called me *sorcière*. What does that mean?"

Tap-tap-tap. His fingers started up again and his expression hardened. "It means sorceress."

Raven stopped eating. "Sorceress." When he said nothing more, she snorted. "Well, that's ridiculous."

"Raven, has there been anyone in your family with powers?"

"Of course not."

"Are you sure? Any strange events, family stories that can't be explained?"

"Dead bodies in the attic? No, we are not Anne Rice's Mayfair Witches. We are a normal American family."

"Hmmm." Gabriel sipped his wine.

"They were wrong." She shrugged. "I'm sure the Casket Girls make mistakes."

"Not often," he mumbled. He pushed his risotto around his plate. "I am drawn to you, Raven." He shook his head.

"But?"

"I am drawn to you like I have never been drawn to a human woman. If you are a witch, if you have power, my tooth will bring it out in you. It will make you far more powerful."

"You don't think it's true though."

"It would explain your psychic abilities, and it would mean... it would mean you might have the power to break Crimson's curse."

Raven paused with her fork halfway to her mouth. "But I'm not, Gabriel. I can't be. I might be able to find the spell, but I'm not a witch. Believe me, if I was, I would have saved myself when I was dying."

His fingers stopped tapping and he gave a low chuckle. "In Paragon, I would have been forbidden from saving you if you were a witch. The gift of my tooth would imbue you with dragon magic. While this magic is fairly harmless inside a human, inside a witch, it could make you more powerful than anyone should be. Dragon-witch pairings have been outlawed in Paragon since the early fourth century when the Witch Queen of Darnuith attempted to overthrow my uncle." He toyed with the ring on his finger. "Of course, in retrospect, she might have done us a favor if she'd succeeded."

Raven sat back in her chair and sipped from the glass of white wine that was waiting for her, courtesy of Juniper and Hazel. "It's a good thing I'm not a witch then."

"Mmm-hmm," he said, nodding but not breaking eye contact.

"But if I'm not a witch, what does that tell us about the symbols on my arms when you touch me?"

"Nothing," he said.

"Okay." Raven drained her glass. "Why do you think it didn't happen to Kristina? She had powers. If the tooth brought this out in me, why not her? Why not Agnes or Richard?"

Gabriel went absolutely still, all levity draining from his features. "I don't know."

Raven paused. Something didn't add up. Being here in

this apartment reminded her of a detail Agnes had mentioned. "Kristina has your tooth. That first night you saved me, you told me you had followed our bond. Why can't you use your bond to find Kristina?"

Gabriel's expression hardened. "I don't want to talk about Kristina." He stood, his body seeming to fill the room. "It's late, Raven. I'll call Duncan to take you home."

CHAPTER THIRTEEN

R aven didn't sleep that night. Her libido had gone from blazing inferno to bucket of ice in record time. And worse, after the way Gabriel reacted when she asked him about Kristina, she couldn't help but be suspicious. Why didn't he want to talk about her? Unless he knew more about her disappearance than he was letting on. As much chemistry as there was between them, her guard was up, and it would stay up until she knew what secret he was keeping from her.

Her suspicions only multiplied when Gabriel wasn't at Blakemore's the next day. Agnes said he was on a buying trip. His absence bled into a quiet and uneventful weekend where Raven spent far too much time in her room or sitting on the roof, staring at the stars and thinking about him.

He returned Monday, but he was different. Distant. He stopped in every afternoon to see her, but there was no more whispering in her ear. No stolen touches. He asked about the books and that was all. By the next Friday, she'd logged thirty-six grimoires, completing the section in the catalog, but when she showed the potential curse-breaking spells she'd bookmarked to Gabriel, he shook his head at every single one.

"How do you know they won't work? You haven't tried any of them." She snapped the grimoire in her hands closed in frustration.

"I can read the magic," he said. "Look at the ring. Do those spells look like the key that fits this hole?"

"What the hell are you talking about?" The last spell was a list of ingredients. It wasn't a key at all.

"Don't read them, Raven. Feel them. Take them in." He gave her a pitying look and shook his head. "Never mind. Just keep doing what you're doing and trust me."

"Okay," she said flatly.

"How is your... reaction?" He pointed toward her arms.

"If you're talking about the burning, itching and crawling feeling, it happens every time I open one of these." She pressed her hand into the cover of the grimoire in front of her. "If you're asking about the markings, I don't know. It only comes out when you... touch me."

For a minute he stared at her, eyes smoldering as if they were back in his room and he had her against the wall. But then his expression turned on a dime and he headed for the door like the library was on fire. "Don't forget to pick up your paycheck on your way out."

Paycheck. That's right, it was Friday. One good thing about today. She planned to split her earnings between her mom and Avery. She owed them. She wondered how much it would be. Gabriel had never disclosed how much he'd pay her, and she'd only worked two weeks, but anything was better than borrowing money from her family again. She finished logging the book she was working on and locked the room before jogging downstairs to Gabriel's office.

"Your paycheck, Raven." He handed her a paper check. Antiquated. But then when you were a five-hundred-year-old dragon with a total of four employees, she supposed setting up direct deposit wasn't a priority.

She looked at the check. Looked again. Her lips parted. "Uh..." Her gaze darted between him and the check. "This is for four thousand dollars."

"That is correct."

"I've only worked here two weeks."

"I gave you a raise. I felt you deserved it, considering." He stepped closer, his gaze flicking to her arms. "Considering you have skin in the game. You're important to me, Raven. I want you to be happy here. I want you to stay and do what you were hired to do, nothing more."

"What is that supposed to mean?"

"It means exactly what I said." The tapping was back, and Raven reached for his hand, but he slid it into his pocket. "Don't you have a weekend of adventure to get to, little witch?"

Little witch. That was new. Did he believe what Delphine had said, that Raven was a sorceress? "What's this all about? Why won't you let me help with your hand?"

Richard rushed into the doorway. "Gabriel, there's a man out front making an offer on the seventeenth-century armoire. He's agitated. I need you."

Gabriel gave him a little nod, then turned back toward Raven as he moved for the door. "I'll call Duncan to take you home."

"We're running out of time, Gabriel. I could stay late. I could keep looking."

He smiled sadly. "We had a deal, Raven. I've required too much of you already. You're no good to me exhausted. Go home. Rest. Live your life."

Raven tried to tell him she wasn't tired at all, that with a break for dinner she could go another hour or two, but he was already gone.

۞

IT TOOK EVERY OUNCE OF WILL INSIDE HER, BUT RAVEN refused to dwell on Gabriel's hot-and-cold routine that weekend. She could tell he wanted her. More than that, he liked her. He'd said as much, said he was drawn to her like he'd never been drawn to anyone. So then why had he refused to touch her since the night they visited the Casket Girls? No, it wasn't the Casket Girls. He'd kissed her after that. As she played back the night in her head, she realized he'd turned to ice after she'd asked about Kristina. What secret was Gabriel keeping about her?

Warning flags flew in her head. His reaction wasn't normal. Maybe Gabriel was dangerous. No matter how drawn to him she was, she needed to remember how little she actually knew about him.

"You're doing great, Rave," Avery said from beside her, breaking her from her reverie.

Raven glared at her. She was not doing great. She wasn't keeping up with the other kayakers at all.

Once she'd paid her mother and Avery part of what she owed them, she'd used some of her massive paycheck to do something she'd always wanted to do, kayak through the alligator-infested waters of Manchac Swamp. Although Avery had sworn she would never go, Raven succeeded in convincing her when it became clear she'd have to drive her anyway, forty minutes each way. Raven offered to pay, and Avery crumbled like an overbaked cookie.

Manchac Swamp kayak tours were well known in New Orleans, but before Raven had become ill, she'd always dismissed them as something only thrill seekers took part in. The swamp had a reputation. Skimming along the surface of the water at eye level with reptiles longer than she was tall rightfully terrified her. Not to mention it had long been rumored the swamp was haunted by the ghost of voodoo priestess Julia Brown.

As legend had it, Julia had worked as a *traiteur*, a folk healer in Louisiana tradition, in the town of Frenier that bordered the swamp. She was the closest thing to a doctor the area had ever known, but she was also creepy as hell. Eyewitnesses said she used to sit on her porch singing, "When I go, I'm taking you with me" over and over. She foretold her own death in 1915, and the day they lowered her into the ground, a hurricane swept in from the Caribbean, surging thirteen feet and bombarding the area with 125-mile-per-hour winds. The storm flattened the town of Frenier and the surrounding area. People still said it was Julia who did it, Julia and her voodoo. Some believed she haunted the bayou to this day.

Raven was more afraid of Julia than the alligators. Her experience with Gabriel had sealed her acceptance of the supernatural. Even if she hadn't believed in the ghost of Julia, just two years ago a skeleton had been found on the shores of this swamp. It turned out to be a 1915 hurricane victim whose body had likely been freed from its place tangled in the cypress roots and muck at the bottom of the swamp, the bones surfacing like a bad memory. Alligators and dead bodies aside, there were the mosquitos and biting flies. And the paddling. She wasn't crazy about the paddling.

But Raven needed this. She needed to stare fear in the face. She needed to use her body in a way that showed it was healthy. She needed to prove to herself that she was alive and nobody's prisoner, free to be as crazy as she chose to be. It was either this or she was getting a tattoo, and she'd never liked the thought of needles.

"Try holding your elbows higher," Avery said. Poor Avery. She was stuck babysitting. They'd fallen to the back of the group, so far back she couldn't make out what the guide was saying anymore. Raven skimmed her oar along the water, trying her best to use her core instead of her arms as their guide had suggested. But her kayak moved at a snail's pace, and she was already exhausted.

The problem was, although she was healthy again and had graduated from physical therapy, it had been years since she'd participated in any outdoor activity. She hadn't ridden a bike in five years. She'd never been kayaking. Her body was soft and her heart and lungs were out of shape. But she was here. She was doing this. Wasn't this how life started again, with the first try?

"I'm not going to win any races, but I won't get stronger if I don't try," Raven said, as much to herself as to Avery.

"You can do it. Don't worry about them. We're all going to the same place." Avery smiled supportively. Her curly black ponytail had expanded in the humidity, turning into a pom-pom at the back of her head. Raven sensed her own shorter haircut was wild too and pushed her bangs back with one hand. She should have worn a headband.

Using her paddle like a rudder, she navigated around a cypress tree and gazed longingly at the tour guide up ahead. He was pointing his paddle at something offshore. She paddled faster, hoping to gain some ground before she lost sight of him altogether. As hard as she tried though, her form was sloppy and she was working twice as hard to go half as fast.

"Rave..."

"I'm trying, okay." Raven sat up straighter and squared her shoulders. "I can't get this thing to move."

"Rave..." Her sister stared over the front of the kayak, eyes wide. Raven slowly turned her head. An alligator at least ten feet long was watching her from the shore with interest. Although its body didn't move, the vertical slits of its eyes did. That cold reptilian stare locked onto her. She stopped paddling.

Too fast for a creature that large, the alligator slipped into the swamp with the splashless stealth of a predator. Absolutely silent, it became instantly invisible aside from its snout and eyes. A few yards from her kayak, it dove.

"Where did it go?"

"Don't panic," Avery said. "Hold still. They're usually not aggressive. He's probably as scared of you as you are of him. He's swimming away, I'm sure."

Raven froze, the arm of her paddle across her lap. Her gaze locked onto a fat drip of water rolling down the paddle's blade and she lifted it slowly, meaning to swing it inside her vessel. The drop fell into the water with a plop. Suddenly the swamp rose beside her, the water surging with the alligator as it thrust and twisted. Rows of razor-sharp teeth opened inside a long, deadly snout that snapped her paddle. The plastic splintered and was wrenched from her hands. Worse, the gator's scaly body brushed the side of the kayak as it reentered the water, tail thrashing.

Raven's kayak rocked onto its side. Avery screamed and reached for her, but she was too far away. Raven was going over. Capsizing. The alligator was out there, and she was about to join it for a swim. Almost parallel to the water, she gripped the side of the kayak and took a deep breath in anticipation. Her heart pounded against her breastbone. Her mind raced with terror.

The swamp rose again. Raven could swear she saw a brown hand, a woman's hand, surge from the surface. Yes, there was a woman under the water, her long black curls floating around her head, her black eyes staring up at Raven, her full mouth smiling. Raven grabbed her outstretched hand. Light. So much light. Raven's skin lit up with symbols the same as when Gabriel touched her. She locked her arm, hand in hand with the woman, and held on.

She shouldn't have been strong enough for this, but the woman was pushing back, holding her out of the water. An unnatural force shifted her weight in the opposite direction. The kayak tipped and then the bottom slapped the water so hard her teeth clacked together.

"Holy shit, Raven! Are you all right? I thought for sure you were going over."

"Did you see her?"

"The alligator? Yeah. I couldn't miss her." Her hands were trembling.

"No, not the alligator. The woman."

"What?"

Raven looked at her sister, feeling as if she were having an out-of-body experience. All she could see was the brown hand rising from the water and those arresting black eyes. She searched the swamp beside her. The alligator was gone, but there was a skinny brown stump protruding from the water, the top of which roughly resembled a hand. She rubbed her palm.

"Nothing." Raven shook her head. "That was close."

Avery stared at her with unmasked concern.

"Hey!" the guide yelled, moving toward them at a speed she'd never seen anyone paddle a kayak.

Avery stared at her. "Damn, Raven. That was so weird. When you went over, there was a flash of light like the sun was magnified off the water. It was blinding. I've never seen anything like it."

Raven turned toward her. "You saw that too?"

"How could anyone miss it?"

The trees beside them moved. Raven bristled. Without a paddle she was helpless. But it wasn't another alligator. It was Gabriel, and he looked pissed.

"What are you looking at?" Avery asked.

Raven didn't answer. The guide hooked on and began towing her to shore.

~

WHAT WAS SHE THINKING TAKING SUCH A RISK? GABRIEL waited at the dock, his head burning, although the January weather was temperate. All that fire came from the inside, from the anger and terror that had drawn him here at supernatural speed. He gazed at his ring, at the dark eye at the heart of it, now bigger for the use of the power. When Raven's terror had shot down their connection like a bullet, neither God nor the devil could have kept him from her. He'd landed in the swamp near her, then flew here to the dock when it was clear she was no longer in danger. Still, he wouldn't be happy until she was out of that damned kayak.

The group of adventurers paddled nearer, and he held out his hand to Raven.

"Uh, er. Give me a second to help," the tour guide said. "Well, okay, that's one way to get out, I guess." He laughed nervously as Gabriel lifted Raven straight out of her kayak as if she weighed nothing.

Gabriel ignored the guide and took Raven by the shoulders. Why was she taking unnecessary risks? Didn't she know how much he needed her? Didn't she realize how valuable she was to him, to the world?

But as he looked at her, that tug was back, his dragon sniffing and chuffing close to the surface. She smelled of tears and panic, and when she met his eyes, she started to cry. Without a word, he wrapped his arms around her and tucked her under his chin, against his chest. "You're okay," he whispered. "Everything is okay."

Her tears soaked his shirt as she sobbed.

"Are you Gabriel?" A woman who resembled Raven came up behind her on the dock. She was dark-haired and blue-eyed but curvy and taller. Confidently, she held out her hand.

Raven lifted her head. "Gabriel, this is my sister, Avery. Avery, Gabriel Blakemore."

He shook her hand, but didn't release Raven.

Avery noticed. She gave him a strange, quirky smile. "So, uh, what are you doing here?"

Raven's eyes widened as she looked between him and her sister. Her lips parted while she tried to think of an excuse.

"Raven and I have a date," he said. "I came to pick her up. Couldn't wait." He kissed her on the temple.

Avery's eyebrows shot toward her hairline. "You're dating my sister—your employee?"

The way her mouth twisted told him everything he needed to know. Avery was the type of woman who assumed things about a man, assumed that every man was attracted to the same kind of woman, and only under the same sort of circumstances. It bothered Gabriel that her question seemed to assume that Raven was less than worthy of his attraction. Nothing could be further from the truth.

He gave Avery a lazy smile. "I'm enamored. Do you have a problem with that?"

Raven looked up at him from the shelter of his arms.

"No wonder your paycheck was so big," Avery murmured under her breath.

If Gabriel didn't have a dragon's hearing, he would have never caught the comment, but he did. He coughed into his hand to hide his laugh.

The guide appeared beside them. "Your life vest, please." He pointed at the floatation device Raven was still wearing.

"What kind of tour are you running?" Gabriel snapped, his anger rising to the surface and cracking like a whip. "She could have been killed. Why weren't you with her? Why hadn't you taken precautions and guided them away from known alligators?" Without even meaning to, he'd placed himself between Raven and the guide, backing him up to the edge of the dock.

"I, uh—"

"I don't want to hear it. You are lucky she is uninjured. I'd have your head—"

"Here." Raven shoved the life vest into the guide's hands and firmly thrust him in the direction of the shore, her other hand pressing into Gabriel's chest.

The man didn't hesitate. He took off toward the parking lot where other guides were helping him load the kayaks into his company's truck.

"Gabriel, it wasn't his fault," she said.

He looked down at her, again surprised by how she tamed his anger with a touch of her hand.

Avery peered at them. "Well, okay then. Are you coming back with me or going with Gabriel?"

Raven's gaze darted between Avery and Gabriel as if she couldn't make up her mind. Gabriel sighed. This was awkward. He hadn't meant to ruin her time with her sister.

"I'm going with Gabriel," she said.

His heart swelled.

With a little wave, Avery took off toward the truck, leaving him and Raven alone on the dock. Raven whirled on him as soon as her sister was out of earshot.

"What the hell are you doing here?" she asked.

Gabriel straightened. "I felt your fear. I thought you were in trouble, so I came."

"I can take care of myself, Gabriel."

He scoffed. "Can you?"

"I'm here, aren't I? You didn't actually save me from anything, did you?" She placed her hands on her hips. Her face changed and she lowered her chin. "Um, actually... Did you?"

"No. You got lucky." Okay, now he was raising his voice. "What sort of lunatic goes kayaking in a swamp full of alligators?"

"Oh, that's rich. You take me to see three zombie-vampire women who want me dead, but you think the alligators are dangerous? Ha!"

"I didn't know the Casket Girls would attack you. I wouldn't have taken you if I'd thought they were dangerous."

She popped a hip out. "And people take this tour every day. This is the first time this has happened. It's January. The alligators barely move this time of year."

"Why do you need to engage in such behavior?" His

fingers were tapping now, and he started to pace the length of the dock, growing more agitated with every step.

"I told you I need to do things. I have to feel like I'm alive. I can't sit in your damned cage all day."

"It's not a cage!" he boomed. He heard the truck pull away. The wind was picking up. A storm was brewing. Strange. There was nothing in the forecast.

"I'm alive, Gabriel, and I plan to make the most of every moment I'm here. What do you care anyway? This is the most you've spoken to me in a week."

He looked away. "I was giving you space."

"Bullshit. You have been avoiding me ever since I asked you about Kristina!"

"I told you I don't want to talk about Kristina."

"I heard you the first time. The problem is, I'm doing her job and I'm the one having the side effects. Who knows what will happen to me? You won't tell me anything about Kristina. What if whatever happened to her happens to me?"

Rain started to spit from the heavens, although above it all the sun was still shining. *The devil's beating his wife* is what the locals would say. Gabriel had always found it a strange expression, but the weather pattern seemed fitting as the tension between them grew.

"I can't tell you about Kristina, okay? I can't. But you are safe."

"How do I know that?"

"Because I told you I'm going to keep you safe!"

"But you didn't keep *her* safe. Did you have something to do with Kristina's disappearance?" Raven shouted. She had to. The wind was howling now.

How could he respond? She wouldn't want to hear what he had to say. But then they each had other things to worry about. The storm was threatening to sweep them both off the dock.

"Why won't you let this go?" he asked.

"Why won't you talk about her? What are you hiding?"

Gabriel's gaze caught on something in the water. "Raven, behind you."

"Behind me? What are you..." She turned and saw what he had seen. Alligators. A dozen of them. They were lined up in the water, staring at her.

"Why are they doing that?"

"I don't know." He held out his hands to her.

She stood her ground, balancing on the edge of the dock in the howling wind, an army of alligators behind her. "Tell me you didn't kill her."

Gabriel shook his head vehemently. "Why would I kill her?"

"Tell me!" Lightning cracked across the sky.

"Raven, I did not kill her." He held her gaze, willing her to believe him. "I never hurt her."

Her shoulders softened. He opened his arms and she ran to him.

The wind stopped, then the rain. Gabriel studied the alligators as they turned and swam deeper into the swamp. He looked down at Raven, the symbols glowing again, all the way up the back of her neck. There were more. They were spreading. He had no idea how to stop them. Worse, he was sure that what the Casket Girls had said was true. Raven was a witch. He had broken an ancient law when he cured her and invested her with his power.

As sure as he was breathing, it was she who had caused the storm and she who had called the swamp creatures to her aid. Raven was already using magic she didn't even know she had in her. He had to find a way to get her to acknowledge what she was. If he didn't, she'd never understand the nature of her power or how to control it. She could end up hurting herself or someone else.

A horn blared from the parking lot. "Duncan is here," he said. "Let me take you out for something to eat."

"No," she said. "Take me home."

CHAPTER FOURTEEN

R aven was relieved when Gabriel dropped her off at
the Three Sisters without argument. It wasn't that
she didn't want to spend time with him. On the contrary,
she was sure she was doomed to think about him all night
long. No, it was more the principle of the thing. She'd said
she needed weekends off to live her life. He'd agreed to that,
then showed up to chastise her as if she were a child for
doing something people did every day. Yes, she'd had an
unusual and frightening experience, but that wasn't her
fault, and he wasn't her father. She'd come too far to put up
with that controlling crap. He didn't own her, and refusing
dinner was a way for her to prove that.

After realizing her mom and Avery were working downstairs, Raven showered and changed into a pair of jeans and
a T-shirt. There was something she wanted to do, and they
wouldn't approve. Neither would Gabriel. It wasn't good
enough to hear Gabriel say he hadn't hurt Kristina. She
needed to know what had happened to the girl.

SHE KNOCKED ON THE DOOR OF A LITTLE YELLOW bungalow and crossed her fingers that someone would be home. It wasn't hard to figure out where Kristina had once lived. Her father had taken to the internet, looking for any information leading to her whereabouts. He'd commented on every story concerning her disappearance and had been easy to find.

The Kane house was walking distance from Raven's, although she never came down this way. She wondered if Kristina or her dad had ever visited the bar. A few long moments passed and she knocked again. This time she heard footsteps. The door opened to reveal a potbellied man with thinning gray hair. He scratched the section of his belly that poked out from the bottom of his T-shirt.

"Help you with somethin'?" he said. His words slurred a little, and Raven thought she smelled a whiff of alcohol on the air.

"Are you Mr. Kane?"

"Mr. Kane was my father, sweetheart. I'm Joe. Joe Kane. You sellin' something?" His eyes raked over her, and for a split second she thought the tone of his question was the faintest bit inappropriate, as if he were asking if she were for sale.

"No," Raven said firmly. "I'm a friend of Kristina's. I'd like to ask you a few questions. I'm worried about her."

He stared like she was growing a second head.

"Is something wrong?" she asked.

He coughed. "Oh, uh, it's just I wasn't aware my daughter had any friends. She was sort of a loner. Never brought nobody home."

"Oh, she had friends. Good friends. I don't know why she wouldn't have mentioned me." Raven caught herself babbling. She shut up and waited.

"What's your name?"

"Jenny Ryan." She felt a gut instinct not to tell him her real name. She didn't want this conversation to get back to Gabriel, and changing her name seemed essential to ensuring as much.

"Come on in." He held the door open wider. She followed him into a family room that smelled like cat urine and looked like it hadn't seen a vacuum in months. Raven couldn't tell if the sofa was gray or just dirty. The shades at the front of the house were closed, and what little light remained outdoors was pinched from the room, leaving only the glow of a table lamp between them.

This was definitely Kristina's house though. She recognized her likeness from the missing-person article she'd found on the internet. The entire fireplace mantel was covered with pictures of her, as were the walls and the little side table. Baby pictures of her in the bathtub, as a child running through the sprinkler, a teen in her cheerleading uniform, a young woman going to prom, and the portrait her father had used in the article she'd read on the internet. She had long, sleek dark hair. Her oversized amber eyes and straight white smile were undeniably pretty in a subtle, unassuming way. She was taller than Raven, curvier. Had Gabriel found her attractive? Raven noted absently that Kristina had gone to the same high school but graduated a year before Raven started. She gave the father an appreciative nod as she took in the pictures and then perched on the stained edge of the filthy sofa.

"Can I offer you a beer?" he asked, scooping his half-empty Miller High Life from the side table. "I'd offer sweet tea, but a conversation like this calls for something stronger. Maybe even stronger than beer."

"No, thank you." Raven rubbed her palms on the thighs

of her jeans. "I was wondering if you could tell me what you remember from the day Kristina went missing?"

His face fell, and he gave her a scrutinizing look. "I thought you said you were Kristina's friend."

"I was. I mean, I am."

He snorted. "Couldn't have been very close or you would know she wasn't living here at the time she went missing."

"Oh? I guess she didn't tell me she'd moved out." Raven shifted nervously. She'd assumed, based on the article she read, that Kristina was still living with her father.

"Hmm. That's surprising. She was so proud of herself the day she left. Said she was moving in with that Blakemore fella. Couldn't get enough of him." He looked down into his beer.

Raven froze. "Did you say she moved in with Gabriel Blakemore? Like to live?"

He screwed up his face. "How well did you know her? Yeah, she moved in with him. Told me she was better off without me. Wanted out of this dump. Not my fault I can't work 'cause of my back. Didn't talk to me again after that. Next thing I knew, she was missing. He stole her away from me, and then she disappeared." He mumbled incoherently and took a swig of his beer. "I told the cops I think he done something to her, but they don't listen. I've got my eye on that place though. Blakemore's rich, but I'm watching. One of these days he's gonna slip up, and then I'm gonna prove he's keeping her from me."

Raven frowned. He made it sound like Gabriel had Kristina locked up in a dungeon somewhere. Something didn't add up though. "I thought you were the one who filed the missing-person report? If she wasn't living here or talking to you, how did you know she was missing?"

He curled his lip. "I used to stop in there regular to make sure she was safe. One day I went by and she was gone. That asshole said she'd moved out and didn't leave a forwarding address. Bullshit. He knows. He knows something he's not telling the cops."

Raven's head was spinning. Had Kristina moved out or gone missing? Or both? And why hadn't Gabriel mentioned she'd lived with him? Unless he had something to hide. She sighed, and her shoulders sagged with the release of her breath.

"Well, thank you," Raven said. "It was good to see her pictures and talk about her. I'm worried about her."

"How did you say you knew Kristina again?"

Had she said? She couldn't remember. She glanced at the pictures on the mantel, focusing on the one in the BFHS Falcons cheerleading uniform. "We went to school together," Raven blurted. "High school. I hadn't seen her in a while, which is why I hadn't heard about her moving out. We spoke occasionally though when she would come in to the... hair salon. That's what I do for a living. Cut hair. I'm a hairdresser. Kristina had some beautiful hair." Raven trailed off, a big stupid smile on her face.

Kristina's father stood up and snagged the picture from the fireplace, running his thumb along the glass cover. "Were you a cheerleader, Jenny?" He stroked his daughter's picture with the tips of his fingers.

"Yep. We were on the team together." Why had she said that? She could kick herself. He'd probably seen his daughter cheer. Would he remember Raven wasn't on the team?

"I used to love that little skirt. You could almost see her ass when she bent over."

Okay, that was a weird thing for a father to say about his

daughter. Raven planted her hands on her thighs and stood. "I need to go now. Thank you for your time."

"I still have it, you know."

She took a step toward the door. "Have what?"

"The uniform. Why don't you put it on for me, Jenny? Relive the glory days?"

"Mmm. I don't think so, no." Her stomach twisted. The way he was looking at his daughter's picture was wrong, and when he looked up at her, that wrongness came right along with the eye contact. Raven turned around, reached for the doorknob, and pulled it open.

His hand collided with the door, slamming it shut.

"Let me go, Mr. Kane," she said evenly. He was right behind her, but she did not remove her hand from the doorknob.

"Stay. Have a drink."

"No, thank you."

He yanked her hair back and slammed her head and chest against the door, his body crushing her from behind. "You girls are all alike. Don't know your place."

She whirled and pushed him hard in the chest. Her knee landed in his crotch for good measure. She wasn't as strong as him, but it was enough to make him recoil.

"Bitch!" He lunged for her.

Raven thrust both hands in his direction. It was a reflex, nothing more. His body flew across the room as if she'd shot him from a cannon. He smashed into the opposite wall, denting the drywall, and crumpled to the floor. The oddest part? Raven never actually touched him. It was almost like pushing a red rubber dodgeball. He was on the other side, and when she'd crushed it between them, the pressure had shoved him back. But there was nothing there. Nothing to see but a fat man flying across the room.

She did not waste the opportunity to escape. Without checking to see if he was okay, she slipped out the door and ran. She didn't stop running until she was upstairs in the apartment above the Three Sisters with the door locked and bolted behind her.

～

GABRIEL WAITED IN HIS OFFICE ON MONDAY MORNING, his fingers tapping on his desk until his knuckles were sore. Raven's fear had cut through him like a knife the day before last, but he'd forced himself to stay away from her. That day on the dock, she'd made it very clear she didn't want him to save her. Out of respect, he'd kept his distance and was relieved when her fear abated quickly.

But after a long Sunday of not feeling anything down their bond, he was desperate to see her. Anxious to know she was okay.

"You should have something to eat," Agnes said from the door. The old bird was a force to be reckoned with in a red silk blouse and wide-leg black pants.

"I'm not hungry."

"Have you tried telling her how you feel?"

He slapped the desktop with his tapping hand. "How I feel? There's nothing to tell. I'm bound to her; that is all."

"Bullshit, Gabriel. You'd have to be blind to think your bond with her is the same as the one you share with Richard or me. You light up whenever you see her."

"That's anger, Agnes."

She made a sound like air going out of a tire. "You know, barring a miracle, you might not be around forever."

"Thank you for the reminder," he said sarcastically. "You are short for this world as well, granny."

164

She scowled. "Make fun, but at least I loved before I died. You have a chance, and you're running from it like you're allergic."

"I am allergic. Terrible love allergy." He gripped the arms of his chair to keep from tapping. "I haven't known her long enough to love her."

"How long does it take?" Agnes rested her chin on the fingers of her left hand.

He cleared his throat. "It's been over five hundred years for me and it hasn't happened yet."

"Five hundred years, and now it's right in front of you and you're willing to let it pass you by. You've been alone too long. You don't realize how good it can be to have someone in your life."

"It can't be love. It takes years to fall in love. Months at least."

"I knew I loved Harry fifteen minutes after I met him."

"Fifteen—"

"He bought me a copy of *Pride and Prejudice*. Brought it into the office where I was working as a secretary, all wrapped up in paper and string. He said it was his favorite. It was my favorite too. All the other girls got flowers. He brought me books." She looked wistfully over his head.

"Hmm. I gave her a roomful of books. Will she fall into my arms?" *Raven wouldn't want a book*, he thought. *She'd want an adventure.*

"Gabriel." Agnes's voice was serious now. "Tell her how you feel. Take a chance. While you still can. Tell her."

"Tell me what?" Raven appeared in the doorway, very much alive and well. He met her eyes, and goddamn it if his mind's tail didn't start to wag like a dog's.

"You're late," he said, but there wasn't room for anger in

his voice. His mind was too full and distracted with assessing her hunched shoulders and pale face.

"Sorry. I... wasn't feeling well last night. I couldn't sleep and I got a late start. Duncan waited for me. He probably called you."

No. He did not, Gabriel mused. He stood and approached Raven, noticing that Agnes had leaned against the doorframe and was watching them as if she had a tub of popcorn in her hands. "Agnes, do you mind?"

The old woman got the hint and left with a roll of her eyes. He closed the door behind her.

"Are you feeling well now?" he asked.

"Fine. Just tired." She rubbed her eyes.

"Is it the markings?" he asked, wondering if this was a symptom of the magic he saw awakening within her.

"No... yes... I need to tell you something, but promise me you won't be angry."

He quirked an eyebrow. "That would be an empty promise. I'm already angry. I have a feeling whatever you are about to tell me is something you should have shared with me a day ago."

Her mouth opened and her words stuck in her throat. "You felt it down the bond?"

"Of course I did."

"You didn't come."

"You told me not to. As I recall, you violently opposed my impinging on your freedom by trying to rescue you on your day off."

"Uh, yeah. Thanks." She frowned.

"What happened?"

"I went to see Kristina's father."

Gabriel's fingers began to tap and he paced away from her, feeling the dragon rise and roil in his torso. "Why would you do such a thing, Raven? The man is dangerous!"

"I found that out the hard way."

"I bet you did. Did he..." Gabriel's voice cracked. "Was he violent? I will tear his throat out! I swear I will."

"No!" Raven's eyes widened. She placed a hand on his chest and steadied him. Instantly the crawling sensation ceased and he stopped tapping. "I'm not physically hurt, Gabriel. He pulled my hair but he didn't hurt me. Actually, I may have hurt him."

He stroked his thumb over her jaw and watched a trail of symbols ignite in the wake of his touch. "He's twice your size. Are you secretly trained in the martial arts, or is there more to the story?"

"I pushed him away." Her throat bobbed. "Without touching him."

A smile spread over Gabriel's face. "You used magic."

"It felt more like it used me," she said. She turned and paced the length of the office, rubbing her palms together in circles. "I didn't try to do it. I could have killed him. And now, afterward, it's like there's a monster sleeping inside me. Do you have any idea how that feels?"

He tipped his head and gave her an irritated look. "I think I have an inkling."

Color bloomed in her cheeks. "Uh, right. Sorry."

"I'm excited for you. We can work with this. I can teach you. With practice, we can solve the riddle of your power. We'll take it apart and put it back together until we understand it. Once you understand it, you can control it." He rubbed her shoulders and moved in close.

She pulled away from him and put space between them. "What happened to Kristina, Gabriel?"

He groaned. "Why are we talking about Kristina?"

"Her father told me she came to live with you. You were the last person to see her alive."

"Her father, the man who attacked you? You are going to trust him over me?"

"Why won't you tell me? If Crimson took her, Crimson could come after me. If the magic killed her or made her crazy, that could happen to me too. Did she have symbols on her arms? Did you have a romantic relationship with her? Were you sleeping with her?"

Her voice grew more strained with her agitation, and tears formed in her eyes. Everything in Gabriel clenched. That note he heard in her voice was jealousy with an undertone of anxiety.

He was not a patient dragon. When he hated something, he killed it. When he wanted something, he either bought it or took it. He'd made exceptions for her because he thought it would please her. Now he could see that wasn't what she needed at all.

"Raven," he barked in a low sharp voice, "stop."

She stopped. He swept into her, digging his fingers into the hair at the back of her head. Her lips parted at his hold on her, but she did not speak.

"I did not sleep with Kristina. I did not kiss her or love her. She never had symbols on her arms, even when I touched her to shake her hand or to nudge her shoulder. She was a medium and would have noticed any new powers. I cannot tell you what happened to her right now. You will have to trust me on this. But, if you are patient and drop it for now—"

"Gabriel, I—"

He kissed the words from her mouth, fast and hard. "If you are patient and let it rest this week, I will reveal all to you on Friday night. A date, Raven. No games. Come out

168

with me, and I will explain everything I know about Kristina. I cannot answer what you ask here and now, but if you come with me, I will show you what you need to know."

Her eyes searched his.

Everything about her turned him on: her lips, her closeness, the way her body conformed to his. He wanted to take her, here, now. To force the thoughts she was having out of her mind by filling it with pleasure, by filling her. But he wouldn't force her. She was already his. She just didn't know it yet. He had to bide his time, let her come to him when she was ready.

"Do you trust me, Raven?"

She lowered her chin and looked at him through her lashes. "Yes."

"Friday. Come with me Friday. Until then, let this go." When she didn't answer him right away, he tugged gently on her hair.

She lowered her shoulders and slashed a hand through the air between them. "Yes, Gabriel. I will go out with you on Friday."

"Good," he said. He kissed her then, firmly. It wasn't a question but a claim. Everything he gave to her mouth was a statement, a chant of *You are mine. You will always be mine.*

She melted in his embrace, her arms going around his neck and one of her feet skimming up the outside of his lower leg. It took all his strength to pull away, but now was not the time or place. Not the way he wanted her. He smiled, steadying her on her feet. "Friday night." He walked to the door and opened it for her.

It took her a moment to gather herself. She smoothed her hair and straightened her clothes. "Yes. I— I'll be in the library if you need me."

CHAPTER FIFTEEN

R aven needed a glass of ice water. Not only to drink but to dump over her head. The way Gabriel had kissed her had ignited something inside that she was having trouble extinguishing. Her body ached for him. The brush of her clothing against her skin was oddly arousing. Her bra felt tight, and she squelched the urge to strip out of it. If he hadn't stopped, she would have let him have her there on the desk in his office. No way could she have stopped him. It had been over five years since she'd been with a man. There had never been any man like Gabriel.

Didn't that make her an idiotic female? As far as she knew, Gabriel had done something hideous to Kristina and was going to do the same to her Friday night. Only, she no longer truly believed he had hurt her predecessor. Oh, he was capable of killing. She admitted that much. But he wasn't a killer. He was her defender and protector. He'd always backed off when she'd asked him to. Didn't it mean something that he'd respected her wishes to stay away Saturday night?

With a sigh, she unlocked the library and propped the

door open. She plodded to the kitchenette and filled a glass with water to dribble on the soil of the African violet Gabriel had brought her. She drank the rest, trying her best to quiet her mind. All her desire for Gabriel would be pointless if she didn't break his curse. He'd turn to stone. Even if her cancer didn't come back, she'd never be the same. He'd scored a mark across her heart, awakened in her a love of mystery and a belief in magic. How could she return to a world of drink orders and essay exams? The life she'd left behind didn't fit her anymore. Her family's love had become a too-tight hug that threatened to crush her wings.

"Fix him," she whispered to herself, scanning the grimoires. She needed more time, time to solve the puzzle that was Gabriel. She was in a room full of magic. There had to be a way. Approaching the shelf where she'd left off, she ran her fingers down the spine of the next book on her list, then pulled it from the shelf. Opening it on the desk, she instantly noticed it was different. There were no lists of ingredients like before. Instead of being a recipe, the spells in this book were a combination of symbols and incantations. She couldn't read it—this one was written in Spanish —but she stared at the page and something occurred to her. She returned to the last grimoire she'd reviewed. She knew what these were. *Potions*, she thought. The entire section she'd been working on contained books about potions.

Rushing back to Kristina's log again, she found that, yes, every book she'd flipped through so far was in the same section. She hadn't put it together before. Light flooded her brain and she laughed. It was so simple, so obvious, but she'd completely missed it. This was the system Raven had been looking for. The books weren't sorted alphabetically or by language or by the Dewey decimal system. They were sorted by the type of *magic* contained within them.

The Casket Girls had said that the cure for the stone had to come from the snake whose venom infected it. What if they meant the type of magic? Crimson was a voodoo priestess. She hadn't cursed Gabriel with a potion, she'd used... well, whatever it was that voodoo practitioners used. A voodoo doll? A spell brought about through dance? Raven knew almost nothing about the religion. But she was willing to bet there was a section in this library dedicated to the practice. That's where she needed to start.

She paged through the catalog until a word in a title caught her eye: *vodou*. Raven went to that section of shelf, noticing the titles were familiar. This was creole. She didn't speak the language, but so many things around New Orleans borrowed from it that it was instantly recognizable. She pulled the first grimoire from the section and opened it on the desk.

Her fingers tingled as she touched the pages. This magic felt different. It rippled through her and made the hair on the back of her neck stand up. *What was happening?*

She yanked her hand back from the book and lifted her head. Someone was in the room. There was a shadow beside the bookshelf, long and thin. Squinting, she leaned over to see who was there. There was no one. The light was wrong. The window was behind her, but the shadow was stretching toward her. She stared at the dark thing. It blinked at her.

With a start, she realized the thing was not human. Maybe it was one of the oreads. She hadn't asked Gabriel what they looked like.

"Hello," she said to it. "Can I help you with something?"

The two circles of light that were the thing's eyes widened, its mouth forming a perfect *o*. It shot like a dart straight toward her. She screamed, more out of shock than fear as it passed through her like an icy wind. She spun around to see it dive into the ventilation shaft.

"What happened? What's wrong?" Gabriel stood in the doorway staring at her. "I heard you scream."

She rubbed the place where the thing passed through her. "What do oreads look like?"

"Like mountain nymphs." He shrugged.

She spread her hands.

"Er... similar to your human depiction of fairies. Pale. Large eyes. Gossamer wings. That is, when they allow you to see them."

Raven tore a sheet of paper from the back of the ledger and sketched what she'd seen. She held it up in front of his face. "Do you know what this is?"

Gabriel grimaced, his eyes darting between her and the drawing. "You saw this?"

"I couldn't have drawn it if I hadn't. The thing flew straight through me."

"Raven, I'm not sure how to tell you this."

"Quickly. You're freaking me out."

Gabriel shook his head. "That is a demon."

❧

CRIMSON ROLLED OVER AND RUBBED HER EYES. IT WAS early. Not even ten in the morning. She'd been up most of the night performing a completely fake ritual for a couple that had renewed their vows. It was exhausting making that shit up. It had to look real without actually doing anything at all. Ironically, it would have been easier and less draining for her to do the real ritual, but no way was she going to call on the spirits to help every traveler who tossed a few Cnotes in her direction. She needed to save her real power for herself.

"This better be good," she said to the demon standing over her. She'd nicknamed this one Chuck. Not that demons used names. These entities, she'd learned, weren't identities in and of themselves, but hollow and dark energy. They absorbed, drained, and fed off human experiences, creating none of their own. No personality. No soul. If you took raw desire and coupled it with a bottomless pit of need, you'd have a demon. Still, she'd named each one for her own purposes. It helped her tell the demons apart. This one seemed oddly shaken. That worried her. There wasn't much on this side of heaven and hell that could shake a demon. She reached out to touch the thing so it could show her what had happened.

Images flashed through Crimson's brain. The girl, Raven, sat behind a desk, a massive book open in front of her. She looked up, straight at the demon. Her blue eyes flared. Crimson felt what the demon had felt, a tug of immature power deep in its torso.

"Hello. What can I do for you?" Raven said, addressing the demon directly.

Whoosh. Chuck passed right through her on his way back home, and what he saw inside her was the most terrifying part of all.

"Interesting," Crimson said, stroking the back of the demon's head. "Not only can the girl see demons, but her body possesses a strange mixture of raw magic. It seems Gabriel's tooth has awoken something in her. Something I haven't seen before."

The girl wasn't entirely human. Raven had power, power she hadn't yet learned to use. After the way the demon had reacted to the name Tanglewood inside the

Three Sisters, Crimson suspected that Raven came from a long line of powerful beings. She hesitated to use the word *witch*. The traces of magic the demon had sensed as it passed through her were broader than traditional witchcraft. Perhaps sorceress was the better term. Perhaps something more.

"Tanglewood," Crimson said, and the demon hissed as if she'd burned it. She narrowed her eyes. "What do you know about that name? Show me."

The demon refused, squealing and drawing away. Crimson grabbed a white ash root from her nightstand and stabbed it through the demon's toe. It cried out, but now it wouldn't be going anywhere. As it twisted and thrashed, she removed her nightshirt and began massaging her breasts, tracing around her nipples with the tips of her fingers. She spread her knees. The demon settled its full attention on her again.

This was why it was important to use names. She remembered Chuck's desire was sex. The demon couldn't get enough of it.

"Show me what you know about Raven's family," Crimson demanded, arching her back.

The demon reached out an oily hand and touched her. As the images flashed through her head, Crimson's eyes widened. Even she hadn't expected this. The demon was wise to be afraid.

When she'd seen all of what it had to offer, she removed the ash root from its foot. It crawled to her, its hands slithering around her breasts. She allowed it to mount her. What she paid the beast was well worth the information, and it would keep him coming back to her. It would allow her to bend the demon to her will. It had always been this way. Her natural ability to seduce demons had informed her magic on all levels. After all these years, they were a part of her and always would be.

As the dark thing filled her up, she thought it was about time she got to know Ms. Tanglewood better. Much better. She might be the answer to swaying Gabriel into giving her what she wanted. More, the girl might be the permanent solution to her little aging problem. A dark and wonderful idea filled her mind. But it would be tricky. Crimson would have to find a way to lure the girl to her, and then she'd have to make her an offer she couldn't refuse.

CHAPTER SIXTEEN

Gabriel rushed to Raven's side. Her knees gave out, and she sat down in the chair behind the library desk as if she was testing the sturdiness of the legs. He'd never been so relieved that the antique was stronger than it looked.

"Please tell me you keep demons on staff to clean during the night?"

"No. Demons aren't friendly creatures. It shouldn't have been here. Before the curse, it couldn't have been. My protective wards are failing." He held up his ring to the light.

Her eyes snapped to his. "Why was it here? Why was it watching me?"

"I'm not sure." Gabriel knelt down in front of her and took her hands in his. "But the bigger question is how were you able to see it?"

She scoffed. "It was right there. How could I miss it?"

Putting this off was no longer an option. Gabriel had to make her see what she was. As much as he feared how she would take it, that she might even leave him, she had to face the truth. "Ordinary humans can't see demons, Raven. You did. You saw the demon because the Casket Girls were right about you. You have power."

She shook her head. "No." Her eyes darted around the room and then settled on his. "What kind of power?"

"You are just what they said you are. A witch. When I fed you my tooth, I was hoping you were psychic. I had no idea you were a sorceress. But those markings on your arms? Those are symbols, writing. That's your magic coming to the surface, magic that was always inside you."

For a long while she said nothing. She stared at the book, then at her hands. Gabriel braced himself. He would not stop her if she tried to leave. He'd promised her freedom, and he would always be true to his word. But his chest ached at the thought of losing her.

"Raven, say something."

She chewed her lip. "Can you read this grimoire?"

He stood and looked down at the book. "Haitian creole. Yes." He marked the page with his finger and closed the cover, then opened it again. "The title means 'The Spirit of Voodoo.' This is a book about summoning spirits."

"And what is this spell?" She pointed to the page she'd been perusing.

It had been a long time since he'd read the language, and it took him a few minutes to translate the page, but once he had, he smiled. "This is a spell to make the unseen visible. This is a spell to allow you to see demons."

Raven held up her hands. "I felt it enter my fingers."

"You felt the spell—"

"Gabriel, what if the symbols on my arms aren't magic that is in me coming to the surface? What if it's magic I'm absorbing?"

"The longer you've been in this room, the more it's spread."

She nodded, looking excited now. "What if every spell I touch becomes... a part of me?"

The implications barreled into him, and he wished he had a chair to land his own ass in, because his knees felt like they could give out at any moment. He settled for using the bookshelf to hold himself up. "You absorb any spell you touch."

Her mouth gaped. "Saturday, in the swamp, when I touched the stump to keep myself from capsizing, I saw a woman in the water. I think it was Julia."

"The alligators and the wind."

"I absorbed her magic from the swamp."

Gabriel's eyes widened. "I wonder..." Intently, he searched the titles on the shelf along the far wall and flipped to a page at the center. He held the book out to her. "Try this."

The grimoire was written in Romanian, one Gabriel had collected long ago when he'd visited Budapest. Raven wouldn't be able to read it or understand it, but if her power held the qualities they thought it did, he'd know soon enough. He watched, breathless, as she placed her fingertips on the page.

"It tickles," she said. "Whoa." The look on her face was pure wonderment as she levitated off her chair, floating higher above the desk.

"How do I get down?" she asked with a laugh as she drew closer to the ceiling. Gabriel quickly read the spell on the next page.

"Think about your feet," he said.

Slowly she sank to the floor. "This is real," she said. "We've figured it out. I absorb magic. That's what I do. The reason it took me so long to notice is I was in the potions section."

"Yes." He nodded. "This is a very powerful gift. The possibilities are endless."

Her face was brimming with excitement as she squealed and waved her hands at him. "Bring me another! Something good."

Gabriel scanned the shelves and nabbed a smaller leather volume from the front of the library. He flipped to the spell he was looking for and placed it in front of her. "Try this."

She placed her hand on it. "Oooh, it's cold."

Gabriel turned his palm up and caught a snowflake as it fell from the ceiling. Awestruck, Raven traced her fingers through the cold and damp in his palm, and then her gaze climbed to the ceiling, which was now spitting out snowflakes like a Hollywood machine.

He pulled her out of the chair and whirled her down the aisle, dipping her, elated at the pure joy in her eyes. Big, fluffy flakes of snow drifted from the ceiling and caught on her lashes. She giggled.

"It's all you," he said. "You're making this happen."

"How?" She sounded breathless. "All I did was touch a page."

The snow tapered, then stopped altogether. He set her on her feet. "Every spell you come in contact with, you soak up. I've only heard of one other witch like you, and she lived in Paragon. The truth is I'm not sure of the extent of your abilities. But you are powerful, Raven. Truly remarkable."

She moved closer to him, and he thought she looked... happy. The anxiety had drained from her face and a shallow smile graced her lips. There was hope and joy in her expression, like she'd opened a new toy. Gabriel understood he'd broken one of Paragon's oldest and most serious laws by saving her, but he didn't care. The way his body was responding to the sight of her told him he would have done it all over again, even if he'd known in advance she was a witch.

She swept her hands through her hair. "Let me touch your ring." She reached for his hand.

He pulled it out of her reach. "What if you absorb the curse?"

"Do you think that would happen? I don't think so. I made it snow today; I didn't turn into snow. I'll simply soak up the magic behind the curse. Maybe I'll understand it and then be able to break it."

"It's too risky. We don't know how your magic works yet."

"Stop fighting me. It's not going to—" She sprang forward and grabbed the emerald before he could protest.

Although he hastily drew his hand away, it was too late. The smile faded from her face.

"What's wrong? Did it hurt you?" he asked.

"Not as much as your pulling the damned jewel from my grip did." She rubbed her palm. "I felt something, but I don't think it's the curse. Let me touch it again."

He raised an eyebrow at her. "Begging to touch me? I think I like these new powers."

Expression flat and clearly annoyed, she held out her hand and didn't say another word. Reluctantly, he placed his fingers in hers. Her thumb stroked over the stone, her focus going blank, then distant. She shook her head.

"I can sense the curse, but it isn't like touching the books. It's like a black hole. It doesn't give me anything."

"Or your natural abilities are smart enough not to ingest poison," he said. "You said you felt something."

"I see a door." She waved a hand dismissively, her eyes focused on the wall. "Not an actual door, an... opening. Through the opening is an island. Red rock... a volcano... jungle."

"That is Paragon."

Her gaze met his. "I think I could use this ring to send you back. You wouldn't need the ring's magic if you were back there, right?"

He frowned and looked way from her.

"You already knew that. You've known all along you could go back."

"Yes."

She dropped her hand. "So you can survive! If we run out of time and we haven't broken your curse, you can go back."

He shook his head. "No, I can never go back."

"Why not? Gabriel, this is life or death."

"I told you, there was a political uprising—"

"So go back with your tail between your legs and toe the line. A new regime is better than turning to stone."

"You don't understand. It wasn't a new regime."

"Help me understand."

It had been a long time since he'd talked openly about Paragon. He didn't welcome revisiting the old memories. Still, she deserved an explanation.

"Over coffee. Come."

As Raven had come to expect, a coffee service was already in place when she entered Gabriel's apartment. An urn of coffee, cream and sugar, along with a plate of warm blueberry scones waited for them in the dining room.

The oreads seemed to anticipate Gabriel's every need. She wondered again what they must look like, but she'd never seen one.

Gabriel filled her mug. "Cream or sugar?"

"Just cream. One."

He did the honors, then handed her the mug. She took a long, fortifying drink.

"You were saying, about Paragon."

He stirred his coffee. "Dragons have ruled Paragon since the dawn of time. Our citizens are made up of a variety of supernatural beings: witches, vampires, fairies, elves, and other dragons of mixed blood. But my family has ruled from the Mountain since Paragon's earliest days. We were installed as rulers by the Goddess of the Mountain herself."

"Your family? Are you saying you are Paragon royalty?" She had to set down her mug so that she wouldn't drop it.

He leveled a sober stare on her. "The goddess left us a tablet of laws, ancient magic that directed my family's rule. The first and most important law was that no individual dragon was allowed to rule for more than two thousand years."

She snorted. "Two thousand years?"

"Purebred dragons are immortal."

Raven blinked, suddenly breathless. "I guess I knew that on some level, but I can't wrap my head around it. Wouldn't there be too many dragons if all of them lived forever?"

He sipped his coffee. "You are a smart woman, Raven. Yes, there would be. If not for two simple facts. First, dragon offspring are rare. And second, immortal or not, we can be killed."

She chose a scone from the pile and took a bite, hopeful

that if she remained quiet, he would fill the empty space with additional explanation. She was not disappointed.

"Dragon females are rare in our population. Precious. Even if a female dragon succeeds in laying an egg—"

"Wait, you hatched from an egg?" Raven felt her jaw pop open like she was a cartoon character.

Gabriel shrugged. "Dragons are similar to your reptiles when it comes to reproductive biology."

She closed her mouth. It opened again.

"As I was saying, dragon eggs are rare, and many eggs never develop properly, so dragon children are even more rare. Too, although we are naturally immortal, we can be killed by unnatural means. Magic"—he held up his hand and wiggled his ring—"certain types of enchanted metal. There are five kingdoms of Paragon, all five ruled by dragons who make their home in and around the Obsidian Mountain. This area is called the kingdom of Paragon, the dragon kingdom. Over the centuries, we've warred with Darnuith, the kingdom of the witches; Everfield, the fae kingdom; and Nochtbend, the kingdom of vampires. Although we've always maintained control, dragons have died in these wars. So, you see, the dragon population has held steady at a few thousand individuals for tens of thousands of years."

Raven pondered his description, wishing she had a map. "What's the fifth kingdom?" she asked. "You said there were five, but you only named four: Paragon, Darnuith, Everfield, and Nochtbend."

He broke off a corner of scone and popped it between his teeth. "The fifth is Rogos, the land of elves. Elves are wise creatures and have never in their entire history gone to war. They keep to themselves. As far as I know, they've never killed anything."

"So every two thousand years the current king and queen step down from their rule." Raven tried to put it all together.

"Yes. This is what has always come to pass. At the coronation of the eldest son of either the king or queen—"

Raven waved a hand. "Hold up. Wouldn't a son be from both king and queen? You do need a male and a female to reproduce, don't you?"

Gabriel chuckled. "Of course we do, but a king and a queen of Paragon would never mate with each other. It would be an abomination."

"Why?"

"They are brother and sister."

Raven dropped her scone and leaned back in her chair. "Go on."

He sighed. "I forget that kings and queens in your world were also lovers. In my world, as I mentioned, dragon children are rare. The king and queen are always brother and sister, and each of them takes a consort, a husband or wife from the dragon community. Both are of royal blood, and thus both can produce heirs to the throne. This gives our ruling class double the chance of producing another male and female heir, the oldest of which will inherit the throne."

It made sense when he put it that way. She raised an eyebrow. "Were you the oldest?"

He shook his head. "No. My brother Marius was the oldest of my siblings. There are nine of us, the largest number of eggs to be successfully incubated by a dragon. My mother was Eleanor, the queen; my father was Killian, her consort. Our uncle Brynhoff never took a consort, but the council of elders didn't push it because there were nine of us: eight males and a female. The crown was safe.

"Over three hundred years ago, the scheduled coronation of my older brother Marius was to mark his transition to king. The next day, my sister Rowan's coronation would install her as queen. But instead of stepping down as the goddess demanded, my uncle murdered my brother in cold blood. We believe he also murdered Killian and our mother. We don't know for sure because our mother used magic to send the remaining eight of us here, but all indications are that they died as well that day."

"Dear Lord. Gabriel, I'm so sorry. That's horrible. Your own uncle betrayed you, and you've been forced to hide here all these centuries?"

He nodded. "The worst part is that our mother sent a message with us, warning us to stay apart in this world for our safety. We don't even have each other anymore."

Her heart felt heavy and her mind immediately jumped to Avery. What a cruel fate to have family but to never enjoy their company.

"So you see, I can't go back to Paragon. Not now. Not ever. Because my murderous uncle is still in power and I am now the eldest offspring. There is a price on my head. If he ever found out where I was, he would devote all his resources to ending me."

"You're now the heir to Paragon." The implication made her mouth go dry. "You're... you're a prince!"

He bowed formally. "I was. Now I'm a purveyor of antiquities. A dragon with an expiration date." He tapped his ring.

Her breath caught. "So, where do we go from here?"

He leaned across the table. "You keep taking in what magic you can from the library. You and I will practice using it."

"All right." It was all so overwhelming. She had so many questions they crowded each other to get to the front of her mind. But when she opened her mouth to ask them, all she could think was that he suddenly looked exhausted. "Are you feeling okay?"

"I need to rest. The curse draws my energy."

She wrapped her hand around his, the warmth from his skin seeping into hers. Their eyes caught and held. His stare traveled all the way to her toes and everywhere in between. "I'll get back to work. Thank you for this." She forced herself to look away, toward the tray.

The corner of his mouth twitched. "I didn't make the coffee."

"No." She drew a deep breath. "Thank you for giving me another chance at life. For helping me discover who I am... what I am."

"Raven, there is so much more to you than this. You can thank me for the tooth, but I didn't make you who you are."

CHAPTER SEVENTEEN

I t took all Raven's willpower to leave Gabriel and return to the library. She'd never in her life experienced a stronger attraction. Her body was alive with it. And then it dawned on her. As a dragon shifter, Gabriel *was* magic. Was her desire to be near him and the tingling when he touched her the result of her growing affection for him or simply a side effect of her power?

And what of her previous vow to keep her distance until she knew for sure what had happened to Kristina? Damn, she was a mess. Her heart had set its sights on Gabriel, and the damned organ was far louder than her brain. She loved the way he watched over her and the way he listened when she spoke, as if the entire world revolved around her. She loved that he was powerful enough to save her when needed, yet had obeyed her wishes to stay away when she'd asked. Her attraction to him was intense enough to be almost painful. Yet he never used that attraction against her. He was honorable and loyal, she supposed. But there was something more; she felt connected to him, as if that little piece of him inside her was the last piece to an intricate puzzle, the key to becoming something greater than she'd ever expected.

She hurried back to her desk and the grimoire open on it.

She heard his door open and his footsteps descend the stairwell outside the library. Where did he go every afternoon? He always needed to rest around the same time each day, but he never did so in his apartment. He simply disappeared, reappearing in the early evening. While he was gone, Agnes and Richard ran the shop. Neither of them said much about his absence, other than "He's resting to counteract the curse." Was he truly napping the entire time in some secret room somewhere?

She flipped the pages of the grimoire, the same one with instructions on how to make it snow. The next spell she absorbed made a gale-force wind blow through the room. It knocked books from their shelves and scattered papers everywhere. She slammed the cover closed. The wind stopped. She cleaned up the mess.

She was tidying the last corner of the room when it dawned on her that Gabriel would be asleep all afternoon. She paused, the spine of a grimoire in her hand. Delphine had said that the antidote for Gabriel's curse must be made from the venom of the snake that'd bit him. The grimoires in this room might not hold the answer, but Crimson's magic did, and Raven was a witch who absorbed magic. She grabbed her purse and cardigan, locking the library behind her.

Richard and Agnes were both with customers, and she thought she could slip out the front door without being noticed, but Richard's hand landed on her shoulder even as he smiled at the man he was helping and excused himself.

"Where do you think you're going?"

"Having lunch with my sister," Raven lied. It was better if he didn't know the truth.

"Have Duncan drive you," he said.

"It's close. I can walk."

Richard frowned. "Gabriel won't like you going out unprotected."

She tipped her head and pecked him on the cheek. "Then don't tell him, silly. You know what? If I'm not back in an hour, you can send out the cavalry."

He scowled, but when she strode quickly toward the door, he didn't stop her.

Crimson's shop was called Hexpectations Voodoo Emporium and was on Dumaine Street, about four and a half blocks from Blakemore's. Raven rushed toward it on foot, hoping it wouldn't rain. The sky was overcast and there was a chill in the air—winter in New Orleans. She pulled on her sweater and wrapped her arms around herself against the chill. The idea of calling an Uber crossed her mind, but with traffic the way it was, it would be faster to walk.

A few minutes later, she found what she was looking for. The wooden sign for Hexpectations had a painting of a voodoo doll with a pin through its heart. Nice.

She paused a few doors down from the shop. It was well known that Crimson owned the place. She ran local advertising for her touristy voodoo-ritual gigs. It was very possible that Raven would see her behind the counter when she walked in. Crimson knew who she was, even if she didn't know what she was. She might be opening a can of worms doing this, but if she could touch anything in the store with Crimson's magic in it, she might be able to absorb it and use it to help Gabriel. She had to give it a try.

Tucking her hair behind her ears, she steeled her resolve

and went in. A bell chimed over the door, and a strong herbal scent met her as she crossed the threshold. It smelled like a combination of eucalyptus, peppermint, and something sour, almost as if Crimson was trying to cover up the smell of sour milk with essential oils.

Thankfully, she was not alone in the store. A group of Japanese tourists, five men and two women, laughed and talked near the cash register. Raven played with a crystal in a bin near the door while nonchalantly glancing toward the cashier out the corner of her eye. A goth-looking teenaged girl with a septum piercing leaned against the back counter. She snapped her chewing gum and stared at her phone.

No Crimson. Raven relaxed a little. None of the crystals were giving her a hint of magic. She walked down the aisle, randomly picking up items. She touched gris-gris and mojo bags, dolls, herbs, candles, books. Up and down each row, she examined the items for sale. Nothing spoke to her. There were no tingles. Her skin did not glow under her sweater. There was no change in the air or the temperature.

How could this be? Crimson's shop was a magical dud. How could the voodoo queen of New Orleans not leave a trail of magic in her own shop?

"Can I help you find anything?" the goth girl asked, looking annoyed. The Japanese tourists had left, and now Raven was the only one there. The girl probably thought she was planning to steal something.

"Do you sell daggers, like the kind you use for root work?"

"Uh, the owner might keep some in the back room, but it's locked when she's not here." The girl pointed at a door behind the register. The heavy panel of wood was covered in symbols and surrounded by dried herbs. Raven concentrated on the door, and for a moment, she thought she could hear it whisper to her. She considered rushing past the girl and touching it, but honestly, she wasn't going to get answers from a locked door.

"Are you not allowed in there?" she asked.

"No one is allowed in there but the priestess herself."

"What about the priestess herself?"

Raven whirled to find Crimson standing behind her. Her ample bosom and flowing skirt seemed to fill the aisle, and Raven suddenly felt boxed in.

"She was looking for an athame," the goth girl said.

Crimson's gaze never wavered from Raven. "You're Gabriel's new girl."

Raven forced down her fear and held out her hand. "Yes, I am. You must be Crimson." Her voice was high and soft, not a hint of suspicion or animosity. Would Crimson fall for it?

"Aren't you a sweet thing?" Crimson shook her hand, smiling a wicked smile.

Raven waited for Crimson's magic to send tingles into her hand. Instead, her palm went cold. Crimson was like a vacuum. There was no magic in her, just darkness. Emptiness. A vast and awful absence of energy. Raven had never realized how full of life everyone else was until she touched the thing that was Crimson.

"Nice to meet you," Raven murmured.

Crimson showed her teeth. "Come to the back room and we'll select an athame just for you." Her voice was syrupy and came out through a plastic smile.

Raven retracted her hand. "No, thank you. I've changed my mind." Her heart was hammering now.

Crimson's eyes turned hard and cold. "Lost your nerve, witch?"

Raven took a step back.

"That is why you need an athame, isn't it? You're a witch."

"So?" Another step back. She bumped into the goth woman who snapped her gum.

"You'll never break my curse, Raven. Tell your master to give me what I want."

"No."

She narrowed her eyes. "He might do it in exchange for you." Crimson reached for her.

Everything slowed, becoming crystal clear. Raven's heart sped up to the point that her chest hurt. There was a moment of darkness when she thought she had passed out, a dropping sensation as if she'd jumped off a tall building. And then she landed on her feet behind Crimson, magic curling around her like smoke before it vanished like a snuffed candle.

She moved for the door, her limbs feeling oddly elastic. It chimed when she opened it. Crimson whirled. Their eyes met. Raven bolted into the crowd on the sidewalk.

Gabriel was waiting for her when she walked into Blakemore's. He looked like hell. Wherever he went in the afternoons really did a number on him. Had he been sleeping on the curb of an underpass?

"I'm sorry," she said.

His face contorted, eyebrows becoming dark slashes, his jaw painfully tight. "Are you done trying to tear my heart from my chest, Raven? At least for the day?" His voice was too low, too steady.

"I... yes."

He turned on his heel and disappeared through the double glass doors at the back of the store.

CHAPTER EIGHTEEN

Gabriel didn't show himself again until the next afternoon, and by the stony expression he wore, Raven knew he was still angry.

"I said I was sorry," she repeated.

He paced toward the window in the library, running his fingers along the frame and gazing out over Royal Street. "Dragons collect things, Raven. It's in our nature. The more valuable the possession, the more closely we guard it."

"I'm not your possession. You don't own me. You can't buy me. I'm a human being."

"No. No, I can't. I can't even bind you. With one thought, I could call Agnes and Richard to my side. They'd come running. I can't call you. I can't tell where you are."

"Good." She crossed her arms over her chest. "Frankly, it's creepy you can do that to anyone with or without their permission. I'm a free woman, Gabriel. I'm here because I want to be here. I want to help. But I'm not a thing to be hoarded or protected."

He looked at her over his shoulder, the light from the

window framing a stunningly attractive profile. She tangled her fingers over her stomach.

"Do you know what part of the bond remains?" he asked softly. "It was the way I found you, both on the day you were attacked in the alley and in the swamp."

Raven licked her lips. "You mentioned before something about my fear."

He nodded. "Yes. Your fear. It cuts through me like a knife. I cannot rest. I cannot think." He stepped closer to her, desperation leaching from him. Her chest was heavy with the weight of the emotion building in the room. "Don't you see how much I care for you? Have I ever treated you like a possession, even though it is in my nature to do so? Have I ever hurt you?"

She thought about it. "No."

"Then stop hurting me."

"I have never intentionally hurt you, Gabriel."

He winced. "Your fear feels like being shredded with razor blades. It feels like taking a stroll through a blender."

Raven's hands pressed into her stomach. "I am sorry. I didn't know."

"Please, Raven, for your sake as well as mine, be more careful."

She moved toward him and placed her hand on his cheek. The idea that he'd felt shredded by her fear made her feel absolutely wretched. She wouldn't be his prisoner, but she also refused to be his torturer. "I will be more careful. I am sorry."

He nodded. "Thank you."

"There's something I have to tell you about yesterday, about where I went and what I found out."

He leaned on the library desk, his hands coupled near

his waist. "Please, tell me why you were frightened for your life... again."

Okay, a little more attitude in that comment than necessary. "I went to see Crimson."

Gabriel stood and whirled like he was searching for something or someone to break. "Why?"

"I wanted to try to absorb her magic. I thought if I could get a taste of what she was, I might be able to reproduce it, take it apart, and use the pieces to break your curse."

"What happened?"

"There is nothing magical in her shop. Not a single thing. I think she keeps anything with any power behind an enchanted door in the back. But she was there, Gabriel, and when I touched her, I felt null energy."

"Null energy?"

"I don't have another word for it. I felt like there was something in her that ate magic. I couldn't absorb it because there wasn't anything there to absorb. There was just this gnawing, black, perpetually hungry thing inside her that wanted to destroy everything. All it wants is darkness. There's just... nothing."

His face turned grim. "That's unfortunate."

"There must be some way to undo what she's done. If you gave her what she wanted, she'd undo the curse, right? Pull that darkness back into herself? She wants you. She wouldn't end you on purpose."

"It seems so."

"We just have to think of another way."

His fingers began to tap against his thigh and she took a step closer and gathered his hand in hers. The tapping eased.

"You're the only thing that helps," he said. His full,

focused attention made her feel like the center of the universe. The symbols on her arms began to glow.

"We will find another way, Gabriel. I know how you're feeling. I know what it's like to be out of time and staring death in the face. I can sense your despair, the way you want to shed this curse like a chain and take your life back. When I was sick, I wanted to blow out the walls. I wanted freedom so badly I would have chewed my own arm off to get it. But you saved me from that, and now I will save you from this. I will find a way, even if I have to go to Paragon myself and forge you a new ring."

He touched her forehead with his lips. "Thank you, Raven. Thank you."

THE NEXT AFTERNOON, GABRIEL BROUGHT HER A GIFT. The box was wrapped in shiny black paper with a gold bow. She opened it to find a length of knotted rope.

"My birthday isn't until April. What did I do to deserve a frayed length of knotted rope?"

"You became a witch," he said. "I made this for you to practice with. Untie it. I'll tell you in advance that these knots are not the kind you learn to tie in the Boy Scouts. I've magically bound each one with increasingly more difficult spells. Only an expert at countering magic can untie all six. You will have to examine the knot to determine which spell I've placed on it, then find the counterspell in your internal arsenal or in these grimoires. Then you will have to apply that counterspell to the knots."

"Ha ha, very funny." Raven examined the knots. "Was wrapping this like a gift supposed to make me feel excited about spending my days untying knots?"

"You can take them home with you to practice."

Raven tried not to look disappointed, but she'd gotten excited when she saw the wrapped box. This was not the gift she'd had in mind. It was also not the practice she'd had in mind. When Gabriel said he'd work with her, she expected one-on-one interaction, not a take-home test. She picked up the rope.

"I won't be in tomorrow," he said.

"Why?"

"There's something I need to take care of."

"That's not vague or anything."

He approached her, his power bumping into her before he did. She was so much more attuned to it now. It licked her body like a thousand tongues of fire, not an unpleasant experience. She moved closer until there was less than an inch between them and his heat practically enveloped her.

"If I tell you something, will you keep it to yourself?"

"Of course I will," Raven said. Now she was concerned.

"I'm going to see a lawyer. If we can't fix this, I want my affairs to be in order."

She chewed her lip. "We're going to fix this, Gabriel. We will."

The smile he gave her was sexy enough to melt her dress. "I hope you're right. Spending more time with you once we've put this Kristina mess behind us is definitely on my priority list."

Yes, Kristina, Raven reminded herself. It was getting harder and harder for her to remember to be cautious with Gabriel. He kissed her gently on the cheek, then left the room before she could take her next breath.

The days that followed moved quickly. Raven absorbed book after book. Once she finished the voodoo section, she was able to untie the first three knots, but nothing she'd absorbed helped her sort out her feelings for Gabriel. By the time Friday rolled around, she had one last practice knot left to be untied and an awkward date with Gabriel to look forward to.

He arrived as he had every other afternoon, just before five. "Duncan is waiting downstairs."

She stood from the desk and tossed the length of rope into her purse. "I'm ready."

"No, I don't think so."

"Excuse me?"

He held out a shopping bag to her. "You'll want this for where we're going. You can change in my apartment."

"Where are we going?"

He gave her a slanted grin. "Change. I'll meet you downstairs." He opened the door to his home for her, and she made her way to his bedroom before opening the bag. It was a dress. Well, part of a dress. The actual amount of material seemed a yard shy of a full garment. It was royal blue, sleeveless, and had leather trim along the neck, criss-crossing over the waist and along the hem. He'd included a black lace bra and panties, which was a good thing, because the ones she'd worn to work that day would have shown. Still, she was sure she didn't have the boobs to fill the thing out. She slid the expensive fabric over her skin, noticing the way the material skimmed her body. This was the difference between being rich and being middle class. Raven didn't own a single piece of clothing this perfectly made.

For a second, she felt guilty about accepting the gift. Then she decided it wasn't necessarily a gift. She could give it back tomorrow. And this was work related. Tonight she would learn what had happened to Kristina, and perhaps she could use that information in some way to advance her understanding of magic. Besides, if she succeeded in breaking Gabriel's curse, she would have earned the cost of the dress five hundred times over.

She smoothed the fabric and looked at herself in the mirror. The dress fit perfectly, almost as if it were made for her. She'd put on some badly needed weight since she started at Blakemore's, which helped, plus the dress was cut to flatter, cinching in her waist and giving her chest some lift. Gabriel had included a pair of strappy high-heeled booties that made her legs appear longer than they were.

Turning in front of the mirror, she had to admit the look was flattering on her. She wondered how he'd managed. She freshened her makeup and brushed her dark hair. Was it just her, or had it grown out significantly? It was almost down to her shoulders now. By the time she finished primping, she felt sexy and sophisticated, although she wasn't completely sure she could pull the look off. Wherever Gabriel was taking her must be upscale. She hoped she'd fit in.

She slung her purse over her shoulder and strode out of the apartment. Gabriel hadn't left her the key, but the door locked behind her. *The oreads*, she thought. Carefully balanced on the unfamiliar heels, she descended the stairs.

"Sweet child of mercy, you look hot," Richard said, snapping his fingers and throwing back his head. "Mmm-hmm, that dragon is going to burn up when he sees you, miss thing."

"I must agree," Agnes chimed in. "The dress suits you."

She thanked them both before stepping out the door.

Gabriel was waiting, leaning against the car in a pair of jeans and a black button-down that made his eyes look even darker than usual. He scanned her from head to toe, then pushed off the car to meet her on the sidewalk. A deep rumble met her ears. Gabriel's purr. "You look enchanting," he whispered in her ear. "I think that's the appropriate compliment for a witch, don't you?"

He opened the car door and helped her inside, then rounded the back to slide in beside her. Duncan pulled into traffic.

"Where are we going?"

"I wouldn't dream of ruining the surprise."

"Now you're just being annoying."

"It's one of my better qualities." He inched closer to her until the outer edge of his pinky finger grazed her thigh just below the hem of her short dress. That touch might as well have been a blowtorch for how it made her blood pump.

"I've almost solved the knots," she said, glancing at Duncan. The man had both eyes on the road. Thank heaven for small favors. She was sure she was blushing, and although he couldn't see it from the outside, her need made her feel like she was wearing a neon sign. She wanted sex, wanted Gabriel so badly that her body felt like a raw nerve.

"You've come a long way in a week." Gabriel seemed to read her mind. He pressed the button for the privacy divider.

"You didn't make it easy for me. The first one was about applying the right force, simple enough. But the second one required heat to loosen the bond. For the third knot, it was necessary for me to lengthen the rope, the fourth to shrink the binding agent holding it together, and the fifth... the fifth one was very tricky."

"You figured it out."

"Barely. It was an illusion. A very good one. I tried for over a day to untie a knot that wasn't really there. All I had to do was destroy the artifice and I had it."

"What do you make of the last one?"

"I'm not sure yet. I think it has something to do with focusing energy though."

"Oh?" His eyebrows shot up.

"The spell you've put on it seems to be tightening the knot again and again, like a song on continual loop. I need to break the repeat mechanism. Then I should be able to untie it."

"Clever, clever girl," he said. He slid his hand over her knee and traced tiny circles along her skin.

She watched as his hand swept higher up her thigh. Long, lengthening strokes that ran from her inner knee up under the skirt of her dress, stopping short of her black lace panties. He'd seen them, picked them out. The thought of them in his fingers made her squirm. Her breath came heavily. She licked her lips and inhaled his smoky scent. A little higher and he'd graze her sex. Her body longed for it, ached for it. Her nipples hardened within the lace of her bra, and her hips circled, moving his hand up her thigh.

"What happened to waiting until you trusted me about Kristina?" he asked, his sinful mouth drawing close to hers. A dark grin played at the corner of his lips, and he watched her through hooded eyes.

It almost killed her to hold her ground. "Tell me. Tell me now where we're going and what happened to her."

"I can't. I can only show you. And we are about half an hour from our destination. What shall we do for thirty minutes?"

He trailed his fingers closer and grazed the seam of her underwear. Raven closed her eyes, her breath coming out in a shaky exhale. She had to be soaking wet. Her body was a throbbing bundle of need.

"Would you like me to stop?"

His fingers climbed again toward the apex of her thighs,

and this time she shifted her hips. He obliged her with a long stroke over the thin material that covered the center of her sex. The rumble in his chest grew louder.

"Oh, Raven, you are wet," he said, brushing his lips against hers. "Tell me what you want. Should I stop or give you a taste of what will happen when you are mine?"

She licked her lips, then tried to catch her breath. No amount of effort could remind her of why she wanted to wait. All her mental energy was focused on the tangle of nerves so close to his fingers. His touch was exquisite torture. Lord help her, she was weak. But there was no other answer she could give than to raise her fingers to the nape of his neck and drag her nails through his thick dark hair.

"You must tell me, Raven. I've promised I wouldn't take anything you weren't willing to give. I am nothing if not a dragon that keeps his promises." His skin felt hot against her own, and his dark eyes smoldered with red fire.

"A taste," she said. "Give me a taste."

❦

THE POSSESSIVE GROWL THAT ESCAPED GABRIEL'S throat was a bit premature. After all, she'd asked for a taste, nothing more. She wasn't his. Not really. Not yet. But she'd asked for more and he intended to give it to her.

He caressed the back of her knee with his fingers, which then climbed toward the moist lace that covered her sex. Slowly, so slowly. His mouth hovered over hers. Jasmine and vanilla formed a heady scent in the small space, and he wondered if it was her magic coming to the surface. Perfume didn't grow stronger with excitement. Magic did.

He worked his fingers under the lace. When she moaned in response, he claimed her mouth, drinking that moan in with a kiss that she returned with abandon. She gently clawed the back of his head with her nails.

"So wet," he whispered into her mouth, dipping a finger into her and circling. She raised her hips to drive him deeper as her tongue darted over his bottom lip. He returned the gesture, deepening the kiss and showing her with his tongue exactly what he wanted to do to her.

She tipped her head back and whimpered between kisses, her hips moving faster now. Gabriel's own arousal was threatening to tear through his jeans, but this wasn't about him. It was about her. About showing her how perfect it would be if she were his. He wanted to make her sing.

He kissed his way down her neck to her breast, skimming his teeth over the thin material of her bodice. Her nipple pearled under the heat of his breath. He dipped a second finger into her, working slow, languid circles. He watched her carefully, committing every flush, every roll of her hips to memory. She writhed closer to him, her petite body grinding against his fingers. How he would love to be inside her, buried in her. Once she said the word, he would mark her as his mate. He slid an arm into the arch of her back and lifted, his fingers diving deeper, his thumb massaging in quick hungry circles as he ravaged her neck with his mouth.

That was all it took. She arched in his arms, the symbols in her skin lighting up in unison as her orgasm tore through her. He held her through the aftershocks, then gently removed his hand, lowering her to the seat and straightening her dress. When she looked at him again, her eyes were bright with astonishment.

"You asked for a taste." He flashed her a smug grin.

"Wicked, wicked dragon. You knew if I had a taste, I'd want the entire meal."

The car slowed to a stop.

Gabriel shook his head. "We're here."

❦

THE BREATH LEFT RAVEN'S LUNGS IN A DEEP SIGH. What Gabriel had done to her body had wiped her mind. Gone were her former anxiety and misgivings, replaced by a deep sense of relaxation and a strong desire to curl up and take a nap. She'd never had an orgasm with her first lover. He'd been seventeen and had all the self-restraint of a rabid weasel. Gabriel was sex on legs. He was a dark wind that blew through her. He was the flame and she was the moth.

If she didn't find out soon what had happened to Kristina, she would weep. She was too sure, too incredibly lost to Gabriel, to accept that he had hurt her predecessor. It would break her if she was wrong about him. Her heart would not survive it.

Raven allowed Gabriel to help her from the car. Duncan had pulled over in front of a club, very exclusive by the looks of it. The place was called Bacchus, a familiar enough name for New Orleans, but she didn't recognize it as anywhere she'd been before. Not surprising. Most of her post-drinking-age adulthood had been spent in a hospital bed.

"Come on," Gabriel said, guiding her toward the bouncer.

"Gabriel, there's a line. A very long line."

"Not for me," he said.

The bouncer saw him coming and immediately dropped the rope. "Good evening, Mr. Blakemore. Your VIP room is ready."

Gabriel placed his hand on the curve of her back and guided her into the crowded and dimly lit club. "Upstairs."

On the way up the metal-and-glass staircase, Raven looked over the railing at a stage that was already set for a live band. "Who's playing tonight?"

"Blue Radio."

"*The* Blue Radio?" Raven turned to him excitedly. Blue Radio was one of the most popular groups in the country at the moment. Tickets for their concerts sold out instantly. It was unusual they'd be playing in an intimate venue like this. Even more unbelievable that she was present to hear them. "I love them. I've had a thing for them ever since their David Bowie tribute concert."

"The owner of this club is a friend of their new manager. No one knows they're here. Only the fortunate patrons who get in tonight will be lucky enough to see them. Including you." He winked at her.

Truly excited now, she followed him to a small room overlooking the stage. His VIP room, she supposed. Dark wood lined in red velvet, the room provided privacy from the hall via a heavy black curtain. Although she could see hundreds of other patrons, she felt secluded here, above it all. A server knocked on the wall beside the curtain before entering and asking if they wanted anything from the bar. She ordered a martini. Gabriel ordered whiskey.

The drinks hadn't even arrived yet when Blue Radio took the stage. Along with the rest of the crowd, Raven leaped to her feet. As soon as they began their set, she sang along, swaying to the music.

"Do you want to dance in the pit?" Gabriel asked her, pointing to the area in front of the stage. "I can get us down there if it pleases you."

Raven scanned the crowded dance floor below and shook her head. "No."

He laughed. "You'd rather dance up here, alone?"

She turned to him. "I'm not alone." She reached for his hand. When their fingers touched, the symbols on her skin came alive. "Anyhow, I'd rather be here with you than down there, worried about someone seeing these."

"You plan on touching me then?" he asked.

Raven became acutely aware of why they'd come here. She was supposed to be asking about Kristina. But for some reason she didn't want to. She almost didn't want to know. Everything about tonight was what she wanted, what she had prayed for. An adventure. A piece of the life she'd missed before. The music, the man, the energy of the roaring crowd below them. She didn't want it to end.

Somehow she found the strength to say the name. "Kristina." It came out of her in a burst and caused her eyes to tear.

He took her hand. "I can see this is a hard limit for you. So let's get it out of the way."

"Just tell me. I have to know what happened. It's eating me alive."

"Come." He took her hand and led her toward the stairs and then into an employees-only corridor. The music grew louder as they descended a long concrete ramp. By the direction of the sound, Raven thought they must be behind the stage, or under it. Where was he taking her?

There was a woman in a suit standing at the end of the ramp, her hair bleached white and cropped up the back of her neck. From behind, Raven could tell she had her arms crossed. She was tapping her foot, and the muscles of her shoulders seemed tense.

When they approached her, she said, "I hope you can

appreciate how dangerous this is for me. He will kill me if he ever sees me again."

"I know," Gabriel said. "I am sorry, but I need this of you."

The woman turned around. "Which is why I'm here. I owe you one, Gabriel. This is it."

Raven squinted, taking in the slope of the woman's nose and the high cheekbones, the amber eyes. Aside from the cut and color of her hair, she looked exactly like the picture on her father's mantel.

"Kristina?"

"Shhh," the woman said. "If you want me to tell you anything, you will not use that name, and when you leave here, you will never think of me or look for me again. That name, that person, is dead. Do you understand?"

Raven narrowed her eyes and nodded.

"Good." The woman who had once been Kristina uncrossed her arms and slipped her hands into her suit pockets. "If you need to address me, you can call me Jezebel. I'm Blue Radio's manager. I'm here for tonight, and then you will never see me again. Understand?"

"Jezebel," Raven repeated. "Nice to meet you. I'm Raven."

"What do you want to know? You have five minutes," she said sharply.

Raven turned to Gabriel. "Can we have a few minutes... alone?" He made a face as if she'd injured him, but with a quick bow of his head, he receded up the ramp and out of sight.

"Did Gabriel have anything to do with your disappearance?" Raven asked.

"Of course he did," she said. "He helped me vanish so my father couldn't find me and kill me. I'll spare you the details. All you need to know is my father is abusive and dangerous. Gabriel tried to take me under his wing. I stayed with him for a while, but my father tracked me down. He stalked me endlessly. Did Gabriel tell you my father tried to set Blakemore's on fire?"

"No." Raven frowned.

"Luckily, dragons have a handle on fire. Gabriel contained the blaze. After that, it was clear the only way I was ever going to be free was to fake my own death. Gabriel got me this job and arranged for my new identity. And he promised to keep my secret until my father's death. He's the only one who knows, Raven. I told no one else. Not even Agnes or Richard. I couldn't risk it. Now you know too. I hope I can count on you to keep your mouth shut."

"I won't say a word."

"Three minutes," Kristina said. "The band is finishing their first set."

"Why did you draw my family crest on the library catalog?"

Her eyes widened. "What's your family crest?"

"It's a twisted version of the tree of life."

Kristina hung her head and laughed. "That was the symbol the spirits sent me of the one who would break the curse. I kept asking them who can stand up to Crimson? Who can find a way to bring magic back to the ring? And they kept sending me that symbol."

"But what does it mean?"

"Gabriel doesn't know this, but the day I sketched that symbol, I came to understand that my being there was keeping the one who could break the curse from his life. If I'd found a way to stay, or taken a job closer to Blakemore's, I might have been able to keep searching for the cure. But the spirits were adamant that the symbol I'd seen represented the one who must do it. It's you, Raven. The symbol represented you. You are the only one who can cure what ails his magic."

"You mean I will find a spell to break the curse."

She shook her head. "*You* will break the curse and restore the ring. You can't do one without the other."

Raven felt like she'd had the wind knocked out of her. "No. I haven't practiced magic long enough for that. I can barely untie a knot in a rope. I can't fight a voodoo priestess. I can't restore dragon magic to a ring that's not even from this world."

The woman stared at her. "Weren't you once as good as dead?"

"I was dying when Gabriel saved me, yes."

"Listen up, zombie Barbie. I speak to the dead, and what they are telling me is that you are way more powerful than even Gabriel right now. Your magic is getting stronger while his is getting weaker. I'm not sure what's up with your little-miss-helpless routine, but you need to have a good look at yourself and admit what you are."

What did Kristina want from her? Raven spread her hands. "I know what I am and what I can do. I can absorb magic when I touch it."

The woman shook her head. "That's the icing on the cake, sweetheart. The tree I sketched, I had no idea it was your family tree, but I did know it was someone's. I traced it back to a woman who was burned at the stake for being a witch in the mid-1700s. If I were a betting woman, I'd bet that you are her descendant. You're a witch and you have a dragon's tooth charging you from within. And unless I'm blind, you two are more than boss and employee."

Raven blushed.

"You are capable of saving the man and the dragon. Let

yourself go. Stop saying you can't. Stop putting limits on yourself. If you love him, you'll try harder. You'll try anything."

"How? Tell me how!"

"If I knew how, I would've done it myself. I can tell you one thing; I doubt very much the answer is in that library of Gabriel's."

"You have to help me. I'm not strong enough to figure this out, but maybe together—"

"Pssh. Sorry, love. I can't risk it. I'm supposed to be dead, remember?"

"But aren't you bonded to him? Won't you die when he dies?"

She shook her head. "Take it from a medium, everyone dies. I'm not the one he needs or the one who can save us." She glared at Raven for a beat, then turned back toward the stage. "Now, you better go find Gabriel before he gets testy with me for keeping you from him. The way he looked at you, I thought he'd rather kill me than leave you."

Raven paused. "I feel the same way."

"Then I suggest you tell him so. While you still can."

CHAPTER NINETEEN

Gabriel waited near the backstage exit for Raven to return. Would she understand that he could not have revealed Kristina's secret, even to her? It was not in a dragon's character to break a promise. Kristina was his friend and his bonded servant. Although he'd freed her from the expectations of the bond for her protection, he would not free himself from his responsibilities to her. He could only hope and pray that Raven would understand that and not be angry with him for hiding it from her all this time.

He heard her before he saw her. Her footsteps fell rapidly and her heart pounded. Worried, he rounded the corner to meet her. She barreled into him at a full run, and he caught her in his arms and twirled her around to stop her momentum.

"What's wrong?" he asked.

She placed her hands on either side of his face. "You didn't hurt her."

"No."

"You set her free."

"Yes." His jaw hardened. "She was no good to me anyway with that father of hers constantly screaming in my face and scaring away my customers."

"You are a good man, Gabriel Blakemore."

"Dragon. I'm a dragon. You can't forget that. I'm not safe and I'm not human. I can't give you that. Not ever. Even if we break the curse."

She inhaled and tugged his head toward hers. "Safe is overrated." Her lips crashed into his as hard as her body had, and he absorbed the impact with pleasure. The dragon enjoyed it too, rousing from its slumber and begging him to claim her, to mark her as his mate. It was instinct, as primal as his need to eat or drink. And it was rare. In Paragon, dragon males outnumbered females eight to one. It was common enough for males to seek sexual release outside their species. But rarely did they bond with them as their mate. Usually it was only about sex.

Raven was different. She'd always been different. He wanted her. All of her. Her body, her soul, and her heart.

"Say you will be mine," he demanded into her lips. "Tell me you accept me as your mate and give yourself to me."

She retreated, seeming to fight with herself over the notion.

"I don't want to be owned. I won't be caged."

"I wouldn't dream of caging you. It would be like caging the wind."

"But you would own me." She moved away from him, crossing her arms over her chest.

He dropped to his knees on the concrete corridor. "Don't you understand you already own me?"

"What are you doing? Get up."

"You have ruled me since the day I walked into your

hospital room. You wicked girl, will we never be equals? Will you keep me at your beck and call, broken under your will until I am no more?"

"What are you talking about?"

He tipped his face up to hers, humiliated but helpless to stop the words that tumbled over his lips. "I gave you everything you asked for. Your freedom, my distance, the truth about who I am and what I've done." He pointed toward where Kristina had been. "Still you hold yourself back from me. Hold yourself over me. I am not your lapdog, Raven."

"You want me to be yours. To commit to you. But what does that mean? Will you suffocate me? Imprison me?"

"No." The word fell bitter from his lips. "Be mine. Trust me. Dragons do not mate lightly, Raven. This isn't about sex. This is about forever."

She gazed down at him, her body trembling, and he wondered how it was he was scaring her when he was the one on his knees, submitting to her will. Placing her hands on his shoulders, she steadied herself. "Yes, Gabriel. Yes."

❦

ON HIS KNEES IN FRONT OF HER, GABRIEL HAD TAKEN A submissive posture, but Raven knew better than to assume he was harmless. There was a dragon coiled at her feet, a magical entity normally powerful enough to tear her apart. Binding herself to him was as terrifying as it was exciting.

No sooner had she said yes than his expression turned to hunger. He rose slowly and wrapped an arm around her, pulling her flush against his side. "Come with me," he whispered in her ear, and the words were seductively smooth and laden with promise.

Raven thought he would take her back to his VIP room,

but instead she found herself swept from the Bacchus and into the atrium of the building next door. All she could hear was the rush of blood in her ears and the pounding realization that she was his. She was bound. And the oddest part was, she wanted to be. Something deep inside her finally felt wholly alive in his arms.

Gabriel slipped a card into a slot near the elevator and the doors opened. He ushered her inside.

"What is this place?"

"I have an apartment here."

"You— Why?"

"I told you the owner of the club next door invited Blue Radio. That is me. I own Bacchus. I keep this place for the times I have responsibilities here and have to stay late."

She paused as the elevator doors closed. "You invited Blue Radio here so that I could meet Kristina and know she wasn't dead."

"I couldn't tell you. I'd promised her. I had to ask her to do it. Thank the Mountain she agreed." Gabriel pushed her against the wall of the elevator, smoothing his hand along her side, his thumb grazing the bottom of her breast. Raven melted into him, parting her lips as his kiss landed on her mouth. The tangle of tongues and limbs that followed was almost violent. His mouth worked hers, thrusting and stroking against her tongue in a rhythm that was undeniably sexual. She fisted his hips and pulled him against her with all her strength, feeling the hard length of him press into her belly. His mouth was a brand, scorching hot against her lips, her throat, and all she could think was it wasn't hot enough. She wanted more, everywhere, over every inch of her body.

The ding of the elevator brought her to her senses. As soon as he whirled off her, Raven smoothed and adjusted her dress. Gabriel gave her a seductive smile and interlaced his fingers in hers. The doors opened. The hall was empty.

"Thank the Mountain," he said. "With the size of the erection you've given me, I might have frightened someone."

Raven ran her fingers along the length that challenged the fly of his jeans. He was hard enough it must have hurt inside the heavy denim. He growled, and then that deep rumbling purr started again. She took it as a challenge, running her fingers along his length again.

Quickly he keyed into a room to their right. The door wasn't even closed before he had her in his arms. He swept her off her feet and carried her into the room closest to the door: the kitchen. He lifted her, setting her bottom on the edge of the marble island. She wrapped her arms around his neck and kissed him again, his heavy purr rattling her mouth, her throat. God, she wanted him, wanted to feel that scorching tongue against her flesh.

His hot fingers moved like tongues of fire up the outsides of her legs and under her skirt. It reminded her of standing too close to a bonfire. When the flame flickered, it would almost hurt. Her skin prickled beneath his touch but then adapted, wanting, needing more. The throbbing between her legs had become a heavy weight. She needed him to fix it, to end this torturous ache.

He snapped the sides of the black lace panties and tore them from her body.

"Oh!" was all Raven could think to say into his mouth. He backed up a step and unbuttoned his shirt. Underneath, his chest was a work of art, all lean, corded muscle, golden peaks, and deep shadows. She reached out and ran the tips of her fingers down his front and over his abs. "I want you, Gabriel. So badly."

He looked at her through his lashes as he gently lowered her onto her back on the island and used his folded shirt to cushion her head. The marble was deliciously cold against her hot skin. His hands skimmed along her thighs as his lips trailed from her jaw, along her neck, the mound of her breast, over the thin material of her dress and lower.

"Gabriel..."

His lips brushed her inner thigh. She thought she might combust at the feel of his hot breath against her. Reaching for him, her fingertips nestled in the silky strands of his hair.

"Please, please," she whimpered. He was so close. She needed him.

His response was a growl and a warm, wet lap of tongue up her center. She arched and moaned, the tips of her breasts tingling with the electric need that shot up her torso. His purr grew louder, vibrating against her center as his slightly rough tongue darted inside her. His teeth gently grazed her flesh. She gripped the edges of the island, her legs crossed at the ankle behind his back. She was so close to the edge, she bucked her hips, desperate for release. Instead, he slowed, then pulled away.

"Gabriel, please!" she cried.

"Say it," he demanded. There was no misunderstanding what he wanted. It couldn't have been clearer to her.

"I am yours," she said. "All yours. Just yours."

The pressure and intensity of his mouth increased along with the vibration of the purr. Sparks of light exploded behind her closed lids. The orgasm took hold of her like the rumble of a passing train. She jackknifed off the marble and released a cry of delight that drew out another possessive growl from Gabriel. Before she'd even come down from the high, he'd swept her off the counter and whirled her through the apartment to the bed. Her dress went flying, and then talons landed on her bra. *Talons*. Sharp and sinister, the claws had sprouted from his knuckles, his hands becoming something not quite human. He traced the tip of that talon along her belly and drew a sharp, cool line around her nipple.

"Don't be afraid. I would never hurt you. Tell me if you want me to stop," he said.

She grabbed his wrist and pressed her lips to the side of the sharp appendage that once had been his index finger. "Don't you dare stop."

With him hovering over her, she felt small, dwarfed by his size, but not threatened. There was a part of her, even now, that pictured him on his knees and she knew—knew on a deep, psychological level—that Kristina was right. She was powerful, and right now, she was his equal. She hadn't meant to do it, but she'd claimed him as hers long before she'd agreed to be his. So as he slid that talon between her breasts and sliced her bra away, she didn't fear him. She reached between her knees and tugged at his belt.

Gabriel helped her remove his pants. The sight of him above her was glorious, his erection long and thick, almost intimidating. Almost. She wrapped both hands around him.

"You wicked, wicked woman," he hissed through a smile. The noise he made next was more animal than human.

His wings fanned out over her as he laid her back. "You are mine, Ravenna Tanglewood. I claim you."

She met his gaze, her nails digging into his silky hair. "Yes. I am yours."

He joined with her then, his arms braced on either side of her head. She closed her eyes and moaned. When she opened them again, Gabriel's smoldering gaze met hers, his smoky scent the strongest it had ever been. It seemed to sink into her skin.

"You're mine, Raven. Mine," he whispered in her ear.

She wrapped her arms tighter around his neck as his body moved above her.

"You're mine too," she said breathlessly.

He didn't let up. His heat filled her until blissful tongues of fire rushed through her veins. Another release barreled into her. His came on its heels, and the feeling sent her over again, both of them on some sort of blissful ride that wouldn't end.

When they finally came back to earth, she was covered in his smoky scent, her heart pounding. And she'd never felt closer to anyone. Her heart was warm and full to overflowing. Gabriel pulled her against his chest and wrapped his wings around them both.

"I love you, Raven," he whispered against the back of her neck.

Raven burrowed her face in his chest. "I love you too," she whispered.

He closed his eyes. She stroked the side of his head as he drifted off.

Funny, Raven wasn't a bit tired. She thought she could run a marathon. She slid out from between his heavy arms and the shelter of his wing and headed for the shower. With the warm water pouring over her, she assessed her body. Scratches curved along the side of her left breast, teeth marks grazed her throat, and her sex was blissfully sore. She lingered in the hot spray, but nothing seemed to calm the building energy inside her. Antsy and vividly alive, she dried off, then went in search of her dress.

Gabriel was still asleep, so deeply he didn't rouse when she passed the bed. Raven scooped up the dress and put in on, relieved it hadn't been torn. That was saying something, considering her underwear was in ribbons. Oh well, she didn't need underwear to take a walk. She slipped on her heels, borrowed Gabriel's apartment key, and left him a note.

As soon as she emerged from the building, she took a deep breath of night air. Delicious. The city throbbed with energy that crackled around her. She started walking, picking up speed. She weaved between the people on the street.

Raven broke into a run, her legs loose and strong. The city blocks flew by. Laughing, she pumped her arms, amazed the booties she wore, with their four-inch heels, didn't even pinch her feet. They felt like athletic shoes, and the way they absorbed her weight, almost as if her feet weren't completely striking the ground. Like she was flying. This was freedom. This was life unadulterated. Life with no limits.

She was so caught up in the rush that she didn't notice the truck backing out of the alley.

The bumper struck her hip and her body flew. The traffic, the buildings: it all became a silver rush, and then she collided with the pavement and rolled into the opposite curb to the sound of screeching tires.

Gabriel is going to be pissed, she thought. She'd promised him she'd keep herself safe, and now she was... What was she? She raised her head. The dress was shredded and she wasn't wearing any underwear. Great. The truck driver was yelling at her to stay still. He was calling 911. Her shoe was missing. Where was her other shoe? Oh, in the middle of the street. She sat up and cracked her neck.

The truck driver dropped his phone.

Raven looked down at herself. No blood. No pain. Not even a scratch. She held her hand out to stop traffic and limped across the street, scooping up her other shoe. Ruined, just like the dress. She hoped they weren't expensive. Who was she kidding? The ruined clothes were the least of her problems. Gabriel was going to be livid.

"Are you... Are you okay?" The truck driver shouted at her, his hands shaking.

"Fine!" she yelled back, removing her remaining shoe and running barefoot for Gabriel's building. "Don't worry about it."

Minutes later, she ignored the stares as she held her dress together as much as possible and walked through the lobby to the elevator. At least she'd kept ahold of the key. She was back in Gabriel's place before she could cause much more of a stir.

"I know what you're going to say, Gabriel, but I'm fine. I didn't even bump my head." She turned the corner and stopped dead. He hadn't moved since she'd left him. Absolutely still, wings limp, he lay in the same position he'd been in when she slipped out of bed hours ago.

And it didn't look like he was breathing.

CHAPTER TWENTY

"Gabriel! Gabriel!" Raven shook his shoulder. "Breathe!" She lowered her ear to his lips. Shallow but there. "What's wrong? Gabriel, please, I don't know what to do."

His eyes fluttered. "Richard," he whispered.

Raven shook him again. "You want me to call Richard? You need an ambulance!"

He squeezed her hand and mouthed, *Richard.*

She grabbed his phone off the nightstand and used his finger to unlock it. She thanked her lucky stars when Richard's face popped up in the recent calls list. She tapped the number.

"O dragon, my dragon! What can I do for you at this late hour?"

"Richard, it's Raven. There's something wrong with Gabriel."

"Where are you, darlin'?"

"Next to a place called the Bacchus. I don't even know the address."

"Never mind. I know where it is. I'm on my way."

Raven hung up the phone. "He's on his way. Stay with me." He was curled on his side, his knuckles near his lips, pale skin barely darker than the sheets. She couldn't miss the contrast of his ring. Almost completely black. A deep sense of dread weighed on her. The magic that had protected her, that had filled her with energy—it had come from somewhere, from him. She'd drained him. She'd absorbed his magic without realizing what she was doing. And now he was barely alive.

She thought about trying to put the energy back where it came from, but she had no idea how to do that. What if she tried and ended up taking more by mistake? No. Richard would know what to do. She removed her hand from Gabriel's shoulder, afraid to keep touching him.

"I'm sorry," she gasped, tears streaming now. "I didn't mean to."

His eyes fluttered again. "Not your fault," he mumbled. "Curse."

Thankfully, it wasn't long before the door flew open and Richard and Duncan rushed in. Richard took one look at her torn dress and frowned. "Did he do that to you?"

"No!" she said. "I did this to him." She gestured toward Gabriel's motionless form. "I was hit by a car, but I'm fine."

Richard's brows dipped.

"I'll explain later. Do something. Help him!"

"Room," Gabriel mumbled.

Richard nodded. "Right away. Duncan, give me a hand." Duncan slipped his arm under one shoulder and Richard took the other. They stood him up between them.

"Wait," Raven said, realizing he was completely naked. She quickly pulled on his boxers. "What about his wings?"

Gabriel groaned and his wings retracted into his back, completely gone.

"Quickly. Out the service elevator," Duncan said. The older man grunted with the effort of helping to carry him.

Raven held the door. A quick ride down, and Duncan's car was waiting near the garbage bins at the back of the building. They loaded Gabriel into the back seat with Raven.

"What is this room he's asking for?" Raven asked.

Richard sighed from the passenger's seat. "Maybe it's better— I like you a lot, Ravenna, but Mr. Blakemore has secrets I don't exactly feel it's my place to divulge."

Gabriel's hand landed on Raven's. "With."

She looked down at his pale hand on top of her own. "It looks like Gabriel wants to share this particular secret with me."

Neither Richard nor Duncan said a thing, but they exchanged glances in the front seat. They arrived at Blakemore's, but Duncan pulled into an alley down the road. A privacy gate opened at the touch of a button, and they drove into a courtyard. Ravenna recognized it as the far end of the one where she'd had breakfast with Gabriel, the one behind Blakemore's. Duncan parked, and the men helped Gabriel out.

"Try to remain calm," Richard said.

"Do I look like I'm freaking out?" Raven shouted in a tight, high-pitched voice. They led her through the doors opposite the entrance to Blakemore's. Raven halted. She was standing in a room as big as a warehouse, and it was filled with *treasure*. Gold coins and loose gemstones, silver urns with gracefully sloping handles, strings of pearls larger than teeth, twinkling chalices, and jeweled goblets. Treasure beyond her wildest dreams was stacked in a heap at the center of the room: a mountain of wealth. There had to be millions of dollars of valuables in that stack. Her jaw dropped.

Duncan and Richard placed Gabriel on the pile and backed away.

"What are you doing? You can't just leave him there." She rushed forward, but they grabbed her arms and held her back.

"Wait for it. Trust me, you don't want to be too close," Richard said.

"What's happening to him?"

Gabriel's body started to seize, his back bowing over the treasure. His knees went rigid, then snapped, bending in the opposite direction. Talons sprouted from his knuckles and his toes. His jaw elongated and his skin... his skin tore and stretched until Raven had to look away. There was a series of popping sounds, a wet splat, and then a huff as if someone was operating a massive bellows.

Raven opened her eyes. The dragon before her was as dark as the man it had once been, with black scales that reflected emerald in the light. Its nose was covered in bony projections, its head dominated by two intimidating horns. The body was long and graceful, ending in a tail barbed with bone. On its back sprang two membranous wings, tiny scales sparkling like diamonds along their frame.

Raven had known Gabriel was a dragon, but until that moment she had never appreciated what that meant. He was gigantic and terrifying. His teeth were longer than her entire body. Everything about his presence was fierce, overwhelming, monstrous.

He craned his long neck and lowered his head, placing his chin on the floor in front of her.

"I think I'll leave you two alone," Richard said.

Duncan gave her a little bow before slipping out after him.

Trembling, Raven faced the beast that was holding intensely still before her. She took one step, then another. "Gabriel?" The creature's black eyes trained on her, red and brown flecks glistening in the light.

She reached out and stroked his nose and then his neck, giving him a scratch behind the ear. He wrapped a wing behind her back and nuzzled her. When he raised his head again, bright green caught her eye. His heart glowed through his chest, the same color as his emerald ring.

"Does this help you?" she asked.

He snorted and nudged her shoulder.

"This is where you go in the afternoons, isn't it?"

The massive head bobbed.

She placed her hands on either side of his snout and kissed his scales. "Rest. Get better."

He nudged her again. What did he want?

She smiled and looked into those giant black eyes. "I am yours, Gabriel, still. And you are mine. Rest. I will be in the library when you wake."

He pulled his reptilian lips back and then lifted his head. Like a marine mammal entering water, he slipped into the mountain of treasure and disappeared.

⁂

THE DRAGON OPENED ITS EYES, SAFE IN ITS MASS OF treasure. The vibrations from metal and stone that surrounded him were both soothing and healing to the beast, but it was time for him to leave his sanctuary. His mate was unguarded, somewhere out there in the world, and the desire to protect her was far stronger than his desire to remain safe. It was stronger than any yearning or fear, including the fear of death.

Gabriel burst from his hoard, naked and in the shape of a man again. He raised his hand. His ring was still dark at the center, but the sliver of green around the edge was larger than before. Not much time left. Two weeks until Mardi Gras. Two weeks to save Raven. He no longer had the luxury of believing he could save himself too.

He crossed to the bag Richard had left him and dressed in a freshly laundered suit. His phone was in the bottom, charged and tucked inside his shoe. Cradling it in his palm, he sighed. He'd promised himself he would never do this, but he had no choice.

With a few taps, he dialed a number he hadn't used in a decade. It rang three times before a click signaled the call had been answered. "To what do I owe the pleasure, *brother*?"

Thirty minutes later, Gabriel sauntered into the library to find Raven asleep at the desk, next to a stack of grimoires almost as tall as she was. She'd changed her dress and was wearing sweats and a *Hamilton* T-shirt that was too big on her. Tiny, she looked tiny against the massive stretch of mahogany beneath her, utterly fragile. It was dark outside again. Late. He must have slept all day.

"She's been here since early morning," Richard said from behind him.

Gabriel brought his finger to his lips and gestured for Richard to join him in the hall.

"Let her sleep for a few more minutes," he said.

"She said she, uh, drained you." Richard tugged at one of his ears.

"She's mine," Gabriel said, and even he could hear the smile in his voice.

"Is that some kind of kinky dragon thing?"

Gabriel raised an eyebrow. "It means we are mated. Together. Bound physically and spiritually. She gave herself to me."

"Oh." Richard scratched his jaw. "Because it almost seemed like she came close to killing you."

Gabriel pointed a knuckle at him. "She absorbs magic. I should have anticipated that. It wasn't her fault."

"Still, maybe you two should, you know, take precautions in the future. Like, um, avoid having her absorb your energy until we fix this thing with your ring."

"What are you saying?"

"It's just, you know, the look in your eyes is something I haven't seen before. I know you want to be with her again, but that would be dangerous. You were out of commission for two days."

"Two—" Gabriel looked at his phone again. Richard was right. He thought he'd slept twelve hours. It had been thirty-six. "Fuck."

"Exactly what I think you should avoid for now."

He sighed. "I'll find a way to fix this."

"There's something else."

"Why do I have a feeling I'm not going to like it?"

Richard pulled out his phone and tapped the screen. A YouTube video played. Raven, dressed in the blue dress he'd bought her, flew across the highway and slammed into the curb. She slapped the cement like a rag doll, and for a moment Gabriel couldn't breathe. That fall would have snapped the bones of any human. But then he remembered she was uninjured in the next room. Sure enough, she sat up in the street, her blue dress shredded but not a single drop of blood or an abrasion on her.

"Thank the Mountain my power protected her."

Richard rubbed his forehead. "You might want to ask the Mountain for a few more favors Gabriel, because the internet is lighting up over this. It's already been shared 1.5 million times. Everyone is out looking for the real Wonder Woman."

"Has anyone recognized her?"

"Not yet. Luckily the angle was bad and the recording is shaky."

"Let's hope that luck holds out. None of us needs the type of scrutiny this would bring upon her."

"That's what you're concerned about? Not that Raven is newly immortal and you're running on fumes?"

Gabriel swatted the idea away. "I'm relieved she was able to protect herself."

"Okay," Richard drawled. "That's all I have for you. The mail's on your desk, and Agnes is closing up shop. Good luck with the—" He made his hands dance around each other. "Oh hell, just good luck. Remember, you are playing with all our lives."

He turned on his heel and jogged down the stairs toward the back entrance.

"He's right, you know."

Gabriel whirled to find Raven standing beside him.

"We can never do that again. I almost killed you."

Forcing a confident smile, he said. "Never say never. I'm not ready for that to be our last night together."

She smoothed her black curls behind her ears. "I'm not ready to watch you die again."

"I wasn't dead." He moved closer to her.

"I could barely feel your heartbeat."

"I have an idea, Raven."

"I'd love to hear it. I've been combing through that

229

library for two days straight and have yet to come up with a single lead."

"That's because there isn't a single book in that room that contains any information on how my ring was made. There's only one place where that magic exists."

"Paragon," Raven said.

"Paragon. Unless Brynhoff has moved it, there is a copy of my mother's book of magic in the palace library. If I take you to Paragon and get you to her book, you can absorb her magic. You won't have to break the curse. You can make me an entirely new ring."

"I thought you said you couldn't go back there. You said there's a price on your head."

"Yes, but Paragon has a masked festival this time of year. It's similar to Mardi Gras actually, but exists to celebrate the Goddess of the Mountain. In a few days, everyone will be wearing masks. We can slip in and get you to the book."

She contemplated the idea. "But if you need a ring to stay here, won't I need one to go there? Won't the atmosphere kill me?"

"I was worried about that at first. I would never have thought to do this if it wasn't for last night. I mean, two nights ago. You absorbed dragon magic from me and it made you stronger. Paragon is made of dragon magic. I do not think you are in any danger, although if you start experiencing any symptoms, we will leave immediately."

"You want me to go to Paragon." She placed a fist on her hip. "Where we will be in danger of being murdered if anyone figures out who you are."

"Yes."

She shook her head and laughed, her eyes twinkling. "When do we leave?"

CHAPTER TWENTY-ONE

Raven had never been so relieved. Gabriel was back to normal, as normal as a man who turned into a dragon could be. Considering she'd been afraid she'd killed him—death by sex—it was a weight off her shoulders to have him back to his old self. Only, the clock was still ticking. Crimson's curse was still eating its way through Gabriel's magic, and Mardi Gras was now less than two weeks away.

She prayed that Paragon would provide the answers they needed.

She stumbled through the door to her apartment above the Three Sisters and came up short. Both her mother and Avery were waiting at the kitchen table. The looks they gave her were so sharp they hurt.

"It's late," her mother pointed out.

"Again," Avery said.

"On a Sunday night." Her mother sipped from the glass of sweet tea in front of her and looked at Raven out of the corner of her eye.

Raven scowled. "You don't have to wait up for me." The shifting and head rubbing that ensued told her that was nowhere near what was going on. "Has something happened?"

"We know you're sleeping with your boss, and we are very concerned," Avery said. "We're here to talk some sense into you."

"First of all, none of your business." The red tide of anger swirling in Raven made her ears hot. "Second, yes, Gabriel and I are a couple. I'm an adult; he's an adult. Why in the world would you have a problem with him? A couple of weeks ago you were telling me he was New Orleans's most eligible bachelor."

Avery reached over the table and grabbed something off the chair next to her. She held up the torn blue dress. "What kind of sick shit is he into? Did he hurt you?"

Raven laughed. "Oh my god, seriously? No. Gabriel did not do that. He would never hurt me."

"Then what happened to it?" her mother asked, still unconvinced.

Raven crossed into the kitchen and started pouring herself a glass of water while she thought of a suitable lie. "It was run over by a car. I dropped it in the street while it was still in the bag. He bought the dress for me. I felt bad about it." She raised her shoulders to her ears and sighed. "Gabriel and I are getting serious. In fact, I might be staying overnight there on a more regular basis."

The two looked at each other, her mother wringing her hands atop the table.

"Oh, come on! I am twenty-three years old. I've been sick the majority of my adult life. And now I have someone I love, who loves me in return, and you guys are going to give me a hard time about it?"

"You're in love? Really?" Avery's voice was soft now, warm. Her eyes twinkled.

Although the words had tumbled from her lips before she realized what she was saying, Raven's mind turned them over and over. In some ways, it seemed like the bond between her and Gabriel was stronger than love. But it was important to say these things. It was important to know these things. And she was in love. Truly.

"Well, Raven? Are you in love, really in love? Not just saying that?"

"Yes. I'm in love," she replied, absolutely sure. "And honestly I feel like this is the one. My last and final love. The man I'll spend the rest of my life with."

That made her mother smile and Avery right along with her. Her mother rose from the table and pulled her into a hug. "Then I guess our work here is done."

◈

SHE HAD TO FORCE HERSELF TO SLEEP. RAVEN HAD THE strongest desire to go back to Blakemore's and climb into bed beside Gabriel. Unfortunately, that was a bad idea for a number of reasons. First, she wasn't sure how her power worked. Could she drain him in his sleep simply by touching him? Second, she needed her rest. She couldn't learn to control her power if she was falling asleep at her desk. She needed to be sharp.

In the morning though, she dressed in record time and treated herself to the breakfast her mother had whipped up before she left for work: scrambled eggs with spinach, onion and mushroom, bacon, and fresh fruit. Raven couldn't remember the last time she'd been this hungry, but then she hadn't eaten much since she drained Gabriel. She'd been too concerned for his welfare to eat. She made up for it now, stuffing herself.

"My god, where are you putting it all?" Avery asked, when she saw what little was left in the pan. Raven had eaten enough for three people. "Are you storing it in baggies for later?"

"I was hungry," Raven said, then added the excuse her father used to use when they gorged themselves at the table as kids. "Growing girl."

"That's the truth," Avery said. "I've never seen anyone's hair grow so fast. It's down to your shoulders already."

Raven crossed the kitchen to check out her reflection in the hall mirror. Using her fingers, she combed her hair into a ponytail and fastened it with an elastic. Silky and strong. She knew the new growth wasn't natural, but the last thing she wanted to do was cut it.

"I think it's just the curl straightening," she said. "It was tighter before, but the weight of the length is making it appear longer than it is."

"What?" Avery asked.

Raven chuckled. "Hair can only grow so fast, Avery. What other explanation could there be?" Digging in her closet, Raven found a backpack and put in a few outfits. She wasn't sure when they were going to Paragon, but she decided it was better to be ready than to end up somewhere without underwear again.

The ding of her phone told her Duncan was waiting downstairs. "My ride's here. See you later." She kissed her sister on the cheek and headed for the door.

"Wait, Raven!" She turned around to find Avery holding a fancy envelope. "This came for you yesterday. I forgot to give it to you last night."

"Thanks."

"You know what that is, don't you?"

She shrugged. "Wedding invitation?"

Avery laughed and shook her head. "Look at the seal."

Raven turned it over. "Krewe Prometheus."

Prometheus was one of the newer krewes, the New Orleans term for an organization that sponsored a parade or ball during the carnival season, newer than Bacchus, Rex, or even Orpheus. She didn't know much about them. She smiled. There was only one person who could be responsible for this invitation: Gabriel. He was the only one she knew who was rich and important enough to be invited to something like this.

Raven carefully opened the square envelope and slid an expertly folded piece of card stock from the interior. It fanned out into a lacy, three-paneled die-cut work of art. Raven cleared her throat and read, "Krewe Prometheus commands your presence at a masquerade ball at the Emperor's Palace on Saturday, February tenth."

Raven's eyebrows shot up and her chin dropped as she looked back at Avery. Being invited to a krewe ball was a huge deal. None of them had ever scored an invitation before.

Avery cracked a slow, lopsided grin. "Looks like you're going to the ball, Cinderella!"

RAVEN RACED INTO BLAKEMORE'S AND HEADED straight toward Gabriel's office. The entire ride over she could think of only two things: telling him she loved him again and asking him about Krewe Prometheus. But when she rounded the corner and barged through the heavy wooden door, Gabriel wasn't there. Someone else was, leaning up against the antique desk. A blond man, tall and narrow, with eyes a blue that reminded her of deep water.

He flashed a smile that could send any red-blooded woman to her knees. Under the shiny, refined exterior, the smoky scent of dragon seeped from the man and coated the back of Raven's throat. The smell was similar to Gabriel's scent but different. Almost cloying.

She covered her nose with the back of her hand. "Have you seen Gabriel?"

"You must be Ravenna," he said.

She knew one thing for sure: he wasn't from New Orleans. His accent was Midwestern with a hint of that same exotic quality Gabriel's had.

"How do you know who I am?"

"Aside from the fact that you are covering your nose because as a mated female, my scent is repulsive to you, my brother cannot stop talking about you. I could probably mold you from clay after our conversation this morning."

"You're Gabriel's brother?" Only then did she notice the ring on his finger, a sapphire roughly the size of Louisiana. His was square-cut and sunk into a thick platinum band that made the stone unapologetically masculine.

He bowed formally and extended his hand. "Tobias. It's a pleasure to meet you."

She raised her hand to shake his but was met with a growl that rattled her bones. Before she came close to touching Tobias, she was swept off her feet and placed behind Gabriel, who crouched and bared his teeth. She'd never seen him like this. Even in the form of a dragon, he hadn't looked this deadly.

"You invited me here, Gabriel. Remember?" Tobias raised his long, tapered fingers defensively. A vigorous laugh rumbled from his chest. "I was simply introducing myself in the human fashion. I will not touch her without your permission."

Raven stroked her hand over Gabriel's back. "It's good to see you," she whispered. It was more than good. She felt a physical lightness in his presence, and for a split second, they were the only two people in the world. Gabriel turned to her, and she smiled from the deepest part of herself. When his face softened, she kissed him squarely on the lips.

Tobias cleared his throat. "Now that we've cleared that up, should we talk about why I'm here? I didn't leave my patients in Chicago to watch you two smooch. What's the emergency?"

Gabriel motioned for his brother to take a seat in one of the two chairs in front of the desk. "Tobias is a pediatric heart surgeon at Northwestern in Chicago. We lost touch in the beginning. All of us did, before the age of cell phones. But Tobias and I reunited a few decades ago."

"Reunited is a stretch. We bumped into each other at a Sotheby's auction when we were both bidding on the same Kerry James Marshall painting."

Gabriel sighed. "The one that got away." He dragged the second guest chair to his side of the desk before Raven could sit in it.

"What are you doing?" she asked.

Tobias chuckled. "Mated male dragon. He doesn't want you to sit next to me. He's afraid our pinkies might bump."

Gabriel growled. Raven squeezed his hand. "It's okay. I'll sit with you. I'm right here."

Tobias rolled his eyes.

"Seriously, what is this all about?"

"I'm dying, Tobias." The room grew quiet enough that Raven could hear herself breathe. "A local witch cursed my ring. If I don't break the curse, I will run out of protective magic by Mardi Gras."

"Fucking witches. Do you need me to help you deal with her?"

"Not exactly." Gabriel leaned back in his chair, his fingers still threaded with Raven's. "It is too dangerous for us to attack the witch herself. She's too powerful and too careful. But Raven is more than my mate. She can absorb magic."

Tobias's eyes locked onto her, and then he was out of his chair and across the room. "She's a witch. You mated a witch."

Gabriel flattened his lips into a straight line. "Yes. Although I'm not sure *witch* is the right word for what she can do. Sorceress, maybe."

"Under Paragonian law, I would be expected to kill both of you. This is an abomination."

"We're not in Paragon," Gabriel said. "And she is not the type of witch the law was written for. She is not from our world."

Tobias paced the office a few laps but eventually returned to his seat. "What do you want from me?"

"I believe that if Raven is given access to mother's grimoire, she can absorb her magic and replace my ring. Although the curse will not be broken, it won't matter. I'll have a new ring."

"But Mother's grimoire is in—"

"Paragon, yes."

Tobias laughed louder. "You must be joking. You want me to help you return to the world where our mad uncle wants us dead, to raid a heavily guarded palace and find our murdered mother's grimoire, all so that a witch, in a forbidden mated relationship with you, can steal our mother's magic and use it to make you a new ring?"

"Yes."

Tobias rose. "I'm sorry you are dying, Gabriel, but the curse has gone to your head. I cannot help you." He turned to leave.

"I would owe you," Raven blurted. He turned to look at her. "I can absorb any magic. There must be something you want that you can't do for yourself. Maybe I can help you in return."

The muscles in his jaw tensed. She'd struck a nerve. "Can you heal?"

She licked her lips. She wasn't sure. She'd never tried it before. "If you give me the spells, I am sure I can wield them."

Gabriel flattened his hand on the desk. "If it's healing you want, I have Maiara's amulet. I will lend it to you."

The look Tobias gave him might have cut through iron. "You recovered it?"

"I did."

Raven had no idea what they were talking about, but it didn't seem the time to ask.

Gabriel sensed her confusion and explained. "Maiara was an indigenous guide four of us befriended in the early days. She helped find a place for each of us to settle in what is now the United States. She left her amulet to our brother Alexander before she was taken and killed by a warring tribe. But when her people recovered her body, they took it from him and burned her with it. I recovered it from her ashes, but by that time Alexander had left our group and has never been found. I've had it ever since."

"You don't know where he is? Even now?" Raven asked.

Gabriel's eyebrows rose. "We don't know where five of our siblings are."

"Our mother ordered us to remain separate. We came here in 1698. All eight of us arrived in Crete. Mother left us a message to spread out across the globe. Four of us migrated north. We assume they are still in Europe somewhere. The other four came to the New World. But we lost track of Alexander. Only Gabriel, Rowan, and I keep in touch at all."

"Rowan?" She looked toward Gabriel.

"Our one and only sister."

"Oh."

Gabriel glared at Tobias. "The amulet for your help. I would do it myself, but with the curse as far along as it is, I'm not strong enough to hold open the portal."

Tobias leaned forward, cupping his face in his hands. "This is suicide."

"Just get us there, brother. I'll do the rest. You can stay safely outside the city. If something happens to us, you can flee."

The way Tobias rubbed his palms on his thighs, Raven thought he must be a dragon at war with himself. His fear was unsettling. Going to Paragon was a risk, she knew, but clearly it was even more dangerous than Gabriel had led her to believe.

"Tell me again why you can't go after the witch who did this to you? Have Raven absorb her magic and break the curse?" Tobias said through tight lips.

Raven frowned. "I tried that. The curse Crimson has placed on this ring isn't normal magic. It is the absence of magic. It's a black hole, a spreading nothingness. When I shook her hand, it was more of the same. She was hollow, for lack of a better word. I don't know how she's doing it, but I can't absorb it. It's just not there."

"So, what you are saying is I am your last resort."

"Yes," Gabriel agreed.

"Would you give me Raven in exchange?"

Raven's eyes widened. She felt Gabriel tense beside her, his magic gathering like a storm around him. If looks could kill, Tobias would be writhing on the floor. By the smug look on his face, Tobias knew exactly what he was doing. Raven glared at him.

"If I let you have Raven, there would be no reason for me to live. I'd let the curse have me."

Her blood ran cold. The admission broke her heart.

"What about you?" Tobias asked Raven. "If I asked you to leave him in order to save him, would you do it?"

Tears gathered in her eyes. "You're an asshole."

"Answer the question."

"Yes." The word came out like a croak. "It's more important that he lives."

Gabriel growled.

"Relax, brother. I apologize. My comment was in bad taste. It was a test to see if this mating was both real and mutual. All I want is the amulet and I will help you."

Beside her, Gabriel's muscles relaxed.

Raven wasn't satisfied. "Why would you question the mating bond? After the chair and Gabriel almost flying across the desk every time you look in my direction, I would think it was obvious."

"Obvious that he's bonded to you, not the other way around. Our compulsions don't work on witches. I needed to know you are invested." Tobias blinked.

"I'm invested," she snapped. She tucked herself into Gabriel's side. "When do we go?"

"I would recommend today," Tobias said. "Time in Paragon flows at a different pace than here. We will lose Earth days on this mission, if we are lucky enough to keep our heads attached to our shoulders. If we're going to do this, we get in, have you touch Mother's book of spells, and then get you out as quickly as possible."

"Sounds good to me," Raven said.

Tobias turned his attention on Gabriel. "She'll need something to wear and a bit of cosmetic enhancement to pass as a Paragonian."

"I packed a few outfits." She pointed at the bag. "What's the weather like there?"

Both dragons looked at her as if she was out of her mind. "Any clothing made here would stand out, I'm afraid." Gabriel's fingers tapped beside her, and she stopped them with her own. "I have one of Rowan's dresses in a trunk upstairs. She left it with me. She couldn't bear to look at it."

Tobias lowered his chin and gave Gabriel a hard look, but neither said a word.

"Enough talk, let's get on with it," Gabriel said.

Tobias adjusted the sapphire ring on his finger and rose from his chair, a wicked half smile twisting the corner of his mouth. "Would you like me to help Raven get dressed?"

Another feral growl escaped Gabriel's chest.

Tobias grinned at her and laughed under his breath. "It never gets old."

CHAPTER TWENTY-TWO

Every part of Gabriel's body was crawling with the need to shift. With his ring's power diminished, the beast was always at the surface, and it didn't help that Raven's beauty seemed to be growing exponentially by the minute. If Tobias kept looking at her, Gabriel was going to gouge his brother's eyes out with a spoon.

Some logical part of him recognized that this was his mating instinct kicking in. She had finally given herself to him. She was *his*. When a dragon came upon something of exceptional value, they guarded it with everything they had: mind, body, soul, and magic. He wouldn't hesitate to injure his own brother to protect her.

Fucking Tobias. This particular brother always did have the face of an angel. Human women flocked to the man, and unlike Gabriel, Tobias had developed a taste for the species. He'd had a few long-term relationships over the decades, although he admitted to Gabriel that he'd never revealed his true nature to anyone. He'd never trusted anyone enough. Yeah, if he looked at Raven again, Gabriel would punch him in the balls.

"How do I look?" Raven asked. She emerged from the bathroom dressed in his sister's gown. It was red, perfect for Pyre Night. Tight around the waist and flaring from the top of her hips to the floor, gauzy material covered her breasts and gathered at the base of her spine where it flowed like a train behind her. The dress was backless to allow for wings that his love didn't have. She carried the matching elbow-length gloves in her hand.

"You look stunning," he said. His tapping fingers and crawling insides stilled. With everything he was, he focused on her. "One more detail." He grabbed the box he'd fetched from storage and opened it. The red ruby inside was the color of blood and as big as his thumb. He removed it from the box and tied the gauzy strip of fabric it was attached to around her neck.

She touched it lightly with her fingers. "Thank you. It's lovely. And... big."

"It's from Paragon." How did he explain to her that jewels there were part of the landscape? He'd have to let her see for herself.

"I have a mask for you too, for Pyre Night."

"What's Pyre Night?"

"A celebration of renewal in honor of the Goddess of the Mountain. At the end of our Paragonian year, the citizens of Paragon remove old or worn things from their homes, things they don't want anymore, and burn them in the streets. They wear masks to hide their identities, lest someone see the sadness of releasing old things or be offended that they are purging themselves of a past gift or a shared remembrance. It's a popular holiday, similar to New Year's Eve here."

"It sounds exciting." Raven lifted the skirt of the red dress and watched it flutter out from her legs before settling around her feet. "I know what you and Tobias meant now about the difference in clothing. This material is as light as spiderwebs. It's like wearing a whisper."

He grinned at that. "It's called vilt. This material was woven from the nests of vilt worms that are about the size of your cattle. We raise them for this."

"Like silk."

"No. Not exactly. Silkworms in your realm are destroyed in the making of silk. Vilt worms are cherished. They spin the nest and the nest is used for the cloth, but the vilt worm lives on. They can live thirty years or more if cared for properly. It's one of our top industries."

"You talk about Paragon like you still consider it your home. After three hundred years of exile, you still used 'our.'"

Gabriel ruminated on the notion. "I suppose it will always be my home in a way. I know we are going back there for a specific purpose, Raven, but I can't pretend I am not excited to show you where I come from."

"I'm excited to see it." She took his hand. "You look very handsome, by the way, in your costume de rigueur. I love the sash. It's different from the human version but equally as sexy."

"You find me sexy?" He pulled her against him and kissed her, her red lipstick smearing beneath the pressure and intensity. She didn't complain or try to stop him. Her body melted into his, and the scent of her arousal was a brand upon his heart. He knew she could drain him within an inch of his life, and still he was ready to mount her. Death be damned.

"Are you two ready?" Tobias said from the door. "We are wasting daylight."

Gabriel pulled back, panting.

"Give me a minute to freshen up," Raven said, ducking into the bathroom.

Gabriel wiped his mouth, his fingers coming away red. He walked into the kitchen and wet a towel to clean up.

"Are you sure about this, Gabriel? You know it is dangerous, for all of us." Tobias leaned against the counter and crossed his arms.

"There's no other way."

"I'm concerned. You are newly mated. That makes you volatile. Whatever you do, no matter what happens, you cannot reveal yourself for who you are. That would be disastrous."

"I'm not an idiot, Tobias." Gabriel tossed the towel on the counter.

"No. You're a dragon with a permanent hard-on for his female."

"I'm ready," Raven said, emerging from the bathroom and looking as radiant as he'd ever seen her.

Tobias slipped on his mask, silver with gold flames that gave his face the qualities of a bird, elongating his nose and bringing out the burnished quality of his blond hair. Gabriel donned his as well, a classic black with gold details. Raven's was red leather, and when she tied it on, Gabriel's cock twitched at the thought of her wearing it while he was inside her.

Tobias's hand landed on his arm. "Ready, brother?"

"Ready."

They each hooked an arm through Raven's, Gabriel suppressing his aggression at Tobias's touching her. It was strictly necessary in this instance. Then Tobias raised his ring and drew a large sapphire circle in the air.

And the way was opened.

WHEN TOBIAS CIRCLED HIS RING, RAVEN SAW THE resulting magic as if someone had crossed two live wires. There was a crack, a rumble and hiss, followed by a blinding flash of blue. The room ripped down the middle as easily as tearing a sheet of paper. The edges curled, reality rolling in on itself. At last, everything around her changed.

The world had become a tropical jungle at twilight. It felt like New Orleans in August, hot and humid, like you could wear the air as a blanket. But she could breathe normally. The environment wasn't killing her. That was a good sign.

"Welcome to Paragon," Gabriel said. His smile was brighter than the sun—the two suns, now that she did a double take—currently setting on the horizon.

"Gabriel, your ring!" It was solid green again. Vibrant.

"I don't need its magic here. Not in the same way. Don't be fooled. The curse will return as soon as we do."

"This is where we part ways," Tobias said. "I will wait here for your return, as agreed. You have twenty-four hours. If you are not back by then, I'll assume you've been found and leave without you."

Gabriel nodded.

"Overflowing with brotherly love." Raven sneered, but Tobias didn't seem to notice.

Gabriel chuckled and pointed at the red, rocky mountain in the distance. Smoke bloomed from the top. The volcano was active. "The Obsidian Palace is built into the side of the mountain. We will have to journey through Hobble Glen to get there. It isn't far."

"It looks like the goddess isn't happy with the current

administration," Tobias said, thrusting his chin toward the mountain.

Gabriel's expression went flat. "The law is the law." He offered Raven his arm.

She slipped her hand inside the crook of his elbow, and they started down the path toward Hobble Glen. The village in the distance was different from any human town Raven had visited. At first she thought the rustic cottages looked almost medieval with their slate roofs and stone masonry. But as they neared, her higher elevation gave her a bird's-eye view. The cottages lined both sides of a network of streets that branched out in a circular pattern from what looked like a central square. She got the impression of standing on the outer edge of a pie.

The volcano rumbled ominously behind the backdrop of the quaint village.

"What did you mean when you said 'the law is the law'?" she asked.

"Do you remember me telling you that our traditions are based on a law handed down from the mountain goddess at the beginning of time?"

"I remember."

"According to our holy scrolls, no ruler may remain on the throne for more than two thousand years. Brynhoff broke that law when he murdered my brother and forced us into exile. The goddess is angry. That"—he pointed at the billowing smoke from the volcano—"is a warning. Tobias and I have never seen the volcano active. If it erupts, Paragon will be consumed."

Great, Raven thought. *One more thing that might kill us.*

They descended into the valley. She was thankful that Paragonian fashion called for soft leather slippers and not high heels. She would never have been able to navigate the terrain in human footwear. These shoes were made for comfort and for walking, as was the dress, it turned out. The material provided its own air-conditioning, billowing around her legs and causing a faint breeze to caress her body under its folds. That was necessary in the heat. It had to be ninety degrees.

Gabriel tried to teach her about the plants and fauna lining the trail, but she couldn't hold it all in her head. He claimed a yellow fruit they came across tasted like oysters and pointed out a small rodent with four sets of ears. There were green plants with tiny spiky leaves Gabriel said were used as weapons and others whose foliage could be used as an umbrella. Everything, including the flowers, was new, if not outright bizarre—both fascinating and overwhelming.

Things only got stranger when they broke from the jungle and Raven saw the village of Hobble Glen up close. Truly, it was something out of a fairy tale. Each of the stone cottages was decorated with gemstone walkways and ornate doorways that made use of wood, stone, and metal. Electric lights were strung over the street, and a fountain bubbled at the center of the square in the distance. A motorized vehicle that looked more like a horseless carriage than a modern car zipped along the road behind them.

Gabriel pointed to one of the cottages. "The front doors are important. Paragonian families use them as a sort of crest. When there is a marriage, an element of each family's door is incorporated into the door of the newlywed couple. The patterns become extremely complex over time. No two are the same."

"The craftsmanship is incredible. And the jewels! They must cost a fortune."

"The craftsmanship isn't cheap, but gems are ubiquitous here. You can purchase a raw sapphire for the same amount as a gallon of milk in your world."

Raven's mouth gaped. "Truly?"

Gabriel kicked the dirt. "There are rubies here."

Raven gawked at the twinkling spots of red in the dirt. She cursed. "And all this time, I thought this gem hanging around my neck was priceless."

He chuckled. "Oh, it is. Not because it's a ruby, but because it is enchanted with an illusion charm. It provided my sister with unparalleled beauty. It is making you appear Paragonian."

"What does that mean? You look the same."

He turned around and ran a hand up the nape of his neck. Three V-shaped ridges rose along the top of his spine. He turned back to face her and removed his mask, pointing at his right eye. There was now a pattern of darkened skin curving in a double crescent near his temple.

"You hide them?"

"On Earth, yes. Although to be fair, your kind frequently alters their appearance in strange and unusual ways. I doubt I'd get a second look in this form."

"And because of this, I have them too?" She touched the stone.

He smiled. "Yes. It will also allow you to understand our language. Thankfully, my sister added that particular enchantment so that she could eavesdrop on the elves at Marius's coronation."

Raven desperately wished she had a mirror to see what the markings looked like on her face. They strolled closer to the central fountain in the circular city. As Gabriel had mentioned, Pyre Night was well underway. Fires burned in the streets, surrounded by revelers. Gabriel greeted people as they passed, smiling beneath his mask. Raven did the same.

"What do people usually burn?"

Gabriel placed his hand on her back, taking advantage of the dress's low back to run his thumb along her spine. "Old clothing. Expired food. Broken things. Sometimes pets."

"Pets?"

"Ones who have died recently. It's a way to send their souls back to the Mountain."

"And the mountain is like a god?"

"The Mountain is our goddess. She is the mother of all dragons. We come from the stone. That's why each of my brothers and I have a ring like this that houses our power. This is where we come from and where we go if we are killed."

"This isn't what I expected." Raven shook her head as they entered the throng.

"Oh?"

"I thought everyone would, um, be like you were in your special room." She didn't want to come out and say "shifted" or "dragon" in case someone was listening.

He smiled. "Actually, this is the form we live our lives in," he whispered. "Our other form is for extreme circumstances: battle, some kinds of magic, breeding."

Her eyebrows shot up at the word *breeding*. Did that mean Gabriel couldn't have children except with another dragon? She was distracted by the thought when she noticed men looking at her. A lot of men. She tugged at Gabriel's arm. "I think there's something wrong with my illusion."

He laughed. "Females are rare here, and you are as

beautiful as they come." He pulled her to his side. "Would you like to try tribiscal wine?"

"There's wine?"

"The best in the five kingdoms. Come, let me get you a taste." He stopped at a cottage with a sign that read THE SILVER SUNSET INN. The place was charming, bustling with people sitting at long wooden tables covered in candles. Gabriel bellied up to the bar and drew out a purse full of coins from his pocket. Gold coins. He held up two fingers to the bartender, and they exchanged a few words. Gabriel paid and the man slid two frosty beer glasses across the bar, filled with a dark purple beverage.

"Try this," he said, handing her one.

She tentatively took a sip. "Delicious. It tastes like sunlight."

"The tribiscal fruit only grows at the top of the mountain, closest to the sun."

She drank a little more. "Mmm."

Gabriel moved in close. "Will you excuse me for a moment? I'd like to ask a few questions of the people here. I haven't been to Paragon in three hundred years, and it might be wise for me to know more about what we're walking into."

She nodded. "Good idea." She watched him navigate the tables and sit down beside a heavyset male.

"Are you here alone, my dove?" a male asked from beside her. He was too close, his eyes fixated on her as if she were something to eat.

"No," she said, smoothing the hair over her ear. "Excuse me." She stepped away from the bar, looking for Gabriel. He was engaged in a heated conversation. Another set of eyes caught hers, and a third male started for her from across the bar. Damn. She felt like a sausage thrown into a dog kennel. She sipped her drink and turned on her heel, slipping out the door and into the street where she hoped to blend into the crowd until Gabriel was finished.

The fires were raging now. To her right, a man in a mask threw a box onto one of the large pyres that burned every few yards down this stretch of street. He was laughing hard enough that tears streamed out the bottom of his mask. His buddy kicked the box deeper into the flames and handed him a drink. Everyone was purging their belongings, laughing or crying as the blaze consumed their offerings.

Her head swam a little from the wine and she slowed down. It wouldn't do to be drunk when she was trying to absorb the queen's magic.

The door to the bar opened behind her and one of the men stumbled out, raising a finger. "Miss, a moment of your time."

She pretended not to hear him and crossed the street, looking for someplace to hide until Gabriel was done. She glanced up to find a cauldron-shaped sign hanging above her head. She swaggered to the entrance. The sign had no name written on it, but wasn't the cauldron a universal sign for magic? As she neared the door, she thought it must be. An enchanting odor called to her as strongly as Cinnabons across a crowded mall. It smelled of metal and lavender and coated the back of her throat like a milkshake. This was where she needed to be.

She took another sip of wine and entered. Once inside, she spun around and looked back toward the Silver Sunset. The man was still standing outside the door. He hadn't followed. Good.

Shifting back and forth on her feet, she blinked rapidly in the dim light. The place was crowded with statues, amulets, dried plants and fruits. Symbols lined the walls, and a fire burned under a cauldron at the center of the room. It was the cauldron that was emitting the wonderful smell. She staggered toward it and inhaled deeply.

"You shouldn't be here," a low, undeniably female voice said.

Raven roamed deeper into the shop. "Hello?"

"It is considered bad luck for a female to be in my shop. They say if you stay too long, the magic will render you barren."

"What happens to the men?" Raven asked. A hiccup parted her lips, and she laughed aloud.

Shifting skirts came from her left, and then a figure broke from shadow into light. The figure was humanoid but not human. Not dragon either. Her exposed skin was dark purple and scarred in a pattern of swirls that Raven found only half as intriguing as the gossamer wings that protruded from her back. The wings were the same pearlescent silver as her eyes. With a sharp nose and a shock of silver hair, the female looked beautiful but dangerous, like a poisonous spider or a venomous reptile.

"You should not be here."

"You said that. But just so you know, I'm already barren. Chemotherapy fried all my eggs." She hiccupped again and swayed on her feet. Okay, she was definitely drunk. What was in this stuff?

The purple female's eyes narrowed. "Why are you here?"

"Honestly, I smelled what you were cooking and wanted to find out what it was. Whatever you're brewing smells delishhhhhious."

In a flash, Raven's back was shoved against the shelves. A silver dagger pressed into the base of her throat. She dropped her glass and it shattered on the stone floor.

"Why are you here, witch?"

"What?"

"You want to know what's in the pot? Twinkle root. My very own fairy-made witch-detection system. Dragons can't smell twinkle root, but witches can. Witches find it irresistible."

"I don't know what you're talking about."

"Oh, I think you do. There's a price on your head, witch, and I'm going to cash in. Abacus!" A silver birdlike creature flitted to her side. "Take a message to the Mountain. I have the one who was foretold."

The silver creature darted through a small opening near the window. Raven tried to sidestep the fairy and was met with a strong arm and a blade digging into her flesh. Her head was throbbing now, the inebriation from a moment before wearing off. She groaned.

"You drank the tribiscal wine, didn't you? Stupid mistake. It's highly intoxicating to your kind. No wonder you revealed yourself."

Where was Gabriel? She had to get out of here and find him. The dagger pressed harder into her throat. "Do not move. I will not let you destroy Paragon."

"Why would I want to destroy Paragon?"

She bared her pointed teeth. "Remain silent."

Raven could bear no more. She was beginning to worry about Gabriel. Reaching up, she grabbed the fairy's wrist and focused on the female. This was a magic creature, and Raven absorbed magic.

The fairy gasped, then tried to jerk her arm away. Although the knife receded from Raven's throat, she did not release the fairy witch. She guzzled her magic like it was Kool-Aid. The winged creature paled while her own skin began to take on a purple hue. That's when she let go. It wouldn't do to have to walk Hobble Glen the color of a grape.

The fairy crumpled, holding her throat.

"I'm sorry," Raven said, genuinely empathetic for the creature now sinking her cheek into the floor. "You left me no choice."

"You... no... ordinary... witch." The fairy's labored breathing made her words sound strained.

"No. I'm not." Raven had turned to leave when the door burst open and three men barged in wearing matching red-and-black uniforms. Two seized her arms. The third was a man as big and dark as Gabriel. He approached her carrying a silver rod.

"What's that?" she asked, meeting his black eyes.

He thrust it against her bare shoulder. Light flashed and everything went dark.

CHAPTER TWENTY-THREE

G abriel cursed under his breath. That absolute torment of a woman was going to get herself killed! He watched Scoria, the captain of the Obsidian Guard, bind Raven's wrists behind her and then flop her onto the back of his mountain horse as if she were a sack of grain. The beast, which was the size of an earthly equine but far better on rocky terrain, tossed its head back at the abrupt weight of her body slapping its shoulders. Raven couldn't be comfortable, but she did not struggle.

Unconscious, he thought. Two officers Gabriel did not recognize mounted the steeds behind her, and all three galloped toward the mountain.

Making himself invisible, Gabriel took to the sky, his wings a faster mode of transport than his feet. There were wards around the palace. He'd have to be close to the guards to sneak through undetected. He still wasn't sure how he would pull it off. He cursed Raven again. Of all the foolish things to do. Scoria was Brynhoff's right-hand man. He wouldn't be easy to overcome.

The horses scaled the rocky terrain on cloven hooves.

Even by air, Gabriel had a hard time keeping up. Up ahead, he saw the air shimmer and poured his last ounce of energy into his flight. He dove, swooping in next to Raven, turning sideways to bring his body as close as possible to Scoria's horse. He was so close his wings brushed the man's cheek, and Gabriel held his breath when the captain's gloved hand swatted at the air as if chasing a fly.

Magic buzzed against Gabriel's skin as they passed through the barrier, and then the world opened up again. The palace stretched before them in all its splendor, its expansive veranda welcoming them, glistening with polished obsidian and the shimmer of gold and jewels. The entire floor was a mosaic of emeralds, rubies, sapphires and amethysts as well as other precious stones pieced together to depict a dragon curled around a fruit tree.

The sight of that family crest made Gabriel's chest hurt. Once upon a time, this had been his home. As a child, he'd played on this floor.

He hated his uncle then. Hated him with everything he was. For three hundred years he'd convinced himself that he never wanted to return to Paragon, that he could be happy remaining on Earth forever if he had to. Now he wondered if there wasn't a small part of him that wanted a crack at taking back the throne. Perhaps more than a small part of him wanted vengeance.

The guards dismounted and Scoria pulled Raven off the horse's shoulders. It was all Gabriel could do to keep from slitting the man's throat as he manhandled her toward the throne room. It made his skin crawl and his talons itch to see another man's hands on her. At least she was awake again. Her eyes roved as she wildly searched her surroundings.

He followed close behind the guards. The two enormous wooden doors that led to the throne room opened slowly, their ornate carvings dating back thousands of years. Those doors had been here since the dawn of Paragon, back when there was order and not a dictator. He slipped through behind the guards. At the front of the room on a dais, Brynhoff sat on one of two gilded thrones. The other was empty. Had he finally taken a mate?

"Your Highness, we have secured the witch whose coming the seer has foretold. We bring her to you. We apprehended her in Aborella's apothecary." Scoria thrust Raven forward, still gagged, still wearing her mask. Brynhoff leaned forward, sniffing and scowling at her.

"She smells of dragon. Are you sure she's a witch?"

Raven mumbled loudly through the gag.

"Let her speak," Brynhoff demanded. "I want to hear what she has to say."

No sooner had Scoria untied her gag than Gabriel's beloved launched into a tirade. "Of course I am a dragon. I am no witch! These men accosted me as I was trying to participate in Pyre Night. What is the meaning of this?"

Scoria placed his hand on the hilt of his sword, and it was all Gabriel could do to maintain his invisibility and his distance. If he got too close, Brynhoff might recognize his scent.

Brynhoff crossed one leg over the other. "What proof do you have this woman is a witch, Captain?"

"Aborella pointed her out herself. Said this woman drained her of her power."

Raven gasped in convincing outrage. "Me? Do I look like I could drain anyone of anything? Believe me, if I had the power of a witch, I wouldn't allow myself to be bound like this." She turned her shoulders to show the king how uncomfortably her wrists were tied.

"I don't recognize you. I thought I was aware of all females in my kingdom. What is your family line?"

"I am the youngest daughter of Roosevelt," she said, and Gabriel had to smile. Roosevelt was the name of the bartender at the Silver Sunset. She must have heard his name spoken at the bar. He was indeed the owner and drunk most of the time, but he did have children, legitimate and illegitimate. "I am Freya. I am rarely allowed out in public."

Scoria grumbled in protest. "She is lying."

But Gabriel could see the lie was working, in no small part because Brynhoff was likely taken with her beauty. His uncle leaned back in his chair, a flirtatious smile crossing his face.

"Relax, dear lady. There is one sure way to settle this. Show us your wings." Brynhoff circled his hand and scanned her lasciviously.

Gabriel ground his teeth.

"Excuse me?" Raven said, her voice cracking and breathless with what Gabriel suspected was real fear. "I am not the type of female who shows her wings to strangers."

Good girl, Gabriel thought. That was exactly what a female of his species would say.

"Do it, young one, or I will be forced to treat you as the witch they say you are."

Brynhoff, you fucking bastard, Gabriel thought. Raven swallowed so hard Gabriel could see her throat bob from across the room.

"Can you untie my hands at least? The positioning is uncomfortable."

Sweat dripped down her temple. She was working on something. Gabriel could feel it down the bond. In fact, there was so much magic coming off her, he was surprised his uncle couldn't smell it. Then again, Gabriel couldn't actually smell it either. Raven must be doing something to cloak her scent.

"Do it," Brynhoff commanded.

With a sneer, Scoria sliced through the ropes binding her wrists with his sword. She rubbed each one with her opposite hand, and then, as if by some miracle, two fleshy wings emerged from Raven's back. Gabriel had no idea how she was doing it. The necklace she wore might provide some assistance with making her appear more beautiful, but it could not make a viewer see wings that were not there. They looked convincing, although he noticed they seemed to hang limply from her back. He wondered if she could actually move them.

"Happy?" Raven said, succeeding in making her voice sound both humiliated and angry.

Brynhoff waved again. "Yes. Good. Put them away, dear."

The wings began to refold, then disappeared before they were even near collapsing into her back. Gabriel inhaled sharply, but it seemed the others in the room didn't notice the failed enchantment.

"Darling?" Brynhoff yelled toward the sanctuary behind the throne room. "Can you come here? We have a situation."

So his uncle *had* taken a consort. Gabriel wanted to vomit. To think a female of his species was supporting this murderer... this dictator! What kind of dragon would do such a thing? Unless he was forcing her? Gabriel ground his teeth, the hilt of his dagger hot and heavy in his hand.

There were footsteps, and then Gabriel nearly dropped to his knees. His mother, Eleanor, stepped onto the dais. She was very much alive and dressed in royal garb!

Gabriel's stomach clenched. How could this be true? He'd thought she was dead. If she was alive, why hadn't she sent for him and his siblings? All at once, his world stopped and spun in the opposite direction. His mother paused to kiss Brynhoff on the lips before crossing to the empty throne, her citrine ring glowing like a star.

❦

ALTHOUGH RAVEN HAD INSTANTLY DISLIKED KING Brynhoff, she had reason to do so. This was Gabriel's uncle, the man who had killed his oldest brother, Marius, rather than relinquish the throne. He was as smug and pretentious as Gabriel had described. His embroidered robes and crown of jewels made her physically nauseous. Still, the hate that flooded her when the royally garbed woman stepped to Brynhoff's side was both stronger and completely unfounded. Raven had never met this woman and could only assume she was Brynhoff's new consort, a replacement for Gabriel's mother whom he'd killed.

The woman had hair the color of a starless night and eyes that seemed to bore into her. She was lanky, and her above-average height gave her a noble grace that belied her otherwise harsh angular features. It was her scent that made the nape of Raven's neck prickle. An acrid stench like melted plastic that turned her stomach. Dark magic. She'd remember that stench always. Repulsed, Raven had to breathe through her mouth so she didn't vomit.

"I don't know you," the woman said to Raven. "Why have you come to Paragon?"

"I didn't come here. I live here." Raven lied slowly, steadily. The secret to a good lie was to trick one's mind into believing it was true, if just for a moment. Raven pictured herself working in the backroom of the Silver Sunset. "As I said before, I am Freya, the daughter of Roosevelt of the Silver Sunset. I was minding my own business when these three men accosted me and accused me of being a witch. I am no such thing, and I wish to be returned to my father."

"She has shown us her wings, Eleanor," Brynhoff said. "She is a dragon."

The one called Eleanor's eyes narrowed. "It is a sad story you tell me, girl, but you must understand, my most powerful seer, Aborella, foretold that a daughter of Circe would visit our realm this Pyre Night. She would come with thievery on her mind and death in her heart. We cannot take any chances with such a menace."

"Circe—" Raven said, keeping her voice neutral. "I am not a descendant of anyone named Circe."

"No. As a dragon, you wouldn't be. Do you know the story of Circe?"

"Not as well as I am sure you do, my queen," Raven said.

"Empress!" Eleanor snapped. "Do not insult me."

"My apologies, Empress." Raven bowed her head.

Her stomach clenched. It was obvious by the crown on her head that matched Brynhoff's that she was royalty, but if this woman was calling herself empress, that meant she and Brynhoff had taken on additional power since Gabriel left Paragon. How had the monarchy changed in three hundred years? She eyed the citrine ring on the queen's finger, so much like Gabriel's emerald.

"At the beginning of time, when dragons roamed only in their beastly forms, there existed a powerful goddess named Circe. Circe was skilled at witchcraft. Some would say she was the most powerful enchantress of all time. She lived on a magical island in a realm far, far away from

Paragon. She took a human as a lover and bore a son, but unbeknownst to her, the lover who warmed her bed belonged to another goddess. The other goddess threatened to kill the boy, and Circe desperately needed a way to protect her son."

Raven tried her best to control her reaction. Circe? From Greek mythology? This was Earthly folklore. She bit her tongue.

"Desperate, Circe beseeched the mother of all dragons, Balthyzika, to help defend her son. In return, Circe promised the dragon and all her descendants the ability to transform into what we are today. This pleased Balthyzika, as dragons were once treated as monsters and hunted for their magic. The dragon protected Circe's son, who lived a long, full life and bore many children. Circe followed through on her promise, giving dragons the ability to shift into our common form." Eleanor pressed her hand to her chest. "So you see, a descendant of Circe is the most dangerous witch of all. What Circe has given, a descendant can take away."

"But why would she?" Raven asked.

"Do not question me, girl."

"Freya," Raven said. "Please excuse my ignorance. There is little time for study working for my father."

"Yes, as you've pointed out, you've been quite sheltered," Eleanor drawled.

A silence fell across the throne room. Raven coupled her hands in front of her hips and shifted on her feet under Eleanor's weighty gaze. "Can I go now?"

The empress stood, her red-and-gold robes folding around her as she crossed her arms and descended from the dais. She approached until she was standing in front of Raven, less than an arm's length away. The empress inhaled deeply through her nose. Silently, Raven cursed. Eleanor was smelling her.

"Remove the mask. I want to look upon you so that next time I converse with Roosevelt, I can tell him how I met his lovely daughter Freya."

Raven raised her hands to untie the mask.

"I must tell you, Freya. That dress and mask remind me of one I've seen before, one I commissioned for my own daughter, in fact."

Raven stopped. "How is that possible?"

"I was just asking myself the same question. You see, I commissioned the gown you are wearing for my daughter, Rowan, to wear to my son's coronation over three hundred years ago. You never forget something like that. I was involved with every detail of its construction."

A chill crept up Raven's spine and made her scalp tingle. If Rowan was the empress's daughter, that would mean... "It couldn't be the same dress, Empress. It must be a coincidence."

"How do you know Rowan?"

"I don't!" Raven protested. It wasn't a lie. She'd never met Gabriel's sister. Still, her voice was shaking. She was starting to panic.

"Lies! How do you know my daughter?" the empress shouted.

"I. Don't."

All at once, the empress drew the sword from the dark guard's hand and swung it at Raven's neck. Raven had just enough time to gasp before an invisible force stopped the empress's arm. *Gabriel*, Raven thought. He must be invisible. She inhaled his unmistakable smoky scent.

The empress's eyes widened, her lips beginning to tremble with rage. "What is this? Scoria, kill her! Kill her now." Bereft of his sword, the guard reached for her with his bare hands.

A burnt plastic stench rolled off the empress, stronger than before. Magic. The empress was casting a spell. Calling on the same magic she'd used in Crimson's shop, Raven shot forward, grabbed the invisible mass that was Gabriel, and folded space around them. There was a moment of total darkness, the now-familiar dropping feeling, and then she was behind the empress, behind the thrones, and feeling like she might pass out from weakness.

The echoes of the empress's screams filled the room around her as Raven tumbled toward the floor.

CHAPTER TWENTY-FOUR

Gabriel caught Raven before her head slammed into the obsidian. He swept her into his arms and spread his wings. Unable to maintain his invisibility much longer, he sought out a place to hide, trying to remember the layout of the palace after so many centuries. As silently as possible, he flew into the back hall and raced for the library. Lucky for both of them, Scoria and the rest of the Obsidian Guard seemed to be concentrating their search at the front of the palace, likely assuming Raven would use her power to escape, not to move deeper into the interior.

The door to the library was open, and Gabriel carried Raven inside as quickly and quietly as possible. Things hadn't changed much, thankfully. The furniture had been reupholstered but was in all the same places. He navigated the maze of bookshelves and gently rested Raven on the chaise near the window.

"Wake up. Raven, please. Wake up." He brushed her cheek and checked over his shoulder. Thank the Mountain they were alone. He stood and paced. Something was wrong. Her breath was shallow and her skin was deathly white. She was ill, but why? Had she overused her abilities when she drained Aborella and then transported him to safety? Perhaps she needed to rest.

He left her to search for the grimoire. The multicolored spines of the ancient tomes that made up the royal library passed by in a blur as he worked his way up and down the aisles. In the end, he couldn't miss it. His mother's grimoire was at the center of the room on a pedestal, its misshapen leather cover showing its age. He approached it cautiously, only noticing when he was directly in front of it that a shimmer of magic protected the pages. This was no surprise. Eleanor had always kept the book warded to defend it against unauthorized reading. He rushed back to Raven.

"Raven," he whispered. He lifted her shoulders. "Wake up, darling. I've found the book. It's time for you to do what you came to do." She did not rouse.

He pressed his hand to her forehead. She was burning up, her breathing almost nonexistent. She needed a healer. He looked back at the book, then at her, and finally at his ring. He could try to steal the book or he could carry Raven. It would be impossible to leave with them both.

Gabriel closed his eyes. It was a death sentence to leave the book behind, but there was no other choice to make. Raven was far more important to him than his own life or any hope of extending it.

"I've got you, Raven."

Moving fast, he turned the crank to open the window above the chaise, just enough for him to squeeze through. He gathered her into his arms and climbed onto the sill. This wouldn't be easy. He hadn't used this much magic in centuries and was too tired to cloak them both in invisibility. The palace was heavily guarded. His only hope was to use the element of surprise.

He kicked off the sill and flew away from the castle, the library, and his best hope of breaking the curse, racing for Tobias with Raven in his arms. The shimmer of the protective ward surrounding the castle came into view and he dove as he had before, swooping down directly toward the guards who blocked his way. The black uniforms turned, aimed, and released their arrows. He twisted and tumbled through the air, crashing through the line. With Raven in his arms, he could not use his fists, so he fought with everything he had left. His legs, his wings, his head. He bit and tore at the cheek of a young guard who collapsed in a bloody spray.

At last he broke through the shimmering magic and took to the air again. Pain shot through his leg. He looked back to see an arrow piercing his flesh. With a curse, he flew faster until he saw the clearing in the jungle where they'd arrived. Thank the Mountain. Tobias was still waiting as promised. He threw Raven into his brother's arms as he made a rough landing. Good thing too. His leg gave out and he tumbled to a stop. Everything hurt.

"I see you've made friends," Tobias said, setting Raven down to tend to Gabriel's leg. He did not hesitate to break the arrow and pull each side from the wound. The pain was so intense Gabriel almost lost consciousness. It might have been better if he had. As it was, he experienced every moment of agony as Tobias rid him of the arrow and pressed a hand into the wound.

"We have to get her home. Now," Gabriel said. "She's sick. I think she's dying."

Tobias nodded. "Considering the circumstances, you'll let me touch her?"

"This is no time for jokes, Tobias. Get us out of here."

His brother scooped Raven up and tucked her against him with one arm. Gabriel grabbed his other. Tobias's sapphire circled and the night split, its sections curling away to expose pure light. In a heartbeat, they were back in his apartment above Blakemore's, Raven unconscious in Tobias's arms and Gabriel's leg gurgling blood. Tobias set Raven on the bed and then helped Gabriel move to her side.

"Maiara's healing amulet is in the box on my dresser. Bring it to me."

"Yes, I will allow you to borrow *my* amulet," Tobias said. A growl followed the statement. He found the amulet in the box and tossed it at Gabriel, who immediately tied it around Raven's neck.

"Really? You're bleeding out, brother," Tobias said.

"Aren't you a doctor?"

Tobias left the room and came back moments later with two towels and a bowl of warm water. He stuffed one on the underside of the wound and pressed the other on top. "Pressure. Don't let up. If you were human, you'd need a hell of a lot more. Let's hope you have enough magic left to heal yourself or Raven will have to help me plan your funeral."

"Don't be dramatic."

"By the looks of your ring, can I assume you didn't find the book?"

"Oh, I found it, but Raven was already unconscious. She's running a fever. I had to get her out of there."

"Did anyone see you?"

"No."

"So we went to Paragon for nothing?"

Gabriel winced as he pressed harder against his still bleeding wound. "There is something. Something I must tell you."

"That doesn't sound good."

"Raven was taken to the throne room to face Brynhoff. I was invisible, watching, waiting to save her."

"You idiot. He might have scented you."

Gabriel nodded slowly. "Mother was by his side."

"What?" Tobias paled. He stumbled back, catching himself on the dresser.

"She didn't die, Tobias. She is ruling by his side."

"No. This can't be true."

"She's calling herself empress. I watched her... kiss him."

Tobias coughed into his hand as if the thought made him sick. "Why?"

"Power. Plain and simple. I spoke to Riviera in the Silver Sunset before Raven was arrested. The council of elders has been disbanded."

Tobias growled.

"He didn't know it was me. I cloaked myself thoroughly, including my voice."

"What else did he say?"

"Only that the volcano is getting worse." Gabriel lowered his chin. "The Mountain is angry, Tobias. When I saw our mother..."

"Stop." Tobias held up a hand. "We're back. That's all that matters."

"For now," Gabriel said.

Tobias chuckled darkly. "Honestly Gabriel, I don't hear from you in over a decade and now this. Careful, brother. The next thing you know, we'll be sharing Christmas."

※

Once, when she was maybe six or seven, Raven had wanted to go horseback riding. They'd lived in rural Michigan then, two houses down from a woman who owned a mare and her colt. Raven scaled the fence and lured that young horse to her side with a piece of apple, straddling his back the same way she used to straddle tree branches. Her scraped knees hugged his bare back, her hands coiled in his mane. The horse took her for a ride, racing across the neighbor's meadow, leaping and bucking under her weight. Raven clung to him, flat against his back, until he tired himself out.

She was never thrown, but when she finally dismounted, every inch of her body ached, and bruises dappled the insides of her arms and legs. She felt like that now, like every muscle fiber, every bone, every cell of her body and inch of her skin had been stretched and beaten into submission. It was in this state of anguish that she became conscious, waking on the bed beside Gabriel, a moan emanating from someplace deep within her. Her head pounded and tears streamed from the corners of her eyes.

"Praise be," Gabriel said. Turning on his side, he caressed her face, her neck, her arms as if he were searching for a physical cause of her pain. "Does your head hurt?"

She couldn't fathom speaking above the internal pounding, but she gave him the smallest nod, careful not to rattle her brain any more than she had to. In response, he hooked his finger under a leather cord that was around her neck and removed the white amulet he'd used before on her, the one he'd said was for healing. As soon as it was off, the pain in her skull ebbed, but its elimination did nothing for the excruciating ache that lingered in the rest of her body.

"Everything hurts, Gabriel," she whispered. "What happened to me?"

"I don't know." Gabriel placed the amulet on his leg. Raven noticed his thigh was covered in blood.

"Your leg!"

"It's already healing."

"I have some ideas about what happened to you," Tobias said.

Raven turned her head to find him standing by the fireplace. A fire crackled in the grate. It was the first time she'd ever seen it used.

Gabriel cleared his throat. "I filled Tobias in on what we experienced in Paragon."

Tobias groaned. "Yes, I heard all about our dear murderous mother and her insatiable appetite for power. To think how she deceived us all. Such an elaborate scheme."

"Your mother? That *was* your mother." Raven couldn't fathom it.

"Yes. That was Eleanor, and she was not dead as we thought but ruling beside our brother's murderer," Gabriel said.

"It's too horrible." Raven couldn't wrap her head around it. "But she kissed your uncle? Isn't that her—"

"Brother?" Gabriel finished. "Yes. And in case you're wondering, that's not any more acceptable in Paragon than it is here."

The fire crackled.

"She betrayed you." Raven's heart hurt for them.

But Tobias seemed strangely unaffected by the news. He leaned against the mantel, one ankle crossing over the other. "The interesting thing about witches like you is how little most of you know about your own powers."

"Have you known many witches?" she asked.

"One or two over the years," he said. "I had a botany professor for a neighbor once who could not figure out why her early research was horribly skewed from her peers until she realized her very presence was making the plants grow." He chuckled softly.

"Tobias... the point?" Gabriel frowned.

"The point is that Raven is a new witch whose power is to absorb magic through touch, not only the magic of others but the magic produced by a written spell. We took her to a magical realm where she absorbed everything she touched, with no ability to stop the flow of it. She was drinking from a fire hose from the moment she set foot in Paragon. I believe it was the inflow of magic that almost killed her."

Raven held her head and tried to sit up. "I couldn't tell. I didn't feel it."

Tobias shrugged. "Magic can be insidious."

"Did we find the book?" Raven asked.

Tobias glowered at his brother.

"I found it," Gabriel said, "but I was not able to take it, and I needed to get you out of there."

Now her heart hurt as much as her muscles and bones. "You left it behind to save me?"

He kissed her temple. "We will find another way. It is far more important that you are safe."

Tobias cleared his throat. "While I admire the sweet sentiment, it was a terrible risk we took only to leave behind what we were after."

A heavy silence weighed down the room, and Raven's eyes drifted to the fire.

"I need a drink." Gabriel rose and limped around the bed.

"What happened to your leg?" Raven asked.

"Shot by an arrow. It's healing. Where's the bourbon?" He hobbled toward the kitchen.

She sighed heavily. "Pour me one," she called.

She heard two glasses hit the counter and then the gurgle of decanting liquor.

"Is it true?" Tobias asked softly, low enough that Gabriel could not hear.

"Is what true?"

"Are you a descendant of Circe?"

"How should I know? I mean, my god, she's a mythological figure from thousands of years ago. It would be like asking someone if they're related to Ogg the cave dweller." Raven glared at him. "Our family tree doesn't go back that far."

Tobias glowered at her.

Gabriel returned to the room and handed her the bourbon, still holding the healing amulet to his leg. "What's going on here, Tobias? I'll ask you not to stare at my mate like you mean to do her harm."

Tobias shifted his gaze to Gabriel and held out his hand. "We had an agreement. Has your leg stopped bleeding?"

Gabriel removed the amulet and dropped it into his palm.

"Goodbye, brother." Tobias gave a curt nod in Raven's direction before striding for the door.

CHAPTER TWENTY-FIVE

Once Tobias had left the room, Gabriel had a chance to truly examine what had happened. No amount of time apart would change his brother. He would always be the same dragon, both fiercely loyal and at the same time cynical. He could trust Tobias, but he already understood Tobias didn't completely trust him. Clearly he didn't approve of Raven, and his brother probably didn't believe what Gabriel had told him about Eleanor.

Raven rested her head against his chest. "I'm sorry I ruined everything today."

He stroked her hair. "It wasn't your fault. I should have foreseen your reaction to the environment."

"I shouldn't have gone inside Aborella's."

"Why did you?"

"She baited me. She was brewing something called twinkle root. Aborella told me it's irresistible to witches."

"There are other witches living in Paragon."

"Well, I was the only one in her shop." She sighed. "It was irresistible to me."

"My mother said that Aborella foretold your coming."

"Yes, Aborella told me the same thing before I drained her."

"You drained a fully grown fairy?"

"Until my skin turned purple and she was flat on the floor."

He laughed and kissed the top of her head.

"Are you impressed with my mad absorption skills?"

"Maybe I'm relieved it wasn't me this time."

Raven took a deep breath. "I'm so tired. I feel like I've run a marathon."

"Sleep. There's nothing more we can do today. There might be nothing else we can do at all."

"Don't say that."

"We are reaching the end of the rope, little witch. At some point, we need to hold on and enjoy what little time we have left."

Raven sat up, her jaw tightening. "I can't accept that. I won't. If it comes down to that, you have to give Crimson what she wants."

"You can't be serious. She wants my power, Raven. The power that you absorbed when you made love to me, she will draw from me using her brand of magic, only with the curse lifted, that power will be unlimited. She will become even more of a monster, indestructible. Once won't be enough for her. She won't stop until I am her slave."

"I know it's not ideal, but at least you would be here. We could deal with the consequences together. We've tried every other way but the most obvious. We need to negotiate with her."

Gabriel's fist hit the bed. "Do you know what Crimson is? The night I met her, I could smell her power across Bacchus. Don't believe for one second the lie she creates. She is no naive schoolgirl dabbling in rootwork and divination to make a few bucks off passing visitors. Crimson is a mambo. She's terribly dangerous."

"She's our only hope of breaking this curse!"

Gabriel looked her directly in the eye. "No."

Lips twisting, Raven rolled over and did her best to storm off the bed, but the skirt of Rowan's red dress tangled around her legs. She ended up sliding off with a little hop. "Where's my backpack? I need to get out of this thing."

"I saw it in the living room," Gabriel said.

Raven stormed into the next room to find her bag.

"You're clearly hurting, Raven. Lie down and rest." His fingers tapped against his thigh. Fuck. She'd been gone for less than a minute and he was already crawling with anxiety.

"Don't tell me what to do, Gabriel," she said, reentering the room. "I'm a big girl. I can take care of myself. It's my life too, you know. If I think there's a chance of saving you, I'm going to do it. I will not go gently into that good night." Dragging the backpack onto the bed in a way that looked painful and made Gabriel tap harder, she unzipped it and dug through the contents, pulling out yoga pants and an oversized T-shirt. An envelope slid out onto the bed beside her. She picked it up and twirled it between her fingers.

"What is that?" Gabriel asked.

"It's an invitation to a krewe ball next Saturday. I was going to invite you to be my guest, but now that you're acting surly, I'm not sure I want to attend with you, even if it would be our last hurrah."

Gabriel reached for it. "Which krewe?" he asked curiously.

"Krewe Prometheus." She looked confused. "I assumed you were behind this."

He shook his head. "New this year. I've never even met anyone in that krewe."

Tentatively, Gabriel reached out and took the invitation from her, sliding it out from its envelope. As soon as he did, the ink began to smear, twisting in rivulets, then spirals.

"What is it?" Raven asked. She read over his shoulder as the letters re-formed at the center of the card stock.

You've dallied too long.
Your fate is sealed.
Unless you agree
to strike a deal.
One last chance
or lose it all.
Bring your witch;
attend the ball.
No tricks or I will
pull the string,
unravel you and
everything.
Be wise, dear dragon
and consider my proffer
There will not be
another offer.
—Crimson

TIME MEANT DIFFERENT THINGS TO DIFFERENT people. When Raven had been ill, the days in the hospital had seemed endless. She would have done anything to shorten the torment of those long, stretched-out moments of pain. Now the days blinked by. Every moment was a grain of sand trickling down the hourglass to the day she'd have to face Crimson.

Gabriel was growing weaker. He spent more than half the day in his treasure room now. Although Raven would have liked to spend hers curled into his side, she refused to give up. She absorbed grimoire after grimoire. There was nothing in this library that would break the curse. She was sure now. Delphine hadn't been lying. Only Crimson could undo what had been done. But something here might help her defend herself or Gabriel against the mambo. She had to try.

"You look like you haven't slept in days," Gabriel said from the doorway.

Raven looked up from the sixteenth-century tome she was buried in. She folded herself into a wisp of smoke, blew through the room, and formed beside him. "I haven't."

"You've gotten better at that."

"I've been practicing. Tobias was right. I don't know much about my abilities. I've figured some things out. What I absorb doesn't last forever unless I practice with it."

"No?"

"The trick I did in Paragon, with the wings? I can't do it anymore. I absorbed that from Aborella. I could taste her magic in my mouth like a piece of rotting fruit when I made the illusion of those wings grow out of my back. But I can't do it anymore. It's gone."

"You need a mentor. Another witch could help you develop your abilities."

Her eyes roamed over the rows of dusty books. "If we don't find a way to stop Crimson, there will be nothing left to develop."

"I've been thinking about that, Raven. I have an idea." Gabriel strolled deeper into the room, sliding his hands into the pockets of his dress pants. He'd just woken up, but he already had dark circles under his eyes, and Raven didn't miss the way his left leg dragged with each step.

He braced himself on the window frame. "Actually, you gave it to me. I was thinking about the day you almost jumped out the window."

She peered at him through narrowed eyes. "I didn't know you then. I thought you were a psycho. I was just trying to survive."

"Exactly. That's the most important thing, isn't it? Survival?"

No, she thought. *Not anymore.* "What's the idea?"

He turned toward her, the light flowing in from behind his head, burying his face in shadow. "You actually suggested it the day you touched my ring, but I wasn't ready to consider it then. I will go back to Paragon. I will hide in one of the outer kingdoms, anywhere they won't recognize me. Maybe among the elves. It will keep me alive, which will keep the magic inside you, will keep Duncan, Agnes, and Richard alive as well."

Raven's blood turned to ice. While she'd once thought that was a good idea, it now weighed heavily on her heart. "But... I can't go with you. You saw what happened to me there."

"No. You'll stay here and you'll live your life. You don't have to worry about anything. I'll split my assets among you. You'll be a wealthy woman. Everything you've ever wanted will be at your fingertips. You can travel the world. You can go skydiving. Swim with sharks. Whatever makes you feel alive."

"Sharks? Oh God, Gabriel." Her hands were shaking. "I don't want any of that if I can't have it with you."

"It's the only way. You know I can't give her what she

wants. And both of us together aren't strong enough to stop her from taking it. I am a shadow of my former self."

"But if your mother and Brynhoff find you, they'll kill you."

"I will hide. The elves have been known to hide refugees."

She buried her face in her hands. She hated this. Hated everything about the fact that he was right. It was the only way. And someday, when she was powerful enough to control her magic, she could track down Tobias and force him to take her there again. This wasn't forever, but it would take the pressure off. And it would keep him from Crimson.

She nodded her head but couldn't bring herself to say a word. He strode over to her and took her face in his hands, kissing her softly. "I'll call my lawyer and have him finalize the paperwork to transfer my assets to you and the others. I'll have to ask Tobias for help again. I'm not strong enough to make it to Paragon on my own."

Pounding footsteps called their attention to the doorway where Richard appeared panting and out of breath.

"What is it?" Gabriel asked.

"Agnes didn't make it in this morning. I've been calling her all day, but she wasn't answering. I just got a text from her phone." His voice cracked.

"Well? Where is she?"

Richard raised a shaky hand and handed Gabriel his cell. Raven crowded behind him, peering over his arm at the screen. It was a photo of Agnes, bloody faced and sagging. Her pale, aged limbs were chained to a brick wall. Raven gasped and started to cry.

Gabriel read the message that came with the photo.

"Your presence is requested at Krewe Prometheus's masquerade ball. If you don't come, she goes."

Gabriel dropped the phone. Raven caught it and swept it into Richard's hands. She met Gabriel's eyes, her jaw tightening with her scowl. "It appears the choice has been made for us," she said. "We are going to the ball and we are facing Crimson."

CHAPTER TWENTY-SIX

"I can't believe this dress," Avery said. "You are an island goddess."

Raven stared at herself in the bedroom mirror, wishing she could be excited about what she saw. The dress was off the shoulder and floor-length with a slit that ran halfway up her thigh—sexy but sophisticated. But the real star of the show was the color. Gabriel's oreads had designed a layered gown in peacock and teal that ignited the blue fire in Raven's eyes. The bodice was adorned with beads that, knowing Gabriel, were actual precious gems, while the skirt was layered in strips to give it some fullness. It was a masterpiece and, along with the feathered blue mask, did make her look like the manifestation of an exotic island goddess. But she was too nervous about tonight to truly appreciate it.

Gabriel's ring was almost completely black. At a time when they desperately needed it, he harbored little to no power, and Raven was not up to the task of facing a three-hundred-year-old mambo on her own. Crimson had Agnes. If they failed tonight, they could lose everything. Gabriel would turn to stone, and all they had risked would be in vain. Their only hope was to do what Crimson asked them to and pray she would break the curse as promised.

"Why so glum, sis?" Avery smiled at her in the mirror. "You're going to have an amazing time." She added the last pin to secure the back of Raven's hair. It now hung a good inch below her shoulders. Avery had managed to make a gorgeous updo with the help of a hairpiece.

"I was just thinking about how I missed prom because I was sick. Not just mine—yours too. As your sister, it should have been me doing your hair. You've given too much of yourself to me, Avery. Thank you. I can never pay you back, but thank you."

Avery kissed her sister on the cheek. "You're not exactly a burden. So Mom did my hair. I knew you would have been there if you could. We're family. Family isn't always fifty-fifty. It's not supposed to be. When you love someone, you do what you have to do for them and you don't keep a tab."

A horn honked from the street below.

Raven placed her hand on her sister's. If she didn't survive tonight, there was something she needed Avery to know. "I love you, Avery. No matter what happens, I want you to know that I want every good thing for you. I see what you do for me. What you do for Mom. Don't be afraid to do things for yourself too. You deserve it."

Their eyes connected in the mirror. "Wow, you're deep tonight." Avery laughed. "Thank you though. Maybe... someday... I'll—"

The horn honked again from the street and Avery shook her head. "Your carriage awaits." She handed over the elbow-length white kidskin gloves that finished the ensemble.

"I have to go. Whatever you were going to say, do it.

And if you need money to do it, I'll help. Gabriel pays me ridiculously well." She pulled Avery into a tight hug.

Her sister looked absently toward the window. "Must be nice having a driver."

"Duncan is a sweetheart. He almost makes it bearable."

"Bearable? You don't like door-to-door service?"

Raven smiled. "You know, I prefer walking."

"Something tells me if this works out with Gabriel your lifestyle is going to change. Swimming pools, movie stars, baby."

Raven smiled at her sister and grabbed her small beaded purse from the bureau. "Thank you for helping me get ready."

"Wouldn't have it any other way."

They exchanged goodbyes, and Raven descended the stairs to the street where Duncan opened the back door of the car for her. When she slid in, Gabriel gave a long, low whistle. "Juniper and Hazel do nice work."

"They certainly do." Raven's eyes raked over his rugged features and broad shoulders. Gabriel was like a miracle, a seductive presence that made her feel alive every time they were together. His fingers tapped and she took his hand, putting them to rest.

"I'm not going to be able to keep my hands off you tonight," he said. He looked at their coupled fingers, but the words dripped with the promise of more.

"If you are talking about any more than this, it's too dangerous. I could kill you. You don't have any magic to lose." Even to Raven, her words sounded strained. The idea that she couldn't touch him until this curse was broken caused a heavy ache behind her sternum.

"I can't think of anywhere I'd rather die than in your arms," he said.

"Don't talk like that. I can't stand it."

He rubbed his chin. "I think that dress is missing something." He drew a box from the seat beside him. The oreads had provided her with a necklace, a teardrop pendant the same teal as the dress. She wondered what Gabriel had in store for her.

He opened the box. An emerald ring glinted up at her, the same shape as Gabriel's but slightly smaller.

"Oh Gabriel, it's lovely. It matches yours."

"And your dress."

"Put it on." She held out her hand.

"Wait, this ring comes with a question, and your answer determines how long you get to keep it."

"Keep it? I can't keep it. It must be worth tens of thousands of dollars."

"Raven, when I fed you my tooth, I was looking for an employee, someone I could compel to do my bidding and break this curse. What I got was so much more."

"I wish I could have been what you wanted. I wish I could have fixed what was broken for you."

"But you did. You fixed me. My heart."

Oh Gabriel. Her eyes stung.

"After watching my uncle kill Marius, I never thought I'd experience family again, or bond with someone in a way that was stronger than fear, stronger than death. All I wanted was an escape from the horrors I'd left behind in Paragon. I wanted to build an oasis here. I was happy alone. No one here could ever be like me, and there was no one I could trust who wasn't bound to me."

"After meeting your mother and uncle, I can understand why you'd feel that way."

"But then there was you. I tried to bind you, but you would not be bound. And that forced me to trust you. I had to trust you because I could not force you. You are here now because you want to be here, because you care for me. You were willing to die for me."

"I love you, Gabriel. You did more than heal me; you gave me a purpose and a reason to survive. I can't say I haven't been terrified these past few weeks. But when I was lying in my hospital bed, I begged God to either let me live or let me die. No more in between. No more half-life. I've never felt more alive than when I'm with you."

"Love is a human word. Dragons mate, they bond. I wasn't sure I understood the meaning of the word until now. I love you."

She shifted closer to him, wanting a kiss but too afraid of the consequences to actually touch him.

"You said you had a question."

"Should I put this on your finger for a night or put in on for a lifetime?"

"I don't understand. What are you asking me?"

"Marry me, Raven. Take this emerald as a symbol of my eternal affection for you. An engagement gift."

"You want to marry me?" All the oxygen had been sucked from the car, and suddenly the air was close and hot.

He raised an eyebrow. "It may be a short commitment, but it would mean everything to me to know that even for a moment, you were mine in this human way."

"I am yours. And you are mine. We don't need a piece of jewelry or a piece of paper for that."

"I want to marry you, Raven." He shook the box between them. "For the night or for forever?"

She held out her hand and answered directly from her heart. "Forever then."

The cold stone slid onto her finger. Unable to hold

herself back, she eased herself into his lap and wrapped her arms around his neck. "Tell me if you feel anything and I'll stop."

"I feel something," he mumbled into her lips. The kiss was deep, and he stroked his tongue along hers. He touched her knee and worked his hand up her inner thigh. She could feel him harden under her, and then she felt something else; a tingle danced across the surface of her skin.

With both hands, she pushed him away, panting. Gabriel's eyes were wide with fear and yearning. Raven wondered if hers were as well, a mirror of his own, or if there was more there: disappointment that she couldn't block it from happening, utter sadness that the last days they might ever have together would have to be spent at a distance.

As the car began to slow, Raven wiped a tear. Gabriel reached up and thumbed another from under her eye. "Don't cry. It doesn't matter, Raven. Being near you. Having your love. It's enough."

She ground her teeth. Hate was not a strong enough word for what she felt toward Crimson. "For now."

Duncan opened the door, and Raven slid across the seat to take his hand and allow him to help her from the car. Gabriel emerged behind her. He offered her his arm, and she hooked her gloved fingers above his elbow.

"Let's do this," he said into her ear.

They entered the masquerade ball together, knowing they were walking directly into the web of the enemy.

❦

THE STENCH THAT FILLED GABRIEL'S NOSE AS THEY stepped into the crowded ballroom was unmistakably Crimson. Under the scent of perfume and silk, of hairspray and feathers and nail polish and men's aftershave, he could smell the medicinal sewage that he'd come to associate with her and her magic. It turned his stomach.

"I smell her too," Raven said.

"I'm sure she knows we're here."

They entered a sea of ball gowns and masked faces. Above them, aerial acrobats performed for the crowd's entertainment. A woman dressed as a bird hung upside down from a hoop by her feet, reaching for them as they passed beneath her. Across the room, a man danced on a platform with a mammoth yellow boa constrictor wrapped around his body. Scantily dressed servers with trays of drinks and canapés balanced on their hands navigated the crowd.

"There. The black and red." Raven pointed.

Gabriel spotted Crimson, the devil in a red bustier and yards and yards of black lace. Horns protruded from either side of her mask, and the staff in her hand was topped with a realistic-looking skull.

"She's not subtle is she?" Raven moved closer to him.

"No."

Crimson crossed toward them, weaving through the other guests as a widening smile spread across her lips.

"You received my invitation," she said to Raven. "And as I suspected, Gabriel did too."

"Where's Agnes?" Gabriel asked.

"Safe. Although her accommodations are uncomfortable. They will become more so if you are disagreeable."

"What do you want from us?" A low growl rumbled in his chest.

"Straight to the formalities. I'd expect nothing less from

you, dragon." She walked between them, causing Raven to stagger back. "Follow me. It's time we talked."

Crimson led them deeper into the hotel, down the hall to an empty conference room. She flipped on the overhead lights. The taupe walls were jarringly bland compared to the colors of the ballroom they'd just come from.

"Tell us why we're here, Crimson." Gabriel tucked Raven into his side.

Crimson ran her fingers over the skull that topped her staff. "You're almost out of time, dragon. In less than seventy-two hours, the magic of your ring will be depleted and you will die, unless you take me to your bed."

"And I've told you no," he said. "The thought sickens me."

"Yes," she drawled. "You've made that blatantly clear." She paced around the conference table, her red nails dragging along the surface. "And while I could force you, I have discovered another option that is more palatable to me."

Raven shifted beside him. Her gaze darted between him and Crimson as if she might say something. He shook his head.

"What if all you had to do was make love to our lovely Raven here?"

Gabriel's brows dipped. "What are you saying?"

"If sex with me doesn't appeal to you, have sex with her. All I'm interested in is the outcome."

"The outcome."

Crimson faced him, spread her feet, and planted both hands on top of the skull of her staff. "I want your firstborn."

A ball of ice exploded next to Crimson's head. Gabriel turned to see Raven glowing like a star with snow falling around her, turning to hail. He noticed none of it landed on him.

"How dare you even suggest such a thing, you evil gargoyle of a woman?" Raven spat.

"Oh Ravenna, calm down. If you accept my offer and give me your firstborn, you'll have an eternity with your dragon to bear as many more of his brats as you wish. I only need one."

"Why?" Gabriel asked.

"You know why." Crimson began to pace again, licking her ruby lips as if she were hungry. "The child of a dragon and a demigoddess will possess almost unlimited power. Even a drop of blood from such an offspring could level mountains in the right hands."

Raven scoffed. "Demigoddess?"

"As a descendant of Circe, powerful indeed."

Gabriel's eyes widened.

"You didn't think I'd figure it out? The Three Sisters, the Tanglewood name. You are an old dragon, Gabriel. You must have noted the resemblance."

"What's she talking about?"

"He knew you might be a descendant of Circe when he fed you his tooth, dear. You were a long shot, of course. Except you look just like the Circe we both knew. She was the granddaughter of the goddess herself and an accomplished sorceress. Ask Gabriel. He knew her, three hundred years ago, when they burned her at the stake."

"What?" Raven looked at him in confusion.

"It's true that I knew a demigoddess named Circe and I was there when she burned. But she's lying about the rest. I did not know you were a descendant."

"Oh Gabriel, how could you not? Look at her. Those eyes. Do you know what I think? I think you bound her, you seduced her, you mated her, all for the chance that if she could not save you, a child might." Crimson flashed a smile nothing short of evil.

"Why didn't you tell me?" Raven looked betrayed.

"I never suspected, Raven. Not until the Casket Girls."

Crimson laughed. "It's forbidden for a dragon to mate with a witch, you know, where he comes from. Gabriel made sure I knew that, time and time again. It's too powerful a pairing. But it can be yours, Raven, for the cost of your firstborn child."

Raven scoffed. "You never wanted Gabriel at all, did you? It's always been about a baby, about the blood. Sex with him might give you power for a short time, but a child—you want to use our child as your own personal power bank."

"Smart girl. I'm doing you a favor. Carrying this child will enhance your power considerably."

"And then you will rip him or her from my arms. How powerful will I feel then?" Raven said through her teeth.

Gabriel slapped a hand down on the table, cracking the wood. "Crimson, I am not giving you our child."

Raven raised her voice. "Gabriel, we're out of time. We have no choice and she knows it." He looked at her in horror. She turned back to Crimson. "It will take time to get pregnant. Lift the curse now to give us time to be together."

Gabriel shook his head. What was she saying?

"Are you agreeing?" Crimson asked through a wolfish grin.

"I am asking you to lift the curse. Then we can talk."

Crimson laughed. "There's no need to lift the curse, dear. I have a spell that will ensure the pregnancy takes place at your next joining."

"I won't do it unless you lift the curse first and free Agnes."

"But you *will* do it. An agreement between witches is binding. I will do as you ask once you agree."

Gabriel grabbed her hand, "No. No, Raven. Don't."

Raven glanced at him and then at Crimson. "I'll do it."

CHAPTER TWENTY-SEVEN

Raven hated the expression of betrayal on Gabriel's face. He was deathly silent beside her, as he was through the entire car ride. Raw meat to the lion's den, that was what he must think. But there was no time to explain why she'd accepted the proposal. Crimson would never succeed in stripping her of her baby for one simple reason; Raven was barren.

It was something she'd planned on telling Gabriel eventually, something only four people in the world knew. The chemo had fried her internal organs. Her ovaries were dead. She hadn't had a period in years. Nothing Crimson did could make her pregnant. But Crimson didn't know that, and if Raven played her cards right, she would get her to break the curse and then absorb enough of her magic to keep her from cursing him again when she found out the truth.

They entered Hexpectations, and as before, Raven barely detected a trickle of magic. She strolled past the shelves of prepared oils and gris-gris without a single tingle across her skin. All of it fake. All of it useless. Crimson called herself a mambo, but it wasn't voodoo she practiced. Raven knew voodoo from the grimoires in Gabriel's library. Crimson practiced a unique and personal form of magic. That was why Raven could not solve the problem of Gabriel's ring. Only the venom of the snake that bit him could bring about the cure.

At the back of the shop, Crimson paused at the great wooden door Raven had noticed before. There was a ram's skull positioned over it and more carvings than she could take in decorating its surface. Crimson whirled, her staff striking the floor between them.

"Do you know this symbol, witch?" she asked, pointing at a pattern at the center of the door.

"That is the symbol of Papa Legba, the spirit of the crossroads." All at once the tingle of close magic Raven had missed at the front of the shop buzzed across her skin, seeming to twist off the door and curl against her.

"Why don't you do the honors?" Crimson gestured toward the door with an upturned palm.

"You want me to invoke the deity?" Raven asked, perplexed. "Why? If this is your sacred space, you should open the way."

A threatening growl rumbled from Gabriel's chest. "I do not like this game you are playing, Crimson. Is your offer genuine, or is this some kind of trick?"

Crimson pounded her staff against the floor and bared her teeth. "There is no trick, dragon, but I will not be taken advantage of. Your witch has asked me to lift the curse before she does the deed. I need some insurance. If she invokes Papa Legba, it will be her magic holding open the threshold between the spirit world and our own. She'll have skin in the game. It shows me she is serious about our agreement."

"It also weakens her," Gabriel growled.

Raven placed a hand on his shoulder. "I will do it."

His dark eyes conveyed nothing short of torture. "It's a trap," he whispered. She was sure Crimson heard.

"It's for the best," Raven said. She believed it. There was nothing she wouldn't sacrifice to save him. Nothing.

All she had to do was look at the symbol and the incantation came to her. Absorbed from a book and lingering unnoticed in her psyche, it now swam to the surface. She knocked three times on the symbol. "Open the road, open the door, open the gate. We wish to come home, Papa."

On the other side, a heavy thud rattled the wood. Dust billowed through the crack under the door. The lock rattled, and then the hinges squealed as the wood behemoth swung open. The tingle of magic multiplied until her entire body buzzed. The room beyond the door was something else, somewhere else. This was not only a voodoo temple; it was a spiritual realm. The air was magic, the floor was magic, the walls were magic. Raven trembled. If she absorbed too much as she had in Paragon, she'd be doomed.

"Are you waiting for an invitation? Come into my temple, lovers."

Raven did as asked and was aware of Gabriel stepping in behind her, his energy like a flickering candle in this place. She reached for him, tangling her fingers with his. The door closed behind them.

Immediately she felt sick. This was no ordinary temple. She noticed now that what she thought had been meat and herbs hanging along the far wall was a much grislier display. Intestines, a set of eyeballs, a dried hand that might have been a monkey's or a child's. There was a jar filled with maggots, and another with something misshapen and pale gray floating in a green liquid.

The symbol for fertility was painted in blood on the floor. Crimson had made offerings around the symbol: a basket of eggs, a bowl of exotic fruit, a silver platter covered in flowers. The entire thing was ringed in red and white candles.

"Enter the symbol. The time is right to begin," Crimson said.

"First lift the curse," Raven demanded.

"Step inside the circle and I will."

"I need a token of your commitment. Free Agnes," Raven pleaded.

Crimson sighed. "Fair enough." She waved her staff and the far wall dissolved. It was just an illusion. Behind where it had been, Agnes was chained to a brick wall. The old woman drooped from her shackles, bloody and unconscious. Crimson snapped her fingers and the shackles gave way. Gabriel raced to Agnes and caught her before her head hit the floor.

Agnes roused, blinking up at Gabriel. "I knew you'd come," she said. "Don't give her what she wants."

"You have to make it to the front of the store," he said to her. "Duncan is waiting. Go."

Agnes glanced at Raven, who gave her a firm nod. They helped her to the door. Raven saw her limp toward the exit as the passageway closed between them.

"Now you have your token of good faith. Get on with it. Enter the symbol," Crimson said.

Raven stepped over the burning candles, taking her place at the center of the ring of blood. Gabriel did not follow. "I will kill you for this," he said to Crimson. "From this life or the next, you will never rest, you will never be at peace."

She rolled her eyes. "Get over yourself, dragon. Enter the circle and I will lift the curse."

Raven met his gaze and held it. *Trust me*, she mouthed silently.

He stepped in beside Raven, taking her hand. Crimson raised her staff and repeated a string of guttural syllables. There was a flash of light, and then Gabriel's emerald ring blazed to new life. She breathed a sigh of relief.

"The spell is broken," Raven said.

"I've upheld my end of the bargain; now it is your turn," Crimson said.

"You can't plan to stand there and watch?" Raven snapped.

"Yes, that's exactly what I plan to do. Did you think I'd be dumb enough to break the curse and then leave you?" Crimson shook her head. "Oh dear, you do take me for a fool. No, I will be here, making sure my spell does what it was intended to do."

"I won't do it with you watching," Raven said.

Crimson laughed. "Oh, you will do as you have bound yourself to do."

A swell of arousal rolled through Raven, and Gabriel bent over, catching himself on his knees. His eyes shifted to hers, wide with alarm. Now was her chance—if she could absorb Crimson's power, she could turn it against her. Even if Crimson cursed Gabriel again in retaliation, if Raven absorbed her magic, she should be able to break it.

She squatted down and touched the symbol. Fire and darkness spread across her skin, the elements of the spell coming to her one by one. Crimson's magic was layered... layered with Raven's! Raven cursed. This was the trap. When she'd invoked Papa Legba, she'd injected her magic inside Crimson's. She couldn't siphon off the mambo's magic without weakening herself.

Nausea rolled through her stomach even as her need for Gabriel once again took center stage.

"What is it?" Gabriel whispered.

She shook her head. "We cannot leave the circle without making love," Raven said. "And the longer we wait, the more difficult it will be to resist." She grabbed her abdomen as a strange sensation rocketed through her. "Whoa."

Gabriel assessed her and the circle. "She will have our baby, Raven. We will not be able to stop her."

"No, she won't." Another wave of desire blasted through her, and Raven's focus caught on Gabriel's sizable erection. Dreadful need bloomed between her legs. Her nipples hardened behind the cover of her dress, and her breath quickened. Wet and ready, she inhaled his scent deep into her lungs, the ache becoming more than she could bear. She lowered her chin. "Trust me."

The cacophony of Crimson's chanting rattled through Raven's head, the woman's dancing and stomping on the other side of the candles a vivid reminder of the position they were in. Thrusting her staff above her head, Crimson transformed the wooden length into a snake. A boa at least five feet long curled above her, heavy and thick in her hands. She swung the weight of it above her, circling, chanting.

Raven pressed her palms to her ears and shook her head, tears raining over her cheeks. Crimson had outsmarted her. Raven hadn't known this sort of layering of magic was possible. Now there was no turning back from the humiliation of completing the ritual. Would Crimson know when it was done that Raven could not bear children?

Would she then force Gabriel to impregnate her instead? The thought made her sick.

Gabriel's hands landed on her wrists. As she met his gaze, everything she feared she might find in his dark eyes was there: crushing defeat, unmistakable arousal, and a hint of regret. Regret for something he hadn't done yet but knew he would do. They both knew.

Her heart grew heavy even as her sex throbbed. He wrapped his fingers around the nape of her neck. She did not resist when he kissed her or when he began to caress and massage the base of her skull. The chanting around them increased. He moved his mouth down her neck and then up to her ear.

"Take from me," he whispered. "As much as you can."

Raven pulled back and blinked. He was offering his power. If they made love, she would absorb his magic, now unlimited because Crimson had lifted the curse. Perhaps with that added power she could... What? Could she kill Crimson? Anything less than death would not stop the voodoo queen.

The spell around them seemed to throb in her womb, the ritual begging to be fed, to come to fruition. Gabriel didn't bother to undress her. Gently, he lowered her to the floor, pushing her skirt up to her hips. He was inside her in another breath, and her body only wanted it faster and harder. Everything in her drew on him, pulling him deeper, her ankles crossing behind his thighs, her fingers tangling in the waves of his hair, her hips rising and falling to meet his. The hot rush of power that flowed into her was intoxicating, its heady, smoky scent filling her nostrils, filling her with every deep thrust.

She came apart beneath him, her body milking his for every drop he would give her. The contraction of her muscles was nothing compared to the contraction of her power. Her body drank of him, soaked him in, until every cell was singing. She felt invincible.

The candles extinguished themselves.

"It is done!" Crimson yelled, shaking the snake in her hands.

Gabriel pulled out of Raven and, in one explosive movement, transformed into the obsidian-green dragon she'd seen before. His body filled the room, breaking from the circle that had once bound them. Candles scattered. Gabriel's massive jaws snapped.

It happened so fast. He'd shifted and attacked before Raven was off the floor. Crimson's body should have been bitten in half. Instead, her form turned to smoke between his teeth.

"Do you think I'm stupid, dragon?" she said, re-forming behind Raven. The snake she'd been wielding transformed back into her staff.

"Gabriel!" Raven yelled and threw her hands toward Crimson. Purple energy crackled like electricity toward the mambo. Raven's magic decided for her in the moment, the spell to immobilize flying from her fingertips before her brain could react.

With a circle of her staff, Crimson blocked the blow. It wasn't without effort. Raven saw the mambo's knees buckle and sweat bloom under her nose. Crimson cursed.

Raven raised her hands to try again but was swept aside by Gabriel's barbed tail. The dragon was trying to pivot, but his massive size made it difficult. The great bellows of his lungs filled with fire, his chest igniting. Blazing red surrounded his emerald-green heart. Raven felt the temperature in the room elevate, and she scurried behind him.

His fire didn't come fast enough.

"*Fè wòch*," Crimson yelled through her clenched teeth, lifting and shaking her staff.

Her spell landed deep inside Gabriel's open mouth, extinguishing the flame at its source. Raven screamed as the fire within went gray, his shiny black and green armor losing its luster one scale at a time. Her screams came again and again as his neck and front legs turned dull as stone, followed by the long stretch of his torso, his back legs and tail. The transformation crawled up his proud neck and over his head, a spreading concrete disease. His dark eyes were the last to go. They turned on her, glossy with surprise and regret. In an instant, Gabriel, her love, her life, her dragon, was a statue. Gone. Crimson had turned him to stone.

Raven dropped to her knees, the impact driving through her bones and rattling her teeth.

"You stupid, stupid witch. Did you think you could outsmart me? I am hundreds of years older than you." Crimson's teeth gnashed in her direction, her staff waving between them. Raven hardly noticed. Her breath had stopped. Her eyes roved over Gabriel, her brain searching for the spell to turn him back. This pain, this loss, this black hole opened in her chest, it would kill her.

"I'll see you in nine months, Raven. Your baby is mine, promised before Papa Legba himself and bound with your own magic. I warn you, witch, if you try to end this pregnancy or yourself, you will be unsuccessful. You are bound." Spit flew from Crimson's lips.

"I am not bound!" she screamed through wrenching sobs. "You didn't fulfill your end of the bargain. You promised to break the curse."

"I did," Crimson said. "It wasn't the curse that turned

him to stone but my spell. I'm allowed to defend myself. I have upheld the bargain."

Raven's hands trembled. "Fix him. I'll do anything. Fix him now."

"Fix him yourself," she said. She strode toward the back of the room. Raven didn't know what she was doing, and she didn't care. All her focus was on Gabriel.

"No. No!" she cried. Her hands hovered over the cold stone that used to be his flesh. She touched his shoulder and regretted it immediately. The stone turned to dust in her hands. She wailed as the whole of him broke apart, ash raining down around her and sifting through her fingers.

CHAPTER TWENTY-EIGHT

A bomb had gone off. The world was ending, burning down around Raven, everything dead, everything leveled. There was no love left on this planet, no life, no goodness. Nothing but despair. Nothing but horror.

Raven dug her hands into the ashes of what used to be her one true love, her tears falling silently on Gabriel's gray remains, and she could not sort out the storm that brewed within her. Was it the lightning of anger that made her grind her teeth or the agony of loss that beat on her like driving rain, or the wind of change—this idea that she must carry on without him—that was most overwhelming? Elbow deep in the gray dust that was once Gabriel, her fingers bumped something smooth, a bone perhaps. She fished it toward her.

It was an emerald the size of an ostrich egg. She dusted it off and cradled it in her palms, staring at the deep green that glowed bright enough to fill the room with watery light. No, it wasn't the size of an egg. It was the size of a heart. Gabriel's heart.

Raven could taste its smoky magic. This heart was alive.

Deep inside the facets, Gabriel's soul pulsed against her touch. She stopped crying and started thinking.

This was Crimson's temple. Raven stood. Shelves along the wall were laden with roots and herbs and stones. Not what she wanted. Raven needed a book. Crimson's grimoire. Behind her, Crimson was distracted. Raven couldn't see what she was doing, but the scent of dark magic came from the corner of the room where she busied herself. Closing her eyes, Raven inhaled deeply and searched with her senses. When she'd touched the symbol, she'd tasted Crimson's magic. Although it had been layered with her own, she'd never forget it, like saccharine and charcoal, the same signature as the demon she'd met in the library.

The strongest source of Crimson's magic was not Crimson herself, who retained that strange hollow quality, but a spot at the back of the room. Power curled against her now from that spot. Slowly, Raven pivoted toward the source. In a room otherwise packed with roots, herbs, and dried flesh, there was an empty corner. She raised her hand and walked toward it.

One of the knots Gabriel had given her had been an illusion. She'd spent the better part of a day trying to untie the thing when all she had to do to dispel it was use a spell she'd absorbed in a grimoire that smelled of potatoes and made her hair stand on end. She used it now, focusing on that bare corner of room.

A smug laugh bubbled up from her lips as Crimson's grimoire came into view. It rested on an altar stained with blood. A black candle burned beside it, in a candleholder made from a human skull. This was Crimson's altar, her holy of holies, the true seat of her magic. The scent of it made Raven gag: the copper tang of blood, the rot of human flesh, singed hair, and rotten eggs. The last thing she wanted to do was touch it, but touch it she did. She set the emerald on the altar and opened the stained leather cover of that book, laying her hands on one page and then the next, turning quickly, deliberately. The magic poured into her, dark and evil.

"Stop. What are you doing?" Crimson charged toward the altar, and Raven threw out a spell, blocking her from coming any closer. She was surprised when it worked. But Crimson looked tired. Exhausted. Raven was tired too, but she was also grieving. Nothing motivated a woman like grief.

Raven turned faster. She was almost there, almost to the end. "I'm getting to know your magic, Crimson," she said. "It's quite an art you have here. Funny you call it voodoo. It's far darker. Far older."

A crack of magic rang out, Crimson shattering her barrier. Raven called on the magic of the book before her and circled her wrist. A staff appeared in her hand, the twin of the one in Crimson's. She used it to block the next curse Crimson hurled at her. The spell ricocheted into the shelf of herbs. Wood splintered and crashed between them, sending Crimson shuffling back. Raven held the staff like a shield between them. Not a twin after all, she saw now. Where Crimson's was topped with a skull, Raven's held an emerald dragon. She laughed darkly.

"You can't hurt me any more than you already have," Raven said, her voice cracking. She turned the last page of the grimoire and then slammed it shut. "I know your magic and I have nothing left to lose."

"Then you know that I can't reverse Gabriel's death even if I wanted to." Crimson's hands were up, her power crackling around her like static, making her hair float in the thick air gathering between them. Demons fled from the light and flitted into the shadowy corners of the room.

"No, you can't," Raven said. "Your magic only brings death. And now that I know it, I bring it to you."

She raised her staff and screamed the worst of the spells she'd read in that horrid tome. Power like lightning lashed out from her, a spell to kill, a spell to maim, a spell to tear Crimson's head from her body. Crimson blocked it and returned blow for blow. Raven didn't let up; with everything she had she leveled curse after curse. Block, curse. Curse, dodge. Shelves collapsed. Glass shattered. Precious gems rolled like marbles across the temple.

"You can't hurt me, Raven," Crimson yelled, her staff circling to block another blow. "You're a copycat witch. You don't know anything I don't know."

"Maybe not, but I will wear you down, you awful, horrid woman. I will wear you down until there is nothing left of either of us."

Crimson scowled. She was tired. The spell she'd forced on her and Gabriel had drained her. Raven gritted her teeth. If it killed her, she would make Crimson pay. The mambo's eyes darted toward a black box on the floor, fallen from one of the destroyed shelves. She darted for it. Raven attempted a retrieval spell. The box flew toward her. Crimson dissolved into a tornado of black smoke and snatched it from the air. She re-formed with it in her hands.

Lifting a tube of black liquid from the box, she threw it at Raven's feet. "It's time you got in touch with your past," she spat.

Although Raven tried to block it, all her evasive maneuvering did was break the vial before it hit the floor. It exploded in her face. Black smoke surrounded her like a curtain. Her lungs protested with a fit of coughing.

When the smoke cleared, Raven found herself standing on a dirt street surrounded by simple wooden buildings. Her wrists were bound behind her back, and a serious-looking black man held the ropes. Her dress was gone, replaced with a filthy white shift.

"Witch! Witch!" a woman yelled from the crowd.

Simple clothing. Raven's head snapped right, then left, taking in the conditions of the street, the people. French colonial architecture. Dirt road. Horses. Historic dress. The crowd gathered on both sides of the street. Silently, she cursed.

"Burn her, Louis!" a man yelled. He was speaking French, but Raven understood him perfectly.

Raven's gaze snapped to the pile of wood in the middle of the square up ahead of her, a pile built around a stake. She glanced back at her captor who had been called Louis. Raven cursed again. She'd seen sketches of him before, in her history books, and the revelation of who was standing behind her turned her blood to ice. That was Louis Congo, public executioner of New Orleans, which meant that Crimson had sent her back to the early 1700s. As much as she'd loved studying history, this was not the point in time she would have chosen to return to.

"Witch! Burn the witch!" a woman yelled.

Raven searched out the voice in the crowd, her eyes landing on Crimson. The other witch raised an eyebrow and wriggled her fingers in a little wave. Raven concentrated on the knot binding her wrists, sending clear intentions to untie it. She whispered the incantation. Nothing happened.

"Your magic won't work here, Circe," Louis said, shoving her in the back. "The rope has been blessed by the priestess herself."

Raven stumbled forward, the packed earth gritty beneath her bare feet. Priestess. Crimson had charmed the fucking ropes to be resistant to magic. Raven growled and gnashed her teeth, tugging at the ropes like a wild woman. The crowd roared, hurling obscenities. Arms gripped hers and she was wrestled forward, dragged to the stake and bound to it by rough, bruising hands.

"Circe Tanglewood, I sentence you to burn at the stake until you are dead, for the practice of witchcraft and the poisoning of Miss Delphine Devereaux. May God have mercy on your soul."

Delphine... Delphine Devereaux. Raven tried to get her head around what was happening. Crimson had said she needed to get in touch with her past. Clearly she was in the body of her ancestor, Circe, whom Crimson had said was the granddaughter of the goddess Circe and a great and powerful enchantress. Circe poisoned someone named Delphine. Why did that name sound familiar? She searched the crowd. There were two dark-haired sisters—they had to be sisters with how alike they looked—weeping to her right. *Her sisters*, she realized. Circe's sisters. Three sisters. Were these the three sisters her mother's bar was named after?

Raven's mind worked, trying to put it all together as she struggled against her bonds. Her gaze drifted to Crimson. There was someone beside her, someone she recognized. Delphine, the Casket Girl. No wonder she'd reacted so strongly when she found out who and what Raven was. Apparently they had a history, and Delphine fell on Crimson's side of it.

"Burned over her own tree!" a man yelled. A torch was lowered to the branches under her, the blaze catching with a whoosh that sent her heart racing and her head tipping back against the stake. *My own tree,* she thought. The

Tanglewood family tree. She thought of the crest, the tree of life, Kristina's sketch in the back of the library catalog.

She glanced down into the branches, through the flames that licked higher, kissing her legs and burning away her shift. The branches below her glowed red. Symbols appeared in the bark, symbols Raven had seen before in her own skin. Symbols Gabriel had drawn out with his touch. The touch of fire.

Raven watched the last of her shift burn away. There was no pain. No scorching heat. She raised her chin. Was this the end? Had her skin burned so quickly that she couldn't feel it? But when she looked down at herself, her flesh was pale and smooth. Flames reached above her head, caressing her like a lover. Her lover, the dragon. All at once she realized why she wasn't burning and started to laugh. The fire could not harm her. Dragons were immune to fire, and she had absorbed Gabriel's power only minutes ago. Now she also had Circe's. She'd breathed it in, absorbed it through the smoke, through her feet resting on the branches of her family tree.

The ropes binding her wrists should have burned through but they did not. She concentrated on the enchantment as her dark hair whipped around her face inside the inferno. She thought back to the knots Gabriel had given her to practice on. She'd finally untangled the last one, the most difficult, days ago. An infinitely looping tightening charm layered on a strengthening spell had almost been her undoing. Almost. Raven closed her eyes and focused. First she whispered a weakening spell, then a loosening one, then one to interrupt the repeating charm applied to the ropes. Her wrists pulled apart, and the binding fell into the flames.

With a dark laugh, she realized she'd needed this. Needed the flames to reach over her head so she could see herself clearly in them. She was no frail victim, no damsel in distress. She was a survivor, a descendant of Circe. And she was her dragon's witch.

Eyes trained on Crimson, Raven leaped off the pyre, landing in the street to the screams of the voyeurs. Smoke curled off her naked flesh. She strode toward the voodoo queen with malice on her mind.

"Come out and play, Crimson!" Raven yelled. "Everyone gets a turn."

Crimson turned, started to run. But Raven would have none of that. She cast her hand toward the witch, gripping her within her newfound power.

"Delphine, help me!" Crimson called, but the Casket Girl took one look at Raven and ran. She wasn't the only one. The crowd of onlookers was terrified, scrambling over each other to get away from her. Raven ignored them. She lifted Crimson into the air, and with a twist of her wrist, directed the gaping woman's momentum into the fire, closing her fist to hold her against the burning stake. As soon as Crimson's back slapped the post, the flames engulfed her. The mambo howled in agony.

Black smoke billowed from the dusty street, and Raven felt her stomach drop. The crowd, the fire, the executioner, all faded away. She found herself again in Crimson's temple, standing where she'd been, in front of the grimoire. She was back in her dress, although her skin still smoked. Crimson was back too, wheezing on the floor, the majority of her skin blackened and bubbling.

Raven gazed down her nose at her. "What's wrong, darling? Turnabout not fair play?" Demons sifted from the shadows, crowding close, sniffing the voodoo queen's body. "Your friends are here."

"No," she rasped.

Raven could see she was dying, killed by her own magic, by her own power. It would be so easy to finish her off. A stomp of a foot or a crook of Raven's finger could snap the woman's neck.

"Having your magic inside me is like living through a bout of salmonella," Raven said. "Powerful, deadly, and something you never want to experience again." Raven backed away from her, allowing the demons to move in closer. One was spreading her scorched legs, another lapping at a bloody wound on her throat. "I will never practice it. Your power will fade from me and it will die, just as you will die. No one will ever practice this brand of magic again."

A gurgle came from Crimson's throat. Raven could barely see her body now under the pile of demons. Her soul, however, she could see quite clearly. The dark form had left her body and stood small and filmy beside it. The soul stared at her with wordless hate as a band of demons dragged her down into the floor, to the hell that she'd once sought to control, the hell that she deserved. Crimson's soul reached for Raven, her mouth gaping like a woman taking her last breath before drowning. An oily black hand rose up, landed on top of her head, and pushed her down where she disappeared into the deep dark beyond.

Raven stared at the body, scorched and motionless in a puddle of her own blood. Dead. Maybe it was the lingering effects of the woman's magic, but Raven did not feel a single thing, not one emotional whiff of sadness or regret. She would have finished her if she'd had to, she realized. But there was justice in this. Crimson had lived by dark magic and she'd died by it.

Raven whirled, scooping Gabriel's heart from the altar and cradling it in her arm. She opened Crimson's grimoire, tipping the black candle onto its pages. Fire blazed. The pages curled, sending up sparks as the flames destroyed Crimson's legacy. Chin held high, Raven strode from the room and from the shop.

She paused to grab her bag and mask, which were still sitting on the counter, right where she'd left them. To the crackling sound behind her and the smell of smoke, Raven picked up the phone next to the cash register and placed a call to the fire department.

Her second call was from her own phone. "Duncan? I need you. No, I'll meet you at the corner. You won't be able to see me. Just wait there."

The fire was all around her now, but she strolled from Hexpectations without a second thought about the flames. Only days from Mardi Gras, she could hear the crowd of revelers in the Quarter and suspected someone would soon notice the fire. It didn't matter. If anyone was watching the shop at that moment, they would only see the door blow open and a bit of smoke filter into the street.

CHAPTER TWENTY-NINE

Sunrise. Raven felt the warmth on her face as she crossed the courtyard behind Blakemore's to get to Gabriel's treasure room. The peacock-blue layers of her dress fanned out around her with her heavy stride. Her hair was wild, long since freed from its updo. She'd lost the pins and the hairpiece. Black curls stuck to her cheeks and neck.

She was relieved to find the door to the treasure room open. Tentatively, she crept inside. No way would Gabriel have forgotten to lock this room. Everything he'd ever told her suggested that this was too important a place to him, filled with hundreds of years of rare and valuable treasure he would never leave unguarded. At first she wondered if Duncan had called Richard. Then she learned the truth. At the center of the room, in the space before the great mountain of Gabriel's making, two faces watched her.

"Thanks for letting me in," she said. The oreads' skin was as delicate and smooth as pearls and stretched tightly across harsh, pointed features. The two had eyes the color of diamonds and amethyst wings as light and thin as tissue paper. "Are you Juniper?" she asked the taller one. He nodded, his long graceful neck bending slightly toward her. "And you must be Hazel?" The other smiled. "It is a pleasure to meet you both. I only wish it were under better circumstances."

Raven placed the giant emerald on the floor in front of her. The two nymphs gasped. Juniper hissed and flapped his wings. Hazel began to weep.

"He's still here," she said. "He's in there. I can feel him. I don't know if this will work, but I have a memory. Pictures." She tapped her temple and closed her eyes tightly. "I need a blade, preferably silver, and a bowl big enough to hold his heart."

Hazel disappeared and reappeared with a dagger encrusted in gold and jewels. Juniper brought her a deep silver basin.

"Thank you." Raven placed the heart into the bowl. "Stand back."

The oreads scurried away. Raven held her arm over the emerald and sliced. Blood poured out over the heart, filling the bottom of the bowl. Her lips parted and a chant came to her from somewhere deep inside. She let it come.

My love, I give to you life, life from my flesh, flesh from my power, power from the fire, the beginning of all things. My love, I give you life, life from my flesh, flesh from my power, power from the fire, the beginning of all things.

Again and again, she repeated the chant, her body rocking with the words. Her voice was unnaturally low, not hers. The cut on her arm healed. The sun rose and then began to set again, the sounds of music and partying in the streets coming and going with the hours. She swayed and wet herself. Small, delicate hands steadied her. She continued her chant. The sun rose again.

Eventually her body gave out. Her words stopped. The

magic stopped. She toppled to the floor. The last thing she saw before she slipped into the dark river of sleep was Juniper and Hazel pushing the bowl into the pile of treasure, their faces grooved with tears.

She woke just before midnight, the witching hour calling to her heart in a way she couldn't explain. The light of the moon swept through the windows and bathed the treasure room in soft, watery ecru. Her tongue felt like leather in her mouth, and her stomach was hollow. Somewhere outside, a band played. Laughter and voices filtered through the walls from the street.

Tiny hands grabbed her shoulders: Juniper. He helped her up and over to where a table was set. Hazel placed a plate of rice, fish, and vegetables before her and poured her a tall glass of water. Unable to raise her arms, Raven slumped in the seat. Hazel lifted the water to her lips. The sudden slaking of her thirst sent her into a fit of coughing. With help, she guzzled the rest and then swallowed tiny bits of the food Hazel fed her.

The nymph's porcelain features hadn't recovered from her extended sadness. Dark circles marred her eyes, and there was no color in her cheeks. Even her wings had paled.

"No change?" Raven asked.

The two shook their heads.

"It's only been a few hours."

The two nymphs shook their heads harder. Juniper handed Raven her phone, newly charged and overloaded with dozens of calls from her mother and sister. Disbelieving, she stared at the date. If she stared long enough, would it change? Would the truth of what had come to pass be undone? It was Fat Tuesday, two minutes before midnight. It had been three full days since she began the spell.

"This can't be," she said.

Both nymphs visibly sagged.

No wonder the music outside seemed so loud. Mardi Gras. Raven watched the time roll over to midnight, then stood. She would sleep in Gabriel's bed tonight and deal with the repercussions of what had happened tomorrow. She rose and turned toward the door.

The tinkle of falling metal stopped her in her tracks. With trembling hands, she turned slowly, searching the pile of treasure. A goblet fell off the top of the mound, rolled down the side, and bounced across the floor before bumping into her toes.

"Gabriel?" Tears overflowed the dam of her eyelids.

The pile shifted, the mountain splitting like a curtain as a massive head broke through, nostrils flaring over inter-locking teeth. The dragon's dark eyes burned under a set of bony horns, its sleek, scaled body slipping from the treasure and moving toward her, talons clicking on the marble floor. The dragon she'd come to love stood gloriously whole before her, its emerald heart glowing in its chest as it should be.

She dropped to her knees, tears streaming now, harder and faster than she could ever remember crying. It was through blurred vision that she watched him shift, that gigantic body folding and breaking, rearranging itself into a man composed of light and shadow, curves and hollows.

Wiping the tears away, she saw him clearly only when he bent over to sweep her off the floor and into his arms.

"Gabriel." Her voice cracked.

His eyes searched her face. "I am here, little witch. Yours once more."

She wrapped her arms around his neck and allowed him to carry her home.

318

GABRIEL CONVEYED RAVEN ACROSS THE COURTYARD and up to his room, loving the weight of her head against his chest. He needed to eat and to shower and to make love to her until she screamed his name and promised him she was his forever, not necessarily in that order. His chest swelled when he saw she was still wearing his ring.

Raven was in the same dress he'd left her in three days ago. The skirt was soiled and sweat caked her hair. Her needs came first. He carried her into the bathroom and started the shower, seating her on the closed toilet lid. Within the confines of the dress, she looked thinner, hollowed out, as if the boning of the dress was all that was holding her up.

"We both need a shower," he said. "And something more to eat."

"I'd like a shower," she said weakly, her eyes searching his face.

He pressed a kiss to her forehead.

"Crimson is dead. I killed her."

"Good." Gabriel frowned. "Do you think her spell was successful?" He glanced at her abdomen.

"No. I'm barren, Gabriel. I can't have children because of the damage my body endured during my cancer treatment. I wanted to tell you, but there never seemed to be the right time."

"No children, ever?"

She shook her head. "No."

"Was that why you agreed to Crimson's proposal?"

"Yes."

"Smart."

"Do you still want me?" Raven asked. "Even if it means

319

you won't have children? You're the heir to Paragon. If you are with me, your line will end with you."

He leaned in close, taking her face in his hands. "I still want you. I will always want you. We are not in Paragon, and honestly, the fact that you are barren will make things easier. The mating of a dragon and a witch is forbidden primarily because their progeny would be too powerful. We won't have progeny for anyone to be concerned about."

A moment of silence spread between them.

"What was it like?" she asked suddenly, her hand coming to rest on his arm. He noticed that the paint on her nails had melted in places and looked scorched in others. He had questions himself. There was no reason to hold anything back from her. Deep inside, he understood that what had happened was miraculous and irreversible. They had both destroyed and recreated each other. There was no word for the type of intimacy they shared, and he would do nothing to damage it.

"It was pure light, like standing in the sun. I didn't expect that. We are taught in Paragon that we return to the Mountain when we die. I always assumed the heart of the Mountain was dark and dank, that death would be like sleeping. I was wrong. It was standing in the sun, or in the heart of a flame. There was softness and a breeze. The smell of cherry blossoms. The sense of being surrounded by company, although I don't remember speaking to anyone. It was not unpleasant."

"Oh." Raven's tone sounded surprised and a little sad. "Are you upset I brought you back?"

Gabriel was quick to allay her fears. "No. No, Raven. The entire time I was there, a tug right here"—he tapped his sternum—"bound me to you. I thought of you. I desperately wanted to help you, to return to you. I simply could not.

This bond between us became my pulse, my heartbeat. I knew if I let you go, my heart would stop and I would cross over permanently to that place. But I refused. As long as I felt the pulse, your pulse—or was it mine kept beating by you?—I was alive."

Tears scored Raven's cheeks and he wiped them away, the bones of her face hard and sharp against his thumbs. "What happened to you, little witch?"

"I absorbed Crimson's magic to try to undo what she'd done to you, but everything about her practice was destruction. She knew nothing about bringing life. We fought and she sent me back in time, into the body of my great, great... I don't know how many greats, but she was my grandmother. I was in the body of the granddaughter of the goddess Circe, a demigoddess who also went by that name, Circe Tanglewood, on the day she was burned at the stake."

"I think I remember that day," he said slowly. "I stayed away. I could not stand the injustice of it."

"Crimson was there with Delphine. Delphine was Circe's accuser."

"That evil crone." A growl rumbled in his chest.

"I was tied to the stake and they tried to burn me, just as they must have burned her. I was living her death."

"Fuck, Raven. How did you survive?"

"They burned her over the branches of the Tanglewood tree. It's our family crest. Gabriel, Circe never had a grimoire. She recorded her spells, all the knowledge about her magic, in the bark of that tree. Every branch was covered in symbols. I breathed in the smoke and took all of them in. All of them. She was... powerful. She'd brought that tree from someplace called the Garden of the Hesperides."

"But the fire..."

Raven laughed. "It couldn't burn me. I'd just had sex with you. I was brimming with dragon magic. The flames barely tickled my flesh. I escaped and threw Crimson into the flames. I watched her burn alive."

"Praise the Mountain." He reached around her and helped her unzip her dress. It took all his effort to remain impassive as he witnessed the ashy smudges on her skin and the way her ribs showed. He pulled her up to help her out of the dress and her undergarments.

"It was Circe's magic that brought you back." Her blue eyes blinked fresh tears away. "Old magic. The same magic that brought your kind into being."

He repositioned her naked body in his arms and wiped her tears away. A hard swallow preceded his next question. "Do you still hold that power within you?"

"I'm not sure. I feel weak, like there is nothing left." She was pale. Too damn pale.

"You must take from me, Raven."

"But—"

He held up his hand, showing her the ring, its center filled with nothing but green light. "I am immortal again. You cannot drain me. You will not hurt me."

In response, she tipped her head and welcomed his kiss.

"Not so fast, dirty girl."

He adjusted the temperature of the water and turned her into the spray, eliciting a small squeal from her. She smiled. Pure radiance, he thought. He smoothed back her hair under the water and delighted in the way rivulets traced over her shoulders and down her breasts, dribbling off the hardened tips. With a growl, he leaned her against the shower wall.

"You're purring again," she said.

He glanced at her while he soaped a washcloth and

began scrubbing one of her arms. "I do not think it is a purr."

"What would you call it?"

"A mating trill," he said after some thought.

"Purr is easier to say."

He turned her in his soapy arms and washed her back, circling lower, over the mound of her hip, between her legs. She inhaled sharply, and the sound in his chest grew louder.

"Purr it is then." Pressing against her from behind, his lips brushed her ear, his tongue licking the sensitive area behind it before nibbling gently on the flesh. His hands circled her waist, one slipping around to her belly and up to knead her breasts while the other journeyed lower, massaging her sex from behind. He rubbed and circled until her hips bucked urgently against him.

"Please," she said over her shoulder. "I need you."

He had to lift her to get under her, supporting her with his forearms behind the knees. He turned her so she could grip the top of the shower door for support. In one slick thrust, he was inside her, forcing a moan from her. Her breasts were pressed into the glass, and Gabriel enjoyed a lovely view of her open and panting in the bathroom mirror. He growled and worked her harder, his wings spreading to help him with balance.

"Open your eyes," he said, his voice thick and low.

She did as he commanded, meeting his gaze in the mirror. While she was balanced in his grip, she skimmed a hand down her chest and pinched her nipple. He loved it when she touched herself. He kissed her over her shoulder, watching as she moved her hand lower to settle between her legs.

Tight and slick, he felt her come apart like a shower of stars, and he followed her over the edge. Her body tensed and twitched in his arms. His knees bobbed with the draw of energy that followed, a buzz and pulse that had him shifting to hold her around the waist and ease her onto her feet. He found her sex and drew out her orgasm with his fingers, holding her against him while the aftershocks sent tremors through her flesh.

"Oh God, Gabriel," she panted. She steadied his hand, breathing deeply against the shower glass. After a moment, she turned around, her cheeks flushed, her lips full, her eyes no longer hungry but bright.

"I love you, Raven," he said. "You are mine."

She smiled and reached up to circle his neck. "You are mine, Gabriel, and I love you too."

He slipped his hand down to hers, where the emerald he'd given her hugged her finger. He held the gem between them. "Marry me."

She gave a breathy laugh. "Yes. A million times yes."

CHAPTER THIRTY

R aven removed a stack of jeans from her drawer and placed them into the moving box beside her dresser. Although she'd discussed her move and impending nuptials with her sister and mother, her mother had taken the news far better than her sister, who was in full adult-tantrum mode. Avery sat on the bed pouting and sighing heavily every time Raven packed another item.

"You're being overly dramatic," Raven said when her addition of a stack of sweaters to the box caused Avery to violently flop to her back on the mattress.

"Ugh!" Avery lifted a pillow and pressed it over her face.

"Please don't smother yourself on my account." Raven rolled her eyes.

Avery removed the pillow and slammed it down on the other side of the bed. "Why do you have to move in with him now? Why can't you wait until after you're married?"

Raven shook her head. "I just can't. I can't be away from him." She turned toward her sister, leaning her backside against the dresser. "It's like he gave me life after cancer drained it all out of me. He breathed air into my lungs. He brings me joy. Life is short. It's too short to wait when you know for sure. I will never take another day of my life for granted, Avery. Right now that means living with Gabriel."

"Fine." She still sounded pissed.

"Well, I hope you'll get more enthused about this soon. It would be depressing to have a maid of honor who wasn't excited about the wedding."

It took a moment for Avery to process what Raven had said.

"Will you be my maid of honor, Avery?"

Avery sat up and released a high-pitched squeal. "Yes! Oh, Raven it will be gorgeous. Navy-blue bridesmaid's dresses, pastel roses, white satin ribbon."

"Um, who's getting married here?"

"Sorry," she said, touching her lips. "It's just, I can see it. Almost like I'm standing there." Her eyes drifted toward the wall.

Raven giggled. "It does sound beautiful. I'm not ruling it out."

Avery clapped her hands and smiled like she was high. "So when can we start shopping?"

Raven resumed packing. "In a few weeks. I'm going to Chicago with Gabriel for a little while. He has a brother there named Tobias whom he'd like to tell about our engagement in person. We can start planning as soon as I get back."

Avery went completely silent.

"What's wrong?" Raven asked. Her sister looked like she might cry.

"You're finally going to get to fly in an airplane," Avery said. "You always said you wanted to."

Raven grinned, remembering what it was like to fly

wrapped in Gabriel's arms. She supposed nothing would ever top that experience. Still, she was looking forward to the airplane and to all the other first-time experiences she'd missed when she was sick.

"You know, I can honestly say every day with Gabriel is a new adventure."

"Speaking of new adventures, have you told Dad?"

Raven paused, the pile of clothes in her hands suddenly feeling heavier. "Not yet. But I will, after I get back from Chicago."

She could see the disapproval in her sister's expression, but to Avery's credit, she didn't say a word.

"Don't wait too long. You know I can't keep a secret."

Raven raised her eyebrows. "Okay, as soon as I get back."

"Good. Now that that's settled. Let's talk about our, I mean your, wedding."

Raven rolled her eyes but indulged her sister. She didn't get another word in for the rest of the evening.

❧

GABRIEL HANDED HIS KEYS OVER TO RICHARD WITH A firm handshake. "I trust that while I am gone, you will run this business the same as if I were here."

"Considering what you're paying me, I'll run it however you want me to run it." Richard scrubbed his woolly hair with his hand and gave him an open smile.

"You still have to answer to Agnes. I've given her control over the books and all the financial accounts. Treat her well. She now writes your paycheck."

"It's all right. My girl Agnes and I will handle everything, Gabriel. Don't worry about a thing." He tossed the keys up, caught them again, and then slid them into the pocket of his perfectly tailored trousers. "After what the old broad has been through, I plan to be on my best behavior for a while."

"Don't you dare," Agnes said from the door. "I expect you to be as ornery as ever! I can take it. I survived a direct attack from the former voodoo queen of New Orleans." She flexed a muscle.

Richard glanced in her direction. "As I was saying, me and mama Agnes, the slayer of all things evil, will take care of everything.

"Thank you, both of you." Gabriel fished a few documents from his desk drawer and slid them into his carry-on.

"How long do you expect to be gone?" Richard asked, eyeing his suitcase seriously for the first time.

"I'm not entirely sure."

"I thought you said you and Raven were engaged? I can't say I know much about women, but I thought they liked to plan these types of things. When's she gonna do that with you traveling for... you're not entirely sure how long?" His brown eyes twinkled under his arched brows.

"I agree," Agnes said. "Girls Raven's age want to plan big, elaborate weddings with their families. You can't be jet-setting all over kingdom come when you have a wedding to plan." She waved her hand dismissively.

Gabriel assessed his longtime employees and friends and decided it wasn't fair to keep them in the dark. He lowered himself into the chair behind his desk. "I have family all over the world. Seven brothers and a sister."

"No shit? You've never mentioned them before. Don't your kind like to get together?" Richard asked.

"We were misinformed about the hazards of our coexistence. I'd like to rectify that, but this is something that must be done in person. The circumstances are, shall we say, delicate."

"Does Raven know what she's getting into?" Agnes asked.

Thumbing the corner of his mouth, Gabriel thought about that. "As much as she can understand now. The rest will have to come. Some things a person can't understand until they live them."

Richard nodded slowly. "Okay. I gotcha. Good luck with that."

Gabriel scowled at the man's tone. "You don't approve?"

"In my household, things tend to go better for me with my husband when everything is out on the table."

Agnes nodded. "Take it from me. A relationship, especially a new one, requires honesty."

"Everything *is* on the table," Gabriel said seriously. "It's simply a matter of fact that Raven currently does not have the context to understand our reality."

Agnes nodded. "Try your best to explain it to her."

Gabriel lifted his bag onto his shoulder. "I will take it under consideration."

"Before you go—" Richard spread his arms wide.

Gabriel embraced the man, thumping him on the back, and then Agnes, who waited patiently with her arms open.

"Thank you, Richard, Agnes, for everything."

"Anytime, dragon," Richard said.

Agnes kissed him on the cheek.

Gabriel headed for the street where Duncan was waiting.

RAVEN GRIPPED THE ARMRESTS ON HER SEAT WITH AN intensity that left her knuckles white and the muscles in her forearms sore. An alarm chimed overhead as the plane pitched left and then right, tossing her against her seat belt. She chewed the gum Gabriel had given her and pressed the back of her head into the seat. There was an oxygen mask in the ceiling. Why would she need an oxygen mask?

"Try to relax, Raven. It's just a little turbulence. Everything is fine. Look out the window. You're missing the clouds." Gabriel placed a gentle hand on hers.

"I think I'm fine staring at the ceiling, thank you."

"I thought you said you'd always wanted to fly?" Gabriel said.

"I'm beginning to think what I really wanted was to have flown, like in the past. I'll be fine after we're safely on the ground."

"Can I remind you that I can fly without the plane? If we go down, I will break through the wall and carry you to safety."

She scoffed. "And what about the rest of the people on this flight?"

He ran a knuckle across her cheek. "You are an encyclopedia of magical talent. You must have a levitation spell in there."

Closing her eyes, she sifted through her brain. Her fingers relaxed. "Yeah, I do."

"Good. Now look at the clouds. We have first-class seats. You might as well enjoy them."

She opened her eyes and took a long look out the window. "It's like a bed of cotton candy."

Gabriel's grin reflected back at her in the window. He took her hand and began massaging life back into it. He paused to play with her engagement ring.

"Now that you're no longer catatonic with terror, I was hoping we could talk," he said.

"About what?"

"Tobias. I'm not sure how he'll react when we show up on his doorstep. He left abruptly and not on the most pleasant of terms."

Raven shrugged. "All you can do is try. If he doesn't want to hear about our engagement, we simply won't invite him to the wedding."

Gabriel stared at his fingers intertwined with hers.

"There's something else, isn't there?"

"We need to convince Tobias that what we saw in Paragon is real. All my siblings need to know what our mother did to us. They need to understand the peril our home is in."

Raven balked. "What? I thought this was about getting Tobias to come to our wedding?"

"It is. But it's also about having a witness. I have an obligation to tell the others about Eleanor. They need to be prepared in case she retaliates."

"Do you think that's likely?"

"No. She doesn't know who you are or where you came from. Still, I would want to know if one of the others was in my place."

"This isn't something for a quick text or phone call, huh?"

"No." He glanced down at his feet. "Most of us haven't spoken in hundreds of years, Raven. I was only able to contact Tobias by phone because we bumped into each other not so long ago. The rest of us went our separate ways long before cell phones or surnames. Tobias knows where Rowan is. Beyond that, I have little to go on."

"So... this trip is about persuading Tobias to get involved

and to help us track down your other siblings so that we can tell them your mother betrayed them?"

"Yes."

"And you want me to help you." Raven crossed her arms over her chest.

"Yes."

"Gabriel, why didn't you tell me this before? Why make me believe this was all engagement related?"

"Honestly?"

"Honestly."

"I was afraid I would frighten you. After your experience in Paragon and then with Crimson, I wanted to give you a few days freedom without another thing to worry about."

"And you are telling me now because..."

"Richard told me to. He said human partners do not like having information withheld for their safety and comfort."

Raven pursed her lips. "For a gay man, Richard knows a lot about women."

"Are you angry with me?"

She gave an exaggerated sigh and leaned over to kiss his cheek. "No, although Richard is right. You should tell me these things. As your soon-to-be wife, I should be the first to know your innermost thoughts. You don't have to be afraid to share with me. I know what I've signed up for. I'm all in, baby."

He threaded his fingers with hers and leaned back in his seat. "Good. Because you've never known turbulence until you've seen my family together."

THANK YOU FOR READING THE DRAGON OF NEW ORLEANS. Gabriel and Raven are on their way to Chicago to convince Tobias to help them find Gabriel's siblings. Tobias isn't comfortable at all with his supernatural roots, but can his coworker, Sabrina, awaken the dragon within? Maybe. She certainly ignites his inner fire! Sometimes we can't deny our history or our nature.

Find out more in the second book in the Treasure of Paragon series, WINDY CITY DRAGON. This book takes place in Chicago and features Tobias and Sabrina, but you'll see more of Gabriel and Raven as well. Turn the page to read an excerpt of WINDY CITY DRAGON.

WINDY CITY DRAGON is available now.

SIGN UP FOR MY **NEWSLETTER** TO BE NOTIFIED **when new books release!** https://www.genevievejack.com/newsletter/

WINDY CITY DRAGON

THE TREASURE OF PARAGON BOOK 2

USA TODAY BESTSELLING AUTHOR

GENEVIEVE JACK

CHAPTER ONE

Winter in Chicago cut deep. It raged with wind that snapped and cold that gnawed, a four-month attack by Mother Nature that ravaged the city like a relentless, icy beast. For Dr. Tobias Winthrop, whose core temperature was normally a blistering 113 degrees, the cold was both shocking and harmless to his constitution. Dragons couldn't freeze to death or catch human ailments. He hadn't suffered so much as a cough in over three hundred years.

Nor had he pondered his dragon nature in decades.

All that had changed when his brother had phoned him out of the blue weeks ago. Gabriel had needed his help combating a life-threatening voodoo curse. Although Tobias had done all he could for his brother and his mate, Raven, he hadn't heard from the pair since.

He was afraid to look too closely into his brother's fate. If his queen mother's warning to stay apart from his siblings wasn't enough to keep him away, Gabriel's forbidden relationship with the witch Raven was. Tobias had sacrificed his principles to try to save his brother's life. Besides tacitly accepting their forbidden relationship, he'd broken his mother's rule to stay away from his sibling. But the turbocharge on his slip and slide into hell had been helping them go back to Paragon. All these years, he'd worked tirelessly to put his dragon past behind him and become the healer he was meant to be. Helping Gabriel had ripped a scab off a wound he'd thought had healed. He vowed again to do his best to blend in and live as a normal human would.

Except this one time.

Tobias toyed with the amulet in his pocket. Helping his brother hadn't entirely been a selfless act. He'd asked for one thing in return, a healing amulet that once belonged to the indigenous guide who had led him and his siblings through the wilds of early America. With any luck, the amulet would save a child's life.

Despite decades practicing medicine with superhuman precision, one case had been his nemesis. He hesitated outside room 5830, looked both ways to confirm the hall was empty, then slipped inside his patient's room.

The child, Katelyn, slept curled on her side, the tubes and machines she was wired to lording over her tiny body like the appendages of a mechanical monster. Her pale blond hair curled against the pillow, her eyelashes softly feathering her alabaster cheeks. He frowned at the dusky-blue rim of her bottom lip.

Katelyn suffered from a complicated condition. A nasty, yet-unidentified virus had infected her heart and was slowly, torturously bleeding her life away. A heart transplant was her best chance of survival, but it was risky. No one understood this virus; therefore no one could say if it would attack the new heart as well. Active systemic infection was a contraindication of a heart transplant. As long as the virus was in her blood, she would not get the heart she needed.

Without his help, Katelyn would die.

Sick children died every day. Tobias should have faced the inevitability of human death and dealt with it as all doctors did, with grace and acceptance. Instead, he'd sold his soul for a miracle. Silently, he removed the one-of-a-kind, ancient healing amulet from his pocket and positioned it around her neck.

By the Mountain, he was pitiful.

Her eyes blinked open, and she drew a heavy breath through her nose. The oxygen tube there cut a line across her cheeks, and the air bubbled in the humidifying chamber with her effort.

"Hi, Dr. Toby," she said in her sweet child's voice. Her giant blue eyes locked onto him. Total trust. Total innocence. She did not question what he was doing even though he and the nurses had poked her limbs with needles and performed every manner of painful procedure on her over the past several months. She showed no fear. The brave girl only thought to say hello. No tears. No complaints.

"Shh," he said. "I didn't mean to wake you. I need you to wear this special necklace for a few hours. I'll be back to get it later."

"Why?" She looked down at the pearlescent white disk against her skin.

"It's a secret."

"Where did you get it?"

"Where do you think?"

"It looks like a seashell. I think you got it from a mermaid," she said between breaths.

Who was he to deny a sick little girl a fantasy?

"Our secret," he responded, placing a finger over his lips. "I'll be back later to retrieve it. The mermaid king loaned it to me for one night only."

"Whoa." Eyes wide, she strained to smile. "Really?"

"Close your eyes, Katelyn," he said. He was relieved when she obeyed. "Good girl. Now, dream of a mermaid kingdom. I'll check on you later." He tucked the blankets around her.

A few hours with the amulet should heal her, although he couldn't recall it ever being used on an illness like this. If memory served, Maiara, the native healer who had created the amulet, had used it mostly on injuries, not illnesses. It didn't matter. Indeed, he had no other choice but to try. His own magic wasn't right for this situation. Dragons could heal but only by binding, and binding one so young would be unforgivable. No. This was his last hope. He was sure it broke all sorts of ethical boundaries.

It was not like Tobias to break the rules. He wasn't proud of his newfound flirtation with rebellion. Not one bit.

He left the room, completely distracted by his conflicting emotions on the issue, and slammed right into a blur of red and surgical green careening down the hall. Coffee splashed. A box flew and skimmed across the floor. He squatted down to retrieve it.

"Sorry," he said. "I didn't see you." When he handed the box back to the nurse he'd collided with, he did a double take. Sabrina Bishop. He didn't work with her as often as he'd like, but when he did, the experience was memorable.

Sabrina reminded him of cherry pie—fresh, sweet, warm. She was the type who always asked about a patient's feelings, who held a parent's hand during a procedure, who spent way too much time talking to the hospital chaplain.

Her hair, which was the bright red of maple leaves, and her milky complexion didn't hurt the comparison either. He frowned at the coffee stain on her scrubs. "Let me get you something for that."

"Never mind. I've got it." She rounded the corner of the nurses station and took a seat behind the desk. Grabbing a fistful of tissues, she set the red box he'd retrieved down on the counter and dabbed at the spill.

"Animal crackers?" Tobias eyed the snack box, the corner of his mouth twitching upward. "Are those for you or a patient?"

She flashed him a smile. "For me. Why?"

"It's just I haven't seen anyone over the age of five eat animal crackers in a while... like ever."

Leaning back in the chair, she raised her chin and stared down her nose at him. "I'll have you know I do it as a mental health exercise."

He snorted. "How is eating animal crackers a mental health exercise?"

"Have you heard the saying 'How do you eat an elephant? One bite at a time'?"

"Sure."

"Well, how do you eat animal crackers? One elephant at a time." She tore open the box and popped a cracker into her mouth. "It makes me feel like I've accomplished something."

He narrowed his eyes and shook his head. "That makes no logical sense."

"Logic is highly overrated, Doctor. You should ditch logic in favor of magic."

Their eyes caught and held. Her use of the word *magic* unsettled him. It hit too close to his open wound. Could she see through his facade to who he actually was, not human but dragon? Did she suspect he'd just slipped a healing amulet around the neck of a dying girl?

He pushed off the counter. "I should continue my rounds."

"Sad case, huh?" She gestured toward Katelyn's room with her head.

"We work in a pediatric hospital, Sabrina." He cracked his neck and sank his hands into the pockets of his lab coat. "All cases are sad. Children do not belong in hospitals."

She popped another cracker in her mouth and stared at him with a piercing green gaze that seemed to cut straight to his soul. Was she assessing him? The look on her face was strange, unreadable. He didn't need this right now. If a woman like her pulled the right string, he might unravel like an old, worn sweater.

"Well, I should, er—" He moved away from her.

"Doctor, can I talk to you for a moment in private?" Sabrina gestured over her shoulder with her thumb.

He gave her a confused look. "We *are* alone."

"It's important. I need to show you something." Sabrina pointed toward the corner stairwell. She led the way, holding the door open for him. Reluctantly, he followed her, trying to avoid noticing the way her scrubs hugged her backside. The tips of his fingers itched to stroke the silken red length of her hair. This was probably not a good idea.

He hurried after her.

Only when they were both in the stairwell and the door was closed behind them did she address him. "You don't have to pretend with me." She stalked toward him.

He retreated, keeping space between them until his back hit the wall and he could go no farther. "What are we talking about?"

"You don't have to act like you don't care about these kids. You're not some kind of medical machine."

"Miss Bishop—"

"I watch you, Tobias. I see how much you love these kids, how much it kills you each and every time you can't fix a patient's heart. You say it's all part of the job, but I can see that it's an act. The more you deny it, the more it's going to eat away at you." She stepped in closer. By the Mountain, she smelled good, like honey and moonlight.

Tobias's body responded. It had been decades since he'd been with a woman. Decades since he'd trusted anyone enough to be intimate. Trust was difficult when you were an immortal living among humans. Relationships brought with them complications, the risk of exposure, the reality that he could never truly share who or what he was with anyone. How could you have intimacy when the other person wasn't just a different gender but a different species?

"Thank you," he said curtly. "If I ever need a shoulder to cry on, yours will be the one." He shifted to the side to walk around her but she blocked him with a hand to his chest. Her eyes searched his. A circle of heat bloomed where she touched him.

"Nothing rattles you, does it?" she said softly. "Nothing raises your blood pressure. Sometimes I wonder if you *are* a robot. Do you have a beating heart, Tobias, or are you made of chips and wires?"

"I am not a robot," Tobias said firmly. His pulse quickened. Could she feel that? He had no control over it or his growing erection. He needed to get out of this stairwell. "Sabrina, this is—"

Without warning, her lips slammed into his. The kiss was hard, searching. He didn't have the strength to stop her even if he'd wanted to. Something primal and urgent caused

343

his hand to tangle in her hair and his tongue to sweep into her mouth. By the Mountain, she tasted good. He forgot where he was, forgot *who* he was.

All too soon, she planted both hands on his chest and pushed him away. "Not a robot." She panted, breathless. She wiped under her bottom lip.

He opened his mouth to say something, anything, but his mind had gone completely blank. Should he tell her the kiss was inappropriate? How could he when he desperately wanted to kiss her again? She placed a finger over his lips before he could say a word.

"Look me in the eye," she commanded. He did and was surprised when her green eyes glowed a bright, silvery blue. "You will not remember this. If anyone asks what we did in here today, you will say we talked about Katelyn. We never kissed. You will wait here for five minutes and then go about your business." Her eyes stopped glowing, and she smiled sweetly up at him, her cheeks rosy. Was it his imagination, or did her skin look more vibrant than a moment before? "Thank you, Dr. Winthrop. I find our talks incredibly refreshing. You have a good heart."

She turned on her heel and strode from the staircase with a new pep in her step. Tobias blinked once, twice, three times. He pressed two fingers into his lips and chuckled under his breath. Was she a witch? No. He would have smelled her if she was. But she was something. Something that didn't realize her mind control had no effect on him.

He wiped a thumb over his lips and grinned, striding for the door. "Miss Bishop?" he called as he opened it. She was gone, but there was someone else at the end of the hall, someone he hadn't been sure he'd ever see again, and the sight of him was a bucket of ice water on his libido. He made no attempt to disguise his scowl.

"Hello, brother," Gabriel said. "Aren't you going to welcome me to the Windy City?"

꒰ꓗ꒱

CONTINUE THE STORY AND GET YOUR COPY OF WINDY CITY DRAGON *wherever you buy books!*

MEET GENEVIEVE JACK

USA Today bestselling and multi-award winning author Genevieve Jack writes wild, witty, and wicked-hot paranormal romance and fantasy. Coffee and wine are her biofuel. The love lives of witches, shifters, and vampires are her favorite topic of conversation. She harbors a passion for old cemeteries and ghost tours thanks to her years attending a high school rumored to be haunted. Her perfect day involves a heaping dose of nature and a dog. Learn more at GenevieveJack.com.

Do you know Jack? Keep in touch to stay in the know about new releases, sales, and giveaways.

Join my VIP reader group
Sign up for my newsletter

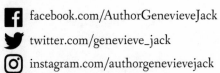

facebook.com/AuthorGenevieveJack

twitter.com/genevieve_jack

instagram.com/authorgenevievejack

bookbub.com/authors/genevieve-jack

ACKNOWLEDGMENTS

Every once in a while, I am reminded that it takes a village to release a book. Sure, as an author, I write the stories, but my tribe and editorial team make those stories better. The idea for The Dragon of New Orleans came to me in my sister's hospital room. She was at Northwestern in Chicago being treated for Acute Myeloid Leukemia, a disease likely brought on by her previous radiation treatment for breast cancer. To cure her, doctors would slowly kill off her bone marrow, meaning she was without much of an immune system until they could grow it back. She spent over thirty days confined to a special ward at Northwestern. That's where she named her IV pole "Mr. Drippy".

Visiting Sue in the hospital, I desperately wanted magic to be real, and if I'd had a wand, I would have waved it. She did endure chemo and the resulting loss of her hair and even having an ill-timed root canal while going through everything else. And when she got better, I swore I'd put Mr. Drippy and stupid cancer and magic into a book. This is that book.

A big thank you to Anne Victory for her mad editing

skills. This book is far better for her attention and encouragement.

Also, you may have noticed that a ton of research on New Orleans went into this book. Thank you to Deanna for beta reading an early version. Deanna lives in NOLA and helped me stay true to the location.

Finally, thanks to Tara, Kate, Brenda, Laurie, and Sara for being my writing tribe. Releasing a new book is a lot like giving birth. Good friends help you breathe through the pain and give you the confidence that what you're putting out will be loved as much as you love it. Thank you all for being there for this one.

Finally, to my dear readers, thank you for coming on this journey with me. I hope you know that although many things bring me inspiration, in the end, I write for you.

Made in the USA
Columbia, SC
21 June 2021